Nowhere to Run

AMY WALLACE

HARVEST HOUSE PUBLISHERS
EUGENE, OREGON

Unless otherwise indicated, all Scripture quotations are taken from the *Holy Bible,* New Living Translation, copyright © 1996, 2004. Used by permission of Tyndale House Publishers, Inc., Wheaton, IL 60189 USA. All rights reserved.

The Scripture on page 188 is taken from the New King James Version. Copyright © 1982 by Thomas Nelson, Inc. Used by permission. All rights reserved.

Cover by Garborg Design Works, Savage, Minnesota

Amy Wallace is represented by MacGregor Literary, Inc. of Hillsboro, Oregon.

Cover photos © Chris Garborg; Author photo by J. Collin Atnip

NOWHERE TO RUN
Copyright © 2012 by Amy Nicole Wallace
Published by Harvest House Publishers
Eugene, Oregon 97402
www.harvesthousepublishers.com

Library of Congress Cataloging-in-Publication Data
Wallace, Amy, 1970-
    Nowhere to run / Amy Wallace.
        p. cm. — (Place of refuge series ; bk. 2)
    ISBN 978-0-7369-4733-6 (pbk.)
    ISBN 978-0-7369-4734-3 (eBook)
    1. Mennonites—Fiction. 2. Policewomen—Fiction. I. Title.
PS3623.A35974N69 2012
813'.6—dc23

                                 2012004600

To my prayer team

Without your love, encouraging notes, and prayers, my stories would not exist. You all have prayed me through every aspect of life and reminded me every week that the reason I write is to glorify God, to experience His smile. I thank God for each of you and pray you experience God's smile and rejoice in the reality that your prayers have changed my life and the lives of readers forever.

When I am afraid, I will put my trust in you. I praise God for what he has promised. I trust in God, so why should I be afraid? What can mere mortals do to me?

PSALM 56:3-4

Our deepest fear is not that we are inadequate. Our deepest fear is that we are powerful beyond measure. It is our light, not our darkness, that most frightens us. We ask ourselves, Who am I to be brilliant, gorgeous, talented, and fabulous? Actually, who are you not *to be? You are a child of God. Your playing small doesn't serve the world.*

MARIANNE WILLIAMSON

ACKNOWLEDGMENTS

Every book carries with it a piece of my heart and copious amounts of my blood, sweat, and tears. This story also bears the fingerprints of all the amazing people listed below. You all have not only shaped and brought life to a work of fiction, but richness and joy into my life as well. Thank you!

My beloved family deserves an award for taking up all the slack left by my time spent locked in my writing cave to create this story. Not only that, but you prayed me through the ICU and back to work and a major surgery and back to work—all within four months' time. Without your love and smiles, I wouldn't have found the strength to keep putting one foot in front of the other or continue typing out a story one keystroke at a time. Thank you for believing in me and locking me in the basement to finish my work. I love you guys—all the way to Jesus.

My phenomenal prayer team prayed me through another story and a tough time in my life. Thanks to them, my family and I made it through. They have continued to storm the gates of heaven on your behalf and mine. They have wrapped this story, every line and word, in prayer. Thank you all for reflecting Jesus's tenacious love in all you do!

Thank you, Chip, for your faithful prayers and friendship. Knowing you are on my side kept me going when the going threatened to swallow me whole. Jen and Sharon, you all did it again! Your critiques and questions made this book better than I imagined possible. And your friendship continues to lead me deeper into Christ. Thank you a million times over!

Once again, I'm honored to be part of the Harvest House family! Kathleen, you made editing fun and challenged me to grow. I'm forever and joyfully indebted to you for your wisdom, humor, and prayers. From phone calls filled with laughter to mochas and substantive edits, you provided a cherished glimpse into what stellar could be.

Special thanks to the many experts who shared their stories, vast knowledge, and time to make this book all that it could be: Marshal

Tom Fitch and the Shipshewana Police Department, thank you for taking the time to read this story and add your sage advice and encouragement (Go CARDS); Gene and Gwen Newcomer, the real owners of the beautiful Songbird Ridge Bed & Breakfast; Gretchen and Lavon Miller, our amazing hosts, who were willing to answer a plethora of weird non-Mennonite questions and who made our stay in Shipshe wonderful; Alvin Miller—our time at Davis Mercantile created some of our fondest memories of Shipshewana; the welcoming and gracious tour guides at Menno-Hof; Owen Wingard, owner of Owl Toys; Cletus Lambright and his daughter Valerie—we loved spending an afternoon with you both at Lambright Woodworking; Vonda Yoder and Delilah and Caspar with Wanna Cabinets and Furniture; Detective Mark Mynheir; Edward Panu; and Joe Karpf.

And finally, to the One who is Light in the darkness, Hope at a hospital bedside, and Peace when storms rage: Thank You, Daddy, for carrying me when life broke and for never, ever letting go.

CHAPTER ONE

Ashley Walters pushed aside the curtains of her bedroom window and peered into the growing darkness. The engagement ring on her left hand tangled in the fabric and she yanked it loose. She should be following her best friend's instructions for finalizing wedding plans, but she couldn't.

Someone was watching her.

Even after a year, she couldn't shake the sense that someone was waiting for the right moment to attack. But she couldn't find him. No amount of police training prepared her for this. No amount of time driving through the Mennonite farmlands or visiting with the gentle people who lived there provided peace.

It used to. But that was before a gunman shattered the calm and left her with more questions than answers. Before the haunting memories caused Brad and Anna and Jonathan to leave Montezuma. Maybe for good.

She scanned the backyard one more time. Just a forest of trees, a new fence, and an empty space in her side driveway where Patrick's car had been parked only a few minutes ago.

She flipped the curtain closed.

Cops always felt like someone watched them. Casualty of the job. Still...

"Ash, come look at the dresses I picked up from your parents. They're absolute perfection." Her best friend, Margo, spun around to show off her rich blue bridesmaid's dress, the long flared skirt dancing around her legs.

"You're stunning. Maybe too stunning. I should have gone with orange or fuchsia."

"Oh, Ashley, please. You shall dazzle them all, darlin'." Margo's *Gone with the Wind* drawl coaxed a smile. "I'm so glad you and your mom chose a flattering dress. Remember Jan's wedding?"

"Ugh. Those dresses made everyone look like pumpkins. I couldn't do that to you and Emma and Kath."

Margo paused in the antique mirror and studied her reflection. "I love this chiffon halter and empire waist. I've never seen this style of dress."

Ashley's phone played the dark and resolute opening of Beethoven's Fifth Symphony.

Margo giggled. "You did *not* assign that ringtone to your mother, did you?"

"Hello, Mom." Ashley shrugged at Margo and turned back to the window.

"Ashley, dear, have you and Margo tried on your dresses yet? What about Kathleen? Patrick said his sister's dress might need more work, but she hasn't answered my emails to confirm. Emma did, bless her. I knew she would. You can't run a bed and breakfast as she does without impeccable manners."

At least Emma raised the standard of their slow-to-respond wedding party.

"I need to know if any further alterations are required. And I need you to answer my emails about last-minute issues from the caterer and florist, and the one from the musicians about the pieces to be played at the reception. I've sent along the top options and would like your input by this weekend."

"Sure thing. I only have the other list of three hundred things you asked me to do last week." Jailing drug dealers and helping keep domestics from turning violent sort of took precedence over napkins and place settings.

"Yes, well. Do get to those this week too, will you? And let me know today about the dresses. That is why you took this week off, am I right?"

"Yes."

"Your father and I want this wedding to be perfect. Our gift to you. You understand that, right, honey?"

She did. And every reminder of that hurt. They'd spent the last ten years in a polite cold war after Eric's death and were now making up for lost time.

"It won't be perfect, Mom." Nothing in life turned out that way. No matter how hard she tried to make that a reality.

"Well, we're giving it our all to make sure everything involved in our only daughter's wedding is the very best."

"I know and love you for it, Mom. It's just overwhelming, and it doesn't have to be. Patrick and I would be happy with a small wedding for family and close friends, just like the reception at Emma's."

"The second reception, dear. Your father and I are taking care of the official one. Your big day will be the social event of the year. You'll love it, you'll see. Only the best." Mom's phone beeped. "That should be the caterer calling about the champagne and chocolate fountains."

"No alcohol, Mom. You promised."

"Yes. Yes, I remember that now. I'll take care of it. Talk to you tomorrow. Love to all."

"I love you too." But her mom had already clicked over to her other call.

Only the best.

If only…

"Did you hear me, Ash? This dress is exquisite."

"It's one of a kind, special made. Only the best." Her words bounced off the silent walls and fell flat. Too much control slipped out of her fingers with every phone call.

She surveyed the backyard for the hundredth time today.

Was he out there? He had been before.

Everything she did now was controlled by those two people. One she loved. The other was a waking nightmare. When would he strike? Would she be ready?

Was he even real?

"Ash?"

She faced her best friend.

Margo didn't turn. Her blue eyes reflected from the mirror and locked onto Ashley's. "Want to talk about it?"

"No." She wouldn't frighten her friend or spoil this time for Patrick or her parents. Especially when she had nothing to substantiate her instincts. Not yet, anyway.

She shivered. "It's nothing, Maggie."

Chester barked and hopped around her feet. Her almost two-year-old Boxer wriggled and licked and scurried around her at the first hint of trouble.

"Silly dog." She bent down and snuggled him close, stroking his chestnut fur. Such a loveable bundle of energy. "He needs to go outside. No more doggie door, so I have to take him out."

"Ash, you changed the locks, the gate, the back door, the security system. When are you going to believe you're safe?"

Never.

Someone had broken into her backyard last year. At least twice. Her fellow officers believed that man was in jail.

She wasn't so sure.

Chester's bark snapped her back into the present, and she hurried downstairs and let her wriggling pup out. Not willing to join him in the oppressive Georgia heat, she stood at the kitchen window. June's temps were brutal. So were the memories.

Movement beyond her back gate caught her attention.

Chester barked.

Her skin pricked with goose bumps.

She grabbed her backup weapon from a safe in the kitchen and headed outside.

Slow and steady she crept down the porch steps and to the fence. Inch by inch, she regulated her breathing and stepped on silent feet.

Chester's low growl rumbled through the quiet.

Lightning fast, she disarmed the keyless deadbolt and flung open the gate.

Chester lurched forward.

An empty side driveway mocked her caution. Nothing moved up or down Vinson Avenue.

Again.

"You need to return to the police counselor, Ash. This is getting out of control." Margo's folded arms spoke volumes. Her designer jeans and flowered tank top didn't soften the worry lines on her forehead.

So much for hiding the truth from Margo. "I'm not crazy. I was jumpy the first few months after he was arrested, but then the edginess went away."

"But it's back."

"I'd rather talk about the wedding." Ashley whistled. "Come on, Chester, let's go inside."

Margo moved away from the door as they entered. "No amount of nagging has motivated you to talk about wedding plans this summer. Do you not want to go through with the wedding?"

"Of course I do. I love Patrick."

"You should talk to the counselor again. She'll help."

Ashley secured her gun and headed to the fridge for a water bottle. "I'm not going back. I respect what Patrick does, but I don't need a shrink. I need to find out who's watching me."

"Talk to Patrick then."

The front door closed. "About what?" Patrick's strong tenor wrapped around her.

He entered the kitchen, Yoder's takeout in hand, and wrapped his muscled arms around her.

For a second, she was safe.

Her stomach growled. She couldn't wait any longer, so she snagged the bag and peeked inside. One sniff and her smile widened. "Steak and potatoes. My favorite. And there's cotton candy ice cream in the fridge."

"So what do you need to talk to me about?" He kissed her cheek and then grabbed plates from the cabinet.

"Nothing." She shot a warning glance at Margo.

Margo clicked her tongue. "I'll set stuff out. Y'all go talk."

Ashley inhaled and worked her jaw back and forth. "Thanks, Mom."

Her best friend mouthed a *Sorry!* behind Patrick's back.

"Come on." He took her hand and tugged her toward the living room. "I've missed you. Talk or not, a few minutes alone would be nice."

As soon as they were out of sight, Patrick pulled her close and nuzzled her neck, planting small kisses all the way up to her lips.

Every one of her nerve endings tingled.

She wrapped her arms around his neck, and deepened the kiss until nothing but Patrick filled her senses.

He pulled back and rested his forehead against hers. "I'm counting down the days."

"Me too." She wanted to be Mrs. Patrick James more than anything else. It was the planning for it that drove her to distraction. Among other things. Her parents' help relieved and suffocated her at the same time.

And no one could help with the haunting sense that someone watched her every move.

"Let's take a walk." He took her hand and squeezed.

"Dinner will get cold."

"At least to the mailbox?" He tugged her forward. "Some fresh air will do us both good."

So would a winter snowstorm.

She unlocked the front door and opened it. "I don't see how you run in this heat. It's oppressive."

Sweat dripped down her back the second they were outside.

"I love it. Gets my blood pumping and keeps me in shape."

That it did.

He opened the roadside mailbox and smiled. "There's a letter from Brad."

She took the two white envelopes he extended.

"Who's that blank one from?"

"Neighborhood kids." She headed back to the shade of the porch.

"The first three were from a couple teens in the neighborhood, advertising yard work services. I just throw them away now."

"They could cut the grass for you, so you could relax when you get home from work."

"I don't mind. Helps me download from the day, so I'm ready to enjoy the evening with you." Back on day shift, she loved the normalcy of coming home and cutting the grass and gardening. Then she'd whip up a meal and share it with Patrick. Life was good.

Inside, she deposited the plain white envelope into the trash and tore into Brad's.

"Let's eat, you two. We have more wedding things to do tonight. Like try on a gorgeous bridal dress." Margo beamed in the candlelight. She'd pulled the shades down to block out the bright summer sun and lit every candle Ashley owned.

Patrick extended his hands the second they sat down. "Lord, thank You for my incredible fiancée and her industrious best friend who keeps us all on track. Thank You for this food and for making the next forty-six days fly by. Amen."

Margo grinned. "Y'all make such a lovely couple. This wedding will be the highlight of the year."

"Yes." Ashley squeezed Patrick's hand. "It will be amazing." If she could push aside the shadows long enough to enjoy the day she'd looked forward to for almost a year.

The letter in her hand crinkled. Between bites of country fried steak and mashed potatoes she deciphered Brad's scribbles. All scrawled and to the point, like a typical fourteen-year-old boy.

She missed him so much.

Margo touched her arm. "So how long has Brad been gone?"

"He and Anna have been in Shipshewana with Jonathan's family since last February. Over a year. They should have come home long before now."

Patrick drank a long gulp of sweet tea, made the way both he and Margo and most Southerners liked. Sugar shock sweet. "What does our favorite teen have to say?"

"An antique fair Anna dragged him to and…" Ashley's mouth wouldn't form the words she'd read on the white stationery.

Patrick's strong but gentle hand enclosed hers. "Everything okay?"

"Brad is moving home."

"That's great." Patrick's smile stretched ear to ear. "Then we can ask him in person to be in the wedding. It'll be good to have him and Anna home again."

"Anna's not coming with him." Her eyes misted. "Brad says…well, I should read it. 'Mamm is happy in Shipshe, helping with Cousin Mark's and Uncle Philip's bed and breakfasts. Cousin Jonathan wants me to stay here and help in his carpentry shop. But I can't. My mom needs me. She said so when she came to visit a few weeks ago. I'm leaving Monday and I'll come by to see you and Patrick soon. I can't wait. I miss you guys. Love, Brad.'"

"He's going to live with Joyce?"

Ashley nodded. "She's his biological mother, and Brad promised last time we talked that she's really changed since she went to visit him at Christmas."

Her one and only meeting with Joyce had been a disaster. The woman's brash behavior and blaming her for dumping Brad on the Yoders' doorstep rankled her. Still. Brad living with her was a very bad idea.

Poor Anna. All she'd endured at the hands of an evil man last year. On top of losing her husband and almost losing Brad. And yet Anna wrote letter after Scripture-filled letter to remind Ashley who God was and to pray for her healing. What could she do for her friend now?

Protect Brad.

"We should head up to Shipshewana and see if we can help." Patrick unsnapped his phone from his belt and called up his calendar. "I could make it work for this weekend."

"I'd love to visit, have wanted to since they left. But…" She flipped the envelope over. "He's probably already here. This was mailed late last week."

"Then it'll be good to see him." Patrick ran his thumb over her hand. "He'll call as soon as he's settled."

"I know. It's just…"

"It'll be okay. We'll pray. You'll see."

"Maybe."

Margo collected the dishes and set to arranging them in the dishwasher.

Patrick stood. "I hate to eat and run, ladies. But I have some work that has to be completed tonight, and you have wedding plans to finalize."

He and Margo must have talked earlier and planned this all out. Her entire week off and Margo would hustle her here and there to make final payments with her parents' money to the hundred people her mother had hired. All for a wedding at Patrick's church and a small reception at Emma's B&B. Of course, there was the guest list Mom had included, bringing the guest numbers into the hundreds. And the formal reception at the country club. Ridiculous. Her chest burned. She hated being managed again.

"I love you. You can do this." Patrick pulled her to him and kissed her soundly.

"I love you too."

And he was gone.

Margo slid her arm through Ashley's. "Let's go try on your gown to make sure the alterations are perfect."

Nothing in life was perfect. Especially wedding planning.

Before Margo could wrangle her ivory, strapless trumpet gown from the complicated packaging designed to keep her dress in perfect condition, a knock at the door saved her. She'd deal with the delicate and understated lace later.

On the way downstairs, she replayed the monstrosities her mother had her try on at the bridal salon. Layers of lace and ribbons, diamond-studded bodices, skirts befitting Scarlett O'Hara. Ugh.

Ashley had won with the simple and classic dress she'd chosen.

Peeking through the living room window, she surveyed the entire front porch and yard. No one was there.

She opened the door to find a crystal vase with two dozen red roses.

Margo slipped past her and picked them up. "Patrick is so thoughtful."

"Patrick brings me tulips. And he doesn't leave them on the porch."

Margo headed to the kitchen. "Here, read the card. This is so romantic."

Not. "The card says *I'll always be here for you.* But that's not Patrick's style. These aren't from him."

"So you have a secret admirer making his move at the last minute to dissuade you from marrying the wrong man?" Margo sighed. "Face it. These are from Patrick to cheer you up from the stress of wedding plans and to take your mind off Bradley's moving in with his birth mother."

"Thanks for reminding me of all that."

"Like you've forgotten." Margo situated the flowers on the dining room table. "I think Patrick's just showing you his ultra-romantic side."

"I'm calling him to find out."

Margo grabbed the cordless phone. "Don't. He's at work, and you're obsessing about every little thing. Take the flowers as the romantic gesture they were meant to be and thank him tomorrow."

"It's not romantic. It's more like playing games."

"It's fun."

No. It sent chills up and down her spine. She hated games.

CHAPTER TWO

"What if I mess everything up?" Ashley twisted her marquise diamond around her ring finger. The rubies surrounding the diamond sparked rainbows over her bedroom wall.

"Be still." Margo zipped up her wedding dress and stood back with a smile. "I can't believe you wouldn't try this on last night. It's amazing."

"I couldn't." Not after the creepy roses. "I needed more sleep." Sleep that escaped her at two in the morning as she stood guard at her window. "You didn't answer my question."

Margo flipped her blonde hair over her shoulders. "You won't mess things up, Ash. And you'd be making a massive mistake if you chickened out now. Look."

She gasped as she looked at her reflection. "It's beautiful. I can't believe that's me." Margo had fashioned her long black hair into a loose updo with her mother's diamond combs.

"You're enchanting. The most beautiful bride ever."

A car's engine rumbled into her driveway. "That's Patrick. I'll go let him in."

Margo about choked. "Oh no you won't." She blocked the door. "Let's get you out of this dress first. I will not allow you to bring disaster to this most special event."

"Old wives' tale. No such thing as bad luck or disaster if the groom sees the bride in the dress before the wedding."

"We're not testing that theory today." Margo set about undoing the fairy-tale magic.

"Anybody home?" Patrick's footsteps ascended the stairs.

"Stay out there, Patrick James." Margo flipped the bedroom door lock.

Chester pawed the wood to get to Patrick. The mutt often chose Patrick over her these days. "Go lie down, Chester."

He obeyed, but trained his sad eyes on her.

"I only have a minute, but I wanted to stop by and see you before I headed into work."

"I'm stuck in here with my evil stepsister."

Margo yanked a comb from her hair.

"Ouch."

"Bless your heart. I'm so sorry that hurt." Sugar sweet, her best friend.

"Sounds like I should leave you two alone."

Ashley shuffled to the door. "Hang on. I wanted to ask you a question first."

Margo wagged her pointer finger. "Do not open that door."

In her slip? Not a chance. She still wished she could see Patrick's eyes when he answered.

"A question? About what?"

Deep breath in. Deep breath out. No use sounding paranoid to Patrick too. Margo was already convinced she was nuts. "Did you leave some roses on my front porch last night?"

"Me? Nope."

"You sure? Margo thinks it was really romantic."

"Maybe they were for her."

"That makes a lot more sense than me having a secret admirer."

"You have a secret admirer? I'm jealous." A chuckle infused Patrick's confident voice.

"You have no reason to be. It's nothing."

"Wish I could see you before I have to go." He tried the handle.

Margo shook her head, a syrupy smile in place.

"According to my evil stepsister, that's not happening this morning. Sorry."

He huffed. "Fine. I've gotta run, though. Love you."

"Love you too."

"See you tonight. Dinner and a movie, right? I'll bring the correct kind of flowers." His footsteps retreated, and the front door opened and closed.

"I told you he didn't leave those roses."

Margo shrugged. "Maybe they are for me. But no one at home knows I'm here except your parents and the folks at work. I doubt any of those people would send me flowers with an anonymous and romantic note."

Donning a jean skirt and maroon tank top, Ashley ran through any possibilities for the admirer's identity. One jumped out and bit her.

"What if the flowers are from Harrison?" Her stomach clenched. But why would her ex-boyfriend pull a stunt like that? They'd made their peace over Eric's death and the rocky ending to their long relationship.

Margo returned the hair clips to their velvet box. "He wouldn't do that. Harrison was and is a gentleman. He knows you're happy now."

"You're right. He's a good guy." Ashley hadn't talked with Harrison since Valentine's Day last year. They'd parted on good terms with the past between them resolved.

A past that included her brother's death eleven years ago. That horrible day didn't haunt her like it had last winter when his homicide case was closed.

But there would always be a piece of her missing, a hole only her funny, protective, annoying big brother could fill.

She touched the photo of her and Eric on her dresser. Harrison had taken it. He was Eric's best friend, always around. A huge part of her past.

"What if I mess things up with Patrick like I did with Harrison?"

Margo patted the space beside her on the bed. "That's what this is all about, isn't it?"

"I have no idea what you're talking about."

"Yes you do. Your reluctance isn't because you're afraid of ruining things with Patrick."

Ashley flopped down beside her best friend.

"It's because you're afraid of being happy."

Margo's words zinged. "I am not. That's ridiculous."

"Is it? Deep down, you're afraid of being happy because you think someone is going to die right before you give in to a joyful future. Like Eric died right before you and Harrison were engaged."

Fists clenched, she jumped from the bed. "That's absurd."

"Don't let Eric's death keep defining you, Ash. Please. Don't let the lies turn you away from the truth. Patrick loves you. You're safe. It's okay for you to be happy."

Margo's misty eyes softened the sting of her words. Maybe she was right. Maybe all the recent notions of someone watching her again and the flowers having a sinister intent stemmed from fear.

She couldn't live that way again.

Her cell phone buzzed. "Hello?"

"Ashley?" Brad's voice filled the phone line. "I'm on your front porch. Do you have time before work?"

"I'll be down in a sec." She ended the call and rushed toward the front door, flinging it open the second she reached it. Then, for a second, she hesitated. Brad's jean shorts and T-shirt made him look so much more like Eric. Same shaggy brown hair and chocolate brown eyes. Sadness tugged at her. "I can't believe you're here." He'd left his Mennonite clothes behind. But he was still Brad. She pulled the taller boy into a hug. "You've grown three inches."

He blushed and motioned to the Mennonite young man next to him, straw hat in hand. "Have you met Matthew Kauffman?"

"Yes." She'd only spoken to him twice. Once after he'd been injured on the Yoder farm. The second time to ask him if Brad could have caused those terrible *accidents*. Then, Matt hadn't answered. Now he was here with his friend. All around her people were healing. When would it be her turn? She stepped back and pointed to the door. "Won't you come in?"

Brad entered, but Matt remained on the porch. "Thank you, but I have work to do on Anna's farm today. I will return this afternoon to pick Bradley up and take him to his mother's."

She closed and locked the door before joining Brad on the white couch. "How have you been? I've missed you."

He popped every one of his knuckles—smallest to largest. "Good."

"How are things with Joyce?"

His eyes lit up. "Much better than when we first met her."

Quiet infused the living room.

"So what are you doing to stay busy?" Drawing teens out resembled a suspect interrogation more than she'd remembered.

"Some cooking. Cleaning. Playing Xbox until Mom gets home."

"Where's Joyce working now?"

"She's a manager at Amelia's Restaurant."

"That's where Patrick took me for our first date."

"Cool. It's a great place."

So Joyce had cleaned up her act. No way could she have landed a job like that without serious work on her people skills.

"When's the wedding? July, right? Nice invitation."

From a teenage boy, *nice* was a major compliment. "July twenty-first. Six o'clock."

"I'll be there. I called Patrick on my way over. He said you two had something to ask me about."

"He did?"

"Yeah. He told me to let you know it was okay to ask." His face scrunched up into a question.

"Patrick and I would love for you to be in the wedding." She should have waited for Patrick, but he must have understood how anxious she was to make sure Brad could be a part. "To be one of Patrick's groomsmen. We'd be honored if you would."

An impish grin spread across his face. Then a grimace. "Do I have to wear a tux?"

"Yep. But it'll be a nice one."

"Okay. I'll do it."

"Great. I'll be right back." She hustled into the kitchen and retrieved the candy dish she'd meant to set out earlier. Margo and Chester played fetch in the backyard.

"Here you go. Your favorites."

Brad picked up a handful of Bob's soft peppermint balls. "Thanks. Mom doesn't let me keep sweets in the house. Neither did Mamm."

"Don't you miss your mother?"

"I love Mamm. But she's happy and surrounded by family."

"You're her family too."

"Yeah, but two of my older sisters live near Shipshewana and she's not working as hard as she did before. It's good for her to stay. I needed to come home."

"Why?"

"I dunno. I've prayed for my mom for a long time. I feel like she needs me. Like she needs to make up for leaving me with Mamm and Daed."

One question nagged at her, but she wasn't sure it was wise to voice it. Even if Brad had shed his Mennonite clothing, the teen was still innocent and had been sheltered from a lot of ugly realities.

"Does she have a boyfriend?"

He crinkled his eyebrows. "I don't think so, no. Why?"

"Curiosity." And protectiveness. A boyfriend at Joyce's house could spell trouble for Brad.

Between work and wedding plans, she'd stick close to Brad and make sure he was safe. He was like a brother to her, and she'd move heaven and earth to protect him.

Patrick drummed his fingers on the florist's counter. An emergency appointment had detained him far later than he'd hoped. Ashley had understood. Now he had the fixings for a late dinner and a movie waiting in the car, and he needed to get on his way. Fast.

"Thanks for staying open late for me, Bea. You're a lifesaver."

"Another customer is headin' this way too, but I'd stay open just for you. Say, Patrick, maybe you should work for me on the weekends. I'd give you a discount." Bea Thompson's grandmotherly eyes twinkled. "'Course you're mighty busy these days. Made a decision on the weddin' flowers yet?"

"Thanks for the offer, Bea." He hated to say what he had to next. "I suggested you, and Ashley agreed. But Ashley's mom put in an order with an Atlanta florist months ago. I found out today when they called to double-check the date and time. I'm really sorry."

"Mama and Daddy's payin'. I know how it goes. Keep the peace on stuff like this. It'll go a long way toward cementin' you in Mom's and Dad's heart."

"Yes, ma'am." He had few options otherwise. They'd survive the next forty-five days and be on their own after that. He hoped.

At least he and Ashley were in agreement on how to survive until the wedding. Then, as Ashley's husband, he'd remind the indomitable Jacquelyn Walters that Ashley was all grown up and could make decisions on her own. Maybe he'd talk with Jacquelyn again about her need for control. She'd listened last time. He stood a little straighter. Yes, he would defend Ashley and help Jacquelyn at the same time.

Bea slipped into the back of her store to retrieve Ashley's favorite multicolored tulips.

The bells on the front door jangled as a stranger in an Atlanta Braves cap ducked into the store.

"Be right with ya."

Patrick turned from the counter and nodded a greeting.

The man's blue eyes widened, and he wiped his hand over his scruffy chin.

Patrick couldn't place him.

The younger man twirled around and raced out the door.

Bea appeared, carrying a vase of tulips and another one filled with two dozen roses. "Where'd he go?"

"Who?"

"The young man that just came in, Mr. Smith or somethin'. I think that's what he said. He's the one I told you I was waitin' for. He's picked up a vase of Vino Rosso roses a couple of times now. Those cost a pretty penny, I'm tellin' you."

"Tulips aren't cheap either."

Bea clucked her tongue. "Nope, they sure aren't. Maybe you should start a tulip fund or somethin'. Gotta keep Ashley happy for a good long while."

"Good idea." He paid for the tulips and waved to Bea as he exited. "See you next month. I'm sure I'll be in here for some comfort flowers a time or two."

His Mustang roared to life and he drove on autopilot to Ashley's Victorian. They'd agreed he'd move into her house and sell his after the wedding. Her painting studio would be impossible to re-create in his brick ranch.

In less than two months they'd be married. Soon he'd be bringing flowers home after work and placing them on *their* dining room table. He could picture it now.

Bright lights swerved into his lane and he jerked the steering wheel to the right to avoid the oncoming car.

The high beams followed, on course for a head-on collision.

Patrick turned into a long driveway and braked hard, his pulse hammering.

The high beams disappeared.

He sprang from the car and tried to catch the license plate, but the car had vanished. He wasn't even sure it was a car. A truck, maybe?

Slamming his hand on his Mustang's top, he growled. He should have catalogued the license plate. Then there'd be one less dangerous driver on the road.

"Lord, please stop whoever was behind the wheel before he or she causes someone serious injury."

His mind switched gears to one of his former counseling patients. Craig Humphrey had sworn revenge for the supposed damage Patrick had done to his marriage. He'd also had a few DUIs last year. But Craig had moved away soon after he severed ties with Patrick's practice, leaving a huge bill unpaid.

He'd hoped that was the end of the trouble. Maybe not.

He shook his head to clear away the dark suspicions. It wasn't probable that Craig had returned to Montezuma to run him off the road.

But just in case, he'd keep his eyes open.

CHAPTER THREE

Patrick was late. Ashley swapped lit candles from the living room with the ones in the dining room for the second time.

Last time Patrick was late, she'd paced the ER waiting room for hours. No. She couldn't start to panic anytime things didn't go according to schedule.

A schedule she never stuck to outside of work. But Patrick did. Like clockwork.

Chester nuzzled her hand and she bent down to pat his warm fur. He flopped over onto his back as he always did. Silly dog.

Some folks believed dogs were like angels. She understood. Chester was always there when she showed any hint of sadness.

She checked the front window. Maybe she should go paint. That would help pass the time and keep her sane.

Patrick's Mustang roared into the side driveway. Such a sweet sound. *Thank You, God, he's safe.*

"Honey, I'm home." Patrick extended a bag of take-out from Amelia's in one hand and another vase of flowers in the other. Tulips this time.

"You didn't have to bring me flowers."

He planted a quick kiss on her lips. "Can't let a secret admirer best me." He placed the flowers on the table and the food on the counter. "Where'd the other flowers go? And where's Margo?"

"The flowers left with Margo. They're both at Emma's. Girls' night with Kath and Emma, watching old romantic movies."

She transferred steaming food from insulated boxes to china plates. Yeast rolls, salads, filet, and baked sweet potatoes. If only she could eat like this every day and still fit into her wedding gown.

"You could join them. When my sister gets a night out, she stays away till the wee hours."

"Susie-Q's still not sleeping through the night?"

Patrick filled glasses with sweet tea and took them to the candlelit table. "She did, but now she's dealing with teething and nightmares."

"It's tough to be almost two."

Patrick grinned and wrapped his arms around her, kissing her neck. And cheek. Then turning his roguish eyes to hers. "So how many little ones do you want again?"

A shiver raced across her shoulders. Maybe Margo should have stayed for dinner. The closer it got to the wedding...

"Maybe three." She slipped out of Patrick's arms. "I've heard that's a good number of kids." She grabbed the plates and hurried to the table.

Patrick prayed and they dug into their steaks. "So how's Brad doing?"

"Okay. He's different. More relaxed, like he belongs in our world."

"But..."

She dabbed her mouth with a napkin. "How do you always know there's a *but* in there somewhere?"

"It's part of my job to read body language and listen for verbal cues." He held up a hand to stop a year-old argument. "You are not a patient or a project. I promise."

They hadn't argued about that in a very long time, but it still rankled her that he could read her so well. Better than most cops. Better than she could read him. That was the real problem.

"Think you could teach me how to do that so the playing field is a bit more level?"

Patrick finished off his steak and sweet potato before answering.

She waited. Silence did a good bit of the work getting criminals to confess. It might work on fiancés too.

Patrick stood and pulled their crème brûlée from the fridge. "So... how 'bout them Braves?"

"Ha-ha. I noticed the bruise on your arm. Baseball practice or another pickup basketball game?"

"You know how it goes."

"Are you going to answer my question?"

"Which one was that?" His smile stirred something inside very different from irritation.

"Are you going to be this annoying after we get married?"

His grin turned mischievous. "Worse."

Some ice-cold tea and a few bites of crème brûlée later, she conceded defeat. For now. "The thing that bugs me about Brad's situation is that people like Joyce don't change overnight. She wasn't a good mom when Brad was three. I doubt she can be that now."

"I disagree. Brad and I have talked about Joyce. Besides, as long as there is breath, there is hope. People can amaze us with their ability to change."

"You forget I go to trial after trial of repeat offenders. People don't always change."

"You're right."

"Can I get that in writing?" She'd learned to use humor to diffuse situations as well as Patrick.

Patrick's thoughtful blue eyes twinkled. "A good student, you are. Try harder you must."

They laughed.

"Nice Yoda. Eric would be proud."

"I'll take dishes if you want to get the popcorn ready and the movie cued."

"Isn't this too late for you? You have patients in the morning, right?"

"Nope. I've had too many late workdays. We needed an evening to ourselves, so I cleared my schedule tomorrow until noon."

"Just for me?"

"Absolutely."

This routine was nice. Peaceful. A good change from her work and crazy schedule of painting until all hours of the night on her days off.

He snagged her hand and nudged her close. "It won't always be boring, you know."

Danger, Will Robinson.

"I'm gonna go cue the movie. Something Jane Austen, right?"

"Anything for you, babe."

"I'll go with the A-team instead."

She scooted into the living room and paused the film at the first preview. A scratching noise on the front porch grabbed her attention. "Is Chester still in the backyard?"

"Yes. You want me to let him in?"

"No."

She slipped over to the front window and peeked out. As usual, no one was there. No creepy bad guy stalked her. It was just her imagination.

Maybe she should check it out though.

Opening the door, she scanned the entire front yard and porch.

A large manila envelope leaned against the house with only her name written on the outside.

Her heartbeat raced. Manila envelopes weren't sinister. Unless they came from the person watching her.

This was crazy. Maybe nothing.

Picking up the envelope, she once again scanned the front yard, every tree and bush. Anyplace a person could hide and still watch her front door.

"What's that?"

Ashley jumped and almost squealed like a little girl. But she didn't. "I...I don't know. I heard something on the porch and then found this."

"You okay?"

"No." She should have told him before now, but she'd wanted to shield him as long as possible from the same jaded suspicion that career cops experienced every day.

Patrick led her inside and closed and locked the front door. He'd picked up her habit well. "Want me to open it?"

She ripped the top flap of the envelope off and peered inside.

Pictures. Nothing dangerous.

She breathed a little easier. "Just pictures. Here, let's have a look." Onto the coffee table poured a huge pile of photos. One caught her eye. Her in a sundress with Eric making bunny ears behind her. Harrison standing by her side. "I don't remember seeing this picture before."

She picked up another photo. Her, Margo, Eric, and Harrison. In high school. Talking outside the cafeteria.

Patrick spread them out. "They're all of you, Ash. Every one of them."

"These photos date from high school to a few days ago, but I've never seen any of them." She shot up from the couch. "Don't touch them anymore, Patrick. I'm getting some gloves."

When she returned, she sorted the photos by general age. High school. College. Police academy. There was even an article about Detectives Karen Everett and Rich Burke closing her brother's homicide case.

Her hands shook as she turned over an 8x10 of her police academy class. On the back was a note.

Acid roiling in her stomach, she unfolded the paper taped to the photo. "I'll always be here for you."

Her mouth dried up and she couldn't think.

"Ashley, Culp is on duty right now. Let's let him deal with this."

"No." She wasn't ready to call in her sergeant yet. Not if she could figure this out first. Culp would just charge in and take over. "I want to keep digging. There could be a clue. I've seen a note like this before. In the roses."

Patrick's face whitened. "You didn't tell me about the note."

"I thought it was harmless." Not really, but she wasn't willing to admit out loud that her initial suspicions were right on target.

The truth remained. She had a stalker.

∽

Patrick held Ashley in his arms. Her whole body shook. "Ash, let me call Culp. We need to let the police handle this."

"I'll call him." She turned her focus to the photos again. "But I need to go through the evidence one more time. Once I call, I won't see these pictures again."

For twenty minutes Ashley sorted and resorted pictures, examining each one in detail.

"There's no clue to his identity in these photos. No threat."

"Even so, he's sending a clear message. He knows you. Well." The statistics ramming around his brain terrified him. Three in four stalking victims were stalked by someone they knew. Weapons were used to harm or threaten victims in one out of five cases. Seventy-six percent of femicide victims were stalked by their partner.

Okay, that was going too far. Ashley had no crazy ex-boyfriend in her past.

Clinical assessment provided no distancing from the impact of those photos. "Ash, can you think of anyone who could have taken these pictures?"

In most of them Ashley smiled or goofed off with friends. Casual, not staged photos. Sharp quality. All of them taken outside. At Ashley's parents' home. Outside her church. At Margo's graduation party. At Eric's funeral. She didn't smile in those or in her police department photos or the newspaper clippings.

"Talk to me, Ash. Let me help."

She sat up and swiped a Kleenex across her cheeks. "What do you know about stalkers?"

"We're not sure that's what this is. Let's not jump to…"

"You're kidding, right? Please tell me you're not going to try and talk me out of what I already know is true. This guy has stalked me a lot longer than most cases. He's obsessed. Very high probability he's dangerous."

"We don't know that." He grasped at brittle straws, but he couldn't give in. Not yet. Denial was safer.

"I've taken classes on stalking because it's become a bigger and bigger problem. I know one in every twelve women will be stalked during their lifetimes. And that a very high percentage of domestic violence stalkers will kill their victims."

He tried on his counselor hat. "So we've taken similar classes and heard similar stats. What type of stalker do you think this is?"

"A simple obsessional, intimacy seeker. He's lived on the periphery of my life for somewhere around twelve years."

"If that's true, he's among the most common and potentially dangerous stalkers." Did he really say that out loud? "I'm sorry, Ash. I didn't mean to dissolve into clinical assessment. I'm scared." Terrified.

"Me too." She deflated into the couch. "I've been the first responder to enough domestic violence cases turned homicides. It's chilling."

"We need to call Culp. If you're right, a number of people could be at risk. Margo. Emma." His sister. Anyone close to Ashley. He hated to push when some sliver of control remained in Ashley's hands as she studied the pictures again. But they had to get the police involved. Tonight.

She pushed the photos away. "I'll call." With robotic movements, she stood and retrieved her cell phone from the end table and speed dialed Culp.

"Yes, this could qualify as an emergency."

Patrick strained to hear Culp's response but caught nothing.

"A stalker. Pictures spanning twelve years. Roses. Notes. He's probably the one who called and hung up earlier today." A pause. "No, the number was blocked."

Patrick's shoulders tightened. She hadn't told him about the phone call.

"Maybe even sent letters, but I threw them away. Figured they were from neighborhood kids about lawn care. The first ones were."

A pause.

"Stupid, I know. I didn't realize they could have been a clue."

Ashley pulled the phone away from her ear. Culp's tenor reverberated through the room. "Do not go anywhere. Hear me? I'll be there in half a sec. Do not mess with those photos anymore either. We can't risk losing or damaging evidence. Understand, Officer?"

Ashley's hand shook, but her voice remained steel. "Yes, sir. I understand."

She stood in place, stock-still, eyes distant. Patrick was sure she still trembled inside.

He did too.

They'd become one of the statistics.

He bit the inside of his cheek until he tasted blood. How could Ashley be so foolish? Those pictures were his prized possessions, and he'd given them to her. To prove how much he loved her.

And there she stood in her kitchen, kissing the wrong man.

Ashley was the only one for him. He'd followed other women, dated one of them. But none of them compared to Ashley.

His mother's dying wish was that he pursue his dreams. She probably meant a criminal justice degree. That hadn't worked out. What he wanted more than that, more than anything, was to free Ashley.

She'd ignored his phone call. Wrongly ascribed his letters to neighborhood teens.

She'd given away the beautiful flowers too. And she'd shared their photos with that…that…he couldn't even think the name. The name of the man who treated Ashley with such absolute disrespect.

Kissing her in public. Keeping her up late at night because he worked too long into the evening. Brainwashing her into agreeing to marry him.

Stealing Ashley from him while he took care of his dying mother.

He didn't have much time. The wedding was next month. He couldn't wait any longer. He wouldn't sit by and watch her ruin her life.

Ashley would thank him.

He'd fix it.

Free her.

Then they'd be together. Forever.

CHAPTER FOUR

Patrick paced the length of the squad room.

"We'll catch him, Patrick. Ease up." Culp remained focused on his paperwork. "Did you plan to stay all day to make sure we're doing our jobs?"

"No."

"'Cause you'll have a few more to add to your watch list soon."

Patrick paused. "What do you mean?"

"I put in a call to the GBI. They'll likely take point in this investigation if things escalate." Culp scribbled notes on a legal pad.

If things escalate. He prayed they would not. "Why does the GBI have to get involved?" Patrick's shoulders screamed for relief. The possibility of calling in the Georgia Bureau of Investigation cast an even darker shadow over an already sinister situation.

"They have resources we don't. Plus, a cop is involved." Culp stopped writing. "They'll help us catch this guy sooner. Before he can do anything else."

Patrick forced his feet to move. He had to keep moving or else he'd start punching walls. No one voiced the details of that "anything else." But they all knew.

Officer Elizabeth Rey cleared her throat. "Don't worry, Patrick."

She ran her hands through her short red hair. "I reviewed the file this morning. Culp is right; we'll catch him."

"How can you be sure? He could go back into hiding for another twelve years." Like that would happen.

"The upcoming wedding has to be the trigger. The stalker will act soon."

That single thought had kept him up all night.

Culp tossed his pen in the desk drawer. "I talked to Harrison Burns and Detective Burke this morning."

Patrick stopped pacing. "I'm sure they appreciated being asked about alibis."

"Give us some credit."

True. Culp was pulling a double shift to work on Ashley's case, and the man had been a cop for almost two decades.

Elizabeth flipped through Ashley's file again. One picture caught his eye. "Did you get the roses back from Emma?"

"Yes. The notes from the flowers and the folder of pictures look like a match to me. But the GBI will determine that for sure as soon as they can."

The roses sparked a memory he'd intended to share with Culp last night. "I think I might have seen the stalker yesterday before I got to Ashley's."

Elizabeth and Culp stared through him.

His face heated. What a bumbler. He should have figured all this out the second he'd seen the nervous guy in the flower shop.

But how? He knew nothing of the note in the flowers. Of Ashley's feeling watched. He wasn't a cop.

Culp stood. "You didn't think that was pertinent enough to mention last night? We could have picked the guy up by now."

"In last night's craziness, my only concern was comforting Ashley."

"She's a cop, Patrick." Elizabeth's blue eyes blazed. "Why would you keep a key piece of evidence from us?"

His jaw ached from clenching. It wasn't his fault the flower shop guy hadn't been questioned.

"I didn't know when I saw the guy at the florist, and Ashley didn't tell me about the notes in the flowers and the pictures being the same until late last night, right before we called you. It's also very possible this hunch might be wrong."

Elizabeth clicked some keys on her computer. "Describe him and what makes you think he could be Ashley's stalker."

"Tall. Caucasian. Tan skin. Younger than me, maybe twenty-five. He was buying two dozen red roses like Ashley received yesterday. When I learned about both notes…"

"Hair and eye color? Car?"

"Blue eyes. Brown hair, maybe. Dark, scruffy beard. He wore an Atlanta Braves cap. I didn't see what he was driving. But he lit out of Bea's shop fast when he saw me."

"Could it be somebody you know?"

Patrick collapsed into a chair. "I didn't recognize him. But someone tried to run me off the road last night too. I thought it might be a drunk driver or a former patient, but he wouldn't know Ashley."

"You didn't think that was worth telling us?" Culp glared. "You're in danger too, Patrick. You have to tell us everything from now on."

He wasn't an idiot. "It could all be unconnected. A coincidence."

"I don't believe in coincidences." Culp turned to Elizabeth. "Let's open a file on Patrick too."

Patrick's shoulders tightened into a vise.

"On it."

Culp returned to his desk. "Give us some names, former patients, anyone with a bone to pick with you."

"It'd be a very short list."

"Like Ashley's. You two are the most loved folks I know."

"The only people on Ashley's list are criminals she testified against. The only one on my list is Craig Humphrey. And the flower shop guy doesn't match his description."

"People can totally change their appearance. Should be easy enough to track down the whereabouts of Mr. Humphrey and have a little chat. I'm running down Ashley's list today too."

"Craig moved away last fall. Collections agencies were after him. I don't have an address."

"We have our ways." Culp grabbed a stack of papers and stood. "Stay alert, Patrick. We've stepped up patrols around Ashley's neighborhood. I'll make sure they swing by yours too."

"Thank you, Sam."

"I'm off to see the chief. I'll catch you later."

When Culp exited the squad room, Elizabeth locked eyes with Patrick. "It's a good thing Ashley's going out of town with Margo this weekend. You should think about visiting a friend too."

"I'm not running away to hide. I need to protect Ashley." He'd already done all he could. He'd checked her house and car for any signs of tampering. Helped formulate a plan for her trip that would alter her normal route. Spoken to her parents about their security system without incurring too many questions.

Elizabeth scowled. "You really should take a weekend vacation. Ashley can protect herself."

"I'm going to help her. She needs me."

"You won't be any help to her dead."

"Thanks for that." He stood and grabbed his briefcase. "I'll be fine."

He prayed that was true.

One question haunted her from last night. Why would someone stalk a cop?

Ashley set down the paintbrush. Nothing but slashes of color filled the canvas. She couldn't concentrate.

Culp had said they'd catch the guy quickly. The stalker had played his hand and police would be there when he made a move.

Her sergeant had also whispered to Patrick last night that the stalker was either stupid or insane. Or both.

Dangerous.

"Ash, are you ready to go yet?" Margo sauntered into the studio, beautiful in a light blue sundress.

She wiped her shaking hands with a cloth. "Go where?"

"To meet Emma, Kathleen, Bradley, and Bradley's mom for a late lunch. Emma called this morning to double-check the time, remember?"

Right. To talk over the order of service. Brad's mom hadn't been happy when Ashley called yesterday afternoon, but she'd agreed to join them.

"Pastor Barnes called. He isn't able to make it down today. Said to email him what we decided, and he'd talk to you later this week."

"I can't believe he's going to perform the wedding. I haven't set foot in his church since Eric died."

Margo pulled her into a hug. "He's known you since you were born. Plus, he likes Patrick. A lot."

Of course he did. Everyone loved Patrick. He was an outgoing optimist who could talk to anyone about anything and set them at ease. Pastor B. believed Patrick was what got her involved with church again. He'd made that clear when they'd visited his home in Atlanta last summer.

That wasn't far from the truth.

"Let's go plan the wedding of the year." Margo smiled, but her eyes had grown older since last night.

So had the ones in Ashley's mirror.

As she stepped onto the front porch, she breathed in the tang of freshly mowed grass and honeysuckle vines. "Let's walk to Emma's."

"I'll wilt in this heat. I'll drive." Margo beelined it for her sky-colored BMW coupe.

"I'm walking."

Margo rushed to block the sidewalk. "It's...well, it's not safe."

So much for forgetting she had a stalker. "I refuse to hole up in my house on my vacation."

"Please. Let me drive."

"This sounds suspiciously like your request for company on your trip home this weekend. It's not your job to protect me. It's mine to make sure you're safe."

Margo turned and headed for her Beemer. "Do this for me. For Patrick. For our peace of mind."

Not because of fear. Ashley followed. "I'm only doing this for your peace of mind."

Her best friend had won this round.

Emma waved from the wraparound porch of the Traveler's Rest Bed and Breakfast. Ashley's home away from home reminded her of languid summer days and lemonade. Innocence and peace.

"Come in out of this heat, girls. Lunch is ready and everyone's seated." Emma's grayish, perfectly coiffed hair and her tailored flowery dress added to the B&B's Southern charm.

Ashley's stomach growled.

"I made extra chocolate croissants for you to take home for Patrick later."

"He's not coming?"

Margo studied her. "Didn't he tell you that when he called this morning?"

"No." At least she didn't remember that. Her stomach coiled into a knot. She couldn't get forgetful again. Not like when Eric died. More than ever before, she had to hold it together.

She had to.

Margo's blue eyes bored deeper. "You told me Patrick would text you if he could make it last minute."

She stepped through the front door and pulled out her phone. Sure enough, Patrick had texted. *Got called into a meeting—can't make lunch. Sorry, hon—will make it up to you.*

At least he was safe.

Brad stood and smiled when she and Margo entered the glassed-in patio. "Thanks for inviting us."

His tan shorts and tie-dye T-shirt surprised her. Brad's new style would take some getting used to.

"I'm so glad you're here. We'll go rescue Chester and you guys can hang out after wedding talk is finished." Ashley extended a hand toward Joyce. "I'm glad you could join us too. I wanted you guys to know what the day would entail."

And to see for herself what kind of mother Joyce had become.

Joyce returned the handshake and half-smiled. "Thanks for the invite."

The women exchanged Southern pleasantries about fashion, the humidity, and what it did to hairstyles.

Ashley refrained from commenting.

Kath pulled her into a hug. "You okay?"

"Sure. Fine." She slipped into a chair between Brad and Kath. "Let's eat."

Emma's chef had stayed to fix lunch and brought out their plates with a grin. "Hope the salmon croquettes and steamed veggies are to your likin'. There's peach cobbler in the oven for dessert."

"Magnificent as always, Jan. Thank you for staying over today." Emma placed her linen napkin in her lap.

"See you tomorrow, Mrs. Emma. Enjoy your visit, everyone."

At Jan's departure, Emma extended her hands. "Dear Lord. We thank You for this scrumptious food, Ashley and Patrick's upcoming wedding, and the beautiful summer day outside. Guide us as we plan and may all we do glorify You. Amen."

Patrick must not have filled Emma in on the events of yesterday. Good. The fewer people who knew, the less panic her loved ones would face.

They all dug into their colorful meals.

Joyce spoke up first. "So, Ashley. Thank you for includin' Brad in the weddin'. You all have done him heaps of good."

"He's like a little brother." Ashley nudged Brad with her elbow. "Our wedding wouldn't be complete without him."

Brad blushed. Such a change from the unsettled, angry youth Patrick had counseled last year. He'd survived so much.

"What do I need to shell out for his tux?"

"Mom." Brad touched her arm. "Don't worry about it. I can afford it. I've been saving up."

Ashley dabbed at her mouth with her napkin. "It's covered. All we need to do is go to Atlanta for a fitting sometime soon."

"Cool." Brad gulped down his last croquette.

Joyce bristled. "We don't take charity."

"It's not charity. It's my pleasure. My parents are taking care of so much of the wedding, I wanted to do this."

Joyce studied her plate. "Well. Thank you, then."

From across the table, Margo winked.

One disaster avoided.

"So why don't you come with us to Atlanta this weekend? Ashley's escorting me home, and we'd love your company." Margo spoke directly to Brad.

"He's busy this weekend, sorry." Joyce cut into her untouched salmon.

"Yeah, I promised I'd help out at home. Maybe next weekend? Would that be too late, Ashley?"

"No problem. I'll see what my day off is and let you know."

Emma pulled out a pen and leather bound book. "While you all finish up eating, I'll jot down a few ideas. Ashley, tell me what you had in mind for the service order."

Conversation turned to all things white and wonderful, and Ashley's mind settled down to details. Safe things like songs, prayers, and candle counts.

Kath scooped up plates. "Want to wash or dry, Ashley?"

Emma rose. "No, girls, you all finish your chat. I'll clean."

"Not today." Kath slid one more dessert plate onto her pile.

Ashley escaped into the kitchen before Emma could argue. "You are one brave woman to cross Emma on her territory."

"She's a softie. But she does too much." Kath peeked over her shoulder. "Besides, it was a good excuse to get a minute alone with you. How are you doing?"

Her future sister-in-law's Irish green eyes pierced through any avoidance attempts.

"Okay. Scared." She couldn't believe how easy it was to talk to Kath. It ran in the James family.

"No more notes or phone calls where he hangs up?"

"No."

The unknown, the waiting, held her by the throat.

"What are the police doing?"

Ashley grabbed a yellow dishtowel and dried the clean dishes. "More patrols. Investigating people I've arrested in the past. Talking with the Georgia Bureau of Investigation to see what resources they can provide to help find this guy."

"This is all so frightening, Ashley. How are you holding up?"

"I'm okay." So not true. "Culp has already run down most of my list of suspects. A lot are still in jail or on probation." Dead ends. She shivered. Not knowing who or what he'd do next pressed in on her. A few more sleepless nights and she'd be a basket case.

In no shape for a wedding.

Maybe that was what he was doing, trying to keep her from the wedding.

If so, he wouldn't win.

Her jaw hurt from clenching. "They'll catch him soon. Or I will."

"Catch who?"

Ashley spun around at the sound of Brad's voice. "Nobody." How much had he heard?

"You sure?"

She took the plate he held out. "Just some police business. Nothing big."

"You look upset."

So much for her confident cop persona. One week off and her training had flown out the window.

Now, when she needed it more than ever.

"I believe Ashley is in trouble."

Bradley's words churned the acids in Jonathan's stomach. Try as he had to forget Ashley and the close friendship they once shared, the thought of her in danger troubled him. He would do anything to protect her, as she had done to rescue Bradley and Anna from harm.

He held his cell phone tighter and turned off the lights in his carpentry shop. Five o'clock Thursday afternoon was time to go home and clean up for dinner at his parents' house. Not time for Bradley to drag him back to a place he had struggled to free himself from.

"Did you hear me, cousin? I believe Ashley is in danger."

"I have heard you." He placed his summer hat on his head and dusted off the wood shavings from his black trousers.

It had been over a year since he had seen Ashley. Her image had almost disappeared from his memory.

Almost.

"Do you know what the trouble is?"

"No. She was talking to Patrick's sister about suspects being still in jail. She was scared. I've never seen Ashley scared."

Neither had he. He had seen his friend angry, hurt, and determined. She had prayed over him when he was in the hospital. Protected his family in ways he never could.

"Did you speak with her?"

"No. I know I shouldn't have listened in, but something was wrong. She saved our lives, Jonathan. We can't just let her face whatever is happening on her own."

"She is a police officer. This is her job."

"I don't think this was police business. No one in town or in our community has heard anything, though."

"You should not be stirring up gossip."

A low rumbling in Bradley's throat carried over the phone lines. The boy hated being treated like a child. This Jonathan had learned to avoid a great deal of the time. "Your asking questions could make things more dangerous for Ashley. This is all I meant by my words."

"I hadn't thought of that."

"If you believe Ashley is in danger, why not ask her to bring you back to Shipshewana?" His conscience pricked. Bradley was not his son, and Ashley's protection belonged to another. This was not his concern. "I am sorry. I know you are following the Lord's direction to be in Georgia. I will pray for you and for Ashley."

"Thank you. I have to go. I will call if anything happens."

Jonathan prayed nothing would happen to Bradley or Ashley. Her wedding was not far away. He bowed his head to pray for Patrick James as well.

Bradley would be in their wedding.

Jonathan would attend with Anna and watch a woman he had once had feelings for marry the man she loved.

"Jonathan, are you sleeping standing up?" Beth Kauffman pulled her cousin's black buggy to a stop in his small parking area. Much different from the minivan she had driven in Montezuma, Georgia. Or the simple cars that other Mennonites from his church drove here in Shipshewana. Beth had opted to use her cousin's rig rather than borrow a vehicle from a church member. It suited her well.

"Sleeping then?" Beth's eyes brightened. Her modest green dress, Mennonite head covering, and bright smile returned his thoughts to the present.

"I am not asleep. Not this time."

She laughed as she tied her cousin's horse to the hitching post beside him. Many Amish frequented his shop and this old-fashioned post was common. So different from Montezuma where Amish horses couldn't manage the heat.

"Will you join me at my cousin's house tonight? The babies are much quieter now than the last time you visited."

Beth had stayed in Shipshewana since Christmas to help her older cousin with the care of newborn twins. He suspected there was more to her staying in Indiana than love of family, but he was not ready to ask questions on that subject.

She tucked a stray brown hair into her prayer cap. "Will you come?"

"*Ja*. I will be there. I must go home first and check to see if my father has need of me this evening. He and my mother have been busy lately, and I do not want them to do so much they injure themselves."

Beth's smile faded. "Have they been sick? I would have brought meals."

"No. They are fine."

"You are a very concerned son. I am sure they appreciate your dedication."

He nodded, growing more accustomed to her flattery. It still embarrassed him, but he had found no good way to dissuade her.

Horse and buggies clip-clopped down highway 5. He had missed them while he was in Montezuma. Their steady cadence spoke of history and family. Simplicity.

Not a life Ashley could ever have become accustomed to, but one that would have kept her safe from the dangers she faced every day.

Dangers that had prompted Bradley to call him. But what could he do besides pray?

Beth stepped in front of him. "You are someplace else today."

He nodded. "News from your home. One of our friends might be in danger."

Beth's eyes widened. "Ashley?"

"Yes."

They stood in silence and watched buggies and cars move up and down the highway.

"There are Beachy churches and some in the Amish districts around Shipshewana who have hidden women in danger." Beth pulled her cell phone from her apron pocket. "I could call and talk to a woman from our church who has done this."

They would help his friend. "This could bring Ashley's danger to our families."

"But we will trust God for our protection. Is that not what we learned from the trouble last year?"

"Yes. You are right." He should not struggle with this fear again. It was his duty as a Christian to help those in need. And Ashley was in need. He would help protect her.

He would pray for the safety of his family and Beth's and the people in Shipshewana. He would trust God to protect them all.

He met Beth's concerned eyes. "I should call Patrick first before you speak to anyone from my church about this."

"*Ja.* That is wise."

Ashley's fiancé could convince her to come for a vacation and stay in a place where she would be safe.

If only she were interested in being protected.

CHAPTER FIVE

I don't think Brad's safe." Ashley turned the keys in her Silverado and pulled out of Yoder's Restaurant.

Margo sat their stash of Yoder's famous doughnuts on the backseat. "You're assuming a lot there. Joyce seemed like a concerned parent. Even you said she's changed."

"So did Patrick last night at dinner. But he agreed we should keep a close eye on things."

"Then keep a careful watch and pray. That's better than getting worked up."

Ashley stared straight ahead. "I should call Jonathan and see if there's any way to get Brad to move back to Indiana. He belongs in the Mennonite world."

Pecan trees arched overhead as they drove toward the Mennonite church.

Margo leaned her back against the door. "Why does it matter so much to you?"

"We've been over this. I was responsible for Brad meeting his mother, and that was a disaster. Now he's turned his back on his culture. He's safer in the Mennonite community." Especially with an unidentified stalker out there watching.

"Sounds like this is less about where he belongs and more about you trying to protect everyone."

"That's what I do, Maggie."

"That's what God does."

Silence reigned as they drove past Anna and Brad's farmhouse and a small Mennonite school. Church members continued to run the Yoders' dairy, still awaiting the day when Brad and Anna would return. Now Brad might never return to his community or Anna to the farm that had been in her family for fifty years. A farm she'd almost lost last year but retained for the sole purpose of passing on to her son.

"What would you be doing right now if you'd married Jonathan?"

Ashley stomped on the brakes. "You promised you'd never bring up that conversation ever again."

"You still drive by his house."

"Brad's house." She pushed on the gas pedal again. "Jonathan was never interested in me, not that it matters. I had a few weeks of a crush going, but he's been my friend ever since. I chose Patrick, and have never regretted that choice."

"So in all your driving through Mennonite farmlands, you've never imagined what it would have been like?"

"No."

"You would have been adorable with a head covering, raising cows and goats and minding a farm."

"The Mennonite belief in nonresistance stands in the way of your daydream. I believe in the second amendment and my duty to protect and serve this community. Had I not used my gun, Brad would have died."

"Without guns that man couldn't have hurt anyone."

Ashley glanced at her friend. "Maybe it's you who wants to become Mennonite. I can take you to a church service."

"Maybe so. I can't help but think about the simplicity of their lives, how little they rush from appointment to appointment. How they don't worry over physical appearance. Aside from their stand on non-violence, they're theologically very similar to us."

"You're forgetting the head covering issue, the fact that they don't celebrate religious holidays, and their very limited use of technology."

Margo shrugged. "True. But we're more alike than different on foundational beliefs like salvation by faith and believers' baptism."

"You've given this a lot of thought."

"Maybe. You have to admit, their lifestyle is appealing."

Ashley pulled onto the side of the deserted road and stopped. "What aren't you telling me?"

Margo batted her eyelashes. "Whatever do you mean?"

"Lying by omission is a sin."

"I haven't lied."

"You haven't spit out the whole truth either. You aren't interested in becoming Mennonite, are you?"

"I've thought about it."

"And now, out of the blue, you want me to consider this lifestyle? Why?"

"No reason. It's just, like you said, a safer community." Margo crossed her arms and lifted her chin. But her pursed lips and determined eyes gave her away. She had a plan, one Ashley would hate.

Like double blind dates or surprise birthday parties. Or something much, much worse...

"This has something to do with Patrick, doesn't it? You two have talked behind my back, haven't you?"

Margo huffed. "I wish you'd listen to reason."

"What are you two planning now?"

Margo wouldn't meet her eyes. "An escape plan, if you must know." She stared out the window.

Ice chilled her veins. They were scared enough to go behind her back and plan a way to drag her to safety against her will.

Maybe she should listen. Margo and Patrick knew her better than anyone else. They'd slipped beyond her tough shell and witnessed the frightened little girl inside. They loved her.

"I have to stay here until this is over. It's the only way I can be sure he won't come after you two or Brad to get to me."

"Patrick is stronger than you're giving him credit. Let him be the protector this time." Margo's voice wavered on the last word.

Tears pricked her best friend's eyes when she turned around.

"I'll talk to Patrick."

"Trust him, Ash. He only wants what's best for you."

Trust someone else to be the protector. Easier said than done.

✑

If Ashley didn't love him, she'd have his head right now.

Patrick hung up the phone and prayed for Margo. She'd called to warn him that Ashley had figured things out and was steamed. Too bad. Ashley needed protecting this time, and that was his job.

He paced between his boxed-up kitchen and equally boxed-up workout room and office. *Decluttering*, the realtor had called it. As if he had that much to declutter. Still, the boxes would go into storage this week and stay until after they returned from their honeymoon.

He grabbed a set of free weights from the closest box. Pumping iron might use up some of the adrenaline filling his veins.

He couldn't avoid the conversation ahead. Ashley would be here soon to discuss his escape plan. The one Margo spilled. The one he'd discussed with Jonathan. Ashley wouldn't appreciate any of it.

But he didn't care. He'd rather have her mad and alive.

Culp had paid Craig Humphrey a visit and the man was furious at being questioned. He had airtight alibis for Tuesday and Wednesday evenings.

So he couldn't be Ashley's stalker.

Patrick set the weights on an end table and opted for inverted push-ups.

More and more unknowns. None of the people who'd made his or Ashley's list could really be the stalker, could they?

So who was he? When would he strike next?

He hated the invasion of fear and helplessness. The waiting.

He banged out fifty pushups.

Someone was out there who could hurt Ashley any second now, and there was nothing he could do to stop it.

As expected, Jonathan had reminded him to pray.

He had. Nonstop, especially in the middle of the night when he couldn't sleep. He almost wished something would happen so they could get it over with.

A knock at the front door jerked him to attention.

He flung his legs to the ground and rushed to the door. Ashley had a key. "Who is it?"

"Craig. Patrick, I need to talk to you. To apologize for what I said before."

How had Craig found his address?

Easy, thanks to the Internet. This wasn't the first patient who'd tried to visit after office hours.

"Please, Dr. James. I…" The locked door muffled the man's voice.

He hesitated. What if it was a trap?

He'd handled Craig's angry outbursts before, and he could handle them now.

Opening the door a fraction of an inch, he maintained a tight hold on the wood. "Craig, this isn't appropriate. I appreciate your need to apologize, but we can talk at the office tomorrow."

A man in an Atlanta Braves hat raised his steel blue eyes.

Not Craig.

The man kicked the door open and shoved him at the same time.

Patrick stumbled backwards.

"You shouldn't have poisoned Ashley's mind. You should have left her alone." He slammed the front door closed.

No words formed in Patrick's mind.

Wild eyes assessed him. "I'll show Ashley."

"Show her what?"

"Don't use your counseling voice on me. I'm smarter than that."

Patrick backed up toward the end table with his hand weights.

"Show her who's the right man, the strongest one. The one who can take care of her for the rest of her life."

Disagree and he'd ignite this stalker's rage. Stay silent, and they'd dance a dangerous dance until Ashley arrived. Then she'd be in his sights. Patrick had to stop him before Ashley arrived.

Then it would all be over.

"No big words to dissuade me from the inevitable?"

Patrick shook his head.

"Answer me."

Wait for it. Wait for him to lunge forward and Patrick could gain the upper hand. He'd taken Tae Kwon Do in college. He could do this.

Ashley's stalker stood still, cold eyes burning into him.

"Don't think you can beat me. Don't even try."

"We'll see about that."

In a flash, he sprang forward.

Patrick slammed the free weight into the man's side, sending him to the floor.

He didn't move.

Patrick waited.

A loud, inhuman snarl filled the room. The man sprang to his feet, red-faced and sweating.

"You'll pay for that."

Stay calm. Stay focused.

The man reached toward the small of his back, and before Patrick could pounce again, he was staring into the barrel of a black handgun.

"Whoa, now. You don't want to make this mistake."

The man smiled. "Yes. I do."

"Let's talk about this." Think fast. Very fast. "Ashley's not impressed by violence."

"You don't know her like I do. She's a good cop. She'll understand."

"How do you know Ashley?" He had to get the man talking so he could make another move. Time was running out.

"What difference does that make to you?"

Patrick lunged forward and tackled the stalker to the ground.

The gun exploded.

Patrick grabbed for the weapon and slammed the stalker's hand against the wood floor until the gun skidded away.

But the stalker was too fast. His head connected with Patrick's face, and he fell backward.

For a second, the room spun.

Ears ringing, brain dazed, Patrick fought to right himself, to get up from the floor. To find the stalker.

Pain slammed into his back, and he fell face-first against the hardwood floor.

"I win, Patrick. I win."

Gasping for breath, Patrick pulled himself to his knees.

A foot slammed against his rib cage.

Then another.

He couldn't block. Couldn't breathe. He collapsed onto his back, his vision blackening.

A calloused hand closed around his throat. "I win, Patrick."

He grabbed at the man's arms, but couldn't pry the icy fingers off his windpipe.

His lungs burned.

Stars blinded him.

His head slammed into the floor. Once. Again.

Searing pain spread over his head. Sliced into his throat. Patrick fought for breath. For strength. He tasted the tang of blood on his lips.

"It's all over."

God, protect Ashley.

He fought to stay conscious. He had to stay awake. He moved his head and stars twisted into blackness.

Then blackness won.

CHAPTER SIX

Ashley tried Patrick's number one more time.

No answer.

She'd agreed to talk face to face about his and Margo's escape plan, but this evening wasn't the time. Maybe after a good night's sleep she'd handle the discussion better.

But she couldn't get ahold of Patrick to tell him.

"He's not answering his cell or home phone."

Margo flipped through channels on the TV. "So go over there without tearing into the poor boy. He loves you. Let him protect you." She turned off the TV. "We only discussed some ideas for your safety because we care about you."

"I know." She grabbed her keys and patted Chester on her way out the door. Now Margo was his favorite.

The drive over took all of five minutes.

One look at Patrick's place and every nerve ending snapped to attention. No lights on.

The front door open.

Scrambling around the console for her phone, she fought the urge to run inside, weapons ready.

It could be a trap.

Someone could still be in there, and she'd be a sitting duck.

But if Patrick was hurt…

Elizabeth's cell rang.

"Come on, Elizabeth. Answer. Please pick up."

"Officer Rey."

"Elizabeth, it's Ashley. I'm at Patrick's. Something's wrong. His front door is open. No movement, no lights inside."

"Stay put. My ETA is less than five minutes. Do *not* go in there."

"I'll try." Ashley shoved her phone in her pocket and exited her truck, staying low in case someone was watching.

Please, God, let Patrick be okay.

Not able to stay still, she hurried to the side of Patrick's ranch. Warm brick pressed into her T-shirt.

Slow and steady, she eased along the east side of the house, staying below the windows.

No noises inside.

She slipped into the backyard and surveyed the entire area. Nothing out of place.

Continuing her perimeter search, she steadied her breathing. Right now she was a cop. Inside would be a different story.

If she found Patrick…No. She couldn't let her mind drift now.

She crept up the back deck and turned the door handle. Unlocked.

The kitchen floor on the other side of the door creaked.

Nowhere to run for cover. She stepped to the side of the door and flattened herself against the bricks once again.

The door flew open.

She pointed her weapon.

Right into the barrel of another handgun.

"Ashley. What are you doing here?" Patrick lowered his XD, his whole body aching with the movement.

But he was alive.

Snatches of memory rocketed through his brain then disappeared.

"What's going on?" Ashley holstered her weapon and then removed the XD from his hand. "Why were you creeping through a dark house with a gun?" She studied his face. "What happened?"

"I don't know." He wobbled on rubber legs. "I think someone broke in."

She rushed into his arms. "It was him, wasn't it, Patrick? But you're alive. Thank God, you're okay."

His ribs screamed in protest. His head swam. Still, he held on to Ashley.

She pulled back, bright red on her hands. "Patrick, you're bleeding. I'm calling an ambulance."

"I'm fine." Why was he bleeding? He touched the back of his head and his knees went weak. Blood streaked his hand too.

He leaned into the porch rail and fought the nausea rising in his throat.

"The ambulance is on the way." She wrapped his arm around her shoulders.

"I'll be okay. I just need to sit down."

She helped him ease down onto the porch steps. He rubbed the burning in his neck and his skin screamed.

What in the world?

Police lights lit up the side of his house. "Did you call the police?"

"Yes." She stepped out of his arms. "Back here, Elizabeth."

Footsteps pounded through his house. The cops were checking for someone. But who? He fought to stay awake.

Officer Elizabeth Rey slipped into the backyard, gun pointed at his head.

His heartbeat skyrocketed. His hands shook, and his head pounded. He blinked to clear his vision.

Someone had done a number on him.

Elizabeth holstered her gun. "Sorry, Patrick. I didn't know what to expect after Ashley's call." She joined them on the back porch. "What happened to you?"

"I don't know."

Ashley pointed into the house. "It had to be the stalker."

Elizabeth's eyes widened. "How do you know it was him?"

"It had to be him. Did he say anything, Patrick?"

"I don't know. Maybe." His head screamed at his effort to think.

A male officer exited his house. "All clear." He stomped down the steps.

Every thud reverberated through his brain. Patrick swallowed the groan rising in his throat.

"You're a mess, man. What the devil happened?"

Patrick couldn't place the officer. Could barely see for the multiple images swimming in front of him.

Elizabeth keyed her mike. "Officer Rey requesting an ambulance…"

"I already called." Ashley studied him again. "They're on the way. I wish they'd hurry."

"No." Patrick shook his head. Stupid move. The backyard spun. "I'm fine."

Ashley steadied his shoulders. "No, you're not. We're going to the hospital."

He didn't budge. "Ash, listen. If a stalker did this to me, you need to go. You need to get out of town now."

Ashley shook her head, then dug out her phone and dialed with trembling hands.

Elizabeth spoke into her mike again and rushed out of the backyard. The world spun. He just needed to lie down for a minute. Face against the wood deck, his eyes blinked shut. He had to sleep. Just sleep.

"Patrick. Stay with me, Patrick." Ashley shook his shoulders. Pain ripped through every muscle.

"Stop. Please." He searched for her hand with his eyes closed.

"The ambulance is on the way."

"No." He fought the nausea and sat up. "I'll go to the hospital on one condition."

"No conditions. You have to go. I'm going with you."

Elizabeth led paramedics into his back yard. "Ashley, ride with him to the hospital. I'll be right behind you."

"No." He could hardly form the words. "Elizabeth…take…take Ashley home. Make sure she leaves. Now. If there's a stalker…Ashley's in danger."

"I'm not leaving you. I'm right here."

Patrick pushed the male paramedic's hands away. "I'm not going unless you promise me you'll leave right now. Please, Ash. You have to be safe."

Ashley ignored him and turned to the paramedic. "Let's go. Hurry up."

In less than a minute, Patrick was hefted onto a gurney and rushed into an ambulance.

His head throbbed. His vision blurred.

"Can you tell me what happened, Patrick?" A man's voice called to him from somewhere to his right. Or left.

No. He couldn't even form the words. Or remember.

Every bump jostled his brain. A needle prick. Someone's hands pulling and kneading his screaming arm muscles.

"Stop." His voice scratched like sandpaper.

"Keep him talking, Officer Walters."

"Patrick." Ashley's cold hand wrapped around his. "I'm here. I'm not leaving you." Her words choked off.

"You…have to…go, Ash. Be…safe."

Beeping, wailing siren. Every sound pierced his eardrums. Why couldn't he just sleep?

Ashley's words scrambled, and he couldn't untangle them. Couldn't respond.

More rattling, banging. A drop. His stomach remained in the ambulance.

More lights. Noises. Loud voices.

Everything faded into pain. Raw. Hot. Pain.

Ashley paced the length of the busy ER waiting room. Why wouldn't the doctor hurry up and let her back by Patrick's side? Where she belonged.

God, why is this happening again? Memories from last year flooded her mind. Patrick in the ER. Bandages covering his hands, his chest. So much pain.

Elizabeth met her in the freezing hospital corridor. "You heard from the doc?"

"Only a fraction of the truth. The doctor says Patrick has a concussion."

"He'll be okay, Ash. Patrick's a fighter."

"Patrick was almost killed by this stalker. And the doctor isn't telling me the whole truth. I can see it in his eyes."

"I'll talk to the doctor, okay? And let you know everything he says. But you need to go. Patrick's right, Ashley. You need to take Margo and get out of here."

"No. I'm not leaving Patrick."

"You two are a perfect match. Stubborn as the day is long." Elizabeth grabbed her shoulders. "But you'll be no help to anyone if this stalker gets to you. We've swept your house. Officers are posted there right now. Margo's waiting in the driveway. I had an officer run your truck over here too. If you pack fast and take off, there's a good chance you can get away and hide somewhere safer. I'll meet you there soon."

"No. I'm not running from this. Patrick needs me. I'll stay and face the stalker if I have to and stop him myself."

"Patrick needs you alive. Please, Ash. Go."

Long minutes of indecision hammered her chest. Patrick would be safe in the hospital, guarded. Margo was not.

"Fine. But you'll come right back here when I leave town and call me the second you know something."

"Will do."

Speeding the short distance between her home and the hospital, she shut off her emotions and shoved the memories into a locked compartment in her brain. She had to get Margo and get her somewhere safe. Then she'd come home and end this before anyone else she loved got hurt.

Cop cars stood sentinel in her driveway. Cops guarded the front porch.

Margo ran from the porch to the side of her truck and flung open her door the second she parked. "Ashley, honey, are you okay? Is Patrick? What's goin' on?" Margo yanked her out of the truck and dragged her toward the house. "Your cop friends won't tell me a thing."

Ashley dug in her heels and stopped Margo in her tracks. "Maggie, calm down." She pulled Margo into a hug. "We'll be fine. We just need to leave now. Have you packed?"

"Yes. What happened to Patrick?"

"He was attacked. By the stalker."

Margo gasped. "Oh, merciful heavens. Will he be okay?"

Time to move. "We'll talk on the way." Ashley hustled into the house and took the stairs two at a time. She shoved everything she could into her suitcase. Gun. Clothes. Toiletries.

Margo banged around in the other room.

Images of Patrick's bruised face and his blood on her hands slipped past her defenses. *God, please let Patrick be okay.* He had to be okay. Tears burned her eyes.

Chester raced into her room, barking and whimpering. "Calm down, boy." She pulled him into her arms.

Hot tears slipped down her cheeks and disappeared into his fur. She should go back to the hospital, make sure Patrick would really be okay. He had been so pale. So weak.

"Come on, Ash. You said we have to go. Let's go." Margo hefted two of Ashley's huge suitcases out of the bedroom.

"I need to see Patrick again."

Margo paused in the doorway. "No. You told me we had to go. Now."

Adrenaline buzzed through her veins. They had to leave. She grabbed her bathroom bag and picked up Chester's leash and her water bottle on the way to the stairs.

Margo searched for her keys. "It's going to be okay, Ash. We'll follow Patrick's escape plan, and the police will catch the stalker. Patrick will meet us soon."

Gunfire exploded right outside her door. "Get down, Margo!" She sprang at her best friend and knocked her to the ground.

Tired squealed. More gunfire.

"Stay here." She unstrapped her ankle holster and flew down the stairs and out the front door.

Elizabeth aimed and fired at a disappearing white sedan.

"I missed him."

Lights flashing and sirens screaming, a patrol car raced past them in pursuit.

"Did you get the license?"

"There wasn't one." Elizabeth holstered her Glock. "Get your bags and get out of here now. He can't follow you when the police are hot on his trail."

She ran back inside and grabbed Chester. "Are you okay, Maggie?"

Her best friend stood at the answering machine, frozen.

"Maggie. We need to go. Now."

"Listen to this, Ash." She pressed the play button.

A gravel-filled voice spoke her name. The hairs on her neck stood at attention. She couldn't swallow. *Don't keep putting people between us, Ashley. Next time they'll die.*

The time stamp said he'd called right before the shooting started. He could have killed Elizabeth.

She grabbed her suitcases and Chester and rushed outside. "Elizabeth, did he take a shot at you or the house?"

"Me. He barely missed."

For the first time, Ashley heard her neighbors' high-pitched questions. Two officers provided crowd control as Culp questioned them.

"We have to catch him, Elizabeth." Ashley handed Chester over to Margo. "What can I do?"

"Leave town." Elizabeth motioned to another police officer. "I need to get back to the hospital and talk to Patrick."

More like protect him. "I'll follow you over."

Elizabeth locked onto her. "Please, Ashley. Be a hero by taking Margo to safety. We'll let you know as soon as we catch him." Then she hurried away.

Ashley stood frozen in indecision. Go back to the hospital. Talk to Culp. Leave.

"Please, Ash. You have to be safe." Patrick's pain-filled words tormented her.

"Wait. Elizabeth."

Ashley caught up to Elizabeth at her cruiser. "He left me a message on the machine." His smoke-stained voice replayed in her head.

"We'll take care of it. Thanks." Elizabeth turned and entered her squad car.

There was nothing left to do.

Nothing but run.

Chapter Seven

Lights off and sedan silent, he crouched in the driver's seat and waited until the sirens died away in the distance. He'd evaded them once again.

Child's play.

The one thing he lacked was Ashley. But he knew where she'd go.

He crept through the silent dairy farm of some Mennonite family, avoiding the farmhouse lights and the cows swishing their tails in a nearby pasture.

No one would think to look for him here.

In the dark, he made his way through the trees and into his favorite hiding place. The abandoned farmhouse had provided a place of refuge when he'd first visited Montezuma. No realtor checked the property. No prospective buyers stopped to examine his home away from home.

It was perfect.

He unlatched the lock he'd placed on the detached garage and opened the door wide.

His silver truck stood guard, strong and ready, exactly where he'd left it for this day. He unlocked the driver's side and climbed in.

Roses wilted in the passenger seat. He'd have to purchase new ones for his meeting with Ashley.

Tomorrow. She'd be ready this time. He'd proven himself to her. This time she'd accompany him into their future.

And they'd live happily ever after.

∽

Ashley struggled to keep her eyes open. Had she driven far enough? Was Patrick home from the ER yet? Was it safe to call?

White lights zipped past her on I-75 northbound. She continued driving south in the left lane, passing Florida license tags one by one. Darkness hid them.

She needed to hear Patrick's voice.

Elizabeth had called a while back to say Patrick was being kept for observation. And the GBI was assigning a special agent to her case. He'd contacted the FBI and would be in touch with her later today. If they hadn't already found the stalker.

Please, God, let Patrick be okay. Let the stalker be in jail. Over and over, she repeated the same prayer. It'd carried her into Florida and kept her sane thus far.

Chester whimpered in the backseat.

"Okay, buddy. An exit is coming up soon. I'll stop there."

Margo stirred in the passenger's seat. "Can we please go through a McDonald's or something? I'm starving."

"How 'bout a Cracker Barrel? Food. A place to walk Chester." Safety in numbers.

"They're closed, Ash. It's almost midnight."

She exited in Ocala and followed the signs to the Cracker Barrel. Maybe someone would still be there and would let them in.

"See? It's closed. Let's go to your parents'. We'll be safe there."

Turning around in the empty Country Store parking lot, she weighed the options. They had to get gas and food and let Chester out. They hadn't been followed. She'd made sure of that, driving off and on the interstate for hours. Slipping through sleepy towns. Speeding down the interstate. So they were safe. For now.

"There's a Steak 'n Shake." Margo pointed across the main street to a white, red, and black building, a beacon of activity on an otherwise quiet street. "I'll get us some burgers and shakes, and you take Chester for a walk."

Chester went nuts.

"You could have avoided the *w* word until we got there."

Margo grimaced. "Sorry." She turned to the backseat and unlatched Chester's crate. "Come on, buddy. Hang on one more minute, okay?" She snapped on his leash.

Ashley snatched at the moment of normalcy and followed Margo's suggestions.

"I'll be right back." Margo sauntered across the well-lit parking lot like nothing plagued her and disappeared into a sea of teens waiting for food.

Ashley knew better. Her best friend only put on airs when life got too heavy.

They should head to Atlanta now. Her parents' house boasted the best security south of the Mason Dixon. Her father was a district attorney and accustomed to death threats. Even if the stalker evaded the police and waited for her in Atlanta, he couldn't get past her parents' security. They'd be safe for a short time. They could sleep there.

If she could sleep.

Chester took his sweet time finding a spot in the small tree-filled area behind Steak 'n Shake.

The heat pressed in on her.

Still, she monitored every car, every person, every movement. One suspicious action, and she'd have her Glock in hand before she could blink.

Cool it. You're a cop. You can do better than this.

Yes, she could. Deep breath in. Deep breath out. She could handle this. All she had to do was get Margo and Chester to safety. Then she'd go home and face the stalker on her turf.

Put him behind bars.

Put herself back in control.

And this nightmare would be over.

∞

This nightmare had to end.

Patrick swung his legs over the ER bed and steadied himself. The room spun. He strained to get a breath. His IV line pulled against his efforts.

He had to get out of here and find Elizabeth. She'd tell him what was happening. No one here would even listen. They just wanted him to repeat the details of the fight. Details he'd forgotten at first. Now he remembered everything in vivid detail.

He'd rather forget.

He needed to know if they'd caught the stalker. He had to make sure Ashley was safe.

"Easy there, Patrick." A blonde woman in a white coat grabbed his arm and nudged him back into the blurry bed. "I've spoken with the doc who first checked you out and had a look at the most recent X-rays and CT results."

"So I can go home now?"

The woman's lips tightened and she drew in a deep breath.

"I don't need pity, doc. I need to go home."

"You're better off than the last time you were here, I'll give you that." She turned away and flipped his chart open.

He couldn't make out a single word. The letters swam and his brain ached.

"Tell me again what happened to you?" She returned to his side. "Last time, it was a—"

"I remember. This time it was a fight. Someone pushed in my door, and we fought. He got the upper hand. Banged my head into the floor a few times. I got messed over bad. Okay? Please, can we be done? I need to call Ashley."

He focused on her nameplate, but the letters wouldn't stand still. Last time she'd wanted to keep him overnight for observation. He couldn't go through that again. They'd already kept him here half the night.

"Well, you have three broken ribs, a concussion, and numerous contusions. You received stitches, and you've remembered what happened. But your concussion and ribs won't get better unless you take it easy."

"But I can go home tonight, right?"

"With supervision. If Ashley can keep an eye on you and wake you every hour, I'll let you leave."

"She's…ah…well…I'll call my sister. Kath or Chip can come back and get me. I'll stay with them."

"I'll get your meds ordered, and we'll get you out of here soon." The doctor grabbed his chart before she slipped through the gray curtain and disappeared.

He searched around the bed for his cell phone. It wasn't there.

Where could he have left it?

With Herculean effort, he sat up again and waited till the spinning calmed down. He could make out a pile of clean clothes and his tennis shoes on the chair next to the bed. Had Elizabeth brought those? Yes. When she took his others for evidence.

His phone had to be in the stack somewhere. The police wouldn't need it.

"Mr. James? I'm here to take out your IV and go over discharge info." A man in blue scrubs entered his room and started to lay out gauze packages on a metal tray on the other side of his bed. "We'll get you fixed right up."

The man's brown hair and blue eyes sparked another memory.

It was him.

Patrick's pulse jumped and the monitors beeped. He had to get out of there. Now.

Ashley let out the first deep breath she'd taken in hours as her parents' security gates closed behind her.

They'd made it.

Sunlight poked out from the mass of pine trees surrounding them.

Margo stretched and yawned. "Long night of driving. You okay?"

"I survived."

"You called your parents, right? They're expecting us?"

"Yes, Mother. I called."

Chester barked.

"Hush. Yes, we're here, silly dog. I'll let you out in a minute. Mom and Dad will spoil you rotten."

Ashley surveyed the forest on either side of the long driveway. Anyone could be waiting out there in the disappearing darkness.

If they could get past security.

But they couldn't.

"He's not out there, Ash. Stop looking for him." Margo shivered. "Just in case, you are going to drive 'round back to park, right?"

"Yes." She'd planned their safe arrival as Margo and Chester slept. She'd changed course in Ocala and headed north, continuing up I-75, past Montezuma, when everything in her wanted to exit and go to the ER to check on Patrick.

No one had called since well before midnight.

They should have by now.

She parked in the garage and let Chester out of his crate. "Hang in there, buddy." She clipped on his leash. No way would she let him or Margo or her parents out of her sight until she'd heard from Patrick. Or Elizabeth.

"I'll grab the bags. You go calm your parents down. I'm sure your mother's a basket case by now. Worryin' about you all night."

She hadn't told them why she was coming. She'd rather not.

"Honey, come on in here and have some breakfast. We've been watching for you for hours." Her mother, dressed in a teal slip dress, beckoned to them with her jeweled left hand. "It's already a hundred degrees out here."

Gotta love Southern small talk. "I'm sorry I woke you all up."

"Anything for you, dear." Mom bent down to ruffle Chester's chestnut fur. "That's my good boy. Are you hungry too?"

Ashley blinked in surprise. "Who are you, and where is my mother?"

Mom tisked. "I adore Chester. You know that."

Off they went to the walk-in pantry. Chester was in heaven.

Dad strode into the kitchen, his favorite trial suit neat and pressed, and tossed the *Atlanta Journal Constitution* on the table. "Nothing new in the news. But now you're here. A bright spot in the day. I'll go get your bags, honey. You wash up. Breakfast is almost ready."

"Will do, Dad."

He stopped to pull her into a hug. "I'm glad you're okay. You'll tell us what's going on at breakfast, right?"

Tears pricked her eyes. So much had changed in the last year. She now had parents involved in her life, caring about her. Comforting her.

It was still so new.

"Yes, Dad. I will."

Margo opened the back door. "I declare. Something smells delightful in here. Thanks for letting us stop over for a spell."

Stop over? She wasn't staying a spell. She was putting Margo on a plane out of here and going back to Montezuma after a few hours of sleep.

Dad beamed. "Margo. I didn't know you'd be coming. Good to see you again." He pulled her into a hug too.

"It's been too long, Mr. Walters."

"Call me Randall." He released them. "I'll fetch your bags and put them in your rooms."

Margo pulled Ashley toward the stove. "Smell that? Dutch pancakes and blueberry muffins. Our favorites. I love your parents."

"Now you do." Ashley scrubbed her hands in the kitchen sink and took a few deep breaths. "We'll eat and sleep. I'll call Patrick first."

"Then we'll repack and stop at my house before we head out tonight."

"What are you talking about? I'm not going anywhere."

Margo stepped to her side and lowered her voice. "We're not staying here. It could put your parents in danger. Remember, I told you earlier? The plan Patrick and I worked out?"

"You didn't tell me anything past coming to my parents."

"Oh. Well, I'll fill you in soon." She turned toward the closed pantry door. "Mrs. Walters, what can I help you with?"

"Margo, what a delight." Mom opened the door and Chester hopped around her. Silly dog. "You and Ashley go freshen up. I have everything under control here. We'll have fruit salad, orange juice, milk, and pancakes or muffins. Ten minutes sound good?"

"Sounds wonderful." Margo elbowed Ashley. "Come on."

Halfway up the plush staircase of her youth, Ashley paused. "You talked to my parents long before I did, didn't you?"

"Whatever do you mean?"

She grabbed her best friend's arm. "'Fess up, Maggie. Now. Mom doesn't make blueberry muffins for me. Those were for you."

Margo pouted. "Fine. Yes, I talked to your mom. I told her we were coming for last-minute wedding stuff. She didn't buy it."

"So you told her about the stalker?"

"Well, no. I told her we needed a place to stay for a bit, and you'd explain when we arrived." She started up the stairs again. "Let's get cleaned up and eat."

Great. She'd put on a happy face for breakfast and then have to rip apart her parents' placid world. Dad would insist on helping and offer money and transportation. Mom would cry and pray.

Things had changed so much since they'd begun dealing with Eric's death. Ten years of cold silence between them, and then Patrick swooped in and saved the day. He'd done so much to help them all heal.

She had to talk to Patrick. Pulling her cell phone out of her purse, she hesitated. He was probably home from the ER by now and sound asleep.

She should wait.

One look at his name in her favorites and she couldn't wait.

His phone rang and rang.

"Patrick James. Leave me a message, and I'll call you back as soon as I can. Have a great day."

Then came the beep. "It's me. I just wanted you to know I love you and am praying for you. Get better fast. I…I wish you were here."

Heavy weights pulled at her every muscle. She needed a nap before she passed out. Just like Patrick needed his sleep to heal.

She'd call back soon.

Maybe they'd both get some rest between now and then. Somehow.

CHAPTER EIGHT

Patrick bolted upright in bed.

Where was he?

Not the ER. Sunlight filtered through lace curtains. Honeysuckle perfume filled the room.

Kath.

He was in his sister's guestroom.

A knock shook the door. "Up and at 'em, big guy. I got food on a tray fit for a king and I can't eat till I wait on you."

Every word slammed into his brain.

Chip flung open the door and returned both hands to the wobbly breakfast tray. "Pancakes, bacon, toast with Mennonite jam, milk for growing bones, and fresh-squeezed OJ."

Patrick's stomach roiled and the room spun. "Can't. I'll throw up."

"Doc said you'd feel that way for a while. But you gotta take your meds. To do that, you need food."

"Where's Kath?" His sister would leave him alone if he told her he needed sleep.

"At the park with Susie-Q. Only way to keep the house quiet so you could sleep in this morning. But Culp is on his way over. You gotta eat and get some of your strength back. You were a mess last night."

"What happened?"

"What do you remember?"

Sometimes he really hated his best friend. "I was at the hospital and this guy came in." His brain hurt. He reached up to press his throbbing temples together.

"Take the meds and the pain will go away."

Right now he'd do anything for some relief. He grabbed the glass of milk and the pills Chip extended his way. After downing them both, he lay back on his pillows. The stitches on the side of his head throbbed.

"What happened after the nurse came in?" Chip studied him.

Patrick closed his eyes. Images from last night attacked his brain. "I hit the guy, didn't I?"

"That you did."

"I thought it was the guy who'd attacked me. Ashley's stalker."

Chip nodded.

"I'm a little fuzzy after that. What happened?"

Plate in hand, Chip sat on the edge of the bed. Even that little movement tossed his stomach. He shouldn't even bother with food.

"Eat a little of the pancakes. All I'm asking. Then I'll fill in the blanks and let you go back to sleep."

"You're evil."

"I'm smart. Kath left me with very specific instructions."

Patrick eased up to sitting again, nice and slow. Then he took one bite. Cinnamon. His favorite. Maybe he could handle a little more.

A minute later, the pancake was gone and he was regretting his gluttony.

"Here's an anti-nausea pill. Thought you might be open to trying it."

Patrick popped the pill into his mouth and took a swig of OJ. It burned all the way down. "Tell me what happened."

"You hammered the nurse, who was innocent, by the way. Guy had been at the hospital all day. He's lived here all his life. Cops talked to him, and he's not pressing charges. You should be very thankful." Chip pulled a chair close to the bed and sat down.

Patrick closed his eyes to stop the spinning.

"They gave you something that knocked you out good. Kath, Culp, and I got you home, and Kath and I have traded off torturing you throughout the morning."

Patrick pondered that a minute. "The evil monkeys from my nightmares. Good to know I wasn't hallucinating too."

Chip laughed. "I won't tell Kath you said that. At least, not for a while."

"Thanks."

A cell phone buzzed somewhere nearby. He couldn't deal with patients right now. Maybe later.

Ashley.

Patrick fought the effects of the medicine. "Where's Ashley? I need to call her. She'll be worried sick."

"Culp talked to her. She's fine. At her parents'."

"Okay." His mind started going fuzzy again.

Chip stopped the buzzing noise and replaced it with his booming voice.

"Go away." Patrick couldn't get comfortable.

"Yep, that was our patient. Ever the chipper houseguest. Okay, right. I'll see you in a sec."

Patrick covered his head with the pillow and wanted to scream. He tossed the pillow to the ground.

"That was Culp on the phone. He'll be downstairs in a minute." Chip moved away. "I'll call him back and tell him to check in later."

"No." He fought the sleepiness dragging him down. "I need to know what's happening. Please. Let me see him."

"For a minute." Chip disappeared.

Patrick closed his eyes. He couldn't stay awake much longer.

"Patrick? You awake?" Culp hitched up his duty belt in the doorway and stepped inside.

"What took you so long?"

"I got here two minutes ago. What do you mean, what took so long?" He turned to Chip. "He doesn't look so good. I can come back later."

"No. Come on, Sam. Tell me what you know."

Culp huffed. "Not much. Ashley is safe at her parents' house. We got some partial prints we're working on. Some DNA evidence from your fingernails and clothing sent off to the state crime lab. I'll let you know when we have something more."

"Who do you think this guy is?"

"Don't know, Patrick. But we'll find him."

"He nearly killed me. And got away. Plus, he's stalked a police officer for years without her knowing. Who would do that?"

"Another cop." Chip's voice was steel.

Culp cleared his throat. "We don't know that, Jackson. You should keep a lid on your guesses. Look, I need to get back to the station."

Patrick's mind spun. Another cop? "Does Ashley know?"

"She's got enough on her mind right now. She needs to focus and work with the GBI agent heading her way soon." Culp paused in the doorway. "You rest up, you hear?"

What if Chip was right? What if another cop was hunting Ashley? What if it was the GBI agent, or someone posing as the guy? Patrick had to tell her. Had to see her. She was in Atlanta with her parents. Only a few hours away.

He had to warn her.

Ashley stared into the depths of her parents' saltwater pool. She should swim. Relax. That was what everyone told her to do.

Margo had gone home to pack. For what, she wouldn't say.

Ashley knew.

Patrick wanted her to run somewhere else. Somewhere far away. But she wouldn't.

Her cell belted out the theme song from Cops. Culp would so love to know that was his ringtone. "Why haven't you returned my calls, Sarge?"

"Been busy. Stalker to catch."

Her first day of work in Montezuma Culp had landed on her hit list. A cocky Georgia cop from the good ol' boys' day. But he'd grown on her. Despite his sometimes lackadaisical manner, Culp was a good cop. He'd had her back many times since that first day.

"Tell me what you know."

"It's hot enough to fry eggs on the sidewalk."

So much for mutual respect. "Don't jerk my chain. I need to know what's happening. How's Patrick? What's going on with the stalker?"

"Patrick's at his sister's. On meds. He'll be fine in a few days."

"And?"

"And we have DNA evidence, the white sedan with bullet holes. We've bagged and tagged evidence from the old Mitchell farmhouse near Yoder's dairy where our guy holed up."

"But no trace of him."

"Not yet. Let me do my job. You stay put until the GBI arrives and then get to someplace where no one but the GBI knows where you are."

"Is that an order?"

"You won't follow it if I make it an order. I'm askin' you as a friend."

Friend or not, Culp hadn't issued an order. She could get away with coming home. Only she could draw the stalker out.

It was the only way to protect the people she loved.

"Gotta go. Do the smart thing, Walters."

"Yes, sir." Clicking off, she smirked. She could obey that instruction. The right thing was protecting her family and friends. Ending the stalker's hiding fit that bill.

Chester barked and ran toward her. She braced for impact and cuddled the squirming furball in her arms. She'd have to leave him here with her parents. In case her next step didn't go as planned.

"There you are." Mother glided down the landscaped path to the pool. "You've slept half the day away. It's almost time for supper."

Her stomach growled. Traitor. She'd barely eaten a bite of breakfast. Too much on her mind. Too much to do.

She had to slip away soon or Margo and her parents would gang up on her and send her who knew where. Or the GBI agent would chime in and manage the whole mess.

First she had to distract her parents.

Then get through the gate.

After that she'd call Patrick and fill him in. She needed to hear his voice, to make sure he was really okay.

Then she'd call her parents and let them know she was safe.

"Mom, I'm sorry to drag you all into this. I just had to get some sleep somewhere safe."

"Of course you'd come home. Now don't worry about a thing. You're safe and sound right here. We have some of Atlanta's finest joining us shortly. And that GBI special agent too, Jim Edwards. He was delayed at his office and will be here as soon as he can. They'll handle everything."

"What?" Ashley glanced down at her faded bathing suit. "I had no intention of talking to Atlanta cops. I need to get dressed."

Mother turned toward the house. "Too late. Rich has arrived. Down here, Detective." She waved a manicured hand in Rich's direction and grabbed Chester by the collar as he started to growl. "You're coming with me, big boy."

"You called a guy I used to date?" She threw on her cover-up.

"He's a good man, Ashley. I knew he'd want to help."

Always confident, Rich flicked a wave their direction and strutted down the steps, his white shirt folded up to the elbow and his tan slacks neatly pressed. A black leather folio tucked under his arm. Very Rich. For once, his tall, dark, and disarming good looks had no effect on her.

Time to put on her professional face.

"Hello, Ashley."

She tugged her cover-up into place. "Rich. Thanks for coming."

Mother patted Rich's bicep as she passed, a growling Chester tucked under her other arm. "You two talk business. Randall and I will be in the house if you need us."

Ashley studied the man she'd dated many years ago. Still Rich, but different. "A wedding ring? You're seriously married?" She hadn't meant to sound so surprised.

"Yep. Tied the knot a few months ago." He motioned to the teak-wood table next to her lounge chair. "Why don't you fill me in on the case before I do a perimeter sweep?"

"Do I know her?"

"Who?" Rich held out her chair.

"Your wife?"

"Oh. No. You've never met her."

Strained silence wrapped around her as Rich slid into his seat and placed his folio between them. Then he leaned back. "Are you going to fill me in?"

"You already know. My sergeant talked to you after I received the packet of pictures. You've probably talked to him and the GBI agents a couple times since then."

"You should have been a detective."

"So, tell me what you know."

Rich slid an eight by ten photograph over to her. "Anyone in here strike you as stalker material?"

"In my academy graduation picture? I don't think so." She studied each face. They'd trained together for months, and she'd worked with a number of them for years.

"What about some of the guys that dropped out?" Rich slid three other pictures across the table to her.

"I don't remember these guys. It's been over six years."

"They dropped out early on, couldn't cut it." He tapped one of a brown haired, green eyed guy. "Some think the stalker could be one of us. I'm not so sure. But maybe a few of these guys would be worth looking into. What do you think?"

Leaning closer, she dug deep into her memories. "Maybe this one? I think his name started with a D."

"Dillon Matthews."

"Yeah, that's him. He creeped out a couple of the female recruits. Asked them out a lot. That's all I remember. Nothing came of any of it, though."

Rich narrowed his eyes. "What about you?"

"No. I hardly ever talked to him. You don't think it could be Dillon, do you?"

"I'll have a talk with him and go from there."

She gathered the photos into a pile. "Thanks for your help, Rich. That means a lot to me, especially with how busy you are."

He slipped the pictures back into his folio and stood. "Always a pleasure, Ash. Hey, how's Patrick holding up?"

"I haven't gotten him on the phone yet. But everyone keeps telling me he's okay." She motioned for him to precede her up the stairs, grabbing her cell phone as she passed her chair. The visit with Rich only deepened her desire to see Patrick. She needed him more than help on this case.

"I figured he'd be up here by now."

"The attack was vicious. I doubt he'll be up and around for a while. It was his idea that I come here." That was the biggest reason she'd left Montezuma. That and getting Margo out of the line of fire.

"Smart man. Can't beat your parents' security. Wish more folks followed their example."

"I agree." She opened the back door and the alarm beeped. "Thanks again for coming. You'll let me know when you have something?"

"You'll be the first." Rich pointed over his shoulder. "I'm parked out front, so I'll just do a quick sweep around the house and then head out to the gate to walk the perimeter."

"Great. See you later, Rich."

"See ya, Ash. Be careful."

"Always." She slipped inside the house and closed the door on yet another set of memories.

"Hey there, beautiful."

Patrick? She spun around. Her fiancé wobbled a fraction as he made his way across the kitchen. "You're here." She rushed into his arms, thankful he didn't groan like last time. "Are you okay? You were supposed to take it easy."

Chip Jackson waved from the dining room doorway. "Yeah, but you know Paddy. He had to see with his own eyes that you're safe."

She pulled back, but Patrick wouldn't release her. He lowered his lips to hers and kissed her objections away.

Every single one of them.

Chip cleared his throat.

She pulled back, but only enough to catch her breath.

"I missed you."

"Brother." Chip shook his head. "You saw her yesterday."

Patrick fixed his eyes on her. "You okay?"

"Yeah. I'm holding up. What about you? What did the ER doc say about your recovery?"

"Let's go sit down in the living room." Patrick slipped his arm around her shoulders, his face growing pale. "My doc said to take my meds, eat, and rest. Two outta three ain't bad."

"Patrick."

Chip wagged his finger at Patrick. "Told you. She's smart and tough. She's got this. You, however, just had stitches, a concussion, and broken ribs."

"Shut it, Chip."

She helped Patrick ease into the couch. "Broken ribs, stitches, and a concussion, huh? You should be in bed."

He shrugged and then winced. "Okay, yeah, probably. The pain pills are doing their job, and this brace around my ribs is making life easier. But I had to see you and tell you what Culp wouldn't."

Her shoulders knotted. "Tell me what?"

"The stalker could be a cop, Ash. Or someone posing as a GBI agent. Be careful who you talk to up here. In fact, you should get going."

A shiver coursed up her spine. She couldn't let this affect her like it was. She had to keep her head. "There are cops here right now. No one's getting through our front gate without someone seeing him."

"Did you talk to them?"

"Yes. I met with Detective Burke. He's doing a perimeter sweep now, then he's going to talk to someone from my academy days. Rich believes he's a person of interest."

"Does Detective Burke have any photos? I might be able to pick the guy out from a picture."

"You remember what the guy looked like?"

Patrick rubbed the back of his neck and winced.

"Maybe you should go lie down." She stood. "I'll throw some sheets onto the other guest bed."

"I'm fine. More concerned about finding the stalker than resting right now."

She hesitated. "I can go find a picture if you think you can ID the guy who attacked you."

Patrick shook his head and wouldn't meet her eyes. "I…I don't know. Maybe."

It was worth a try. The sooner this was over, the better.

No stalker would sideline her for long.

Goose bumps covered her bare legs. "Let me go throw on some clothes and find my academy photo. I'll be right back."

As fast as humanly possible, she donned a pair of denim shorts and a GCPD shirt she'd left in a dresser drawer years ago. For good measure, she slipped her backup in between the small of her back and her shorts and her cell phone into a pocket.

Better safe than sorry.

She hurried down the stairs and into the living room. Patrick looked paler. "You need to rest. Please go crash upstairs. Just for a little bit."

"I'd rather help you." His blue eyes locked onto hers. "Did you bring the photo?"

Unbelievable. "I…I forgot it. I'll—"

Her cell phone buzzed, and she slipped it out of her pocket. "It's Rich. I need to take this."

Patrick nodded.

"Rich. What have you got?"

"Discarded delivery man's garb. I have cops checking security cameras now. Stay inside. All exits are covered."

She swallowed. "You mean he could have beaten me here and hidden all this time?"

"I don't know."

"Where are you now?"

"Working my way around the perimeter."

Ashley's mind whirled. "But the perimeter's mostly wooded area. Are you still going alone?"

"I'll be fine. I'll let you know if…" A loud pop thundered over the phone and then silence. Gunfire?

"Rich? Rich, are you there?"

CHAPTER NINE

Gun in hand, Ashley raced out the front door.

Patrick started after her, but Chip grabbed him by the arm. "Not so fast. She's a cop. She's used to this kind of trouble. You aren't."

His head swam, and he steadied himself on the front porch rail. "She's going to be my wife. It's my job to make sure she's okay."

"You're in no shape to go flyin' into danger."

"Then help me."

Chip hesitated. "I don't know, Paddy."

"I'm going. With or without you."

Chip ran past him. "Let me get my shotgun. I'll catch up to you."

"Call 911 first."

"Got it." Chip raced to his pickup.

Slow and groggy, Patrick headed north, following the landscaped driveway. Sweat dripped down his back and into his eyes.

He could do this. Before yesterday, he could have run a marathon in the time it was taking him to move down the driveway. But he had to keep going. What if Ashley was out there hurt?

At the end of the driveway, he turned left and followed the gate. What had she said? Something about the perimeter. He made his way through the massive pines, searching for any sign that Ashley had come this way.

He pushed deeper into the woods that surrounded the Walters' estate. His breathing came hard and fast.

Leaning against the rough bark of a huge pine tree, he forced himself to breathe in through his nose, out through his mouth.

A clap of thunder exploded further into the forest. He rushed forward.

Gunshots, not thunder.

One. Two. Three.

They grew louder as he ran.

God, protect Ashley. Rich. Chip.

Then silence.

He slowed to a stop and ducked behind a tree.

Voices. Close by.

"Hang on, Rich." Ashley's voice. "Stay with me."

Patrick raced to her side. "What can I do?"

Her hands pressed deep into Rich's bleeding leg. Rich moaned and turned away from Ashley.

Patrick jumped to his other side and nudged him onto his back. "Try and stay still, Rich." He slid Rich's gun out of arm's reach. Ashley's gun remained next to her on the ground.

"Keep him talking." Her voice wavered. She'd been through this before. With her brother.

He focused on Rich. "Tell me what happened. Who did this to you?"

"Did I get him?" Rich's eyes blinked slower and slower.

"Who, Rich? Tell me what you saw." Patrick took a deep breath and forced calm into his tone. "Come on, Detective. Talk to me."

Rich opened his eyes and focused on the sky. "Brown hair, crazy eyes." He sucked in a breath and exhaled slowly. "Ball cap."

"Atlanta Braves?"

Rich nodded.

Patrick locked eyes with Ashley.

Her skin paled and her lower lip quivered. Still she maintained pressure on her friend's bleeding leg.

Sirens wailed in the distance. "They're coming. Hang on, Rich. Keep talking." Patrick touched Ashley's shoulder. "He'll make it, Ash."

She nodded. "Tell me what happened next, Rich."

Rich turned his head toward her. "He fired from the north, and I returned fire."

"Is that when you were hit?"

"No. He shot again…hit me." His eyes blinked shut again.

Patrick shook Rich's shoulder. "Then what, Rich?" He had no idea if he was making it worse or not, but Ashley nodded faster.

"Rich. Keep talking, man. What happened next?"

"Ashley came firing out of nowhere." His voice was just a whisper. "If you hadn't shown up…I'd be dead."

Branches snapped in succession. The paramedics were coming.

"Over here!" Patrick jumped up and almost collapsed. He steadied himself on a tree. "Officer down. Over here. Hurry."

Two men pushed through a thick clump of trees, a stretcher between them.

"I'll take it from here." One of the men slipped his hands over Ashley's. "You can step back. I've got it."

Patrick pulled her back. "He'll be okay, Ash. Let the medics do their job."

"Yeah, yeah. I know." Blood covered her hands and jean shorts. Angry red slashes marked every exposed bit of skin. She must have charged through a tangle of bushes. More than once.

"Let's head back to the house and get you cleaned up."

Minus the trees and sweltering heat, the scene before him resembled Ashley's description of her brother's death. She shook in his arms.

"Come on, Ash." He led her away.

"No, wait. I need my gun." She circumvented the medics and snagged her weapon.

A young officer dressed in a dark blue uniform stepped into their path. "Sir, ma'am, can you tell me what happened?"

Ashley shuddered. "Detective Rich Burke with the Atlanta Police Department was shot by a man we believe has been stalking me."

"And you are?"

"Officer Ashley Walters with the Montezuma Police Department."

Calm voice, but she still shivered in Patrick's arms. "Officer, she's in shock. Can we continue this up at the house?"

Medics raced ahead of them.

Ashley stood frozen. "He has to be okay, Patrick. He has to."

Ashley scrubbed blood from her hands. Rich's blood.

Two people she cared about had been attacked by her crazed stalker. She needed to get away. Patrick was right. She had to run. Far away.

"Ash, you ready?" Margo stood in the kitchen doorway. She hadn't even heard her come in. What kind of cop was she turning out to be today?

"Ready?"

"If you're done talking to the police, let's get out of here. We have a plan to follow."

Ashley dried off her hands. "I'm going. You stay. If he's still watching, he'll follow me. Then you and everyone else will be safe."

Margo stepped in her way. "Ashley Renee Walters, you are not leaving here alone."

"I agree." Patrick placed an older model iPhone in her hands. "This was my personal phone that few people had access to over a year ago. I reactivated it before Chip and I headed here. That way no one but me, your parents, and the police can get in touch with you."

Tears pricked her eyes. As much as she knew she had to go, she hated leaving him.

"Officer Walters? There's something out here I need you to see." The rookie cop from earlier held open her front door. A half dozen cops swarmed her front porch.

"I'll go, Ash." Patrick grabbed both of her hands. "You've seen enough today. Let me handle this one."

She shook her head. "They asked for me."

"Officer Walters?" This time a female voice cut through the commotion. A dark skinned, petite woman extended her hand. "Detective Karen Everett. We spoke last year in reference to your brother's homicide investigation. I'm sorry we have to meet under these circumstances."

"Detective Everett. I'm glad it's you. Have you talked to Rich? You do work with him, right?"

"Yes. I stopped by the hospital before I came over. He should be in surgery now and is expected to pull through fine. From what he said, you saved his life."

This time she couldn't hold back the tears. She'd finally done what she'd strapped on a badge to do: save lives.

She'd also almost cost Rich his.

"If you're up to it, there's something on the porch I believe you should see. I need to know if they're the same type of flowers and handwriting as the other notes." Detective Everett held out her hand toward the front door.

On shaky feet, Ashley followed.

Two dozen dead roses littered her front porch. She could see the note from where she stood in the doorway.

I told you to stop putting people between us, Ashley. Next time, they'll die. Or you will.

Margo gasped.

Ashley closed her eyes. "It's him."

Patrick pulled her into his arms. "They'll catch him, Ash. They will."

Ice filled her veins. She pulled away from Patrick. "I need you to take Chester home. You have a key, so use the food that's there. Will you do that?"

"Yes. Absolutely."

"Keep an eye on Brad too. I don't know if he's in danger, but he could be. And don't answer your door again unless you know who it is. Promise me."

"I'll be fine, Ash. I promise."

She turned to Detective Everett. "I'm going away for a while. You can get ahold of me through Patrick. I'm sorry, I know this puts a kink in your plans, but I have to keep my family safe."

Detective Everett nodded. "I understand."

Ashley led Margo back into the house. "Stay here and keep an eye on my parents, okay?"

"No way. Your parents will have police around the rest of the day. They don't need me. You do."

"I can handle this."

Margo grabbed Ashley's keys off the kitchen table. "No, not this time. Our bags are packed and loaded into my car. I'm driving."

Mom and Dad filed into the kitchen, eyes wide and skin pale. She never should have involved them.

"Mom. Dad. After you get the security situation squared away, I need you to pack for an extended vacation. A cruise, maybe. Will you do that?"

"Yes, dear. Anything you say." Her mom fidgeted with the strand of pearls around her neck.

Dad pulled her into a hug. "Where are you going? Will you be safe?"

Nowhere was safe. "Yes. I'll be fine. I'll call you when we get there."

Margo tugged on her arm. "We need to go. I'll meet you out there."

Ashley turned to Patrick. "I love you. Be careful." She kissed him with a desperation foreign to her before today.

He returned the intensity in full measure.

She broke away and backed toward the door. "I love you, Mom. Dad. I'll see you soon. I love you, Patrick."

"I love you too, Ash."

Minutes later, with the memory of Patrick's watery blue eyes driving her, she gripped the leather steering wheel of Margo's BMW and turned onto West Paces Ferry, entering the frenzy of traffic.

Surely no one could follow her in Atlanta rush hour traffic.

"Where are we going?"

"Head north on I-75." Margo widened the screen of her iPhone and tapped. "We'll stop in Chattanooga for dinner."

An hour up the interstate and Ashley's eyes still darted to her rear-view mirror every few seconds. Her heartbeat raced right along with her speedometer.

"Ash? You're really tense, honey. I know it's been a horrific day, but—"

"He's out there, Maggie. Call Detective Everett."

"And tell her what?"

"Tell her we're leaving the interstate in Dalton, and we have company. Blue Chevy Malibu. He's wearing sunglasses, but I can't tell anything else."

Ashley swerved in and out of traffic. Red lights up ahead forced her to slow down.

Without thinking, she cut off the cars in the next two lanes and flew down a side street. She'd lose him in Dalton.

She ran a red light and Margo ducked down into her seat, arms covering her head.

At the next light, she turned right and headed into a shopping center. Sure she hadn't been followed, she slipped around back and parked behind a Kroger.

"Why are we stopping? What if he finds us?" Margo's voice rose with every word.

"Instinct. We'll wait here a while, and I'll call Detective Everett and a cop friend from Atlanta who moved up here about the same time I left for Montezuma. She owes me a favor or two."

Margo stayed crumpled into a ball.

"Will you be okay if we trade cars with her for a while?"

Margo groaned. "Will you drive her car like you're driving mine?"

"Of course."

"And she'll drive my car like you do?"

"Yep."

In one quick call, she'd connected with Jen and arranged a spot to meet. She also left a message for Detective Everett.

"Let's grab some food in Kroger and get back on the road. We have to meet Jen in an hour."

Margo latched onto her car door. "What if he's sitting in the parking lot waiting for us to move?"

"He's not that smart."

"He got onto your parents' property and shot a detective and then raced away. If your instincts are right, he followed us all the way to Dalton. Sounds pretty smart, Ash."

She should have left Margo at home. Ashley had a detached, emo-tionless place to disappear to in times like this. Margo didn't.

"I should take you home, Maggie. It's only going to get harder until he's caught."

Minutes stretched thin in the hot car.

"No." Margo smoothed her blonde hair into place. "I'm fine now. It won't happen again."

"We can head back."

Margo grabbed her purse and started walking. "No. Let's get some food and meet this Jen. I sure hope her car is decent."

They entered Kroger and Ashley grabbed a blue basket. "Healthy or junk food?"

"Junk food. Definitely. There's chocolate calling my name right this second."

Ashley filled their basket with Reese's Cups, M&M's, chips, sodas, and a bunch of bananas for good measure.

"Evening, ladies. Care to try a—"

Margo screamed.

Ashley spun around and faced the man, her hand on her gun.

A pimple-faced kid in a blue uniform stood there, frozen, a bar-becue meatball extended their way. "I...I didn't mean any harm. I'm sorry."

She scanned the crowd of curious shoppers. Two elderly men stood front and center. A few teens stared.

No stalker in an Atlanta Braves cap. As if he'd still be wearing it.

"Let's go." She tugged Margo's arm and slipped past the group of teens.

They waited in silence in the checkout line and paid for the grocer-ies with no further incidents.

"Maybe chocolate and caffeine weren't such a great idea." Ashley elbowed Margo in the ribs.

"I'm sorry. I know I can't keep doing that." Margo clutched their grocery bag and slowed her stride. "This is all so new to me. The clos-est I've ever gotten to serious crime is NCIS on TV."

"We'll get through it." Ashley stopped at the corner before turning into the loading area. "Stay here. Let me check this out."

She peered around the corner and froze.

A shadowed figure stood by Margo's car.

CHAPTER TEN

A shley modulated her breathing and waited, every nerve ending on fire. The man cupped his hands over his eyes and scanned the car's interior through each and every window.

He was tall, dark haired. Chalky white skin. Lots of bling around his neck. Older, maybe early forties.

A car thief? Or a stalker?

She retraced her steps and pressed her back against the hot brick of the shopping center.

"Let's go back inside," Margo whispered into her ear.

Ashley shook her head and palmed her Glock. "Wait here."

Once more, Ashley surveyed the scene. The man now stood with his back toward her, whispering into a phone. Margo's BMW as yet unharmed, but well within his reach. His next move would determine the success of her attempted escape.

Her gun remained steady.

The man retreated into the building's long shadows.

Then nothing moved.

She waited, heart pounding, sweat beading.

Margo fidgeted behind her.

Ashley glanced at Margo and caught a glimpse of her flashy key ring a second before the quiet alleyway exploded with an ear piercing alarm.

The man jumped and raced away from them.

She grabbed Margo's arm. "Go. Now!"

They rushed to the BMW, threw open the doors, and were speeding out of the alleyway before Margo even had a chance to buckle her seatbelt.

Ashley's hands gripped the steering wheel hard. "I can't believe you set off your car alarm. What if it hadn't worked? What if he came thundering toward us?"

"I freaked. Couldn't stop myself. Besides, it was better than you confronting the man with your gun."

"Call Detective Everett and tell her we lost the Malibu. Also let her know about our friend the skittish car thief."

Margo punched in the number. "What if it was the stalker?"

"He didn't fit the description. But make sure to include all the details. Dalton cops can pick him up and let us know if we can head home."

"I'm having to leave a message. You want to talk?"

Ashley snatched the phone and rattled off the details. "Hope she calls us back soon."

Green lights all the way to the expressway and then a slightly lighter volume of traffic greeted them. They'd meet Jen early and leave Georgia far behind in less than an hour.

Relaxing her jaw a fraction, Ashley replayed the entire incident. "That guy probably never ran so fast in his life."

Margo giggled. "It *was* funny."

"Maybe now." Ashley chuckled.

"See, I can handle myself in dangerous situations." Margo fluffed her hair-sprayed hair.

"This time we got off easy. But please don't do that again. We're running from a violent stalker. If that was him…we need to call Elizabeth too and let her know what just happened."

A sobering silence pressed in on Ashley. How in the world was she going to keep both of them safe?

And for how long?

∽

Patrick checked side mirrors in Chip's truck every few seconds. Nothing but darkness.

"No one's followin' us, Paddy. Lighten up." Chip fixed his eyes straight ahead.

Patrick's brain hurt. Pressure. Fear. Stupid pain pills dragging him down. But he had to see Brad and make sure he was okay. He'd have to tell the boy something of the trouble Ashley was in. Not much. Just enough that Brad would be on the lookout for danger.

Chester huffed and snorted in his sleep.

"You gonna keep Chester at your house?"

Patrick shrugged. His ribs screamed. One more movement to avoid for a while. The list was pretty high already.

"Think I'll stay at Ashley's a while. There are a few repairs I need to do and it's home for Chester."

"Spooked to go to your place?"

"Thanks for the compassion, man. I appreciate it."

Chip glanced his way. "No judgment from me. I'd stay somewhere else too. But I'd stay with family if I was you. You're always welcome with me and Kath."

"Thanks. But I'm okay."

Chip huffed. "Sure you are."

"I'll rest when this is over."

"If you make it that long." Chip stalled any further conversation by pulling into Brad's driveway. "You gonna fake okay for the boy and his mom too?"

"Whatever."

The yellowish siding glowed under the bright porch light. Nothing else had changed since his last visit.

Heavy bass thumped out of a car cruising down the street.

A cat howled in the distance.

Normal sounds.

"Sure it's not too late to pay them a visit?" Chip scooped a drowsy Chester from his crate.

"The porch light is on. Besides, they're night owls, both of them." Patrick made his way up the short sidewalk and onto the front porch, slow and steady. White paint peeled here and there. He should offer to help Brad repaint it. That way he could stick around for a while without raising alarm.

The front door opened before he could knock. "Patrick!" The brown-haired teen rushed into his arms.

Chester yapped all around them.

Gratitude flooded Patrick's heart as he wrapped his arms around the boy. Pain took a backseat. Brad wasn't yet too old to show real affection.

He hugged Brad back. "I've missed you too."

The teen bent down to pick up Chester and then straightened and held out his free hand to Chip. "We haven't met, but I'm pretty sure you're Chip, right?"

Chester licked the teen's face. Brad laughed.

"Yep. Good to meet you."

"Don't let all the flies in an' the air conditionin' out. I ain't payin' to cool the yard." Joyce's words still cut, but the smile she greeted them with had changed. No more flirting, but genuine happiness. Having Bradley home had changed them both for the better.

"Welcome, Patrick. You must be Chip." She waved them to follow her. "Can I get y'all some sweet tea? Just made us a new pitcher this afternoon. And I'll get Chester a bowl of water."

Chip nodded. "That'd be awesome. Thanks."

"I know you'll have some, Patrick. Right?" Joyce exited the living room before he could answer.

Brad sat next to him on the tan sofa, Chester calming down on the teen's lap. Chip took the loveseat.

"The news said a police officer was shot. It wasn't Ashley, was it?" Brad's voice broke at the end of his question.

Chester's ears perked up.

He should have checked in with Brad earlier today. "No. Ashley's fine." Sort of. "She's going away for a while though."

"Why?" Brad's brown eyes widened. "She's in trouble, isn't she? I knew it. I should have asked her more questions."

"What do you know, Brad?" Patrick's shoulders knotted. Brad loved Ashley, but the teen wasn't known for buttoned-up lips.

"She was talking to your sister about suspects being in jail. She was scared. I've never seen Ashley scared."

"Someone's trying to find her." Patrick met Chip's narrowed eyes. "Someone dangerous."

Brad shook his head. "She's going to Shipshewana, right? I told Cousin Jonathan our people up there could keep her safe."

"Brad, you can't tell anyone about this. Understand?"

"I haven't. I know better than that."

Chester yipped.

Patrick smiled. "Sounds like Chester here is defending your honor, huh?"

Brad rubbed the dog's chestnut fur. "He believes in me."

"I do too." Patrick ducked to meet Brad's eyes.

"I know."

Joyce entered with a wooden tray full of plastic cups and a tall tea pitcher. Chester's bowl sat on the edge of the tray. "Here we go. Drink up, fellas." She placed Chester's bowl on the floor and he bounded toward it.

Brad's eyes stayed fixed on Chester, a smile tugging at his mouth.

"Would you all be able to keep Chester a while?"

Brad's whole countenance brightened. "Sure. I mean, if that's okay with Mom." He turned pleading eyes to Joyce.

"We can handle it. How long?" She gulped down some tea.

Patrick followed suit. The sugar-shock tea made him thirsty. But boy, did it taste good.

Chip jumped into the conversation. "Not long. A week maybe? If that's too long, Kath and I can take care of him."

"Why not you, Patrick?" Joyce's brown eyes bored into him. "Is it because you're hurt?"

"How did you—"

"I got a mom's eyes, ya know? We see everything. You limped in here and have been favoring those ribs. You get into a fight?"

More like a slaughter. "Not really. I'd planned to keep Chester at Ashley's, but seeing him with Brad made me second-guess that. They'd both be happier here."

Joyce studied him. "Alrighty then. We'll take good care of him. Won't we, Brad?"

The boy smiled. "Sure thing." He joined Chester on the floor. "We'll have a great time, won't we, boy?"

Chester yipped and hopped around Brad.

Patrick had made the right call there. "Hey, Brad. Why don't you take Chester outside?"

Chester barked and ran to the front door.

"We'll be right back."

When the door clicked behind Brad, Patrick faced Joyce. "Yes, I'm injured. And Ashley is in danger. You all might be too."

Joyce stopped drinking tea and set her cup back on the coffee table. "What kind of trouble are we in and what can I do?"

Her quick acceptance of the situation and willingness to help warmed Patrick all the way through. Then reality chilled him again. "Ashley is being stalked. The guy attacked me and shot a detective in Atlanta."

Joyce gasped.

"But the cops have some leads now. They may have already caught the guy. I haven't heard anything yet."

"Is Ashley safe? Did he get to her?"

"No. She's heading far away to a place where she should be well protected."

Joyce sat forward and licked her lips. "You think this stalker might try to shake us down for information?"

"Maybe. He took pictures of Ashley with Brad a year ago. He must know they're close. If this guy thought Brad could lead him to Ashley, he'd try anything."

"Over my dead body." Joyce stood up and slapped her fist into her other hand. "Ain't nobody gonna hurt my boy. I just got him back."

For a second, Patrick relaxed.

Then he remembered Rich's shooting and the note the stalker had left.

Next time, they'll die.

∽

Jonathan drove his white truck through Shipshewana's quiet streets.

"Have you heard from them yet?" The knitting needles in Beth's hands clicked every so often.

"No. Maybe the police have the stalker in custody."

"I pray that is the case."

He passed horses and buggies clip-clopping in the horse lane through the main tourist area. All the shops had closed long ago. But many of their Amish friends were out visiting.

As he and Beth had been a short time ago.

"Your mother and father seemed very tired, Jonathan. And Anna's eyes are so sad. She must miss Bradley something fierce."

He nodded. "Yes. This separation has been hard for her. I am praying Bradley returns soon. His help with my parents' bed and breakfast was enormous. Anna does much of the cooking, but she has not recovered from her injuries and the trouble in Montezuma yet."

"And your parents?"

"My parents should have sold their small bed and breakfast long ago. I would be honored to take care of them as they did for Mark and me."

"You are a good son, Jonathan."

Beth's encouragement quickened his pulse. They were becoming closer every day. It would be time soon to make a decision.

After this situation with Ashley was resolved.

He pulled into the Amish farmhouse where Beth stayed with her cousin. His cell phone rang in his pocket. He ignored it.

Beth smiled in the faint light. "I should go inside. I do not wish to wake the little ones."

He circled around his car to open her door and help her out. "Goodnight, Beth. I will see you tomorrow for lunch, yes?"

"Yes." She smiled and turned away.

He returned to the driver's side of his truck and pulled his cell phone from his pocket. Patrick.

The phone rang again. "Hello? Patrick?" He pulled out from the driveway and drove down the gravel road.

"Yes. Can you talk?"

"Yes. I have dropped Beth off at her cousin's home. Is there a problem?"

"How does Brad know Ashley is coming to Shipshewana?"

Jonathan stiffened. "The boy has asked every time we have spoken. I would not lie to him. I only told him Ashley was coming up here to visit for a short time."

"He knows she's in trouble."

"You have told him the details?"

A long sigh blew over the phone line. "I told him someone dangerous was after her. I won't lie to him any more than you would."

Jonathan drove back through Shipshewana on State Road 5, passing quiet stores and fewer buggies. There was a long silence before Patrick spoke again.

"She's on her way now, Jonathan. Will the family you talked to be ready?"

Jonathan's stomach tightened. "Tonight? We were not expecting her for a few days. What has changed?"

"The stalker tried to kill a cop. Ashley had to leave earlier this evening."

This news weighed heavy on Jonathan's soul. What trouble was he bringing to his community? To his family?

"My parents had planned for Ashley to stay with them."

"You were supposed to talk to someone from your church."

"They were unable to hide Ashley at this time."

"No offense, Jonathan, but your parents can't be in any shape to protect Ashley if this stalker follows her up there."

On this point he agreed with Patrick. "I will talk to my brother. Mark and his wife, Heidi, do not yet have children. They live close to my home. Between the three of us, we should be able to handle what the Lord allows to come our way."

"I'm praying. Hard."

"As are we. I will talk to you tomorrow, Patrick. Goodnight."

Jonathan hung up the phone and pulled into his brother and sister-in-law's large bed and breakfast. They were full for the weekend. They could not hide Ashley there.

But together he and Mark would find a way to do what they must to protect Ashley.

Heidi opened the front door, her eyes widening at the sight of him. "What's wrong, Jonathan?"

Mark joined them. "Come inside." He closed the door behind them. "Are Mom and Dad worse?"

"No. They are only tired. They will be better tomorrow."

"Then why the late visit?"

Jonathan swallowed and met his brother's worried eyes. "It is time."

CHAPTER ELEVEN

Ashley stirred in the passenger's seat of Jen's SUV. Curling up in an SUV wasn't conducive to rest. Neither was running from a stalker. She'd adjust. For now, she stretched and yawned. Sunlight peeked over the horizon. A few hours' shut-eye between long stretches of driving hadn't been enough.

"Mornin', sleepyhead."

"What do you mean *sleepyhead*?"

Margo braked as the traffic slowed down. "I've driven the last four hours."

Ashley grimaced. "Sorry." She glanced outside at the gray interstate and the city skyline they were driving into. "Where are we?"

"Indianapolis. Want to stop and get some breakfast?"

Ashley's stomach growled. "Guess so." She checked the backseat. "I wish we'd brought Chester."

"That would have turned a twelve-hour trip into a two-day adventure."

"He would have attacked anyone who bothered us."

Margo lifted a perfectly sculpted brow. "Really? He's never been much of a watchdog."

"I've trained him."

Margo cut into the far right lane amid honking horns. "Reminds me of home."

"Early morning commuters everywhere are in a hurry."

"How about Starbucks? It shouldn't be hard to find one downtown."

Twenty minutes later, Margo maneuvered into a parking lot next to a stand-alone Starbucks. The green umbrellas and familiar windows were a welcome sight.

Inside, the place bustled with coffee drinkers ordering in Starbucks lingo. A language she'd learned in Atlanta. The Gwinnett County PD had won the hearts of a few Starbucks workers, and they always gave uniforms free pastries right before closing.

For a minute normalcy reigned.

"What can I get for you, ma'am?" A young fair-skinned blonde girl stared at her.

Ashley pointed to the pastry case. "I'll have two marshmallow dream bars and a venti caramel macchiato."

Margo nudged her. "We have three hours to go. Try healthy?"

Ashley smiled at the barista behind the counter. "Scratch that. I'll have oatmeal and *one* marshmallow dream bar with my caramel macchiato."

She paid in cash and smirked at Margo as she moved to the other counter to await her food.

Margo ordered her usual venti chai tea latte with a turkey and cheddar breakfast sandwich. And a blueberry scone.

"Some healthy." Ashley glanced at Margo's plate as they made their way to an empty table in the corner of the dining area.

"I figured what's good for the cop is good for the friend." Margo grabbed her hand. "Let's pray." They both kept their eyes wide open. "Lord, we need Your peace and protection. Heal Patrick and keep our loved ones safe. Help us get to Shipshewana and find our home away from home quickly. Amen."

"Amen." Ashley turned her focus to the yummy food in front of her. It didn't squelch the guilt hounding her. She should be praying more and reacting less.

She'd tried that, and it hadn't worked. Patrick almost died. So had Rich.

Praying didn't stop all evil.

So she'd do her part to keep her loved ones safe.

Patrick paced behind his office desk.

Nathan Miller, longtime friend and coworker, leaned forward in the leather guest chair. "Buddy, you're acting like a caged tiger—no, an injured tiger. Stop pacing and tell me what's goin' on."

In his mid-fifties, with salt-and-pepper hair, smiling eyes, and a Santa Claus figure, Nathan was Patrick's polar opposite. He'd mentored Patrick and convinced him to join the small counseling office. He could trust Nathan.

"It's nothing. Too much full-contact basketball. That's all."

Nathan studied him.

He refused to squirm under the weight of his lie. He hated the deception, but it was the only way to ensure Ashley stayed safe.

"Where's Ashley? I haven't seen her around in a while."

Smart man. Too discerning for his own good. "Visiting friends. Finishing up wedding details."

Nathan sat back and smiled. "So that's the cause of the nervous energy."

"What?"

"The wedding. You're a goner, man."

"Don't I know it?" His eyes found the clock for the hundredth time Saturday morning. Why hadn't Ashley called yet? She had to be close to Shipshewana by now. He should have gone with her.

"So why are you burning a hole into that clock?"

"Ashley's supposed to have called by now." At least that wasn't a lie.

Nathan stood. "She's a grown woman. A police officer. I'm sure she's safe and having a good time picking up all sorts of wedding whatnots."

If only that were true.

Patrick's cell phone chirped, and he jumped for it. "Hello?"

Nathan waved as he exited and closed the door behind him.

"Patrick. It's so good to hear your voice."

"I miss you, Ash. Please tell me you're okay."

She huffed. "I'm as fine as can be expected. Wish you were here."

"I would be there tonight." He lowered himself into his desk chair. "But it's not safe. Not until they have the stalker in custody."

"I know."

"The second he's found, I'll be at your side again." He shifted to a more comfortable position. "You're there, right?"

Muffled voices filtered over the phone lines.

"Ashley?"

"I'm safe. Apparently Margo has talked to a mutual friend of ours too. And no one bothered to ask me about the change in plans. I hate being told what to do."

He could picture her blazing green eyes and hands on her hips. Independent streak flashing for all to see.

"I love you, Ash. We all do." He inhaled and exhaled. "We just want to be sure you're safe."

"I can take care of myself."

"As my wife, I'd like it if you shared that job with me."

"I know. I'm sorry." Her voice softened with each word. "You've done a great job with this escape plan. No one's followed us since Dalton."

Music to his ears. This crazy plan just might work.

Might being the operative word. He hated the silence and lack of assurance from on high.

Ashley slipped Patrick's phone into her denim shorts. Her gun stayed in her purse. For now.

"We're here." Margo slowed down as the traffic picked up. "Look at those buggies. I've never seen one of those in real life."

A young, Plain woman waved from the buggy right next to them. Ashley waved back.

The Amish and Mennonite businesses were just waking up. "Look, over there. That's Lambright Woodworking."

"How do you know that?"

"From Brad's letters. Lambright Woodworking was his favorite place to hang out. We should visit there sometime."

Margo smiled. "It'll be fun to play tourist for a while."

Right. As long as Ashley kept her mind on the real reason she was here. To protect. To survive.

"Oh, look!" Margo pointed to a store next to the bright red Yoder's Red Barn Shoppes. "Yoder's Meat and Cheese. They have something like a hundred different cheeses there. And meats. And samples."

"You must be ready for lunch."

"I read all about the store and even watched some videos. I have our first few days here planned to the hilt. It'll be fun."

She couldn't fault Margo for trying to forget why they were there.

They passed the Davis Mercantile, Anna's favorite place to shop, and three huge silos before they reached North Street. The area of Shipshewana she'd researched after Brad's last letter.

"Hey, take a right here. I need to stop by the police department."

"Already?" Margo slowed down and turned right. "Can't we check into the B&B first?"

"Are you one hundred percent sure we haven't been followed?"

The question hung in the air as Margo parked next to the one story, light brick building.

"No. Go do your thing in there. I'll stay out here in the AC. With the doors locked."

Ashley exited the SUV and opened the back door to retrieve her small bathroom bag.

"What are you doing?" Margo turned all the way around.

"Getting some mouthwash and running a brush through my hair. Any other questions, Mother?"

Margo pursed her lips and turned around. "Come back with a good attitude, you hear?"

Ashley gathered her emotions and locked them all into their mental compartment. Last thing she needed was to cry in front of Shipshewana's finest.

She found her way to the police department section of the building without asking any questions. That little victory boosted her confidence.

"Can I help you?" A redheaded woman in plain clothes stood up from the front desk. Her laugh lines deepened in a practiced smile.

"I need to speak with the chief. Is he in?"

"I'm sorry, ma'am, but Marshal Taylor is unavailable at the moment. May I take a message?"

"This is an emergency." Ashley modulated her voice and forced civility into it. "I need to speak with him as soon as possible."

The now expressionless secretary returned to her seat, fingers poised above her keyboard. "And your name is?"

"Officer Ashley Walters."

A tall, young uniformed officer joined them, his dark eyebrows raised in a question. "I can take it from here, Lisa."

Lisa held on to her business face, but her eyes burned. "I'm sure you can."

Nothing like an office protector. Ashley understood Lisa protecting the chief's privacy, but she didn't have time for niceties.

The young, tanned man glanced behind him. "The chief is swamped today. But I can have him give you a call."

Deep breath in. Deep breath out. She studied his nameplate. "Deputy Jessup, I'm here to let your PD know a violent stalker could be coming to your town. He's already attacked one man and shot another."

Jessup opened his mouth to speak but closed it fast.

"Think maybe I could see your chief now?"

"Follow me." He led the way to a windowed office. "Have a seat, officer. I'll go give the marshal a call."

Eyes trained outside, she stared at a small public playground and the grove of trees beyond it, trying to formulate a plan for what to say and what to leave unsaid.

Two minutes down.

How many more to go?

She checked Patrick's phone. No calls or texts.

One more look at the clock. The chief's minute hand must be stuck in police station purgatory.

She studied the chief's office. About the same size as Chief Fisher's office back home. Similar framed commendations and college degrees. Marshal Taylor held a Bachelor of Science in Criminology and a Bachelor of Science in psychology from Indiana State University. He was also an Indiana Law Enforcement Academy graduate and a certified instructor.

Family pictures and neat piles of paperwork adorned his desk. She leaned forward to take a look.

"Find anything interesting, Officer Walters?" Tall and fit, Marshal Taylor extended a hand, a slight smile playing on his lips.

Ashley shook hands and returned the smile. At least he had a sense of humor. He wore jeans and a white polo shirt. Normal. But he stood like a cop. Took control of the situation like a man in charge.

"It seems I've interrupted your Saturday plans with your family, Marshal Taylor. I'm sorry for that."

"Call me Tom." He motioned for her to return to her seat. He took his behind the large, dark wood desk. "I was on my way into the office to pick up some paperwork. My family's still eating breakfast."

"Tom. I'm still sorry to interrupt your day. But I'm in some trouble. At least, I could be soon, and want your department to know what you're facing."

"A stalker, you said."

"There are some in Gwinnett County and Atlanta PD and my department in Montezuma, Georgia, who believe this violent stalker could be a cop."

Marshal Taylor tensed. "Do you have a name or any leads?"

"A detective in Atlanta was planning to track down the whereabouts of a man by the name of Dillon Matthews. He dropped out of my police academy class."

"Detective Burke's inquiry was interrupted by a GSW, was it not?"

A massive gunshot wound. One she'd never forget. She studied

Marshal Taylor's expressionless face. "You've talked to my chief?" She should have known. This man had been in law enforcement far longer than she had.

"Yes. And the GBI too." Marshal Taylor shuffled the files on his desk. "Your PD is waiting on the GBI for fingerprint and DNA results. Chief Fisher said the Gwinnett County and Atlanta detectives were running Matthews to the ground. They'll let us know as soon as they know something."

"Did I pass?"

Marshal Taylor smiled. "You think that was a test?"

"Yes." A test of her integrity, how much detail she'd divulge.

"You passed with flying colors. I'm sorry for the situation you're in. We'll plan for the worst-case scenario. That is, if you need our assistance."

"Did my chief insinuate I wouldn't need your help?"

"He might have used the words *independent* and *control* a few times."

She'd thank her chief for that character witness later. "Yes, sir. I'm requesting your department's help."

"Chief Fisher is sending me a copy of the case file. GBI Agent Jim Edwards is making the trip up here too. But no one knew if your fiancé was traveling with you."

"No. Patrick was attacked, hurt pretty badly. We believe by the stalker."

"I'm sorry to hear that."

"Thank you, sir."

Marshal Taylor's fingers clicked over his keyboard. "Can you tell me where you're staying and a phone number where I can reach you?"

"The Songbird Ridge B&B." She rattled off Patrick's cell phone number.

Marshal Taylor scrawled it down on the notepad in front of him, frowning. "I thought Songbird Ridge was full this weekend."

"Oh. Then I don't know what the arrangements are. I'm feeling pretty out of control not knowing the details."

"Your chief was under the impression this hiding plan was your idea."

"No. I...well. I'm going along with it because I couldn't come up with a better one on the fly." She had some other ideas if needed, but she wouldn't share them with anyone. Not yet. Not until she knew for sure who was trustworthy and who wasn't.

He scribbled some numbers on a white index card. "Emergency numbers. Direct line to our police department. If you call here, we'll contact the county dispatch immediately. Also, here's my cell number and the number of our four full-time officers."

"Thank you, sir. I hope I don't need them."

"Me too. One more question. Will you need us to provide security while you're here?"

"No. I'd rather lay low. Too much police presence and too many people will know where I am at any given time. I'd like to avoid that."

"Understandable. You do realize I have to alert all our officers and advise all the officers in the county of the situation. In case of an emergency."

"I understand."

She stood and Marshal Taylor walked her out. "Thank you for coming by. We need to talk Monday morning before or right after you meet with the GBI."

"Yes. I'll be here first thing."

"In the meantime, if you have time, feel free to visit again and meet our other officers."

"Thanks. I might do that. No safer place than in the middle of a bunch of cops, huh?"

He smiled. "Do some sightseeing while you're here. It'll take your mind off of things. Guaranteed."

Nothing would take her mind off where she was.

Or who was trying to find her.

CHAPTER TWELVE

"Move over, missy. I'm driving." Ashley's short time among other cops helped her recenter and remember who she was.

"Well, I'll be. You are one bossy woman in the morning." Margo rifled through her purse.

"I'm bossy all the time, according to you." Ashley exited the small police station parking lot and headed north on State Road 5. "Where exactly is this B&B?"

"We have to check in at Songbird Ridge, but then we'll be staying down the road a piece at the Hidden Creek B&B, owned by Jonathan's parents. They aren't listed and serve as an overflow for Songbird Ridge."

"That makes sense. Marshal Taylor thought Songbird Ridge was full this weekend. Seems everyone knows everyone's business here in town."

"Stop worrying." Margo filed her manicured nails. "No one knows who we are."

"They will before the weekend is over." Ashley's stomach tightened. This wasn't a good idea. "Maybe we should head back to Indianapolis. You know the city, but no one there knows us."

"You're borrowing trouble. Didn't Patrick remind you to trust God for our protection?"

"No."

"Well, he should have. God is our protector, Ashley."

"God didn't protect Rich or Patrick."

Margo turned away.

"No answer to that one?" Ashley hated the acid in her voice. It'd been a while since she'd spent time listening to God. Too often she just talked. Last time she remembered praying, she'd begged God for Patrick to be okay and the stalker to be in jail. Ever since, she'd been too busy staying alive and keeping her friends safe.

"I do have an answer." Margo's blue eyes smiled. A sweet Southern smile. That always meant trouble.

"So tell me."

"Patrick and Rich are alive. They'll recover. And I believe God protected them from a far worse ending. He's protected us too."

Maybe. Her heart agreed with Margo. But she wouldn't say it. She was still too raw inside. She could list in detail what God could have done to prevent the whole downward spiral.

"Turn left here." Margo pointed toward a large, blue-gray three-story country home, complete with a beautiful porch and white rocking chairs.

Ashley parked in the side lot and opened the door.

Miniature horses, goats, and a barn full of large horses greeted her. Maybe it was a good thing Chester hadn't joined them. He'd be all over that barn and making friends with the menagerie of animals.

"Look at those miniature horses." Margo stepped closer. "Aren't they adorable?"

"From a distance."

A young woman in jeans and a T-shirt stepped onto the front porch. She started a little when she saw them.

Did they look that bad to the B&B guests?

"Hello." The woman stepped closer. Her light brown hair was cut in a fashionable bob and she smiled a welcoming smile. Still, Ashley didn't know her from Adam.

"Hello there." Margo extended a hand. "This is such a lovely place. Could you be so sweet as to direct us to the owners? We need to check in." Her best friend's Deep South accent dripped with sugar.

"I'm Heidi Yoder. My husband and I run this bed and breakfast. So I guess you've found what you're looking for."

Ashley stared until Margo elbowed her. "Sorry. We were supposed to meet Jonathan's family. I must have misunderstood."

Heidi smiled wider. "Were you expecting Plain dress and head coverings?"

"No. Well, I mean yes. I suppose I was."

"You must be Ashley." Heidi motioned for them to precede her up the porch steps. "And you must be Margo. It's a pleasure to meet you both."

"The pleasure is ours." Margo's eyes twinkled.

Ashley wasn't so sure. Heidi knew more than she should have. What else had Jonathan shared?

She wanted to go home now more than ever.

The steady beat of horse hooves drew her attention. She turned toward the street. A large black buggy with an orange triangle passed by.

"Our across-the-street neighbors are Amish. They have many visitors from their district. You'll get used to the buggies in no time." Heidi pointed to a very large white farmhouse. No shutters. No electric wires ran to the house. "If you'd like to share a meal with them, they might have an opening Monday. I could check for you."

"They open their home for tourists?" Ashley remembered the disastrous town council meeting where she learned more of what happened to the Mennonites in Montezuma when they'd opened their homes to tourists. Obtrusive questions. Items stolen from the homes.

"Yes. The Millers love it. They're a very hospitable family. Wonderful neighbors too." Heidi turned to face her. "Would you like to meet them?"

"No. I mean, no thanks. I plan to lay low."

"It's good for the soul to rest."

Ashley's soul or mind or body wouldn't rest until her stalker was in jail.

"Can I ask you a question?"

A dark haired, clean shaven man stepped out onto the porch, carrying a full tray.

Heidi pointed to the wicker rockers. "Won't you join us for some lemonade and popcorn?"

The man placed the tray on the wicker table. "I'm Mark. It's good to meet you, Ashley and Margo. My brother and Bradley have spoken very highly of you both."

Mark was dressed much like his wife. Blue jeans and a green polo. So different from Jonathan.

Heidi distributed cold glasses of lemonade and bowls of spicy popcorn. Ashley waited for their hosts to settle into their rockers before she took a bite. "This is so good. Thank you."

Mark stared out into the fields surrounding their house. "Did you have a good drive up here?"

Ashley swallowed some lemonade and locked eyes with Margo before responding. "We traded off sleeping most of the way."

"We were expecting you later this week." Heidi refilled glasses. "I'm sorry we don't have rooms available here. But my mother and father-in-law have a beautiful, quieter B&B."

Ashley squirmed. She couldn't get a feel for how much they knew about her situation. She'd rather not explain. But Heidi knew more about the preplanning than she did. Maybe they could fill in some blanks. "Did you talk to Patrick to make arrangements?"

Margo blushed. "I declare. It's definitely hot out here, don't you think?"

Heidi and Mark stood. Heidi moved to the door. "Let's go inside. It's much cooler in the living room."

Ashley glared at Margo. She'd been in on this whole plan from the beginning and hadn't seen fit to share any details until now. They'd have words later.

Mark and Heidi sat on a leather couch. Margo took a seat in a leather recliner, leaving Ashley the curious rocker. Its dark wood planking between curved branches shouted *uncomfortable*, but it wasn't.

"This is amazing." The words were out of her mouth before she could stop them.

Heidi nodded. "I didn't think it would be comfortable either, but the Amish know how to make hickory oak rockers better than anyone."

Margo leaned forward. "Okay, I hope this doesn't sound rude. But I've met Jonathan and Anna, and y'all don't look anything like them."

Seriously? Ashley lasered Margo, but her friend acted like her question was the most natural one in the world.

She'd rather find out what they know about her and leave the curiosities to another meeting. Or ask Jonathan.

Mark chuckled. "Jonathan told us you two were curious and outspoken. I'm surprised he didn't explain that not all Mennonites are Plain People."

"So you are Mennonite, but you don't wear prayer coverings or plain dresses?" Margo sat forward, like she hadn't a care in the world.

Ashley's radar spiked. Margo was up to something.

"That's right, Margo. We're liberal Mennonites, I guess you'd say." Heidi chuckled at what must have been a local joke.

Ashley took control of the conversation. "I'm sure you get a lot of meddlesome questions, don't you?"

"We don't mind." Mark stood. "But I'm sensing you two are ready to settle in and unpack. If you'll follow me, I'll take you over to Hidden Creek."

Ashley stood too. "Do your parents know I'm a police officer? Or why I'm here?"

Heidi touched Mark's arm. "I should get some snacks out for our guests." Turning to face them, she smiled. "It was a pleasure to meet you. I'm sure we'll see you both again soon."

Mark led the way outside and spoke in a low voice. "Yes, Jonathan explained that you are a police officer and you're here to escape a dangerous man. This is all we know, and we will not share any of it with anyone."

Sufficiently humbled, Ashley smiled for the first time today. "Thank you. I'm sorry for my abruptness."

"I understand."

She doubted that, but appreciated his kindness. "I'll make sure no trouble comes to your family. I promise."

"We'll trust God together for our protection. Yes?"

Yes. And no. Too much was out of her control. She had to regain the upper hand and put her plans into place. Today.

Jonathan's heart beat faster as his brother's truck and an SUV pulled into the guest's parking area.

Ashley was here.

And with her danger could also come at any moment.

Had it been foolish to promise Patrick that his family would keep her safe? It was too late to change plans now. But those plans could place his parents in a dangerous place.

This inner battle had warred since Patrick's first call. He had made the decision to help a fellow Christian in need. That was what he would do.

He straightened his white shirt and black pants and stood at the basement door, waiting for them to enter. As he waited, he took inventory of the large apartment. Two guest beds with clean sheets and towels. Everything was in order. The fridge was stocked with Ashley's favorite chocolate and sodas.

It was time.

He opened the main door and stepped out onto the small porch. The large porch swing moved with the breeze.

"Jonathan!" Ashley grabbed her purse and two suitcases and walked toward him. "I'm so glad to see a familiar face." Her smile lessened. "Thank you for all you've done with Patrick and Margo to provide a safe place to stay."

She wore short blue jean shorts and a wrinkled police T-shirt, her black hair tied back in a ponytail. Even in that, she was beautiful. He prayed silently for freedom from the memories her greeting had sparked and for their safety, the reason she had come in the first place. She would soon leave here and become Patrick's wife.

Beth's gentle smile filled his mind. Yes, God was gracious to have provided hope for a future with someone as perfect for him as Beth Kauffman.

"My family is happy to help you." He took hold of her suitcases and led the way to what would be Ashley's room. "I hope you find everything to your liking. Breakfast will be served each morning when you are ready. There are snacks in the fridge and sodas too. Popcorn and party mix packages on the counter."

The sounds of Mark assisting Margo with her large number of suitcases drowned out Ashley's response.

She flung her purse on the bed and her gun slipped out onto the red comforter.

Words escaped him as his eyes remained on the first weapon that had ever entered his parents' home.

"Would you…I know it is asking something huge for you, but would you please leave your weapon in your SUV?"

Ashley stiffened.

He should have remembered this would be a problem. But it would have been a problem for anyone in their church to have a gun in their home.

"Ashley, this is not our way. I do not believe a gun will keep you or my parents safe. It could put all of you in more danger. Will you return it to your SUV?"

"Yes. I'll leave it in the SUV." She turned to face him. "Unless there's a problem. If the stalker shows up, my gun stays by my side."

"Understood. We will pray that man is caught before he can bring trouble here."

Ashley slipped her gun into the waistband of her jeans.

Footsteps sounded overhead. His parents were coming. "I would like to introduce you and Margo to my parents when you return from outside."

Ashley nodded and hurried outside to store her weapon in her vehicle.

Keeping his eyes focused on his father's slow descent on the stairs, Jonathan rubbed the calluses on his worn hands. His heartbeat returned to normal.

They all met in the living room. He was the only one left in his immediate family adhering to the Beachy Amish Mennonite dress. It had not bothered him until Ashley's questioning eyes met his.

His father stepped forward, his gait unsteady, but his weathered face beamed. He loved having guests. "Philip Yoder. Welcome Ashley. Margo. We are so thankful God has brought you here for rest."

Ashley's eyes teared up.

Margo stepped forward and shook hands. "Thank you for allowing us to stay here. It's so beautiful."

His mother came down the steps, a pitcher of tea and a plate of fresh-baked scones in her hands. The strong hands that had long ago sewn clothing and cooked many meals for those in need now trembled. With age or fear he did not know.

He slipped to her side and relieved her of the scones and tea.

"Thank you, Jonathan." She walked toward their guests. "Welcome. Come have a snack. It has probably been hours since you have eaten."

Ashley smiled and followed his mother to the table. "Would you join us? We'd love the company."

Mark chose that moment to make an exit. "I should be going. See you all tomorrow after church. One o'clock?"

Jonathan nodded.

Everyone waved as he left.

Then the five of them took a seat at the breakfast table. No one spoke.

His parents might attend services with Mark and Heidi and dress in similar styles, but they still sounded like he did, and they still adhered to older customs.

Soon the tea and scones disappeared.

"Those were amazing." Margo wiped her mouth with a napkin. "I should go running later to offset the amount of calories I'll be consuming while we're here."

His mother smiled. "I will take that as a compliment. Thank you. And I will add scones to the breakfast dishes." His mother picked up the plates and took them to the sink.

Ashley joined her. "I'll wash those."

So Ashley had noticed how frail his parents had become.

"Nonsense. You are our guests." His mother proceeded to fill the sink with soap and water.

"It would give me a chance to feel useful. Please?"

Jonathan rose with his father, leaving Margo relaxing at the table alone. "I should be going to my store. There are many furniture orders to fill today." He slipped on his summer hat and waved as he exited.

His father walked out with him. "You know we must not tell anyone about Ashley or why she is in town."

"I was the one who spoke to you about this matter."

"You have told Beth?"

"She heard me talking to Bradley and I told her that Ashley might be in danger. She offered to help. She knows Ashley is here, but nothing else."

"This is good. We must keep details to ourselves, for Ashley's protection. I have spoken to Mark and Heidi also. Our guests have come under our roof. We must pray and do all we can to help them."

"Yes, sir. I understand. I will see you tomorrow after services."

His father returned to his guests. Jonathan walked up the hill to his truck.

Daisy and Donny, his parents' miniature goats, leapt around him as he made his way to his truck parked on the main level, by his parents' garage.

Ashley and Margo would most likely go to church with his parents and brother. He would pick Beth and her two younger cousins up as planned to attend his church near Goshen.

This was as it should be.

It would be better if he did not have an uncomfortable sense that he had just opened his family up to more danger than they had ever experienced.

Danger followed Ashley wherever she went.

He could only pray this time would be different.

CHAPTER THIRTEEN

Ashley stirred in bed, caught in that suspended state between awake and dreaming. Her breathing came in shallow bursts, her pulse thundered in her ears.

She'd been chasing the man in the Braves cap, sure she'd have him in cuffs in seconds. But then he turned on her and raised a knife.

Helpless. Nothing she could do.

Tears streamed down her cheeks.

She fought to wake up, to end the nightmare. But when she opened her eyes, she was in a strange place. In the dark. Her fists and legs bound.

Deep breath in. Deep breath out.

Where was her gun?

Struggling against whatever bound her, she searched her mind for clues. How had she arrived in this place? Had the stalker done this?

Memories poured in. She and Margo had driven all night to Shipshewana. Unpacked. She'd taken a nap. Saturday. Today was still Saturday.

Or was it?

Ears straining to pick up more clues, she laid stock-still and waited. No traffic noises. No footsteps above or around her. Cows mooing. A dog barking nearby.

Once again, she searched her surroundings. Eyes now adjusted to the dark, she could make out a few shapes. A large bed. Small room. Her suitcases on the large trunk at the foot of the bed.

She was in her room at the Hidden Creek Bed and Breakfast.

Kicking her legs and arms, she loosened the bonds that held her.

Sheets. She'd wrapped herself up tight in sheets. So tight she couldn't feel her feet and her hands throbbed.

Twist by twist, she loosed herself and tried to stand.

Pins and needles pricked every inch of her skin.

But she was safe. *Thank You, God.*

Once she could move, she flipped on the light and opened her bedroom door. Late afternoon light streamed in the glass-paned door and kitchen windows. She returned to her nightstand and snatched up Patrick's cell phone. Yes, it was still Saturday. Almost time for dinner.

No calls or texts though. She tossed the phone on top of her suitcase.

"Maggie?" She crossed the tiny hallway to Margo's door and knocked.

No answer.

"Come on, Maggie. Wake up."

No usual moaning and grumbling that her best friend had done during every sleepover in middle and high school.

She opened the door and flipped on the light.

No Maggie.

She rushed outside. No SUV.

No gun.

Searching every inch of their basement apartment, she found no note. No indication of Margo's plans.

Had she left on her own?

Chills shook her shoulders. She was thinking crazy. Her nightmare had spooked her but good, and now everything took on a sinister gleam.

She returned to her bedroom and picked up Patrick's cell. Margo's phone rang and rang.

Ashley hung up when the message started and dialed again.

It went straight to voicemail.

Either Margo had turned off her phone on purpose or it was dead. Margo's phone never died. She always plugged it in to recharge every night.

So why had Margo turned off her phone? Or had someone else done it for her?

Great. The rookie cop spooks had returned. Back then, every bump in the night meant a burglar prowling. Every call was an adrenaline rush.

But not this time. This time Margo had probably left to buy groceries and forgotten to leave a note.

She'd return soon.

Forcing herself to breathe normally, she paced the length of the compact apartment. So much different from her spacious Victorian at home.

Home.

She tapped Patrick's name in the favorites and prayed he'd answer. Six rings and then his voicemail message. She listened, an ache building in her chest. In a month, she'd be married to the love of her life.

Unless the stalker…

No, she wouldn't allow her mind to go there.

At the beep, she infused her voice with confidence and let Patrick know she was settled in and enjoying the beautiful bed and breakfast. "Give me a call when you get a chance. I love you."

TV held no interest. Neither did reading online about stalkers. Or calling her chief in Montezuma. She already knew what they knew thanks to Marshal Taylor. They'd call her when they had something new.

Not able to stay still, she decided on a shower and change of clothes. She'd noted Jonathan's response to her short shorts.

The hot water did her good, but she'd only had time to throw some regular summer clothes into a suitcase, so a complete change in style was not happening until she could get to a store. She chose her only pair of jeans and a simple green T-shirt.

Only fifteen minutes had passed. Time for more pacing.

Thirty bothersome minutes later, the sound of gravel pinging against a vehicle reached her. She sped to the door. Then tamping down her racing heart and loosening her tight jaw, she slipped outside and sat on the porch swing.

Margo waved from the driver's side of a brand spanking new F-350 Lariat. Dark blue.

Ashley stared. Then her blood boiled. What had Margo done?

"Was this why you turned your phone off?"

Margo exited the truck, nice and slow, eyes downcast. "I'm really sorry about that, Ash. I was in the middle of this deal and figured I'd call you right back. But things went longer than expected and I—"

"Where's my gun?"

"What gun?"

Ashley clenched her fists and fought not to scream. Her duty weapon was in that SUV. Her only gun. "The gun in the glove box?"

Margo snapped her little peach purse open. "You mean this one?"

Ashley let out the breath she'd held and grabbed the missing part of her. She checked her full clip. "I have to store this in the truck."

"Try the spacious glove box." Margo beamed. "See? I did good."

Ashley secured her weapon and slammed the glove box closed. "First you ignored my calls and had me worried sick. Then you play games about my gun. I hate games, Maggie. This can't happen again. You go somewhere, you have to tell me. Leave a note. Answer your phone. Something. We're dealing with a stalker here, remember?"

"I remember. That's why I switched out the SUV for this truck. I did the right thing."

Another set of issues slammed into Ashley's brain. "Where's Jen's SUV? And did you pay with a credit card? That puts us on the grid for anyone, any cop, to see."

Margo's tanned complexion faded to white. "I, um. I didn't think about that. I don't carry enough cash to work a deal like the one I did today."

"What deal?"

"If we return the truck in two weeks, we'll be able to trade it in for the SUV with no additional charges."

At least they'd get Jen's SUV back.

Margo fanned herself in the stifling heat. "But you said the stalker wasn't a cop. So how could he find us?"

"I don't know. But no more credit cards. I'd rather play it safe and not invite him up here." Ashley locked the truck doors. "You have the keys, right?"

Margo dangled them in front of Ashley's face. "I'm not the ditz I was in high school."

"I know. I'm sorry."

"Me too. I didn't think about the problems with using credit cards. I'm sorry."

Ashley pointed to the apartment door. "Let's go inside and find something to eat."

"Not too much though. I only bought enough meats, cheese, bread, and cinnamon rolls for a few days."

Ashley's stomach rumbled. "Okay, let's eat."

Margo hesitated. "We...um...have plans for dinner."

"What?"

Margo scurried into the apartment. "Jonathan's picking us up in fifteen minutes."

"Great." A groan almost escaped her lips. This evening had the potential for a great disaster.

Ten minutes of Margo's primping later, Ashley set to pacing again. Then she dabbed on some lip gloss and nixed the idea of applying any more makeup. Before she could run a brush through her hair again, her cell rang.

"Hello?"

"Ashley? This is Marshal Taylor."

Her heartbeat increased. Did he have news that would free her to go home? *Please, God.* "Yes. This is Ashley. Do you have some news?"

He sighed. "Not anything good. I got a call from Chief Fisher. Police there have scoured the Dalton area for the Chevy Malibu that was following you."

"And?" Her hope dwindled with every word.

"Nothing. But it was spotted again in Bowling Green, Kentucky. Fisher believes the stalker may have figured out where you disappeared to and is coming our way soon."

Options zipped through her brain. "What if he's changed cars? We have. Twice. He could be headed anywhere."

"True. But we can only work with the information we have. And what we know is this guy is dangerous, possibly heading here sooner than we figured. Stay alert."

The seriousness of her situation slammed into her for the thousandth time. So did the questions. Top of the list: Where was God in all this? "Yes, sir. And thank you for the warning. I'll see you first thing Monday morning."

"That wasn't Patrick." Margo's jean skirt and peach top, perfect makeup, and bright smile provided a convincing cover for the trembling in her voice.

"No. The police believe the stalker is headed right for us."

"Do you want to cancel and just hole up in here?"

No. She wouldn't hide like a terrified rabbit. She was a cop. She could handle this.

"I'll keep my eyes open for Braves caps and a blue Chevy Malibu." Like the guy would still be in possession of either identifier.

Like staying alert was enough to keep them safe.

Jonathan did not enjoy the curious stares of the Blue Gate Restaurant's customers. True, he had entered with three young women, only one in a covering and modest dress.

He should have encouraged Ashley to stay home. It was the safest choice.

But they were here now, and he must make the best of it. He focused on the high-back oak chairs they were led to by the hostess. These chairs were of the highest quality. He longed to produce such items of beauty and service. One day, if God so willed.

Ashley chose the seat closest to the window and turned so she could see the entire restaurant and outside equally, her back to the small section of wall amid many large windows circling the dining room.

"Well, hello there Jonathan and Beth. How are you and your guests doing?" Edna, an older, Beachy woman and friend of his family, smiled and met eyes with each of the women at the table as she handed out menus. "I'm Edna. Where are you folks from?"

Ashley spoke for them. "I'm Ashley, and this is Margo. We're visiting from pretty far away."

"They are family friends, Edna. Here for a short vacation." He avoided Ashley's eyes. He had not lied, but this stretching of the truth wore on his soul.

"How are your parents doing, Jonathan? Heidi told me they were slowing down lately. Anything I can do?"

Jonathan wished to avoid conversation about his parents. They had cut their visiting friends and spending time away from home drastically in the last few months, and they often spoke of dealing with the aches and pains of age. Their words and actions challenged him to pray and not fear. He spent most of his time afraid. "They are fine. I believe their schedules need to become less full."

"Ah, yes. That goes for all of us." Edna held her pen and notepad ready, her prayer covering in place over her white hair. "Well, back to Margo and Ashley visiting. You should visit Menno-Hof first thing Monday. It's the perfect place to begin."

"Thanks. We might do that." Ashley held up her menu.

"So, what can I get for you? Maybe some homemade loaded potato chips? Thin chips deep fried and loaded with cheese and sour cream."

"Definitely." Ashley's face reddened a slight bit. "Sorry. I'm just hungry and that sounds amazing."

"Is this all on the same check? I should have asked that first." Edna stared at him.

"Yes. One check." Jonathan returned his eyes to the plentiful food choices listed in the menu.

"Are you and Beth going to share an appetizer as well? Like usual?"

Ashley glanced at Beth and then at him before returning her eyes to the menu in front of her.

"Yes."

"Well, Miss Ashley, what else may I get you?"

"I'll have the Amish Country sampler and a slice of chocolate raspberry cream pie."

Edna raised her eyebrows. "That's a great deal of food."

"I'm a…um, I'm sure I'll manage it."

"Good for you. Eat hearty, I always say." Edna turned to Margo.

Ashley had almost shared that she was a police officer. Jonathan was unsure why, but thankful she did not share that detail.

Margo checked her menu one more time. "I'll have the fruit salad."

"Beth?"

"I would like the fruit salad as well. Thank you."

"So I can spend my calories on a slice of old-fashioned cream pie." Margo grinned.

Beth nodded, eyes twinkling. At least Margo and Beth enjoyed each other's company. Ashley only checked her cell phone and studied her surroundings.

"And for you, Jonathan?"

Jonathan added his usual, the country roast beef and an old-fashioned cream pie.

"I'll be back with your order shortly." Edna grinned and then headed to the kitchen.

Jonathan glanced around the room as the women sat in silence. A good number of people in the restaurant wore Mennonite or Amish clothing. Others wore jeans and shorts. None stood out like Ashley though. Her jeans and T-shirt were more fitted than most. He should have reminded her about blending in.

She might have listened if he had chosen words relating it to her staying safe.

Then again, this was Ashley. She would do as she pleased. And Ashley would not have blended in even if she wore a dress like Beth's.

Dear Lord, how am I going to keep her safe?

"How are you doing, Ashley?" Beth leaned forward. "Have you spoken with Patrick lately?"

"No. Well, we had a short call this morning. But I've left him messages and he hasn't called back."

"I am sure he will as soon as he can."

Ashley took a deep breath, her features without expression. "Yeah. I'm sure."

If Beth continued trying to get Ashley to open up, there would be trouble. The two of them had not been on great terms back in Montezuma. And on a good day, Ashley only tolerated a small bit of what she called meddling.

He had pushed her to that limit often when he had lived in Montezuma. He must speak of this to Beth, and pray she understood his intentions. Any talk of Ashley before the recent events had resulted in Beth's questioning his feelings for her.

Beth continued to focus on Ashley. "Do you think Patrick would enjoy visiting up here too?"

"He'd love the atmosphere and the food." Ashley's eyes returned to the window.

"Jonathan and I love this restaurant. It is our favorite place to come."

Margo nudged Ashley with an elbow, then turned to Beth and smiled. "So you two come here often?"

Beth blushed. "When we are able."

Ashley's phone buzzed. "I'll take this outside. Be back soon."

She hurried out the front door and stood outside near their window. Jonathan forced himself to engage in conversation with Margo and Beth, but his eyes returned to Ashley's wildly moving hands and the hunch of her back.

Edna placed hot plates of chips dripping with cheese in front of Margo and next to Beth. "Enjoy, friends. I'll return soon with more."

Ashley joined them right before he began to pray. Her eyes were red and her jaw tense. "Are you okay?"

"I'm fine."

She was not. *God, be with Ashley. Comfort and calm her heart.*

"Were you getting ready to pray?"

"Yes. Will you join us?"

She flipped her napkin onto her lap. "Please, don't let me stop you."

Jonathan did not take anyone's hand as Ashley was fond of doing when she prayed. "Father, we come to You giving thanks for this wonderful food and time with friends. Please be our comfort and protection. We trust You in all things. Amen."

Food disappeared before anyone spoke again.

"This is amazing." Ashley turned to Margo. "Don't you think?"

"I didn't get much. Some human vacuum devoured most of it." A large smile lit her eyes.

"Whatever."

Margo leaned toward Ashley. "What did Patrick say?" Her voice was a slight whisper over the surrounding conversations.

"He thinks I'm losing it. Too paranoid and hurting myself, but safe. He's wrong."

Jonathan wiped his mouth and cleared his throat. "Is it possible you are trying again to control things instead of turning to God? That could cause you much grief. As it has in the past."

Ashley's green eyes blazed. "You and Margo can keep your lectures to yourselves. Brad and Patrick are still in danger. All I asked is that Patrick take Brad away for a few days. Sunday till Thursday. Things should come to a head by then and be over."

Chills passed over his shoulders and he shivered. He was not ready for this danger to come to his family so soon. Especially when Ashley was not emotionally or spiritually ready for the trouble she was facing.

None of them were. But what could he do?

The feeling of being watched caused him to turn around. A few tables away from them, a young woman in jeans and a baggy T-shirt smiled when he met her eyes. He turned back to his table. The woman was one he had met months ago at his church, visiting with a Mennonite family in the congregation. A family who had taken the responsibility for helping her hide. Her life story was a sad and dangerous one, and he had listened and prayed for her. But why would she stare at him now?

Edna delivered steaming plates piled high with food. "Enjoy and eat up. Dessert will be on its way a little later." She smiled at Ashley. "Unless you would like it now."

"I'm good. Thanks." She dug into her food.

Beth ate slowly, smiling at him between bites every so often.

He was thankful she had ceased questioning Ashley and grown more at peace with her presence here. Maybe this outing had done more good than the bad that he feared.

"'Scuse me. Can I talk to y'all for a spell?" The staring woman from earlier—he could not recall her name—stood at the head of their table, her dark hair pulled back in a ponytail.

Ashley straightened, wiping her hands as she assessed the woman. "What about?"

"I'm Candice from North Carolina." She focused on Ashley. "I understand we have a lot in common. I'd like to talk to you sometime." She checked her watch and grimaced. "Maybe tomorrow?"

"Talk to me now." Ashley laid her napkin on the table and stood.

Candice's eyes grew wide and she scanned the dining room. "Please don't get up. I...I need to go. I've been in town too long already. I... um...I need to get back to my home."

Candice's drawl was far more pronounced now. Jonathan held his tongue and waited.

"I'd like to know how you understand we have a lot in common."

Margo tugged at Ashley's elbow. "Sit down. You're causing a scene."

Sweat broke out on Candice's forehead and her hands trembled.

Ashley sat.

Candice stepped away from their table. "Sorry to disturb y'all. Don't mind me. I just lost track of time. I'll talk to you soon, Ashley." She exited the restaurant in a hurry.

Jonathan swallowed hard. What could he do now to remedy this troubling situation? *God, protect Candice and Ashley. Give them peace. Protect them as only You can.*

Eyes narrowed, Ashley leaned toward him. "If your people have hidden women before, how come everyone here seems to know my business? I'm not safe here, am I?"

Jonathan had no answer. Her protection was not under his control. "You are safer here than at your home. Of this, I am sure."

"Then can you try to keep a rein on the motor mouth blabbing my story everywhere?"

His muscles tensed. He could not make this promise any more than he could keep Ashley safe. Candice's interruption and Ashley's reaction had convinced him of this even more. "I will see what I can do."

Ashley's focus returned to the window. Beth's wide blue eyes stayed focused on him.

He had no assurance to give this time. He hated to disappoint Beth like that. Ashley also. *Lord, bring this situation to a safe conclusion. Soon. Please.*

He returned to his last bites of roast beef, eyes on his plate.

Ashley gasped.

"What is wrong?" He followed her gaze to the crowd outside.

"He's found us." She pointed to a young, dark haired man wearing an Atlanta Braves baseball cap.

CHAPTER FOURTEEN

Ice filled Ashley's veins. She'd win this confrontation and take her life back.

The weapon in her ankle holster burned against her leg. In this crowd of slow-moving tourists, she'd have to be careful. Very careful.

"Ashley, don't." Margo grabbed her arm and jerked her back onto the Blue Gate Restaurant's porch. "Call the police here. Let them handle it."

"I can end this right now." Her eyes stayed fixed on the man slowly strolling up the sidewalk in front of the Craft Barn's white exterior. Right within striking distance.

"None of the police involved would be okay with this."

Visitors streamed past them on all sides. Horses and buggies clip-clopped through the traffic light on the main road. Happy chatter surrounded her.

All she saw was a stalker.

The man in a Braves cap turned at the corner of the Craft Barn and crossed the street to a sidewalk on the other side of Van Buren Street. He stopped right in front of Riegsecker's Cabinet Company. Another neat, white building.

"Stay here, Maggie. I'm a cop. You aren't."

She hurried across the street and onto the sidewalk on the other side of the street.

Her heart pounded with anticipation. She would end it here.

The dark haired man glanced around and started down a side street toward some white siding homes.

She followed, catching up to him quickly, right past the furniture store's parking lot.

She grabbed his blue windbreaker and shoved him against a tree. "Who are you?"

The man trembled. "I...I'm Dennis Perkins. Wh...what are you doing. I didn't do anything wrong. I...I'm just goin' home."

"Well, Dennis, you're under arrest for stalking a police officer and attacking my fiancé." As soon as the words were out of her mouth, she groaned. She had no power of arrest in Shipshewana, Indiana.

The whoop whoop of a police car's warning siren filled her ears. Good, they could take over here.

A uniformed cop parked next to them and stepped out of his black and white. He towered over her. "Is there a problem here?"

Obviously. "I'm Officer Ashley Walters. This man has been stalking me. He's attacked one person and shot a detective in his pursuit."

Dennis craned his head around. "I didn't do nothing, Officer. I swear. I never saw this woman in my life." His voice quavered. His face was red and sweat-streaked. His eyes darted everywhere.

He was lying.

The Shipshewana officer slipped his handcuffs out of their case. "I'm Corporal Winslow. I'll just take this gentleman down to the station for questioning."

Corporal Winslow handcuffed Dennis and tucked his head down to assist him into the cage of the squad car. Closing the door, he turned to face her. His intense brown eyes bored through her. Good quality for a cop. But not when it was turned on her. "I'll call Marshal Taylor too. We'll let you know what we find out."

"Thanks." Her breathing returned to normal and her pulse slowed.

Winslow leaned closer. "Next time, call us first. We don't go around assaulting citizens."

The chastisement burned all the way to the bottom of her feet. She straightened to her full five feet, eight inches and glared. "Where I come from, we catch the bad guys any way we can."

He shrugged and turned to his car. "Take care, now."

Watching the police car turn around and head to the station, she clenched and unclenched her fists.

She glanced around to find bonneted women and stern-faced men staring at her from the furniture store parking lot.

Wonderful. An audience. Now everyone who didn't know her before would know her by tomorrow.

But she'd caught the stalker. Now all she had to do was collect Margo for a trip to the police station and make sure the police up here took care of business right.

Then she could go home.

Sunday morning dawned bright and hopeful. Ashley yawned and stretched in the now-familiar bedroom.

Birds chirped outside. The Yoders' miniature goats hopped on the porch and banged into the glass door. They'd done that last night too.

"Rise and shine, Ash. Breakfast will be ready shortly." Margo stood in her opened doorway, blue sundress swaying with her movements. Makeup perfect. At eight o'clock in the morning?

"It's an amazing day. Too bad we can't visit any stores before we head home this afternoon."

"You really think that guy you attacked yesterday was the stalker?"

Ashley stood and faced her best friend. "It was him. And I'm sure Marshal Taylor will call soon to confirm it." He should have called last night after telling her to go home and that they'd handle the interrogation and get back to her. But things moved slower up here.

"Okay, okay. Let's go back to that happy Ashley I just saw for the first time in weeks." Margo held up her hands in surrender.

Footsteps sounded on the steps. Ashley grabbed a summer robe and tied the belt.

"Good morning, girls." Mrs. Yoder set a shaky tray on the small oak dining room table. "I hope you all are hungry."

Ashley smiled and noticed for the second time how weary Jonathan's mother looked. From her eyes down to her toes. "That's a lot of food, but it looks amazing. Thank you."

"I'll see you all in about an hour for church."

Margo slipped into a chair and began filling her plate. "I'll have to go for a run tonight. You with me?"

"Absolutely. If we run, I can justify a huge bowl of fresh fruit and an enormous slice of homemade toast."

"And there's Amish peanut butter." Margo pointed to a light brown, fluffy mass of what she wouldn't call peanut butter. "It's natural peanut butter with marshmallow cream. It's yummy. I had a taste this morning when I was helping Mrs. Yoder with breakfast."

"When did you get up, Maggie?"

"At seven." Margo grabbed Ashley's hand. "Let's pray. Lord, thank You for this beautiful day, this scrumptious food prepared with love, and for the privilege of going to church to worship You with other believers. Amen."

Ashley filled her plate with far too much food. Cheese, meats, toast slathered with Amish peanut butter. But like last night, it was too good to pass up. "Have you noticed how shaky Mrs. Yoder is?"

"Debra's okay. Her doctor says it's nothing to worry about. They just need to slow down and rest more."

"What about Mr. Yoder?"

"Philip is fine. Still working too hard. Thinks Jonathan worries too much and should pray more. Can you believe that? I can't imagine Jonathan needing to pray more."

Ashley continued eating in silence, savoring the sweet and filling Amish peanut butter and fluffy bread. Nothing like the dry toast she and Chester shared most days. Chester and Patrick both would have loved it here. She missed them so much. And she'd see them soon.

Her phone rang.

Margo met her eyes, concern filling the space between them.

Rushing to the phone, Ashley prayed. "Hello?"

"Ashley, it's Tom. Do you have a minute?"

His business voice gave nothing away. Except that he hadn't used that impersonal tone at any other point. "Sure. What's happening with Dennis? Did you compare his fingerprints to the ones from Patrick's house?"

"Yes."

Of course he had. She shouldn't have asked but waited him out for the information.

"Ashley, Dennis is not your stalker. He's a longtime resident of Shipshewana and the fingerprints didn't come close to matching."

No. No, Dennis had to be the stalker. If not...

"I'm sorry, Ashley. I know you wanted this thing over."

Why would God allow this? "Dennis matched the description perfectly. Braves hat and all."

"There are some Atlanta Braves fans who live up here, you know?"

"Guess so."

"I'm sorry. Truly. We'll get plans in place with the GBI. Then you can rest a little more easily."

Right. She ended the call with Tom and pulled her wallet from her purse. Each picture twisted the knife in her heart.

Her and Eric in high school. Her and Patrick at the High Museum of Art last year. Brad and Chester in her backyard.

"Why would God do this?" Tears threatened. She couldn't get her hopes up again. She'd call Patrick and insist one more time that he and Brad go away for a while. Then she'd go looking again. She'd find the stalker and end this as soon as he showed his face in this small town. She'd be ready.

"Do you want an answer to that question?"

"No." She returned her pictures to their places. "You believe God has a purpose in everything. But not this, Maggie. Not this."

Margo nudged her to sit on the bed and sat beside her. "God works all things together for good—"

"Don't. I can't accept that. Not this time. Patrick's and Brad's and your life are all in danger. Don't you get that? If I don't catch this guy before he strikes again, someone could die."

"Yes, Ash. Even this."

Ashley stood, hands on her hips. "What? Like people say be careful praying for patience or you'll get sacked with opportunities to fail at patience? So I pray for protection for my family and friends and God says, 'Here, have a crazy stalker as a teacher.' No thanks."

"It's not like that. I only mean that God is God over every moment of our lives. He's present in each one too. Using them to draw us closer to Him. Protecting us."

Turning away, Ashley inhaled a sharp breath. "God showing me all I have to be afraid of is not drawing me anywhere near Him. It only makes me see I have to fix it this time. And I will."

"What happened to depending on God like you have been since last summer?"

A stalker happened, that was what.

Patrick couldn't focus on the Sunday morning service. Brad fidgeted at his side. Ashley kept texting. He should have turned his phone off. But then he would have missed if something important happened. And he wanted to hear from Ashley.

Just not her telling him what to do every few minutes during church.

His phone vibrated again. *Please. Leave town. Take Brad. If the stalker isn't here soon, he's coming for you too.*

Comforting. He texted her back. *Pray, Ash. I'll call soon.* He had to get Ashley talking about something else when he called. Help her turn her mind and heart back to trusting God in this situation. His conscience pricked. If he'd have stopped the guy last week when he attacked, none of this would have happened.

The memory of the attack was still raw. So were his bruised muscles and banged-up ribs.

He focused back on the last series of texts from Ashley. Yesterday she'd attacked an innocent man in her search for the stalker. She left that frightening text on his phone earlier this morning.

He'd been in the shower at the time, and she hadn't answered his calls since.

She must be in church too.

He had to talk her back down to reality. A scary one, but one in which she wasn't in charge or stressed and trigger happy at every turn.

A new message appeared. *Please, Patrick. I love you. I need to know you're safe.*

Love you too, Ash. We're fine. Are you at church?

They stood to sing "A Mighty Fortress Is Our God," his favorite hymn. He joined in, waiting to answer the text that buzzed in his pocket.

Brad leaned over. "That a patient or Ashley? Can I text her?"

"Sorry for being a distraction. Let's worship right now. I'll stop texting, and we can talk to her after service, okay?"

Brad smiled. He was almost as tall as Patrick now. Two more inches and he'd hit six feet two like Jonathan.

A deacon from the finance committee led the announcements. Patrick checked his phone.

Shore Mennonite Church with Yoders. Be still and know that I am God plaque is killing me. I can't be still. Someone is hunting me.

So much for worship. He had to step out and call. Texting couldn't match what a phone call could accomplish. Ashley needed him.

The youth group took the stage. He could miss this and be back for the sermon. "I'll be back in a minute. I need to call Ashley."

Brad nodded, engrossed in the youth skit about God's faithfulness.

Patrick stepped outside and eyed the full parking lot for any signs of the stalker. Ashley had him jumpy. How could he help her in this frame of mind?

"Hello? Patrick?"

"It's good to hear your voice. I miss you, Ash. Tell me about the service. I didn't pull you out of it, did I?"

"No. The pastor just finished. A sermon on who we are in Christ and how faith in who He is should be the driving force of our lives."

He chuckled. God was hounding Ashley, trying to get her attention. "Did you listen?"

"Please, Patrick. I need a soon-to-be husband. Not another lecture."

"I'm here, babe. What do you want to talk about? Besides me skipping town."

"You are so stubborn."

The pot calling the kettle black. "Would you sleep better if you knew Montezuma PD has stepped up patrols and has seen no one resembling the stalker this weekend?"

"No. That means little. This guy's watched me for twelve years. He could hide anywhere."

True. It was next to impossible to convince Ashley things would be okay, especially when he didn't know when that might happen. He flipped over to his calendar app. "Would it make you feel better if I asked Joyce about a fishing trip later this week?"

"Do you feel up to that? I'm sorry. I forgot how much pain you were in."

Patrick chuckled. His ribs poked back. "Non-narcotic pain pills are making life easier. I could be up for a few hours on Lake Lanier. But I can't go until Wednesday."

"Why?"

"Patients need me too, Ash. I have to do my job."

"You have to stay alive. I think that's more important." Ashley sighed. "Since no one will let me protect them, and everyone says I should just trust God and wait on Him, I guess I have no choice."

"You always have a choice."

"None of the options are good. Wait on God. Search for the stalker. Throw a fit and make everyone go into hiding like I am."

"Or have faith in God to protect all of us and bring this situation to an end in His way."

Another sigh. But softer this time. Ashley was at least considering his suggestions. The phone talk was working.

"So faith in God or faith in my skills. Tough choice. The former hasn't proved so great for keeping my loved ones safe. The latter has."

"The latter is destroying you."

Silence. He'd pushed too far again.

"I love you, Ash. I'm trying to help."

"I know. I love you too. I should get back inside."

He pocketed his phone and stared into the deep blue sky. *Please God, speak truth to Ashley's heart. She needs you. We all do. End this stalker's hold over us. Keep us safe.*

Like Ashley had voiced before, the words of his prayer barely touched his fear.

CHAPTER FIFTEEN

J onathan drove his old white truck out of Woodlawn's parking area and lifted a hand to wave at other departing families.

Beth sat quietly by his side.

The word *family* echoed in his mind. He had experienced such a peace through prayer this morning. God had made clear through His Word and His people that Beth was the right woman and the time to ask her to marry him was soon.

Still, his insides quaked. Could he follow his heart and enter into marriage a second time? He still missed his wife and their baby, but the memory of their last moments together comforted him rather than crushed him.

Ashley had helped that healing begin last year. She had spoken openly about her loss and how she coped with her brother's death. He had seen the healing God worked in her heart. And he had spoken with Ashley as he had not with others about Mary and their infant son's death. Ashley's compassion awakened in him a spark of interest after two long years of contented singleness. Because of Ashley, he had become aware of Beth's interest in him and was now open to a future with Beth.

He had in front of him an opportunity to help Ashley heal as she had helped him. He could see the fear she attempted to hide, her misunderstanding of God being her protector. Now he must pray and ask God to help him find a way to assist Ashley.

Beth turned to him. "Why do you think Candice avoided us this morning?"

"I cannot know her heart."

"You are right, but her behavior is different. Do you think her husband…"

"I do not know." Nor did he want to continue this conversation. It felt too much like gossip. He understood Beth's need to process an unsettling experience. But he had yet to understand how to listen and keep that from turning into gossip. *Father, grant me Your wisdom. Show me how to love Beth as You love her.*

Beth sat forward. "I am thankful my aunt joined us for church this morning and took Alvin and Gretchen home with her, so that I could have a chance to talk to you about something that concerns me."

Here was his opportunity. *Lord, be near.* "What is on your heart?"

"I believe Ashley should hear Candice's story, and I have invited her to lunch with us at your parents' home."

The beating of his heart stopped for a long second. "Why have you done this? Ashley has enough happening in her life without adding Candice's danger. If Ashley hears about Candice's situation, she will feel the need to rescue Candice and place both of their lives in danger. This is not wise. It was wrong of Candice to approach Ashley. I am not even sure how Candice learned Ashley's name."

"I am sure Candice will explain today at lunch."

"I wish you had not invited Candice today." Jonathan studied the Amish farms they passed and the families gathered there. He must order his thoughts before speaking. To respond in emotion was never wise.

"I wish you did not feel it necessary to protect Ashley."

Beth's words hit him like stones. "We must help Ashley see she is not the protector, that God is."

"Then you must let God be Ashley's protector, not you."

"I am helping a friend, Beth. That is all. Patrick and Margo approached me for assistance. You were willing to help hide Ashley when you first learned of her trouble."

"I was willing to help Ashley together with you. But you have taken it upon yourself to protect her from Candice. To tell her she should stay in your parents' home and not be in town much. You have also not spoken with me about your feelings on this situation."

She was correct. God's conviction stabbed at his conscience. He had attempted to take God's place in Ashley's life, to play the Holy Spirit and help her see the truth. God forgive him.

"You are right, Beth. Please forgive me. My intention was not to shut you out, but I have done this. I was wrong."

Beth smiled a small smile. "I forgive you, Jonathan."

Now his heartbeat thundered in his ears. How was he to involve Beth, speak truth to Ashley as he had felt led to do, and avoid usurping the Lord's place in Ashley's life? So far, he had done such a poor job with all three.

And now, he heard no direction. Maybe he deserved God's silence. Maybe this was God's direction, reminding Jonathan he was not ready to help Ashley with a pure heart. Would he ever be able to do so?

"So, Jonathan, did you tell Beth of your newest customer?" Mark smirked across the table at his brother.

Ashley sat silent between Jonathan and Margo, cataloguing every guest's reactions as the conversations flowed around her.

"I have not." Jonathan bit into a yeast roll and chewed slowly. "It is certainly not dinner conversation."

Ashley's curiosity was piqued.

Heidi, Mark's wife, grinned. "Sure it is." She met her mother-in-law's smiling eyes. "We all think it's hysterical."

Beth wiped her mouth. "Please tell me. I cannot stand the suspense."

Jonathan grimaced. "He wishes for me to make each of his grandchildren an old-fashioned potty chair."

Beth attempted to hide a grin. "How many grandchildren?"

"Twelve."

The table erupted with laughter. Jonathan's parents, Philip and Debra, Beth, Heidi, Mark, and Margo. Even Jonathan chuckled. As did the reserved Candice.

Ashley forced herself to smile. Then stuffed into her mouth yet another bite of the best chicken and dumplings in the world. At least that was what Margo had called them. To her they tasted like sawdust.

She just wanted to go home. Or have Patrick here. Then maybe she'd find a way to laugh. Since that was impossible, maybe she'd poke into Candice's story. Try for the second time this afternoon. The first time, Jonathan had interrupted their conversation at the first question and directed them to the table, seating them as far apart as possible.

Right now, she needed something, anything, to take her mind off of all the happy people surrounding her.

Was she the only one who understood the danger they were in?

"So, Candice, how did you hear about me and my story?"

Candice reddened. "I wanted to tell you yesterday, but I had to get back to my house before anyone got all worked up and worried 'bout me."

"Why would your family be worried if you were a little late coming home from dinner alone?"

Jonathan swallowed hard. "We should talk about this after dinner. Right, Candice?"

"Sure. I know you're only tryin' to keep everyone from feelin' uncomfortable."

Jonathan leaned closer and spoke in a low voice. "Candice is not your enemy. Neither am I, Ashley."

"Then tell me how she knows me."

Mark and Heidi jumped in with another story. Ashley ignored them and fixed her eyes on Jonathan.

"This I cannot answer. It is Candice's story to tell."

"So let me hear it."

Jonathan sighed. "After dinner. When it will not upset my parents. They do not know the details of Candice's story or yours. I wish for that to continue."

"Fine."

What did Jonathan know that she didn't?

Waiting for the answer to that one simple question pushed all of her buttons at once.

Mark nudged his wife, Heidi. "Remember that time we took Jonathan and Beth to the Blue Gate Theater?"

Beth blushed and cast her eyes to her plate.

Jonathan smiled. How could he ignore the tension all around? Tension he'd caused and his brother kept trying to smooth over with funny stories.

Heidi chuckled and shook her head. "It was the most fun I've had in ages."

"Not for me." Beth sighed. "It was awful."

"What happened?" Margo slipped into her high school begging posture. "Please tell us. I doubt I could sleep tonight for wondering what happened."

Jonathan took up the storytelling. "Beth was dressed in her beautiful, simple dress and head covering, as always."

More glances and grins zipped around the table.

"We went to see *The Confession*, an Amish play. Afterward, we stayed and chatted with some of our friends whom we had met there." He flicked a glance at Beth. "And Beth was approached by adoring fans wishing for an autograph."

Mark leaned in. "Beth almost started a riot with people crowding in to talk with the famous Amish star."

Laughter filled the room.

Beth stood and bowed a slight bow, holding her pretty pale blue dress out to the sides. "Can you just see me up on the stage?" She shuddered.

The volume of laughter grew and grew. Even Ashley managed a chuckle. Laughter pushed back some of the darkness that hounded her.

Then she caught Candice staring at her again and sobered. There was no way Candice was involved with Ashley's stalker, Jonathan had said. *Things with Candice are not what you imagine.* Last night, his words and his insistence that Candice posed no threat were enough to keep her from going after this stranger. That...and the fact that no one would tell her where Candice lived. Or Candice's story. *It's best Candice tell you her story herself.*

Now she wasn't so sure. What was this woman hiding? And how much did she know?

"I will fetch the coffee carafe and the chocolate pies." Mrs. Yoder stood and placed her hands on the back of her chair, struggling to catch her breath. "Everyone saved room for chocolate pie. *Ja?*"

Nods all around the table.

Ashley caught Jonathan's eye and tilted her head toward his mother. She mouthed a simple *Is she okay?*

He shrugged.

They'd talk about this later. Mr. and Mrs. Yoder needed a trip to Indy for higher quality medical care.

And she needed answers to the even more pressing issue in the room. Dinner was over and Mrs. Yoder was out of the room. "So, Candice. You said yesterday that you were from North Carolina. But your accent is inconsistent."

Candice blushed again. She couldn't be more than twenty. But like everything else about Candice, even her age remained a mystery. "It's high time I explained a few things."

Jonathan's eyes darted from Candice to the kitchen where his mother had gone. "After dessert, yes?" He turned to Ashley and spoke in a whisper. "This conversation will only upset everyone at the table. Please trust me and wait."

Ashley stared around the blank faces in the room. No one would meet her eyes. Not even Margo. "Fine." Her jaw hurt from chewing up all the words she wanted to say instead.

Jonathan commandeered the conversation and navigated it into his favorite subject. "What did Pastor Michaels teach on today?"

"He preached on how faith in who God is should be the driving force of our lives." Margo elbowed Ashley. "But she was a hundred miles away."

"I was not." So mature.

Margo's eyes twinkled. That always meant trouble.

Mrs. Yoder returned with the pie. Heidi took the trembling dish and coffee carafe from her hands. "Let me help you, Debra. Please."

"*Ja*. That would be nice."

Mark and Jonathan wore identical expressions. Hard. Eyebrows knotted together. Hunched posture.

"This looks wonderful, Debra." As Heidi served up the plates and coffee, the tension in the room evaporated a fraction.

Jonathan returned to the earlier conversation. "Bishop Miller spoke of how to face fear and not allow it to control our lives. He spoke of many fears, and I found my heart burning as he preached."

"So what are you afraid of, Jonathan?" Ashley switched to interrogation mode and waited for his answer. Something he'd done to her many times when they discussed forgiveness and freedom.

Beth raised her napkin to her mouth and coughed.

Jonathan returned her pressing stare. "I am afraid of violent men. Of losing my parents. Of failing at my business. I did not realize before these had such a hold on my thoughts."

Mr. and Mrs. Yoder's eyes saddened. "We do not wish to cause the enemy to gain such a foothold in your life, son. I am sorry."

"All I ask is that you allow me to take you to a different doctor."

Ashley broke in. "Indianapolis has a ton of great doctors."

Jonathan shook his head. "Can we talk of this later?"

Mr. Yoder gave a single, sharp nod. "Yes."

Everyone returned to their chocolate pie. Perfect chocolate heaven, except for the elephants stampeding through the room.

Candice only pushed her dessert around on her plate, her unguarded pout giving away her young age far more than her practiced mannerisms and accent.

Ten interminable minutes later, the meal ended and Heidi smiled at Beth. "Would you help me clean up in the kitchen?"

"Yes. Then you can rest in the living room, Mrs. Yoder."

"Good idea, Beth." Jonathan turned to Ashley. "And Ashley and Candice can help as well."

Ashley's jaw tightened. He'd pay for that later.

Candice buddied up to her and chose drying, right next to Ashley's washing. Maybe she'd finally get those answers.

Heidi and Beth stayed in their own world, storing leftovers and whispering about what doctors Mrs. Yoder needed to see.

She could read lips with the best of them.

"So, Ashley, we finally get a chance to talk." Candice's hazel eyes shone with a foreign emotion. Hope.

"Now you can tell me what you know about me and who you really are." So much for having a nice, stress-free conversation like Jonathan had tried to orchestrate.

"I'm really sorry. I should have explained yesterday. But I'd spoken too soon and made a scene. Neither you or I could risk that. Plus, I really did need to get home. I'd waited around for a chance to talk to you and when I finally saw what time it was, I had to get goin'."

"I'm listening."

"First off, I'm not from North Carolina, but all over. I'm an Army brat. I've always picked up the accents of the people around me. Before I came here, that was Carolina. And the reason I know you're hiding from a stalker isn't because someone blabbed it at church or in town. It's only because I overheard the family who is hiding me speaking about another woman who needed protection. They said she was a cop. I know cops."

She'd been pegged a cop by sitting in a restaurant eating dinner? "How do you know about cops?"

Candice lowered her voice. "There are good cops and bad cops, but almost all of them walk like they're in charge. Like how you came into the restaurant. They sit with their backs to the wall and take account of every person in the room with them."

True. Ashley couldn't deny that. And last night, she'd been so sure the stalker was near. She scrubbed pots with renewed vigor.

"Are you married to a cop?" Ashley pointed her chin to Candice's wedding band.

"No. My brother was a good cop. His friends too. My husband worked in the county jail. Not a good job for him. Being around violent men brought out his violent side."

"He hurt you?"

"Yes. I got restraining orders over and over. Tried to divorce him." Candice lowered her voice again. "But he broke into my apartment and beat me so bad I couldn't move for days."

"I'm so sorry." A fire burned in Ashley's gut. Criminals who targeted children and women, who lorded their size and strength to intimidate and control, deserved to spend the rest of their lives locked up with others just like them.

She should have recognized the signs in Candice. Hypervigilance. Quick acquiescence to any demands. No one wanting to discuss Candice's story. But Ashley had been too focused on her problems to see a young woman in need.

"It's good you got away. How did you know to come here?" Ashley scrubbed the last dish and handed it to Candice.

"I have friends who are related to some of the Amish families up here. They did some asking around and found out a number of women have been helped by the communities in and around Shipshewana. And so here I am."

"Does your husband know where you are?"

Candice wiped up the water surrounding the sink.

"Here." Beth held out her hand for the dishrag. "I can put that in the wash."

"Do you wash clothes here often, Beth?" Ashley just couldn't mind her own business.

Beth glanced at her feet and then back up again. "I have helped Debra with laundry for a few months now." Beth turned and exited the kitchen with Heidi.

"Guess she'd rather be the one asking all the questions."

Candice chuckled. "You and Jonathan seem pretty close."

"No. Not really." A million memories rushed back. "We went through some tough times together with his family, Anna and Brad. They almost died. I was there to help." Speaking of Anna, she hadn't seen her yet. She must be away visiting her daughters. The ones Brad had told her about a lifetime ago.

"So you're the good cop I thought you were."

She shrugged. "I do my job to the best of my ability and pray God keeps the good guys safe." At least she used to. Then Rich got shot. And she had to run. "So does your husband know where you are?"

"Maybe. Everyone's done such a good job of covering for me and protecting me. But my husband always finds me. If he does know, at least he won't come after me at someone else's house. And he won't call until he needs money. Yeah, like I have that in spades. I work in a small office in town."

Jonathan entered the kitchen. "Would you two like to play board games with us?"

Ashley stepped toward him, Candice still behind her. "Want to tell me why you lectured me about fear in front of everyone at dinner tonight?"

"It was what my bishop preached about today."

"Right. And you and Patrick haven't spoken about my spiritual health."

"We have not. But we are friends, Ashley. I was trying to help."

She twisted her diamond and ruby engagement ring around her finger. "You had more to say. You might as well say it."

Candice held up her hands. "I'll leave you two alone."

"No."

"No, don't go." Ashley spoke over Jonathan.

"Okay then. I'll just find a place for these pots." Candice set to work.

Jonathan turned his blue eyes to her. "Ashley, I wished to share a quotation I have held onto for many years."

"Okay." She wasn't going to like this.

"It goes something like this, 'Our deepest fear is not that we are inadequate. Our deepest fear is that we are powerful beyond measure. Our playing small doesn't serve the world.' This is by Marianne Williamson."

"I'm not playing small."

"I believe you are afraid you are not enough to handle this challenge. That is playing small. Hiding who you are."

That hit way too close to home. "I don't agree."

Jonathan's blue eyes held no malice. Only concern. "Then maybe you are afraid that God is bigger than you are, in absolute control. But He wishes to use you to solve this situation with the depth inside of you, not with your gun or your attempts at control."

"Are you finished?"

He nodded. "Yes. I am sorry I have offended you."

"I appreciate your friendship, Jonathan. You helped me learn how to let go of the anger I held onto from my brother's murder. But your ways are not my ways. I am not afraid of my inadequacy or of using a weapon to stop an evil man from hurting my loved ones."

"There is a better way. A way to live freely, not in fear." His eyes searched her face.

"Then why haven't you asked Beth to marry you?"

Jonathan startled as if she'd punched him. She should have bit her tongue and kept her emotions in check.

Instead, she turned to Candice. "I'll see you again soon."

Then she marched through the living room, where Jonathan's family was gathered around a Life board game, and opened the door to the stairs. Not wanting to slam it and ruin everyone's evening, she closed it softly until the lock clicked.

Jonathan's voice filtered through the door. He was right on the other side. "I will return in a moment, Beth."

"Jonathan, do you still have feelings for Ashley?"

The question cut into her. *Please, God, no.* She wouldn't go back there and hoped he wouldn't either.

"No. She is only a friend."

"Then leave her be. God will reach her in His own way. You do not have to push."

Their footsteps trailed away from her. Good. She rushed down the stairs and changed into her running shorts and T-shirt, grabbing Patrick's iPhone and her earbuds from her purse. She still couldn't find her phone. She could have sworn she'd had it on her when they fled from her parents' home.

She'd grown so absentminded again. Little wonder given what she faced.

Right now, she needed to hear something besides the screaming thoughts in her head. She tapped on the first playlist that caught her eye and shoved everything from her mind.

Outside, the air was hot and the pavement hard. Not the way she liked it. Running in the horse lane was worse than the dog parks in Atlanta she'd taken Chester to. Horse droppings everywhere.

She dodged a few piles and opted for running in the grass.

The rush of air across her face spurred her on. So did the fears Jonathan pushed on. And Patrick's bruised face. Brad's piercing eyes. Maggie's nervous energy. The danger they were all still in.

On and on she ran.

Buggies passed her. Cars zoomed by.

Steve Green's "You Are God Alone" blared in her ears. Of course Patrick had this in his playlist. On Steve sang about how God had no need of anything we could give and how in the good times and bad, God was on His throne.

That failed to comfort her. She had to do something. Not sit here and wait for God to show up in His sweet time. That could leave her stuck in Shipshewana forever. No Patrick. No wedding.

She wouldn't risk that. Wouldn't let the stalker steal that from her too.

She turned onto a side street and passed the closed Blue Gate Restaurant. And then onto another. Farther and farther from her worries and fears.

Far away from trouble.

She flipped through the song list for music that matched her mood. She tapped on "Resurrection" by Nicol Sponberg. Quick phrases slammed into her. Heart so cold. All efforts were like chasing the wind. Numb to the core.

Yep. That about summed it up for her. She desperately needed resurrection. She was in the midst of a situation that seemed far beyond redemption. She begged God right along with the lyrics. "Make something beautiful out of all this suffering."

But could He? Would He?

Even this?

Maggie's words haunted her. *"God is God over every moment of our lives."*

"God, if that's true…" She panted as she ran. "Show me by ending this nightmare." Deep breath in and out. In and out. "By not taking away this wedding I've dreamed about for a year…Don't let…the stalker ruin everything."

On and on she ran. Past white, shutterless farmhouses. Past large groups of unharnessed buggies and grazing horses. Past nice brick houses. Past empty clotheslines and closed businesses.

Her legs burned. She needed water.

Slowing down her stride, she glanced around. Where was she?

How in the world would she get back?

His eyes sought his target in the dark. Sunday was a good day for checking up on old friends.

Inside, Patrick packed his suitcase and laughed at the boy holding Chester in his lap. "A trip, Patrick?" The night breeze whisked away his words. "Do you really think you can escape me?"

Patrick should pack his suits and ties. They would do a good job of hiding the bruises he'd put there.

Stupid man. He should have gone to Ashley days ago.

Then they could all be together for the wedding.

In Shipshewana, Indiana. Where Ashley had gone to prepare a place for them.

He would hear her voice tomorrow. If she wouldn't answer, he had another way to get her attention.

One she couldn't ignore.

CHAPTER SIXTEEN

Ashley's mind buzzed with a million thoughts and no solutions. Margo feigned wiping sweat from her forehead and turned in her seat. "May I ask you, Officer Walters, why in tarnation we're sitting in the parking lot of the Shipshewana Police Department at nine o'clock Monday morning when it's close to one hundred and twenty degrees and there's blessed air-conditioning and sublime shopping waiting for us as soon as you're done inside?"

"I'll go in a minute. What are you going to do?"

A twinkle-eyed smile played across Margo's face. "We'll see." Then she ran her tanned hands down her pastel summer slip dress. One of Margo's many tells.

"You're going to check out all the places you want to drag me to, aren't you?"

"Maybe."

"I just want to go home. If there's no movement on anything today, I'm packing up and heading home. Patrick won't be there for days. He's taking Brad on a midweek fishing trip. It should be safe."

"Safe is not up to you."

"Whatever." Ashley retied her running shoes and straightened her jeans. "I'll see you in an hour."

161

Margo grabbed the sleeve of her police T-shirt. "How many miles did you run last night?"

"Ten." She jerked away and headed to the police department. No way would she tell anyone that she'd only intended five miles, but got lost. And every step back to the B&B, she'd searched the darkness for the stalker, sure he was only one step behind.

Or one step ahead.

She needed to apologize to Maggie. Her best friend didn't deserve the cold shoulder and harshness she'd received in the last few days.

But right now she had to compartmentalize everything else and just be a cop.

The second she walked into the police department, the young, tanned man from Saturday morning grinned and held out his hand. Others in the small room, including Lisa, the protective office administrator, took note of her but continued working. "Officer Walters, good to see you again."

"Deputy Jessup." She shook hands and stood in place. Inside, she was charging to the chief's office to get it all over with.

"So, you enjoying your stay in our great town?" He hooked his thumbs on his duty belt.

Be kind. Those words from a past Bible reading shot through her. She'd try, that was all she could promise. "Haven't seen much yet."

"But you've met one of our fine citizens. Dennis, I believe his name was." Corporal Winslow's brown eyes studied her top to toes, a glimmer of humor in their depths. He stood from the desk where he sat in civilian clothes, jeans and a T-shirt like her.

She met him posture for posture. "Yes, I have. Good to know you don't have many stalker residents here."

Both Winslow's and Jessup's faces sobered. Winslow spoke first. "We'll do what it takes to keep you safe and catch the guy."

"I know you will." But she'd do more. With a twist of her marquise diamond, she stood straighter.

"Officer Walters." Marshal Taylor stood in his office doorway and waved her forward. "Special Agent Jim Edwards is waiting in my office. Come on in."

Georgia Bureau of Investigation's finest stood and stuck out his hand. "Officer Walters. Good to finally catch up with you."

Her skin pricked. The Mac truck of a man had a firm grip and an annoying drawl. She wouldn't have pegged him as a GBI agent.

"Special Agent Edwards. Not sure why the Bureau sent you all the way up here."

"Let's have a seat, folks." Marshal Taylor took his place behind his desk.

Agent Edwards took the leather chair farthest away from the door and handed her a yellow notepad and pen.

"What's this for?" She sat on the edge of her chair.

"Figured you'd need to make some notes as we go over our options."

Yet another reminder that she was not the one in charge. "What exactly are our options?"

Marshal Taylor spoke up first. "Special Agent Edwards is now in charge of this investigation. He's aware of all the preparation we've done and is on board with our planning."

"What preparation would that be?"

"All of the officers in the county are apprised of the situation. They're set to come as soon as we need them. We also have a local Critical Response Team. SWAT and hostage negotiators included. The Indiana State Police Emergency Team will assist as well." Marshal Taylor typed away on his computer as he spoke.

"You believe any run-in with the stalker will end up in a hostage situation?" She had already assessed this possibility and didn't like it one bit.

"One of the worst-case scenarios, yes."

"I'd say him shooting and killing anyone who stands in his way is the worst possible scenario."

"True. SWAT is prepared to handle even that situation. We all hope we've no need of their specialization."

She nodded and held every errant comment at bay. A plan had already formed in her mind. One she'd keep to herself.

"In a hostage situation, SWAT will provide site containment support while other CRT officers will control negotiations with the stalker."

"And the shooting scenario?"

Marshal Taylor met her eyes. "So far, this stalker has only shot from the shadows. We don't expect him to come in guns blazing. Do you have information to the contrary?"

She cut her eyes to Agent Edwards, hoping he'd pipe in with something more substantial. He remained a quiet observer.

"No. SPD, GCPD, Atlanta PD, and my PD at home hold all the cards and info. I'm still in the dark."

Taylor rested back in his desk chair. "Montezuma PD, Atlanta PD, and Gwinnett County PD are working overtime searching their cities and surrounding areas for the stalker. Most have pulled double shifts and worked almost all of their off-time. The GBI is working with the FBI to build a profile of the stalker and provide their resources to help us find him."

"I know and appreciate all everyone is doing." Half contrite, half bull-headed, what rose to the surface was the fact that no one had caught him yet.

"Detectives in Atlanta and Gwinnett County are digging deep to find Dillon Matthews. So far, there's no next of kin or friends who've kept up with him since his academy days."

"The fingerprints?"

"In the queue. You know how long those take to process."

"Too bad CSI magic can't help."

Taylor grinned. "Maybe one day. First, I'd like to see officers paid what they deserve for putting their lives on the line every day."

"Me too, sir."

Agent Edwards turned his bald head and black eyes her way. "Back to the case. We need your help building the stalker's profile."

"I have no idea who he could be." Maybe if she could get this guy talking, she could figure things out and stay a step ahead not behind everyone else. "I assume you're digging into my friends and relatives now."

"Yes. And we're compiling and analyzing data on the males in your life from all the way back to middle school."

"How soon will you have a profile?" Somewhere she could focus, a face, a set of mannerisms she could identify.

"It will take weeks."

"Weeks?"

"Like Marshal Taylor just mentioned, everyone working this case is staying busy. If this guy calls or sends more flowers, we'll catch him sooner." Edwards stared into her eyes. "Has he called? Or do you have any information you haven't shared yet?"

Back straight, she tossed the empty legal pad onto the desk. "No. He's made no further contact. And I can't believe you'd ask if I had something more. My friends' and family's lives are at stake. No way would I withhold information." Except for the only plan that would keep everyone safe.

Edwards leaned forward. "I meant no accusation. Just a question. Surely you've considered other possibilities besides Dillon Matthews?"

"Yes. But none of them make sense."

"How so?"

"We're professionals. Our radar picks up any suspicious behavior, right? Even at family gatherings and shopping at the mall."

"True."

Marshal Taylor nodded. "We can't turn it off."

"But even my memories of casual brushes with uncomfortable people leave me with nothing. No one foolish enough to stalk a cop. No one with the potential to hide like this guy's done for twelve years."

Taylor huffed. "We can't look into hearts. Many people hide heinous things there for years and years."

Fascinating. If this meeting wasn't about a stalker, she'd dive into analyzing that one.

Edwards pushed forward. "What about high school acquaintances? People you worked for in college? Your initial list of potential suspects hasn't panned out. This guy could be more embedded in your life. Someone who worked for your parents, maybe?"

"My sergeant asked the same questions. I drew a complete blank."

Edwards scribbled notes on his legal pad. "One of Fulton County's District Attorney's investigators is back at our hotel retracing Sergeant Culp's inquiries. We could narrow our suspects down with any small bit of input from you. Anything. It doesn't matter how irrelevant it might seem to you."

"I told Culp everything and everyone I could think of."

"Last time you spoke with Culp, you were dealing with the initial shock of this entire business. Then the attack on your fiancé and two police officers. I'm not patronizing, but I'd urge you to try again. Give us some names. We want to find him before he finds you."

Closing her eyes, she dug into a lifetime ago. Guys she'd dated, two that asked her out and she'd declined. Could one of them be the one? She couldn't even remember their names, much less their defining features. Since her sophomore year of high school and Harrison, there'd been no other guys.

"I didn't have contact with the people my parents worked for, especially not as a teen. Then it was only a cook and a gardener. And a nanny. I believe the gardener has since passed away."

"What about people you worked for?"

Great. How to explain she wasn't a spoiled rich kid when everything she'd say next proved different? "I focused on college and didn't work. Except for some off and on time interning at my dad's office. But his colleagues were all much older than me, and I had little contact with them besides my dad's secretary."

"I believe Culp has spoken to your father's employees. Nothing suspicious there."

"You're looking into high school acquaintances?"

"Any one from that time period stand out to you?"

"I was involved with the Student Government Association, the honors program, Big Brothers and Big Sisters, and the Baptist Student Union in college. Other than that, I studied. Hard. There were no odd people that I remember, at least not odd in a stalkerish way. Odd political activists, yes. Sad family situations in the Big Sisters program, yes. But no one stands out in a weird, following-me-around-all-the-time way."

Edwards clicked his pen. "We're already working with all those organizations, narrowing down the possibilities. I'll have more for you as soon as I can." He slipped a business card from his wallet. "If you think of anything else, give me a call."

Everyone stood. Taylor walked to the door. "We'll stay in touch, Ashley. Call Agent Edwards or myself if you need anything."

Only she was being dismissed. "I'll let you know."

Mind locked in the past, she waved to the officer remaining and exited the building.

Warm summer air slammed into her. Birds chirped. Tourists chattered up and down the now familiar streets.

She catalogued every person. Every car. Every store.

Her stomach knotted. What good was her hypervigilance?

He could be out there, right now, watching her squirm. But she wouldn't know him if she saw him.

"Just come with me to two places. They are must-sees for anyone visiting Shipshe."

"Shipshe?" Ashley shook her head, in no mood for playing tourist. She had to identify shadows from her past before they found her.

"That's what the locals call Shipshewana. They also said we can't leave until we've toured Menno-Hof. I've also planned a stop at Lambright Woodworking and Davis Mercantile."

"That's three. And the stores aren't even open yet."

"There are friendly people everywhere. You'll love it."

There were evil people everywhere too.

Her stomach growled. "Let's go back to the B&B and get some breakfast."

"I told Philip and Debra not to worry about breakfast today. I figured stores would be open by the time you were done, at least the bakery, so we could grab a bite there."

Ashley climbed into the truck and closed her eyes. She needed sleep more than food. "My guess? They left fruit and muffins in the fridge. And yogurt. And a cheese and meat plate. That's what I want."

"We can go purchase those things directly."

"We can't pick money off trees, remember."

Margo scowled and drove them back to Hidden Creek.

Ten minutes later, Ashley emptied the fridge of all its Mennonite and Amish goodies and dug into the spread on her plate.

"Let's pray."

"You go ahead."

Margo held out her hand. "Lord, we thank You for this beautiful home, scrumptious food, and the friendly atmosphere of this town. May Your presence here wash over us and remind us that You hold us in the palm of Your hand."

Meat slices and the best cheese Ashley had ever eaten disappeared in minutes. "This is so incredible."

"So are the destinations I have in mind for today. I talked to Debra last night about places to see and who to talk to, and I collected brochures so we'll know exactly where to go."

"Home would be good. I know how to get there."

Margo huffed. "Didn't Marshal Taylor suggest sightseeing again? It'll help. You'll see."

Only if she kept her eyes open.

After breakfast, they traveled down State Road 5. Ashley studied the already familiar panorama. Despite her focus, she couldn't miss the black buggies that spoke of a slower, more peaceful life than she could imagine. The quaint shops were filled with handcrafted items and food like nowhere else she'd visited.

Too much playing tourist and she'd be lulled into forgetting. If only…

"It's after ten o'clock. Menno-Hof should be open by now." Margo hummed a hymn and bounced her head side to side.

"Stop trying so hard."

"Fine. But don't spoil all the fun today."

"Sorry. I'll do better." And she would, for Maggie. Menno-Hof's bright red barn and attached white farmhouse drew her in. Maybe Maggie was right. This could provide a good distraction. Even research for the revitalization project now underway in Montezuma.

On entering, the first thing she noticed was the handful of people wandering around the gift shop. "Hope it stays like this. Small crowds would be best."

"Yes. Monday is a great day for playing tourist."

Ashley raised her eyebrow. "What else do you know, Miss Tour Guide Indiana?"

"There's a groundswell of folks who visit Shipshewana on Tuesdays or Wednesdays for the famous flea markets."

So Tuesday and Wednesday would be good days to stay at the B&B. Anyone could be hiding in crowds like that.

"Good morning, ladies. Welcome to Menno-Hof. Come right this way." They followed the spry, bonneted woman to the front desk.

"Where are you ladies from?"

Margo locked eyes with Ashley. "Georgia."

"What part? I have cousins who live down that way."

Ashley took the lead. "Atlanta." She pointed to the hallway next to the desk. "Is that where we start our tour?"

"Well, sure. There should be one starting in just a minute. Have a blessed day."

Another woman met them in the hallway. She dressed more like Debra, simple and modest, in a blouse and tan slacks. "Welcome, everyone. If you'll gather round, we'll begin our tour."

Eight other people gathered around them. Ashley catalogued each one and relaxed a fraction. Their guide smiled to each member of the group. "The first of twenty-four stops is in the theater. We'll watch a short movie on how good fences make good communities."

The second the lights went down, Ashley tensed again. Dark and stalkers didn't mix. She turned sideways in her seat with her back to the wall for the duration of the movie.

Lights on and things settled down inside her.

As they walked on through the other stops, she learned about the beginnings of the Anabaptist movement and the imprisonment and torture of a people whose only "crime" was the desire for a church free from state control.

Margo leaned in to whisper. "I can't believe this. Drowned. Burned at the stake. How could people do such awful things?"

She had no answer for the actions then or now. The ones she saw at work every day.

They walked into a replica of a seventeenth century sailing ship and learned of early living conditions. The reality of such harsh treatment even as they tried escaping persecution fuelled the distaste in her mouth. So much human suffering because a group of people chose to live differently.

In one of their last stops, she read about the history of the Anabaptist commitment to nonviolence. Margo joined her. "Nonresistance is one of the big beliefs that set Mennonites and Amish denominations apart from ours."

"I believe I knew about that. And you're just reading from that brochure to learn more highfalutin' words."

Margo waved her comment away. "I just figured you could use reminders here and there."

"Are you going to comment on dress and worship style differences and the fact that I'm a cop?"

"No, but I'm still surprised that the Anabaptists aren't as different from us as I thought." Margo glanced around. "Do you hear that?"

"What?"

"That humming noise. It sounds like a cell phone."

"It is." Ashley focused on the words swimming together on the plaque in front of her.

"Is it yours?"

"Yes."

"Then why aren't you answering your cell?"

"Because I don't recognize the number."

Margo's eyebrows knit together. "You should answer. If there's an update and we can go home, don't you want to know?"

Ashley clutched the phone until her knuckles turned white. "It could be him."

Chapter Seventeen

H e did what?" Patrick jumped from his desk chair.
       "He called. Twice."

"Did you answer?" She knew better than to engage this guy, but he had to be sure.

"No."

"Then how do you know it was him?"

Ashley remained silent for so long, he was tempted to ask his question again. But he waited. She'd explain when she was ready.

"I don't know for sure. Except for the fact that the second call was from my cell phone. The phone that no one's been able to find since before we rushed away from my parents' home. He had to have picked it up in the woods there. That has to be where I lost it. And he's the only one that would hold onto it and not use it until now."

Patrick's muscles tensed to breaking. "Have you called those numbers in?"

"I am a cop."

"You've also been known to be a bit unconventional, shall we say. I need to be sure you're not going rogue or anything to catch this guy."

Another long silence. Again he waited.

"I've texted my cell phone and the other 770 area code to the

Shipshewana PD, Atlanta PD, Gwinnett County PD and home. The GBI too. They're all on it."

Home. Exactly where she belonged. "And they're tracing the numbers?"

"Yes. They're getting phone records. Maybe they'll trace back to a real name or at least they'll see where he's calling from. That would give us a lead. I'm supposed to continue with Margo's sightseeing plans and sit tight." The words dripped with Ashley's familiar mix of cynicism and fright.

He should be there with her. Or at least find a way to help her manage the emotions she was trying to stuff down. "So tell me about your day. Where are you now?"

"Do not pull that counseling voice on me. I'm not standing on a ledge."

He exhaled and returned to his chair. "You said you would need me to talk you down off the wall. That's what I'm trying to do."

"Your getting angry would help more."

Not smart. He couldn't get lost in her anger again. Then he'd be no use to either of them. "I get that. I am angry. Furious that someone out there is stalking the amazing woman I want to spend the rest of my life with. The beautiful—"

"Don't do that either."

"What, tell you the truth?"

"Patrick."

One word in one special tone and he couldn't help but smile. "I love you, Ash. Only prayer is keeping me from doing to this guy like he's done to me. If I could find him."

"Don't, Patrick. Please don't put yourself in his sights again. I can't lose you." Her voice broke on the last word.

"I'm okay. I haven't found him and he hasn't found me. We're safe."

"For now."

He had to change course or they'd fall into the same pattern they had since last week. Anger. Fear. Loneliness. And long distance I-love-yous. "Tell me about Menno-Hof and wherever else you've visited or are going to visit."

Without even glancing at Ashley's texts all morning, he could recite the steps she took through the white farmhouse and big red barn of Menno-Hof. He should be there with her.

"Menno-Hof was good. Here's something I didn't text to you. Did you know that the Amish believe cars speed up the tempo of life and make people forget what's important?"

"I can see that."

"Me too. But we're keeping your Mustang."

"Absolutely."

"The Amish also believe cars cause their families to be away from home and each other too often." Ashley paused.

He waited, hoping for a normal conversation. For Ashley's sake. He had Chip and Kath to rant to about the helplessness of their stagnant situation. Ashley was surrounded by people who, while gentle and loving, couldn't begin to understand how her mind flipped from one seemingly random thought or sight to another but found the connecting points eventually. They couldn't truly understand what was at stake either.

"Maybe they're right. If I stop for just a second and look around, I could live here. Life is slower. The town rolls up at five o'clock. Time for family and friends. Time to worship and sing."

"We could do that now. Life doesn't have to go at warp speed unless we allow it."

"Yeah, my pretending skills are already getting too much of a workout."

"You're going to Lambright Woodworking next? You'll have to text me if their work is as good as Jonathan's."

"I didn't know you were a fan of Jonathan's work."

Patrick could envision her surprised smile. "Things have changed between the two of us recently. He's even working on some special pieces for me. For Christmas."

"Really? You always plan Christmas presents in June?"

"There's so much you don't know about me, isn't there?" He seldom planned this far ahead. He shopped on Christmas Eve like most of his friends. But calling Jonathan about possible Christmas gifts every once in a while gave him a chance to check in and find out what Ashley wouldn't tell him. "I hear Lambright Woodworking might be the place to find a new easel. I could call that in and you could pick it up. Along with some paints."

"Please, counselor. Do you have any guidelines on the upcoming homework?" Her voice held a tinge of annoyance. But only a tinge. That was so much better than a year ago.

"Too much meddling, I'm sorry."

"You know me well. Painting always calms my mind." She sighed. "But please tell me you didn't call and order all of that."

Nope, he had no earthly idea what she'd have wanted or needed. "If you find something, call me. I'll pay for it over the phone."

"Thanks. I miss you."

"Ditto."

"How's pick-up basketball going? Chip hate it as usual?"

"Yep."

"How many more bruises?"

"None. I haven't jumped in to play full contact. Still on the mend. But Chip, he's dribblin' up and down the courts and shootin' the ball like a master jammer. You should see him."

"I'll never get used to that weird hip-hop accent you fake while talking ball."

"It is not fake." He leaned back into his desk chair. "Just a down-home Southern sports fan. An all-American kind of guy."

"That you are, Captain America."

He loved this momentary lapse into normalcy. He could almost see her smiling, her green eyes only for him.

But after another few beats of silence, he came back to reality. "Ash?"

"Yes, sorry. My tour guide says I have to go visit someplace else now. And you have patients to see. When's the fishing trip?"

Never easily distracted, that was what the woman was. "Tomorrow. It'll be great."

The phone silenced again. An incoming call on her end. "Ashley?"

"I'm here. It's him again. I can't take much more of this. I wish he'd show his face so I can finish it."

"Tell me you aren't going to answer." He should have done more than give Ashley his old cell phone. He should have bought two untraceable prepaid phones and kept track of Ashley's phone.

She didn't answer and the line blipped silent again. "Please don't make contact, Ashley. It'll only make things worse."

"I know. But if he's got my phone, he already knows where I am. He could have even found your old phone number through my phone. If so, he's likely headed this way."

Ashley stepped out of the truck one more time, her phone turned completely off. Patrick would call Margo if he needed them. So would Elizabeth Rey and Marshal Taylor.

All she had to do was wait until the PD had accurate call logs as well as the cell tower location information that would help pinpoint the stalker's location when the call was made. She hoped getting a subpoena was easy in Indiana.

It took everything in her not to turn the phone back on and answer. It would all be over soon after that.

Instead she followed Margo into Lambright Woodworking's front room, filled with cool air and the scent of wood shavings and flowers. A leather couch faced a stonework fireplace with shelves of goods surrounding the entire space.

"Good morning. May I help you find anything?" A young Amish woman smiled at them from the counter.

"I'm looking for a wooden art easel. Do you have any?" Ashley's voice came out calm, like a customer with no care in the world but beautiful furniture. She could pretend easily here with so much beauty surrounding her. Old-fashioned nightlights. Soaps. In the other room in front of her, a huge wooden and iron bed and gorgeous cabinetry displays. When she came back to visit with Patrick, they'd have to look into updating their kitchen.

"I believe we do. I'll show you where." She led them to a large open room full of dining room tables, chairs, and dressers of the finest quality. At least by the high standards of Jonathan's work.

"Look at this." Margo held up a simple burgundy candle and an elegant wrought iron holder.

"Very nice. I can see that in your dining room, Maggie."

"I need to talk to the owner about shipping." Margo was off to another display area. "I could use these simple wooden kitchen tools and those candles for a number of interior redesigns on my calendar. Homeowners would scoop them up in a flash."

"My father will be done with his tour soon." Their Amish host smiled and stopped walking. "I'm sure he'd be happy to speak with you."

"Excellent." Margo clapped her hands and then sobered. "Sorry. Not the right time to be effervescing about work."

Ashley shrugged. "It's fine. I understand. Kid in a candy store and all that."

"Over here are our handcrafted bowls and some wooden toys." She pointed to a nook overlooking a long glassed-in work area.

"Farther down, just through that door, are some unique tables for entertaining and if you head back with me to the main room, you can see a handcrafted king-size bed with a headboard of carved baseball bats. My father crafted it for a major league baseball player."

Ashley followed. The dark wooden bats gleamed between wrought iron posts. Patrick would love that.

"Do you ship large furniture to places like Atlanta?" Ashley tried hard to catch the decorating bug, not terribly difficult to do when shopping with Margo.

"Yes. We ship all over the country."

Margo disappeared around a huge cherry wood buffet.

Ashley turned to the Amish woman. "Thanks for showing us around. I can see we'll be here a while."

"Take your time. I'll be up front if you need anything."

Ashley meandered around the large open room, touching oak dining tables and expensive cherry bed frames. Such excellent quality deserved the high prices it garnered on items like these. But not on a cop's salary.

Turning toward Margo's excited chatter, Ashley spotted a honey oak easel and headed that way. The design was simple, early Americana. She'd come back when this was over to purchase that for sure.

"Margo, look at this." She held out a wooden pitcher, handmade, striped in light and dark brown wood. Its smooth surface and functional but beautiful design touched something in her. She sat it back on the shelf, but it wobbled and fell.

She caught it just before it hit the concrete floor.

"Nice catch."

"Nice butterfingers is more accurate." This time she sat it on the shelf with no wobbling.

"You're a lot like that pitcher, you know?" Margo leaned against the doorframe, facing away from her.

Ashley turned toward the windowed woodworking area. On a lathe, a young man spun a tan piece of hollowed out wood, using a tool to remove the coarse tree bark. Probably making one of the smooth bowls on the shelf next to her.

"I really want one of these bowls and this easel. But I should wait. I always regret impulse buys. How about you, Maggie?"

"I'll see." She turned around. "You aren't even a little bit curious about how you're similar to the pitcher?"

"I'd like to buy this too." She set the easel down and picked up the pitcher again, more careful with it this time.

"Not to get sentimental on you, but I overheard Mr. Lambright giving a fraction of the tour and answering a question about pitchers and bowls."

"Guess that's why the young man in there is making a bowl."

"Mr. Lambright told a story about pitchers in Jesus's time and their usefulness. He's a fantastic storyteller."

Ashley licked her dry lips. "So I'm useful. That's good to know. I'm going to head up front and see if I can put these items on hold. And get some vanilla lip balm."

"Sacrifice. That's what a simple pitcher stands for, don't you think?"

"Not going there, Maggie. I only need one counselor in my life, thanks." She headed up front and paid cash for two sticks of lip balm and the easel. So much for not making an impulse purchase.

Slipping up close, Margo nudged her. "You said you didn't have much cash."

"Dad tucked some into my suitcase. I found it last night."

Ashley's phone burned against her leg. She had to turn it back on. Had to know what he wanted. She should have gone back to the PD and let them listen in on one of these calls. But she shouldn't answer. They'd tell her the same thing. And then they'd take it from there.

Not this time. This time she'd know firsthand what would happen next.

Margo elbowed her in the ribs.

Ashley jerked away. "Stop doing that."

"Stop scowling and stop tapping your phone."

"I need to go back to the PD and let them have Patrick's cell phone. If this guy calls back, they can answer."

"We're going back in a few hours. We can give them the phone then."

"I should go now."

Margo finished her order and made a down payment in cash. "Thank you so much for all your help. I'll be back soon to pay off the balance and collect my smaller items."

They stepped into the heat.

Margo hopped into the driver's side of the truck. "I've talked to Marshal Taylor. They have some of the phone records. They're doing all they can to find out who's calling and where he's calling from. Our sitting there watching them won't help anyone. Besides, we have one more place to visit."

"How can you prioritize shopping over finding this guy?"

Margo slapped her hands on the steering wheel. "My job is to keep you occupied so the police can handle it."

"I am the police." Fists clenched. "Take me to the police department. I need to be part of this entire process. He's coming after me. I need to know what to expect."

"They can handle this unemotionally, and according to their protocol. Without us getting in their way. You and I are going shopping at Davis Mercantile. Pretzels, candles, jewelry. Maybe you can find Patrick a wedding gift."

Anger never worked with Maggie. She'd ignore it. Pleading might do the trick, though.

"Mags, please. Do you know how hard this is? I'm in the dark. Elizabeth won't return my calls. Neither will Culp. Rich probably isn't able. I can't be one step behind any longer."

Margo turned into State Road 5, ignoring every bit of pleading.

"My turn to keep you safe, Ash. Please let me."

While Margo was busy with driving slow and taking in the sights, Ashley pulled out her cell phone and turned it back on.

Three more calls. Three voicemails.

Fingers clenched, she punched the third number down to play the message. Same number as most of the others before.

"Ashley. I know you can't let on that you're still in love with me. Not yet. But I'm coming, and we'll be together soon."

Her stomach pitched. Dangerous and delusional. Great combination.

The next message started with the gravelly voice, but this time his words rose in pitch and volume.

"Answer me, Ashley. You're making me crazy. Don't turn on me now. I need you."

She was making him crazy? Whatever. She searched every inch of her high school memories and couldn't dredge up that voice. She punched the most recent call.

"That's it, Ashley. I warned you."

A vise compressed her chest. Her mouth turned to cotton.

She texted the message content to Marshal Taylor. And asked for permission to answer the next phone call.

If he refused, she'd do this her way. She had to find out the stalker's next step. He wouldn't talk to the police. He'd only talk to her.

The phone rang in her hands.

"Don't answer that, Ash. Please."

Two rings. Three. Four. She'd take the upper hand now.

Five rings.

Her finger hovered over the answer button.

Chapter Eighteen

Ashley clenched her jaw and turned off the phone once again. She wouldn't take the call with Margo around. But later, she could set up a meeting and…

"Stop with the deleterious scrunching up of your face. You almost look as if you're hatching a plan. Do not do it."

"He's here, Maggie. I can feel it."

Margo parked the truck in front of the Davis Mercantile. "I'll call Marshal Taylor and have him send some officers our way."

"I need my gun. Drive back to Hidden Creek." There she could ditch Margo and either take or make the necessary call.

"No. You've been wearing your gun all morning. And if you haven't, it's been in the glove box. Don't try to pull one over on me."

"What?"

"You're wearing your gun. Otherwise, why would you be in jeans when everyone else is wearing shorts?"

Busted. Maggie was getting too smart for her britches.

"I'm not going shopping."

Margo grabbed her purse and stood. "Better to hide in a crowd with cops all around than to hide at the B&B and leave Philip and Debra exposed. They can't defend themselves."

"Faulty logic. Staying here will expose all these people to danger."

"You're right. I'll ask Marshal Taylor to consider posting an officer at the doors so anyone fitting the stalker's description can be questioned."

"Why are you calling Marshal Taylor?"

"Because you won't."

Ashley slammed the truck door and waited for Margo to finish her short chat with the police chief. "I'm not going in there. I'll jog back to the B&B on my own."

"You can't protect me that way."

"Right now, I could handcuff you and make you go back on foot."

A huff and a glare from Margo.

"I do like the new tough guy act, even though it's so not you."

"The people who love you are doing all they can to keep you safe. You don't make it easy."

"It's not your job."

Margo sauntered ahead. "This is not your investigation or plan, so just come with me and shop. We'll get pretzels and candy and Christmas gifts."

Even if she were a detective, she'd have no place in the ongoing investigation. Except to check in and be guarded. Might as well play along for the time being.

On entering the blue-gray building, she stopped and took it all in. The warm honey wood floors, the windowed shops. Children laughing. Flower scents and pine.

"Look at these stairs and this massive tree." Margo was once again in her element.

"It's the trunk of a Douglas fir, nearly four centuries old."

Margo turned. "You know this how?"

Ashley pointed to the plaque explaining more than she had. "It's pretty amazing, reaching up through all these stairs."

"Funny." Margo pointed to JoJo's. "I believe you need food."

She turned on her phone. Nothing.

Margo winced. "Let's get pretzels."

Nice try. "I'm going shopping. Upstairs. Where I hope there's more room."

This time Margo followed her. Right into Aunt Millie's Candy and Nut shop. "I'll eat lunch here."

Margo rolled her eyes. "I'm going over there. The candy counter is calling my name."

Some things never changed.

"Ashley?"

She spun around. "Candice? What are you doing here?"

"I'm glad I caught up with you." Candice's hazel eyes darted to the massive carousel and back to the candy store. "I need to talk to you."

"Why didn't you call?"

"I tried your cell phone, but no one answered."

"Good." She caught Margo's glance and motioned outside. "So how did you find me then? We didn't tell anyone where we'd be."

"I followed you."

"What?" Deep breath in. So that was who'd followed her around all day? "Have a seat and let's talk. You said you knew cops. That doesn't mean you know how to follow them. And why would you?"

"I started at Menno-Hof and asked one of the ladies I go to church with. She said Margo had mentioned Lambright Woodworking."

Ashley couldn't contain a groan. It would be this easy for her stalker to find her.

"Did you ask around there?"

"No. But I saw your truck in the mercantile parking lot and prayed I'd find you."

Candice had no idea of the extent of danger she'd put Ashley and Margo in. She was a civilian. A civilian in trouble, from the looks of her red face and darting eyes.

"Has your husband found you?"

Candice's wide eyes and quivering lip told the story. "How did you know?"

"Body language. You didn't agree to meet him, did you?" Pieces of the puzzle snapped into place. *Really, God? This is why I'm in Shipshewana?*

"Yes. He said he had the divorce papers, and all I had to do was sign them. Then he'd leave me alone, and I could have my life back."

"He was lying."

Candice stood and focused on the nearby steps. "Not this time. Over five years of marriage, I've learned to tell the difference between him lying to me and telling the truth. This time it's for real. You'll see."

"Candice, listen to me." Ashley stood and nudged Candice away from the stairs. "I've been a cop long enough to know abusers like your husband can change their methods but seldom their intent. He's not going to show up today, give you the divorce papers, and leave you alone."

"He might." Candice fiddled with her purse strap.

"We need to get out of here." Ashley pointed to the elevators.

"Candy? That you?"

Ashley turned and stepped in front of Candice. Of course her husband was a lumberjack. What was she thinking? "Turn around and walk back down those stairs or I'm calling the cops."

"I'm here to see my wife. You stay out of it."

"Bad move, telling me what to do." Ashley lowered her voice. "When I say go, run to the elevator. I'll keep him here. You call the police."

"You don't scare me." The lumberjack took a step forward and stopped. "I haven't done anything wrong."

"There's a restraining order out against you, isn't there?"

Candice's husband ground his jaws back and forth.

People in the rooftop restaurant turned to view the show. Others gathered in a small crowd behind the lumberjack.

She had no arrest powers here. No right to pull her gun. Too dangerous anyway in this crowd.

"Candice, listen to me." Ashley's voice was a whisper, her eyes fixed on the lumberjack about to move. "Go. Now."

Candice ran.

So did her husband. Straight for her.

Time skidded to a slow-motion movie.

The lumberjack charged straight toward her.

Ashley's vision tunneled. She only had one shot at this.

At the last second, she stepped to the side and hooked his left ankle, his momentum taking him all the way to the ground. His sweaty shirt in hand, Ashley lunged on his back and hammer-fisted the back of his head.

Out he went.

"Margo! Candice! Let's go." She led them down the stairs shoving stunned people out of the way and didn't stop running until they reached Margo's car. "Keys, Margo."

Candice slammed the passenger door and screamed. "Here he comes!"

From outside, the quaint breakfast scene filled him with memories of a better time in his life. When his mother and father lived and Ashley had vowed to cherish and obey him all of her days.

But obeying she was not.

He'd fix that. Once all the pieces of the puzzle were fit together.

Inside Joyce Stone's little starter home, Chester barked. The predictable mutt did just as he'd planned.

Bradley patted his leg and headed for the door, yet another creature of habit. "Come on, Chester. Good, boy. Let's go outside. Be right back, Mom."

He waited next to the back door, only one step away from forcing Ashley's hand. She wouldn't let her "little brother" be a hostage for long.

The rest she had yet to discover.

The door squeaked open and Chester lit out the back, barking all the time. As soon as the dog turned toward him, he reached out and grabbed Bradley around the neck.

"Stay quiet and I let the dog live."

The boy nodded.

Chester ran at them.

A swift kick with his boot took care of the little menace.

"Let go of me." Bradley elbowed him in the ribs, and he fought against loosening his hold. But the boy got free. And like a foolish child, he ran right to the dog, not the phone.

He kicked Bradley hard in the ribs. "That's for your elbow."

Grabbing Bradley by his T-shirt, he pulled him close. "This is for Ashley." His hard hook landed on the boy's face, and Bradley fell to the ground.

He bent down to retrieve what he'd come for. This was far too easy.

Until something struck him on the back. Hard.

"Run, Brad!" Joyce's screeching assaulted his ears. Her bat connected again on his leg. He inched away further.

His entire back burned.

One more downstrike and he flipped on his back, grabbing the bat and wrenching it from her hands. Slow and steady, he stood, bat raised to return Joyce's stupid attempt at bravery.

"Stop right there." The boy stood fifteen feet away, black handgun shaking in his small, pale hands.

Too much had gone wrong. He adjusted his plans, and lunged at Joyce. "Guess you'll have to do."

"I said stop." Bradley racked the slide and pointed. "I know how to use this."

Sure he did.

Just in case, he used Joyce as a trembling shield. All the way to the edge of the yellow house. "Be sure to call Ashley. Hear me, Bradley? Tell her I said hello."

The boy fingered the trigger.

He tossed Joyce ahead of him and turned to run.

Eyes wide, the last thing that registered was Bradley pulling the trigger. A deafening explosion slammed him to his knees.

Chapter Nineteen

All Patrick wanted to do was sleep. There everyone was safe, not in pain, and wedding plans progressed, one box checked off at a time.

A shrill noise dragged him from the fantasy of normal life. He grabbed for the receiver. "Hello?"

"Patrick! You have to get here *right now!*"

Each screech slammed against his temples. With effort, he sat upright and focused on the phone. The world didn't tilt. Good sign. "Is this Joyce? What's wrong?"

"Yes, it's Joyce. And that stalker just attacked Brad and me and got away. You have to come right now. Hurry."

"What? Talk to me, Joyce. What happened?"

The phone went dead silent.

Stalker. Attacked Brad. In a split second, he was up and tugging on clothes. *Lord, please stop this stalker. Protect Brad. Joyce. Show me how to help them.*

He gulped down a glass of milk with a handful of pills and prayed that would be enough to keep the pain down and his body functional. It would have to do. He had to get to Joyce's home fast.

To do so, he broke every speed limit law. And used his new cell while driving. His office manager's recorded message filtered through his racing heart. She should be at the office any minute now. "Jennifer.

Reschedule all my appointments today and the rest of this week. Sorry. Family emergency. I'll call when I know what's happening."

Jennifer would pray. He should too.

The red traffic light up ahead didn't help this situation. He slammed his brakes and his fist against the steering wheel. He had to get to Brad.

Peace.

The word flitted through his mind. He'd have laughed if there was any humor left inside. Peace? How?

Whenever I am afraid, I will trust in You. In God (I will praise His word), in God I have put my trust; I will not fear. What can flesh do to me?

For a second a Bible verse he'd memorized as a child brought comfort. But what could flesh or mortal man do? A lot. This stalker could take everything that mattered.

Joyce's house came into view, Americus police cars dotting the perimeter. One lone Montezuma squad car stood out. Culp. At least his friend was here and would fill him in on what was happening.

Patrick parked his Mustang and on shaky limbs crossed the street into the early morning fray. Joyce's disheveled brown hair was the first familiar sight. "Joyce?" He hurried toward her.

"Patrick. Thank God you're here." She launched herself into his arms. "It was horrible. He came out of nowhere and was kicking Brad. Yanking him up. Punching him. My boy was bleeding, Patrick. I couldn't handle it."

He glanced at the Americus officer closest to them. "Where's Brad?"

The female police officer standing guard looked him over. "Who are you?"

"Patrick James, family counselor. Friend of the family." He stepped closer, Joyce now clinging to his arm. "I'd like to see Brad."

"Stand in line, sir. There's a bunch of cops talking with him right now."

"Without his mother? He's fourteen, you know."

The police officer adjusted her duty belt. "Another officer just finished taking her statement. She's welcome to return to her son."

Patrick led them away.

A strong hand on his arm stopped them. "Not you. Sorry. They should be done soon."

Joyce's haunted eyes darted back and forth between him and the police officer. "I need to be with him, Patrick."

"Go on, Joyce. I'll be in there as soon as I can."

Intellectually, he got that the police were just doing their job. But right now they were standing in his way of doing his job. Of doing as Ashley had asked and taking Brad someplace safe to hide.

He should have listened.

Should have put first things first and accepted that Ashley had pegged this situation spot on.

But running showed fear. Hadn't Ashley said that too?

"You the one attacked by this alleged stalker last week?"

"Alleged?" Patrick turned to the female officer who hadn't moved since she'd barred his way. Short. Slender. Brown hair. Brown eyes. Still resolutely in his way. "The Montezuma police department, the Atlanta PD, the Gwinnett County PD, and…" He stopped just short of telling everyone right where Ashley hid. "They all believe this is a stalker. A violent one."

Her face remained the same.

The morning sun beat down on them, already scorching the air and heating up the pavement. The heat did nothing for his attitude. "Yes. Last week the stalker attacked me too."

She pointed across the street. "Maybe you should go have a seat in your Mustang. You look a little green."

Great. Adrenaline rush over and he not only helped exactly zero, but now he was being told to go sit down and shut up.

He turned and schlepped to his car.

Culp leaned against it, an obnoxious smile on the uniformed man's hardened face. "You should know by now not to mess with female cops. It never turns out well."

"I'm marrying one, and that will turn out just fine, thanks."

"Let's hope."

Patrick glared. "No. Let's make it happen."

"Nothin' you can do right now, so simmer down. You know we're all doin' everything we can to catch this guy. It's personal for every cop. Trust me, Patrick."

That wasn't enough. He wanted the inside scoop, to hear what Culp and Elizabeth wouldn't tell him. To do something besides pray or hide.

Just like Ashley.

He should have been more patient with her.

"Tell me what happened here at least."

Culp raised an eyebrow.

"Okay, so you don't have to. But you know me, Sam."

"I know you're too close to see the big picture."

Patrick clenched his jaw. They were on the same side. "So tell me what it is and what happened here. Please." That last word burned like acid.

Culp pushed off from the Mustang. "Ashley's a cop and always will be. Crazies like this stalker and what he did here today? We all think about 'em. Have nightmares about 'em. It's our life."

Not Patrick's life. Not Ashley's life if he could help it.

"Now that we got that out o' the way, here's what I know of today. Bradley took Chester out this morning and was attacked. Thirty-something guy kicked the dog and Bradley and then let loose on the kid."

God, why is this happening again? Hasn't Bradley been through enough?

"So how'd he get away?"

Culp chuckled. "His mama wields a pretty mean Louisville Slugger."

"Joyce beat the guy with a bat?"

"Yep."

A new sense of appreciation welled up inside him. A hands-on mom for such a short time and she'd managed to rescue her son from a vicious attacker.

"So if you know all this, why can't I see Brad?"

Culp shook his head and stretched his back. "Ever seen Bradley shoot a gun?"

"What?" Patrick's brain couldn't compute what he'd just heard. "The boy's Mennonite. He's never had a gun in his home."

"Does now."

"Did he shoot the stalker?" A disturbing mix of hope and revulsion rose within.

"No body's been found yet."

"So why is the boy being questioned so long about a gun he probably only shot this one time?"

"Can't say."

"Won't say." Patrick started back for the house. "Let me talk to them, Sam. You know I can help."

Without further comment, Culp took the lead and got him inside the small house.

Joyce's high-pitched screech hit him full force. "What kinda person you think I am? Of course I got involved. Woulda killed that creep. He attacked my boy. Do you hear me? He attacked my son. Nobody does that without a mama gettin' riled. I stand by what I did, and I'd do it again. Only harder."

That a girl, Joyce. Patrick couldn't have pegged that emotion better.

Culp cleared his throat. "Sergeant Woods, this is Patrick James, and he's—"

Brad rushed across the kitchen and into Patrick's arms. "You came. I knew you'd come. We have to run, Patrick. Like Ashley said."

He returned the desperate hug. *Thank You, God. He's okay.*

"Brad, let's finish talking to the police first. They need our help."

Sergeant Wood roughed his Marine haircut and dipped his chin. "You still haven't explained where the gun came from. It isn't your mother's."

Patrick recoiled as if he'd been sucker punched. "Bradley?"

"I…I can explain." The boy studied his tennis shoes.

"Please do." Over a year ago, Patrick would have said this behavior wasn't like Brad at all. But he'd seen the effects of last year's standoff with a gunman. This made perfect sense.

Culp leaned against a wall. Patrick took a chair next to Brad. Both the boy and his mom still shook.

He understood. All too well.

"Brad. Tell me what's going on here. Violence isn't your way."

"It isn't Mamm's way or Cousin Jonathan's. But it's the way of everyone else. Around the neighborhood, the big kids bully the little ones. The cops carry guns to keep people safe."

Sergeant Wood leaned in.

Everyone waited.

Brad sighed. "I know Mamm and I would be dead if it wasn't for Ashley. And if she hadn't had a gun, we'd all three have been killed. I couldn't let that happen this time. I knew this guy wanted to hurt my mom and me. And Ashley. I had to stop him."

Joyce pulled Brad to her and sobbed.

The men exchanged glances. So much weight for a boy of fourteen to carry.

Sergeant Wood's hard features softened. "I can understand that, Bradley. But I need to know where the gun came from. Who sold it to you?"

Another huge sigh.

Patrick braced for more bad news.

"I had this friend…I get now that he was a drug dealer. I didn't know it then. He used to pick me up and we'd hang out with his friends sometimes. He'd pay for hamburgers and cokes."

"Did you buy anything from him?"

"No. Even Mennonite teens know not to buy crack. I'm not stupid."

"I never said you were, Bradley." Sergeant Wood scribbled something on his notepad.

Culp stepped forward. "I can look into the case, but it's likely the person Bradley is talking about is in jail for possession and distribution."

Sergeant Wood nodded. "Let's get back to the gun, Bradley. Tell me how you obtained it."

"One of the guys that used to meet up with Derrick and me lives a mile away. He has two older brothers who still live at home. When Ashley had to go into hiding, I went to talk to him."

"Is it his gun?"

Brad shrugged. "I don't know. He just said I'd need it and could borrow it for a while."

Sergeant Wood stood and motioned for Culp to go ahead of him.

"Y'all sit tight. I need to check a few things, and we'll talk again in a minute."

Joyce's eyes followed the police officers out of the kitchen. Then she turned to Patrick. "They won't charge Brad with anything, will they? He didn't know."

"I didn't know what?"

"That minors can't lawfully be in possession of a firearm." Patrick rubbed his temples. "I don't know what I can do, but I'll talk to Sergeant Culp."

Joyce shrunk into herself. "This never woulda happened if I'd told Brad to stay where he belonged. He was safe up there with his Mamm. He knew nothin' about drug dealers and guns. This is all my fault." Her body shook with sobs.

"Mom." Brad nudged her shoulder, but she didn't budge. "It's not your fault. I met Derrick while I was living with Mamm. I knew about guns too. I'd just never touched one. This is not your fault."

Patrick stayed silent. Joyce would never believe that. And he couldn't even jump in to defend the safety of living in the Mennonite community. They all remembered vividly what happened last year.

"You gotta take him back to his Mamm, Patrick. I'll pack his bags." Joyce jumped up from the table and wrung her hands. "They'll let him go with you, won't they, Patrick? They have to. He's not safe here. He needs to go back to his people."

"I don't know what happens next, Joyce. I don't think Brad's coming with me anywhere though. Not right now, anyway." He turned to Brad. "You may not have many choices right now, but we should all be praying."

The boy's mouth moved, but no words escaped.

"Did you say something, Brad?"

"My mom is right. I belong with my people. I'm not cut out for all this violence and danger." A tear slipped down his cheek. "I can't handle this. But I have to make sure my mom is okay."

Patrick stood and put a hand on Brad's shoulder. "We'll work this out, Brad."

Culp and Sergeant Wood stopped talking the second Patrick walked toward them. "Regardless of what happened and what you all have to do about the gun, Brad and his mom aren't safe. They need to go into hiding until the stalker is found."

"Agreed." Culp pursed his lips. "Problem is, the kid doesn't want to go stay with the Mennonites anymore, and Joyce doesn't have family in Georgia."

"Brad's willing to go back if someone will take him in."

Culp crossed his arms. "I'll go talk to some folks. If Joyce will head up to Tennessee and Brad back into his community while we sort this all out—"

"Find the stalker first. That solves everything."

"Yeah, comin' right up."

"Sorry, Sam." Patrick's mind raced with possibilities. His ribs ached. His temples pounded. But he could do something now to help. "I know who to talk to in the Mennonite community. They'll keep Brad safe and busy with work."

"If you're sure."

"I am. And I'll give you all the details after I get Brad settled in. This is the best thing all around."

"And then what're you gonna do?"

Draw a stalker's fire.

This time he'd be ready.

CHAPTER TWENTY

"You're leaving? Already?"

Patrick turned back toward Joyce's home, Brad rooted to the porch, arms crossed. A few police cruisers drove away. "Sorry, I can't stay longer. I have some things I need to do."

Brad stepped down from the small porch and cupped his hands over his mouth. "Chester! Come on, boy. Chester!"

"Chester wasn't in the house with you this whole time?"

"No."

"Did your mom put him in a bedroom?"

"I thought she did. That's what we usually do when people come over. But I checked, and he wasn't there." Brad lifted up on his toes to peer down the street. "He's never been gone this long."

"Did you look under the bed?"

Brad nodded. "I know Chester too."

"Let's walk around the block and see if he's hiding under a bush or with a neighbor." Patrick headed away from Joyce's house. "Does your mom know you're out here looking for Chester?"

"Yes."

"She was going to let you go alone?" Not her wisest decision. "Is she okay?"

Brad shrugged.

"Was your mom hurt?" He hadn't noticed any bruising or injuries.

"No."

So they were back to minimalism. Maybe he should go check on Joyce. Then again, he needed to get moving on his plans before anyone figured out what he had in mind.

"Chester!" Brad's voice broke. He sped up and searched under the bushes ahead.

Brad had to be a mess inside. Too many memories from last year. Patrick should have stayed longer to help Brad and Joyce. But the longer it took to find this stalker, the worse it'd get for everyone involved. He still jumped when someone knocked on his office door.

Brad returned to his side. No Chester.

"Mom understands the danger we're in. She said she just needed a few minutes to talk to a neighbor, and I should stay close to the house. Cops still there and all. The neighbor's a paramedic or something. She thinks I should go to the hospital."

"Does it hurt to take a deep breath?"

"Yes."

"How about your head?"

Brad shrugged. "I'm fine."

"Did an ambulance come with the police before I got here?"

"Yes. Said I should go to the hospital. But they can't make me."

It'd been a long time since they'd gone down this road. One he'd like to avoid as much as Brad. "I can take you."

"No. I've had cows kick me harder than that guy. I'm fine."

Conflicting emotions and thoughts battled for control. Should he drag Brad home to safety? Was it really safe now? Or keep searching for Chester? Out here in the open where anyone could see and attack again.

He was either getting paranoid or starting to understand what parents experienced every day with every decision. Cops too, day in and day out.

They crossed the street and turned right, heading toward downtown Americus. "Does Chester know this way?"

"There's a park a little ways up here. We've been coming every day."

Brad picked up the pace. "He's probably there. That makes sense, doesn't it?"

"Yes."

The park was filled with kids and parents. Brad rushed to a picnic table on the other side of the swings. Patrick walked over to a group of women. "I'm sorry to interrupt, but have any of you seen a chestnut boxer here this morning?"

The three women blinked and stared. The redhead spoke first. "I haven't been here long, but I haven't seen any dogs not on a leash."

"Did anyone else see him?"

"You the owner?" This woman bounced a baby on her hip.

"He's my fiancée's dog. Have you all seen him?"

Patrick studied the three women, willing one of them to remember Chester. Surely Chester would have come to a familiar place like this one if he wasn't at Brad's.

Otherwise...

His heartbeat kept pace with his racing brain.

Brad hurried to his side. "He's not here." The boy's brown eyes watered. "Where could he be, Patrick? Do you think...?"

He didn't want to admit it. But what if...

Ashley's feet pounded the asphalt in a steady cadence. For a short time, life made sense. She was in tune with her body and mind and only her feet raced.

"Slow down." Candice panted behind her. "I'm not...used to...running...like you are."

The words struck like a barb. She wasn't accustomed to running from problems. She faced them head-on. Fixed things. Arrested criminals. Stopped killers.

Not anymore.

In the last month, she'd run from wedding planning. From a stalker. From Candice's obsessed husband.

Reality grated against her defenses.

"Ashley." Candice's footsteps stopped. "I can't go any further."

Two buggies clip-clopped past them before Ashley reined in her attitude enough to turn and walk back to Candice's side. "We can head back. Breakfast should be ready by now."

"Sorry. I know you wanted to be gone longer."

She wanted to be home. Planning a wedding with Patrick. Holding Chester and watching a Jane Austen DVD.

Or even drawing out Candice's psycho stalker husband.

The police and GBI had tracked her cell phone and the other number back to Atlanta. Then nothing. No calls. No more phone data. The guy had probably taken out the cell battery and tossed everything in an Atlanta dumpster. So the cops back home were still on a manhunt, searching for a shadow. Cops here were now searching for Candice's husband.

And she finally had something she could do to help.

Cars whooshed past them in a steady rhythm now. Soon the roads into Shipshewana would be packed with tourists for Tuesday's flea market.

"We can come back out later." She shielded her eyes from the glaring sun. All around them, green grass and white farmhouses marked their surroundings. She wouldn't get lost again. "We made it what? Two miles?"

"Feels like ten. I should hang out with you more. I might finally lose some weight."

Dark circles lined Candice's eyes. Her brown, almost black hair was soaked with sweat. Still, the young woman clung to hope. It filtered out from every pore.

Ashley couldn't go there. "We can run for as long as I'm here." The company would have been great if not for the added sense of responsibility and vigilance required to spend time with Candice.

Candice checked her phone. "Justin hasn't called again. Maybe it's over."

It was never over. Not with a man like Candice's husband. The lumberjack's determination yesterday and the hate in his eyes said he wouldn't stop until either he or Candice were dead.

Few people understood that reality. So many women died every year at the hands of men who had at one time claimed to love them.

Mercy Givens's bruised face and shaking form flitted through her mind, as it did every time she responded to a domestic call. Mercy had gotten away. Helped send her husband to prison. If Ashley could help Candice see the truth, maybe Candice would be another survivor.

"Are you angry? I could go another mile maybe." Candice worried her lip something awful.

"Not at you. At your husband and all the men like him who will stop at nothing to destroy a woman's life for no good reason."

"Like your stalker."

"Yes." Ashley headed back to the B&B.

"My counselor said anger was healthy, but not if I stayed there. She said anger could help me make the decision to get out and stay out of a destructive relationship."

"Praying helps too." Ashley's conscience pricked. Walk the talk, as her best friend would say.

"I'm not big on religious stuff. I mean, I get that the Amish and Mennonite lifestyle is so peaceful and good because they pray and all. But it's not me."

Ashley shrugged. "Just trying to help."

"Oh, you have. And I appreciate it. I know it was stupid for me to have taken Justin's call after all this time. I just thought he'd, you know, changed."

"They don't change."

Candice's face pinched into a question. "But I thought all religious people believed God could change even the worst of sinners."

That was what Ashley had been taught. What her Bible said. What she'd experienced inside.

Too bad it wasn't what she'd seen on the streets.

"Let's get back and get some breakfast." They retraced their steps in silence. Cars swished past every so often.

No blue Chevy Malibu. As if the stalker was stupid enough to stay in the same car.

Patrick's phone buzzed in her pocket. "Patrick? Please tell me you're headed to the lake."

"Love you, hon. But no."

Candice pointed ahead. "I'll see you back there." She walked slowly away, shoulders drawn in, head down.

"What's happening? I haven't heard an update yet this morning."

Deep sigh. "The stalker attacked Brad."

No. Not again. Brad doesn't deserve this, God.

"Is he okay? What happened? Is he in the hospital? I can be there tonight." She picked up her pace.

"No, but he's safe. Joyce beat the stalker with a baseball bat."

"What?" She wished she'd have seen that with her own eyes. Wished even harder that Joyce had knocked him unconscious and this was all over.

"I know. Joyce stepped up to the plate and came out swinging. She's okay too."

The tone of his voice had lightened, as if he were recounting a funny story. Only one reason Patrick would pull something like that. "What aren't you telling me?"

"A lot you don't need to know right now."

"Then pretend better, Patrick."

"I wish I could."

A growl escaped. Too many more days trapped like a bear and she'd lose it. But then she risked losing everything. She had to keep her head.

"If you can't pretend, then just get it over with and tell me. Please."

"Chester is missing."

Tears sprang to her eyes. First Brad and now Chester. *Really, God? Isn't this enough?*

"Are you searching for him? Could he be hurt?"

"Chip, Kath, and some hunter friends are looking for him. We'll find him. I just...I figured you'd be furious if Elizabeth or the cops there told you before I did."

"You're right." She stalked up and down the buggy lane. "You think the stalker has Chester?"

"The thought crossed my mind."

Tears ran down her face. For Patrick. For Brad. For all of them, including her trusting, loving boxer.

Screeching tires forced her instincts to take over.

Candice stood frozen on the side of the road.

Justin stalked toward her.

At least this mess with Justin was going down as she'd hoped. Planned for.

"Run, Candice!" Ashley dropped the phone and raced toward a brown beater that had passed them earlier. "Get away from him!"

Her Glock was in hand as she ran. "Stop! Police!"

Justin the Lumberjack clamped his hand down on Candice's arm and smiled. "You're too late this time."

With a savage shove, he forced Candice in the car and crouched around to the trunk.

Wait for it. Don't shoot. Wait till the right second.

The refrain repeated over and over in her head as she advanced, gun steady. Time slowed to a crawl. Sweat dripped down her back. She had a bull's-eye on her chest in the wide open middle of nowhere.

But so did Justin.

Candice slapped her palm against the car door again and again. "It's locked!"

"Call 911, Candice. Now!"

Justin chose that second to jump into the car and slam the beater into drive.

He aimed straight for her.

In the flash of a second, she had no shot.

The car lunged forward and she jumped a shallow ditch, landing on her knees.

The brown beater pulled away.

But not fast enough. She had a shot now.

CHAPTER TWENTY-ONE

Patrick roared against the silence on the other end of the phone. "Ashley! Ashley, talk to me! Ashley?"

He'd hung up and dialed again every few seconds for the last fifteen minutes. All he got was his serene voicemail message.

Elizabeth's phone went to voicemail too. Culp didn't answer. Somebody had to know something. He just couldn't get through the blue wall to find out what.

He exited his Mustang and slammed the door. Forget clinical analysis or hyped up bravado. He had to do something more than the failures he'd already experienced today.

He speed dialed the number again.

"Hello. You've reached Patrick James—"

Lord, this can't be happening.

Storming up the steps and into his house, his mind ping-ponged between past and present. Neither offered a second of peace.

An hour ago he'd tried to call the stalker on Ashley's cell phone. It didn't even ring. Nothing. He'd probably already destroyed Ashley's phone.

Then he'd driven around all of his and Ashley's favorite places. No Atlanta Braves caps. No crazy-eyed psycho standing around waiting for him. As if it could have been that easy.

All the while Ashley was being hunted.

He should have been there.

The last thing he'd heard was ice in Ashley's voice as she told Candice to run. Candice, the woman whose violent husband probably had Candice and Ashley in his deranged paws.

He tried his old cell number again.

God, make Ashley answer the phone. Please. Please let her be okay.

The silence from heaven caused him to question his approach. He should be listening to God, not demanding. Waiting on God to direct him, instead of forging his own foolish paths. Maybe even praising God that Ashley and everyone else involved in this stalker's web had so far remained alive and not severely injured.

His weary midsection questioned that logic. So did Chester's missing status. He shouldn't have told Ashley about Chester yet.

No answer on the phone. Straight to voicemail. What did that mean?

One glance at his kitchen clock said he could make it to Shipshewana by midnight. But would he be followed? Would Ashley be there when he arrived?

He had to do something. Being left in the black was driving him insane.

So much for listening for God and waiting any longer.

He threw clothes and medicine bottles into his duffel bag and secured his computer in its case. In the kitchen, he tossed a loaf of bread and some roast beef in a plastic bag. He grabbed a six-pack of Cokes and an unopened bag of chips too. That should hold him over until tomorrow.

And just like that, he was off.

He tried his work cell phone again, still begging God to make someone answer it.

One ring.

He pulled onto North Dooly Street. Ashley had to be okay.

Two rings.

Then three.

Soon the phone would click over to voicemail. And he'd be left in the dark with a growing sense that Ashley was in the middle of a fight for her life.

He just had to get there in time to protect her.

The phone stopped ringing.

"Hello? Ashley? Are you okay?"

"Who is this?" A deep male voice snagged his attention. What kind of trouble had Ashley gotten herself into now?

"He was going to kill me." Candice's once hopeful eyes stared into nothing.

Ashley could only hold her friend as she cried.

Cops surrounded them, all busy with their various tasks. Some taking pictures at the side of the road around Justin's brown beater. Some surveyed the blown-out back tire and skid marks with masked appreciation. One drove off with a steaming Justin cuffed and tucked in the cage of a Shipshewana patrol car.

Dazed and subdued, she'd dragged the not-so-tough lumberjack out of the car and face-planted him on the ground to cuff him. Talk about a high note for the day.

"Officer Walters?" Corporal Winslow's brown eyes studied her yet again. His task had to be the top pick of assignments. "Tell me again what went down here."

She hated being on this side of the badge. "I knew Justin wouldn't stop and that his familiarity with this area would allow him to hide from you guys long enough to attack Candice again."

"How did you know all this?"

"I'm a cop."

"Duly noted. But I need a little more." He tilted his head, his intense eyes flashing. "If you can, that is."

Oh, this guy was doing his job a little too well.

"I've been a cop six years and worked a number of domestics. Some from initial visit to court to a homicide. I've attended numerous continuing education classes, the most recent ones focusing on domestic statistics and stalking behaviors."

"How did you know his familiarity with this area? He's never lived here."

"A hunch. The sense that he'd been watching Candice for a long time." She smiled her sweetest smile. "Do I need to explain that one a little more?"

Winslow laughed. "I think I've got that one covered. Thanks."

Despite the acid still churning in her stomach, she could acknowledge this mountain of a cop before her knew the ropes and was doing a masterful job of keeping his head and getting done what needed doing.

"The last thing I need from you right now is to understand why you made yourself a target and how you pulled it off without anyone getting injured."

"And why I didn't let you all in on it?" She stepped to the periphery of activity, leaving Candice a short distance away with two other officers.

Winslow followed. "That would be good to know, yes."

Deep breath. "I'm not typically a rogue cop. I know how stupid and dangerous that is. But this time, I believed Candice's life depended on seeing the full extent of Justin's hatred and that he'd only attack when he found Candice and me alone. Had I contacted you all, I would have had to stand down and wait for days or months for Justin to make his move."

"You risked your life and Candice's."

Margo picked that moment to butt in. "I knew I should have stopped you this morning." Winslow's eyes dilated the second he laid them on Margo. And why not? A blonde, blue-eyed woman in shorts carrying a bag of sweet-smelling food did that to a guy.

With a quick nod to Winslow, Margo zeroed in exactly where Ashley didn't want the focus—on her. "Y'all have been out here so long, I figured you were hungry. Especially since you and Candice haven't eaten since last night's picked-over dinner. I hoped cranberry and orange scones might help." Margo took one look at Candice and handed the muffins over to Winslow. Then drew a shaking Candice into her arms.

"Those are mine." Ashley snatched the muffins back. "Are we done here?"

Winslow nodded to Margo. "I'm Corporal Winslow, but you can call me Adam. And I'm sorry to have to do this, but I still need to speak with Officer Walters."

Margo offered up a true Scarlett O'Hara smile. "I understand. I'll take Candice back to the bed and breakfast for some food. If that's okay with you."

"Yes, ma'am. I appreciate your understanding."

Margo flicked a more genuine smile this time, then focused on Candice. "Dear Lord, take Candice in Your arms and comfort her like no one else can. Be near to her broken heart."

Winslow's eyes followed their departure. "She's a…"

"Yeah, don't finish that line. I've heard it all, and I'm not giving you her phone number."

"I already have it."

Peachy. Then when this mess was over, Margo could ask Adam here to escort her to a wedding. Just thinking about the wedding for half a second brought a measure of needed normalcy.

"Back to business."

"Can we not?"

Winslow nodded to the arrival of Marshal Taylor. "You can always explain yourself to the top brass if you'd rather. Or to your favorite GBI agent."

"Where is Edwards?"

"Gone down to Georgia. But we can ask him to turn around and head back."

"How about not. It's been a hard day already."

"Yes. So you were saying…"

"Right. I risked my life. But I made sure Candice was safe."

"She was shoved into a car and locked inside by a man with a rope, knife, and shotgun in his trunk. Candice wouldn't call that safe, would you think? Besides that, how could you truly think you had a handle on what would happen? There are an unlimited number of possible scenarios that could have ended with a much different outcome today."

Her stubbornness was annoying even her. She knew the consequences of her choices and delaying them wouldn't make them any better. "When Justin attacked me, I made sure he wasn't carrying a piece. Besides that, he didn't strike me as a guy who took a shot and ran away. More like a guy who solved problems with his fists and let the suspense build before he did it again."

"That meshes with his arrest record and the information we've compiled of his recent stalking incidents."

"So I have a pattern of going running, and I stuck to it. I figured if Justin's been watching Candice, he's made note of my behaviors too."

"Cops should never keep to identifiable routines."

"I know."

"But you did this to draw Justin out? Anyone else you're doing that for?"

She'd just shut up now. Winslow and Marshal Taylor had already guessed her intentions long ago, if not right after today's 911 call. She didn't have to fill in all the blanks for them.

"I also had a hunch Justin wanted to humiliate me and then take his time punishing Candice. If I let him think he was getting away, he'd get sloppy and I'd have a shot."

"But there were cars around. You put them at risk too."

"I'd seen the beater a number of times and knew I'd have time to take the shot at a tire and put Justin in a ditch before he could hit another car."

"You can't have known all that."

"I prayed." Guilt pricked. Okay, maybe she should have prayed more. And listened this time. But she'd been sure God had heard her heart just like He had the last time she was in a standoff situation.

That one had turned out okay.

So had this one.

"I've also practiced hundreds of unusual scenarios in my training and with fellow cops and hunting types off duty."

"Any of those redneck types show you how to stop a moving car?"

"Maybe." She could take offense at friends being called rednecks, but they were what Winslow pegged them, and they'd admit to it proudly.

"You're a woman of many talents, Ashley Walters. But if I were you, I'd advise more of your so-called praying and less Lone Ranger heroics. It's a far better idea to include your fellow officers in your plans."

"I'll do that." When her nightmare was all over.

Alone at last, Ashley's mind blanked into nothingness for one glorious second. She'd about had enough of trouble and danger every time she turned around. First Patrick. Then Candice. Now Brad and Chester. What was next?

She nudged the low-hanging porch swing at the bed and breakfast. Cows in the field beyond a creek answered her questions with the moos of contented animals without a care in the world.

Winslow exited through the basement apartment's glass doors, Patrick's cell phone extended. "I believe this might be for you."

She grabbed it away from him. "Hello?"

"Ashley?" Patrick drew in a ragged breath. "Some cop said you were okay half an hour ago, but I had to hear it for myself, so I kept calling. I've been calling over and over since you started screaming at Candice."

The events of the last hour flashed back through her mind. She'd dropped the phone and grabbed her gun. Then she hadn't given a second thought to calling Patrick back. She'd been too busy saving Candice, seeing Justin taken into custody, and then answering a bevy of questions from both her new friend Winslow and Marshal Taylor. The latter being far less amused and friendly than the first.

"I'm so sorry, Patrick."

"Don't tell me, you caught Candice's husband and were being questioned this whole time."

"Yes." She turned to a listening Winslow and waved him away.

The big guy shrugged and ducked back inside. All too happy with his current assignment. Babysitting her. And Margo.

"Can you tell me what happened?"

"You sure you want to know?" The Yoders' miniature goats frolicked in the backyard, putting on a show just for her.

"Skip the details about how much danger you were in and tell me what happened to Candice. Is she okay?"

"Yes. The Shipshewana Police showed up just in time to apprehend the bad guy and he'll be under lock and key without bail for a good long time."

"What about Candice? What is she going to do?"

"Go stay with her brother in Kentucky. He's a state trooper. She'll be a large part of putting her husband behind bars for good, and after the trial is over, hopefully she can live free."

"How are you doing?"

"Thank you for not launching into counselor speak and asking about my feelings right off the bat."

"You prefer being yelled at first? I'll remember that."

"If you call that yelling, it's fine by me." She'd experienced so much worse on and off the job. "I'm okay. Still coming off the adrenaline and getting my ears chewed off by Marshal Taylor. You'll be happy to know I now have a police babysitter too."

"Full-time?"

"Probably. They're calling in the reserves to cover the loss of active duty manpower."

"Good."

Time for the two questions she dreaded asking. "So how is Brad? Any news on Chester?"

Patrick took his time to answer. Never a good sign. "Brad is safe. Joyce too. I'm sure Culp and Marshal Taylor will fill you in with more details than I can. As soon as they stop stewing over your recent adventures."

"Thanks for the reminder of my doghouse status." Her breath caught and knotted in her chest. "No one found any sign of Chester? Did you check my house?"

"Yes."

"What are we going to do, Patrick?"

"I don't know how you're going to feel about what I have to say next, but hear me out, okay?"

"Patrick, the likelihood of someone listening to our conversation is low, but it's still there. So please don't tell me what you're planning. I just want to know you're finally going somewhere safe."

"I am."

"Do you have any good news for me?" Her little girl voice rose to the top. She hated that voice and the helplessness that accompanied it.

"Rich is out of the hospital and on the mend. Elizabeth did keep me updated on that. I figured she had told you too."

"Nope. I'm glad he's okay. I haven't talked to Elizabeth or Culp in a while. They've spoken daily with Marshal Taylor, though, so I know what's happening there when life isn't so crazy here."

"So will you give your babysitters the slip?"

She almost wished the stalker were listening in, weighing the inflection of her voice and words. Then he'd make his move soon. And she'd be as ready for him as she was for Candice's lumberjack husband.

"I plan to be a model detainee."

"Of course you will."

Chapter Twenty-two

Another sunrise, another day spent waiting. Her phone hadn't rung except for Patrick's calls. No updates about her case. No Chester. No contact with Brad or Joyce or her parents.

Even silent, this stalker held the upper hand.

She wasn't allowed to go running without Winslow, and she just couldn't hack running with a guy who wasn't Patrick.

She also couldn't stomach spending the day playing tourist with Winslow and Margo cutting their eyes at each other and smiling like they had last night. Yuck. This wasn't high school.

Then again, it'd been years since Maggie had stopped working long enough to show interest in a guy. It was time. And Adam Winslow was one of the good guys. Deep down she cheered for her best friend. She just wouldn't let Winslow know or allow either of them to catch the little green monster sitting on Ashley's shoulder.

Ashley slipped the Bible Patrick had given her for Christmas from her lap and onto the porch swing.

On that extra special day, her new Bible had contained a diamond key necklace tucked into 1 Corinthians 13. Patrick had beamed. She'd kissed him soundly and talked of moving the wedding date to December thirty-first. She should have done that.

That happy moment existed so long ago. So long ago she could hardly touch the joy she'd experienced at the love poured out on her.

The Bible drew her back to the present. She read and reread 1 Corinthians 13. Then she just flipped through, not caring where it landed.

"Good morning, Ashley." Winslow sauntered across the visitor's parking lot from the detached guest house, a bright smile filling his face.

"Looks like you slept well."

"I did. I'll have to request babysitting duty more often. It agrees with me."

She directed her attention to the clouds above dotting a bright blue sky. "I'm sure Margo loves being called a baby."

"I was talking about you."

"Don't push me, Winslow."

"Adam, please."

"The threat remains, Adam. You don't know me well enough to go jerking my chain when you're not in uniform."

"Margo filled in a lot of details."

She would strangle her best friend after she finished reading her Bible. Margo might enjoy the fun of flirting with a handsome man and pretending like the world was a dandy place.

Not Ashley.

"I'll leave you to your Bible reading then." Adam reached for the door handle.

"You know Margo's a Bible-believing woman whose loyalty rests with me, not just any guy she dates."

Adam grinned. "Margo and I aren't dating. But be sure to check out Romans 5 this morning." With that, he entered the apartment.

"Whatever."

She flipped to Romans 5 and found a cute little baby blue note from Margo's personal stationery.

Maggie's beautiful script filled the page. *Verses three through six gave me great comfort as I was reading tonight. I hope you have the same experience.*

Rather than seethe that Margo had let Adam in on this little note, she searched the page for the suggested verses.

We can rejoice, too, when we run into problems and trials, for we know that they help us develop endurance. And endurance develops strength of character, and character strengthens our confident hope of salvation. And this hope will not lead to disappointment. For we know how dearly God loves us, because he has given us the Holy Spirit to fill our hearts with his love. When we were utterly helpless, Christ came at just the right time and died for us sinners.

Hope didn't do it for her right now. Neither did Jonathan's preaching about how to conquer fear and how to not play small.

None of it reached the depth of her being. The words and verses and quotations only scratched the surface of her problem.

God had helped her rescue Candice. But He wouldn't bless or in any way condone the plans she'd chosen for the next step of this battle.

Pinpricks of unease made her shiver. She forced the emotion away. What choice did she have?

Faith in herself was all she had left. Despite what everyone else tried to tell her.

The little destination flag on Patrick's GPS drew closer and closer. Adrenaline and excitement shaved the edge off the pain not checked by the Advil he'd just downed with the last of his Mountain Dew.

He'd be holding Ashley soon.

He pulled into the gravel driveway of the Songbird Ridge. No cars filled the small parking lot, so maybe they'd have room for him. Spending the night on another friend's couch didn't hold much appeal.

Exiting his Mustang, he checked out the surroundings. Nice bright red horse barn and large fields beyond. The blue country house met him just like their website, with the illusion of peace and a good night's rest. He hoped the rest wouldn't prove as elusive as the peace.

Jonathan stepped out from the front door and onto the long front porch. "It is good to see you again, Patrick."

"You too." Patrick extended his hand as they met in the middle of the wicker chairs. "How is Anna? Are she and Ashley spending any time together? I'd hoped they'd comfort each other with the recent news, but Ashley hasn't mentioned Anna at all."

Jonathan's features dropped their controlled professionalism for a half second. "Ashley has not seen Anna this trip."

"Why?"

"Anna left for her daughter's home in Ohio the day Bradley left for Georgia. She did not think she could handle returning to the memories after Ashley arrived, so she planned to stay through the summer."

"Being Mennonite doesn't protect you from post-traumatic stress." Patrick checked his watch. Ashley had to be up and going by now. But the chance to help Anna and Jonathan dangled before him. He had to take it.

Jonathan bristled.

"PTSD is real, Jonathan. There's help dealing with it."

"Anna and Bradley both spoke with counselors here. They were fine until news of the stalker reached us."

"So Anna knows about Brad's attack."

"I did not share that with her. But I have spoken to Beth's family. They have assured me that Bradley is well cared for and staying busy indoors."

"Sounds like everyone is tucked into a safe hiding place."

Jonathan motioned to the rocking chairs. "God is our only safe hiding place."

Patrick let that one go. This was how Jonathan handled stress, and Patrick wouldn't take it from him. "How is Ashley?"

"I have not seen her since Sunday. A lot has happened since then." Jonathan's focus shifted to an unknown place down the road.

"Is that where the incident with Candice happened?"

"Yes. Ashley may think she was running in a place where such violence would not hurt many. But she was wrong."

"I'm sorry, Jonathan. I agree with Ashley and believe she did what was best for Candice. The woman's life was in danger."

"Prayer is more powerful than a handgun."

Patrick wouldn't argue this.

Birds chirped overhead. Horses and goats and dogs all added their unique clomping and snuffing to the loud silence surrounding Songbird Ridge.

He needed to see Ashley. "So, can you point me to where Ashley's staying?"

Jonathan stood. "Across the road and down about a half mile. My parents' brick home sits off the road a ways, in between two Amish farmhouses. You cannot miss it."

Patrick returned to his Mustang. He'd check in after three like the website instructed. It was past time to see Ashley.

But he couldn't stop the catch in his spirit that he'd played a fool's game in coming here. Would Ashley agree?

Jonathan walked next door to his large, empty home. The one he had wished to fill with a family someday. That was why he and Mary had built this home with many bedrooms.

The home he prayed he would share one day with Beth.

He unlocked the front door and entered. Silence greeted him. He wished Bradley and Anna would have stayed with him longer. Their company provided the companionship and understanding no one else here could give. They had been through much together.

A soft knock surprised him. He returned to the front door and pulled it open.

"Hello, Jonathan." Beth stood in front of him, her beautiful blue eyes wide. "I just heard about Bradley from my parents. Are you okay?"

"Come. We can have a seat on the front porch." Being alone with Beth in his home, even at a time like this, was frowned upon. He understood and respected the wisdom of his elders in upholding high standards of behavior.

He and Beth sat on the porch swing.

She touched his arm. "Are you okay?"

Beth understood how the news of Bradley's recent attack would affect him. He had seen the boy severely injured twice already, almost dead from the evil plans of a man bent on destruction. Beth had been beside him for the second of those times. And now another evil man had attacked Bradley. The same man who stalked Ashley. The one who would kill any who stood in his way.

"I am not doing well. I do not understand the violence that has come against my young cousin. I do not like the helplessness I felt last year or what I feel right now."

Tears welled in her eyes. "I am so sorry for all Bradley has experienced. What you have gone through as well."

"Thank you."

Beth's bright smile touched the frightened places within him. "God will protect us, Jonathan. He protected Bradley from evil yesterday. We can trust Him."

They sat in comfortable silence.

Beth's words washed over him. He needed her by his side as more than a special friend or the woman he had been courting. He longed to comfort her as well, to draw her into his arms and tell her everything would turn out for good, a truth he believed by faith alone these days. "Beth?" He turned to face her and took her hands in his. "Will you?" His mouth dried up like a desert.

Her eyes sparked with what he hoped was joyful anticipation.

It was time. He would accept this gift from God he had found in Beth and not allow the lie of fear to hold him bound any longer.

"We have not known each other all our lives, but the circumstances of last year threw us together, and I have seen from the first day on that you are a woman of great faith. You have loved and served my parents for many months. They adore you. You made Heidi's work at the bed and breakfast light. You are among the first to volunteer for what needs to be done at church."

"And I have helped my cousin with her twins since their birth. That was a job only God could do."

They laughed.

"Yes. And you challenge me to be more and more of the man God created me to be. I admire that about you."

"You are a stubborn man at times, Jonathan. But you have such a good heart. I wish you could see in yourself what I see in you."

Maybe someday. With Beth's help he might come to see himself as she saw him, as God saw him. Not as unworthy, as not good enough. But as a man after God's own heart. Maybe he'd even become a man who could trust in God as Beth did and not fall into the temptation of trying to take over God's place in other's lives.

"I love you, Beth. Will you do me the honor of becoming my wife?"

Her eyes watered but her lips turned up into a beautiful smile. "Yes. Absolutely." She touched his face with her soft hand. "I love you too."

Sliding closer, he cupped her face in his hands and bent forward, almost touching her lips. "You are a gift." Then he lowered his lips to hers and lost himself in the most perfect moment he could imagine.

"Patrick!" Ashley raced up the driveway and into his arms.

He smiled and wrapped the comfort of his strength and presence around her. Tears sprang to her eyes, but she just held on.

"I've missed you."

She answered with a kiss that deepened until she could hardly breathe.

Patrick pulled back and held her face in his hands. "This is so much better than a phone call."

"Yes."

Wiping the trail of tears from her face, he studied her like a desert dweller getting his first look at water.

She hoped the mirage of okay-ness stayed in place.

"You've lost a lot of weight."

"Please, keep whispering sweet nothings in my ear."

He pulled her close again and kissed the sarcasm right out of her brain. "Maybe we should head inside for some ice cream. Or Amish donuts."

"You need more sweetness?"

"I need you to stop neglecting yourself to try and take care of everyone around you."

She stuck out her tongue. On the inside, though, her whole body breathed in relief. She wasn't alone in this nightmare anymore.

And everyone else was tucked away someplace safe. Or under police hounding. Okay, protection.

They entered the B&B and Margo squealed and rushed at Patrick. "You took your good and sweet time." Margo hugged him tight. "But thank God you're here. Now maybe our dear, gentle, obedient Ashley will return."

Adam stepped forward. "You must be Patrick." The men shook hands. "I'm Corporal Winslow. Adam. Your fiancée's babysitter."

Patrick grinned. "I'm surprised you don't have some scratches and dents for talking like that."

"He should."

Margo huffed. "Adam and I were just fixing lunch. Have you eaten, Patrick?"

"Nope. I'd love some food. So would Ashley."

"Yes, master." Ashley bowed. "I'll obey your every command."

"In my dreams." Patrick pulled her to him. "Actually, I like you just the way you are. Only married."

"I concur."

The four of them sat down at the small oak table to a spread of Amish meats and cheeses, pastries, and fresh fruit. None of it called to her.

"Patrick, will you pray for us?" Margo just had to go and wink at her before closing her eyes.

Patrick took Ashley's hand. "Lord, we come before You overflowing with thanks for Your protection of Candice and Ashley. For friends to share this heavy load with. For working things out so that the people we love are now out of harm's way. Remind us that You are in control, even when life hurts and seems dark. We trust You will bring us all through. Amen."

They all dug into the bowls and platters in the center of the table.

Ashley forced herself to match Margo's amount of food and actually eat it this time. She turned to Patrick after the first bite of meat. "Do you believe that prayer you just prayed?"

Margo shook her head.

Adam continued eating.

Patrick shrugged. "I want to believe it. I figure speaking the truth can only help it get down deep enough to where I believe it again."

She nodded. At least she wasn't alone in the struggle to believe. Time to pull back to the surface a bit. "How was your drive up here?"

"Uneventful. I stayed off the interstate for as long as I could. Then I'd backtrack some and stop at friends' houses when I needed a break."

Adam swallowed a huge bite of cheese and crackers. "You sure you weren't followed?"

"As sure as any of us can be. I tried to follow the advice of cop friends and watched the cars around me closely."

"Did you change cars?"

Ashley could have called that answer before Patrick left Montezuma. "No."

"So maybe you and I need to go tuck your ride into my garage after lunch. No use getting too comfortable."

"As if that could happen." Still, Adam played things safe. She appreciated that fact more than she'd let on. She turned to Patrick. "You think he already knows where I am, don't you?"

"Yes."

So much for the mirage of okay-ness.

"Then we need to go somewhere else. Keep moving."

Adam shrugged. "From all the reading up on this case I've done, it looks like you don't have anywhere else to run where you'd be as safe as you are here with cops in four counties ready to jump at the first sign of the stalker."

Nowhere to run. The truth sliced through the tiny bit of hope she'd secretly held on to. "I guess running would only prolong the inevitable too. He'd find a way to get to someone who knew me, and he'd keep hurting them until I turned up to stop him."

"Which you won't." Everyone focused on Adam.

Patrick spoke first. "You're either brave or stupid, my new friend."

"I'm going with the first. I also have the whole police force behind me on this one. Marshal Taylor, Ashley's boss, Chief Fisher, the GBI, and every PD head involved in this case has weighed in with the same sentiments today."

Ashley squirmed.

Patrick turned his amazing blue eyes on her. "You didn't share that tidbit with me."

"Yeah, well. A girl's gotta keep some secrets. Right?"

"Wrong." Margo fixed her with a glare and didn't look away.

Ashley did. "Fine. Okay. Y'all have ganged up on me and won. I'm here to stay."

"It's because we love you." Patrick took her hand.

"I don't. No offense, Ashley." Adam plunked two fruit filled pastries on his plate. "I like you okay. And you're a good cop and all."

"None taken. And thanks."

"I just hope you'll be a smart cop and let a village catch this stalker." Adam turned his attention to his food.

Patrick studied her again and saw too much.

As much as she loved him and loved having him here, she wouldn't let him stop her from doing what had to be done.

CHAPTER TWENTY-THREE

Patrick woke to the smell of bacon, eggs, and coffee. *Thank You, God, for someone else's cooking.*

Despite how he kept it together in front of Ashley, he hurt. Every nerve ending. Every cell. But he was here in Shipshewana, less than a mile away from Ashley. He could finally do his job and make sure she was safe, heart and body.

Call him a caveman, but he wanted to be the protector. Too bad that wasn't what Ashley most wanted.

He dressed in jeans and a 104.7 The Fish T-shirt. Thankfully, what was clean when he packed proved a good choice. The temps here hadn't reached Atlanta scorching.

Ten minutes later with Advil in hand, he conquered a flight of stairs and entered the small dining area. Two couples shared a table by the window. He set his pills and water bottle down at the only table for two and proceeded to the buffet.

"Good morning, Patrick. How did you sleep?" Jonathan's sister-in-law, Heidi, smiled up at him.

"Great. Thanks. This food is amazing. Sure beats my usual coffee and bagel."

"You'll soon have someone cooking you meals much better than this, yes?"

He caught himself before he laughed. Neither he nor Ashley cooked much. They'd probably flip a coin for who got out of bed first. And he'd let Ashley win every time.

One month left and he could let his mind go where he couldn't right this second.

He turned his attention back to Heidi. "Jonathan wouldn't say, but I hope you'll tell me how Anna is doing."

Having encouraged Brad to explore the possibility of spending time with his birth mother and the news of how hard Anna was taking Brad's departure weighed on him.

Heidi grabbed an empty mug before he could add it to his tray. "Do you like it black?"

"Yes."

"I'll bring it right over if you want to sit down."

He must not have brought his A-game to breakfast. He'd better get some food and meds down before he went to see Ashley.

A quick prayer of thanksgiving and a few bites later, his muscles relaxed.

"Are your injuries healing well?" Heidi set a steaming mug in front of him and took a seat.

He forked a bite of eggs and bacon into his mouth. This he could get used to easy. "I'm doing okay. The doc said I should rest more and stop pushing, so I haven't been running like I'd hoped to at this point."

"Only driving long distances to come to the aid of your loved ones."

Heidi got it.

"So, Anna?"

"Yes. Our dear aunt was still pretty shaken by the events of last year. Then when Bradley chose to move back to Georgia to stay with his birth mother, well, she took that very hard. The time with Hanna's family in Ohio will do her good though. She will be cared for and loved on. That can heal a multitude of pain."

In time. But Anna had been assaulted by a gunman and her son almost killed before her eyes. That kind of trauma required more than some family TLC.

"She was brokenhearted when Jonathan told her about the stalker attacking you, Patrick. Even later, when I spoke with her on the phone, her voice shook as she prayed for Bradley and for you. She was always the steady rock in her family."

Even more reason for Anna to spend time with a counselor who would help her work through all of the traumatic events of recent days. "I'd really like to help Anna."

"It is very kind that you care so much. She admires you and Ashley. I can see why."

"Will she listen if you tell her that I can help find a good trauma counselor in Ohio?"

Heidi stood. "I should let you finish eating before your food gets cold. I will talk to Mark, and we will pray about your kind offer."

That was likely the best he could do today. If he struck out with helping Ashley too, this day would rank up there with a root canal.

∽

Ashley scrubbed the breakfast dishes until they squeaked in protest. "Adam, don't you need to go check in at the police department or something?"

The tall, muscular cop stretched out on the couch and put his feet on the coffee table. "Nope. My job is to be here twenty-four seven until Marshal Taylor tells me otherwise."

Great. Not only did that mean she'd spend another day on pins and needles waiting for trouble with an audience, but she now had her hands tied in terms of doing anything to advance her plans.

Then again, maybe not.

"So what do you and Maggie have in store for today?"

Margo stuck her head out of her bedroom. "We were thinking a Cranium marathon before lunch and a Trivial Pursuit marathon afterward. Sound good?"

Margo closed her door before Ashley could growl her answer. She hated games.

Patrick picked that instant to open the glass doors. "Hello to you too."

"That growl wasn't for you."

"Glad to hear it." He wrapped his arms around her waist and kissed her neck. She shivered, and he pulled back. "Want me to stop?"

"No." She rinsed dish soap from her hands and dried them on a towel before turning around in Patrick's embrace. "That's better."

"I'll say."

"So." Margo sauntered out into the living room in another cute blue skirt and sleeveless top outfit she'd purchased in town at some point. Maggie still got to fly the coop while Ashley was shackled to these four walls.

No one promised life was fair.

She focused back on Patrick and the comfort of his arms.

Margo stood at the center of the open living room and kitchen area. "If Ashley and Patrick are going to play lovestruck honeymooners today, then Adam and I will increase our cerebral function with games."

"Games don't make you smarter." Ashley grabbed Patrick's hand and walked five paces to the living room loveseat.

"They pass the time better than brooding," Margo laid out the Cranium pieces.

"I think we should vary our routine then."

Patrick raised his eyebrows. "And do what?"

"Not go running." Adam threw her a smirk.

"It was you who reminded me cops should never keep to the same routine. If the stalker is here, then he already expects us to stay put and play games like we did all day yesterday. It's what we've done for the last few nights too. Don't you think he knows by now when you go to sleep, Adam?"

Adam chewed on that.

Patrick stood. "Then why don't we go look at furniture?"

"Town should be back to normal size today. It's Thursday. No flea market."

Margo looked up from the game. "Don't you think that makes us better targets?"

"You're the one who wanted to play tourist on Monday." Ashley slipped on her tennis shoes. "Why the change of heart now?"

"Candice's attacks."

True. The attacks had both been very public. "But this stalker is different. He's only attacked people at their homes or on private property. He doesn't use the public as a shield."

Margo folded her arms. "He could change his modus something or other."

Adam and Ashley shared a look. "Operandi." Adam shrugged. "As long as we stick together, I'm up for it." His eyes narrowed. "But you have to promise."

"I'm not an idiot, Winslow."

"That's not a promise."

Patrick chuckled. "Come on, Ash. We all know you're crawling these walls. This is your chance to do something besides play games."

"Why do I feel like I'm being set up?"

Patrick slipped on his poker face. The new thrown-together couple waited.

"Fine. I promise. I'll leave Patrick's cell phone here even."

"No." Adam snapped it up from the end table. "We should keep it with us. Just in case."

She stuck out her hand for the phone and then checked for messages. "Candice called early this morning. I should check in with her." She pressed Candice's name.

"Hello?" Candice's shaky voice put Ashley on alert.

"Candice, it's Ashley. Are you all right?"

"No." Sobs filled the phone line.

"Talk to me, Candice."

"Well…I was doin' okay. But then…well…Justin called me this morning." More tears. "He said he was sorry. That he'd lost his mind missin' me so much. And that he wasn't going to hurt me ever again."

Ashley clenched her teeth. "He's lying. Don't you remember the rope, knife, and shotgun in his trunk?"

Margo shook her head.

Ashley ignored her. Candice had to listen to reason. She had to hear the truth.

"He said he'd sell all his guns and never ever threaten me again. He wasn't really going to hurt me. Just scare me is all."

"That's why he shoved you in the car? The car that had rope and weapons? To scare you?"

"He's my husband, Ashley. You don't understand."

She understood well enough. "You'll be dead if you go back to Justin again. Please, Candice. Don't even think about dropping the charges against Justin. Stay in Kentucky like you'd planned. Start seeing the counselor you found there."

"I…I don't know. I love him, Ashley. He loves me too."

"Real love doesn't hurt like Justin's hurt you. That's not love."

Candice gulped in a breath. "I know you're trying to help. But I have to do what's right. What's best for me and Justin. I hope you'll understand."

"Candice, I—"

The phone beeped, and Candice was gone.

"She's going to drop the charges against her psycho husband."

"We'll pray, Ash." Margo studied her. "That's the very best thing we can do. That and trust God to reach Candice's heart with the truth. He can handle things much better than we can."

Ashley wanted to scream. Pray and wait for one more dangerous situation to explode? How could Candice not see the truth? She'd put her life on the line to help Candice see…for what? So Candice could end up in the morgue anyway.

So much for any of her best laid plans.

Despite her desire to hole up in her room and fume about one more thing she couldn't change, Ashley was glad to leave the B&B. New surroundings would help her avoid any more talk of Candice. And the gnawing reality that she should have done more to help her friend escape her violent husband. But what?

She shoved the whole situation to the back of her mind. Maybe her subconscious would figure out a way to reach Candice before it was too late.

Soon they stood in the small lobby of Jonathan's furniture store. Shiny wood floors and an organized showroom beyond the front desk all spoke of Jonathan's meticulous attention to detail.

Beth and another bonneted woman Ashley didn't know entered from a back room. Beth started and didn't finish what she'd been saying.

Something about how they would share their news soon.

Beth's blush filled in the most likely possibility. "Well, hello, Ashley, Margo. And Patrick. I am glad you are here. I know Ashley has missed you." She turned to Winslow. "I am sorry, I do not know your name. I am Beth Kauffman. This is my cousin Emma."

"Adam. Nice to meet you both."

Emma grinned and ducked behind the counter, busying herself with some sort of paperwork.

Beth played hostess. "Are you all here to see Jonathan?"

"No, just browsing." Patrick turned back to their little group. "I've heard Jonathan has some great dining room furniture. Why don't you and Margo check it out, hon?"

His voice wavered a fraction on the last word. What was he up to?

Feigning interest in a nearby curio cabinet, she listened to the hushed discourse between Patrick and Beth.

"Is it ready?"

"I can go check."

"Will he come out to answer any questions Ashley might have?" Patrick glanced her way.

She scurried off to find Margo.

"Maggie, are you in on this?"

Margo turned on her cute heel, yet another set of fancy wrought iron candle holders in hand. "Aren't these beautiful? And affordable. I'm getting these. They'll fit right into the loft apartment I'm redecorating when I get home."

Ashley didn't bother answering. Once Maggie got lost in decorating ideas, there was no need to.

"You collect candle holders?" Adam's eyes had already glazed over. Poor cop would have been happier at an electronics store.

"Interior decorator. I collect all manner of home furnishings for use in the offices and homes I stage for sale or redecorate."

Ashley tapped her foot. "You didn't answer my question."

Margo pointed to a far wall. "I'm going to check out the sconces and living room furniture. Want to join me?"

Fine. She could distract herself. Running a hand over the smooth finish of an elegant cherry wood four-poster bed, she could imagine it in the bedroom she and Patrick would share.

"Like it?" Patrick placed a hand on her back.

"Yes. I love the Queen Anne style."

"Is this the one you've hinted about before?"

"It's more beautiful than I imagined." She turned to face him. "Is this what you've been talking to Jonathan about? I knew you weren't Christmas shopping early."

"Happy early birthday-slash-wedding present."

"You're kidding."

"Nope." Patrick took both of her hands in his and rubbed his thumbs over them. "I talked to Jonathan the first time you dropped a hint about new furniture. I had no idea then we'd have a chance to see it together before I had it delivered."

She ran her hand over the wood again, a shudder running up her spine. If only Candice would listen to her and be safe. If only the stalker was behind bars. Then she could enjoy this moment properly.

"I am glad to see you like the furniture, Ashley." Jonathan stood at the foot of the bed. "There is also a matching ten-drawer dresser, two nightstands, and an armoire."

"It's incredible, Jonathan. Thank you."

He bowed his head and turned to walk away.

Margo elbowed her. "You should ask fewer questions sometimes, chica. Wasn't this surprise worth the little bit of frustrated impatience on your part?"

"I don't like surprises."

"You liked this one."

"Yes. Yes, I did." She loved the furniture. And even more, the man standing in front of her, his blue, blue eyes caressing her.

Surprises, however, seldom turned out this nice.

∽

Patrick was on top of the world.

The trip to Jonathan's couldn't have gone any better. And now he had Ashley in his arms while Margo and Adam chatted away in the front of Adam's SUV about his growing up and her family.

Only Ashley's restlessness broke the illusion.

Every so often, her eyes would scan their surroundings, finding exits, cataloguing every face that passed them by. She'd done it at Jonathan's when other customers entered. She'd done it at Yoder's grocery too. And when they'd dropped off the food back at the B&B.

She'd likely continue during their stop at Lambright Woodworking. So would he.

They entered the beautiful store that Margo had raved about on the phone. The stone fireplace and elegant furniture caught his attention right off. But the massive bed with a headboard made of baseball bats won out. "Now this is a bed."

"Mr. Lambright made this one himself for a famous major league baseball player." Margo played tour guide for them, waving at the Amish woman behind the front counter.

"Do you remember who?" Adam's eyes grew wide. "This is my kinda bed."

"Sorry. I don't, but I can ask if you'd like."

Adam shook his head. "No. Thanks. Too far out of my price range anyway."

"And it only works if you're a single guy or a pro ball superstar." Patrick wasn't either one. He smiled at Ashley. He'd take their new Queen Anne bed over any other option.

"Want to see the pitchers I told you about the other day?" Ashley led him to one of the back rooms.

232 ᴄ∞ Amy Wallace

"Didn't you buy one of those along with the easel and paints?"

"I was going to but decided against it. Wait a minute. Did Margo and Jonathan help you order one of those too?" Ashley's voice pinched.

"Are you mad at me for the surprise? I know you hate surprises, but I figured the furniture was a good kind of surprise."

"It was."

"Then why did you snip about your friends helping me order something else?"

"Sorry." She tucked herself into his side. "I'm worried about Candice. And the last time I was here I was sure the stalker would keep calling. Then I heard his voicemails. I can't stop wishing he'd just show up so I can end this."

"You and me both."

"We have different ideas about what 'ending this' means."

That they did. Patrick's version included five or six cop cars, Ashley safe at the B&B, and three cops jumping the stalker before she ever knew he was in town.

He'd like the chance to return some broken ribs too.

Not a very Christlike wish. But a very visceral one.

Adam and Margo laughed over another story. A family of five looked around another part of the store, also laughing at some sort of family joke. All around them the world continued as if nothing were wrong. People smiled. Bought furniture and went out to eat without a care in the world.

While Ashley's and his world had come to a grinding halt. A one-day-at-a-time waiting game they both hated.

Thanks to an unknown man playing a deadly round of cat and mouse.

A stalker who could strike at any moment.

CHAPTER TWENTY-FOUR

Ashley groped for the blaring phone somewhere on her bedside table. The one that snatched her from a pleasant wedding dream. Why would Patrick call this early?

"The roosters aren't even crowing yet."

"Where I'm standing, they are."

She recognized that gravel-filled voice. In seconds, Ashley was sitting up and wide awake.

"Come on now, Ashley. I know you've missed me."

She forced her breathing into a normal cadence, her mind scrambling for good options. She'd already blown a basic rule for stalking victims: Don't engage.

"Is *he* there with you, Ashley?"

The venom in the stalker's voice ramped up her heart rate. Still she breathed in and out. In and out. Waiting.

Seconds ticked by.

He couldn't see her right now if he believed Patrick was there. She slipped out of her bedroom and into the living room, waving for Adam and Margo's attention.

She mouthed only two words. *It's him.*

Adam jumped to attention and motioned for the phone.

She shook her head. Right now she had things under control. She needed a better picture of his mental state and intentions for her.

"Tell your ball and chain that you'll be free soon, Ashley. I'm almost done with my plans. All I need is one thing from you. Meet me tomorrow. Slip away from that mountain of a cop before he wakes up at seven and jog three miles north. I'll meet you there. Then we'll be together. Forever."

She had to speak. Find out more information. "Why?"

"I love your voice. So calm. So at peace. I knew you wanted a man who would take care of everything."

She shouldn't have spoken. The stalker's now blissful voice turned her stomach.

"I will answer all your questions soon, my love."

Margo's wide eyes drilled into Ashley's soul.

Please, God. Help me keep them safe.

"If I meet you, will you leave my friends alone?"

"If? Ashley, my love. Tomorrow will be the wedding day you've longed for since you were in high school."

His delusion ran deep and long.

"What if I don't come?"

Adam jerked his head side to side.

She knew what she was doing.

"If you don't come... There is no point discussing that impossibility. I know you're playing tough cop for your friends. I understand. They'll accept us in time. You'll see. I am the one who can truly give you the best. Only the best."

Only the best.

"Why would you say that?"

"Say what? The words you've heard all your growing-up years? Your parents are lovely people. And they were so right. You deserve only the best. The three of us understand each other now."

Oh, God.

"What do you mean?"

"I mean that your parents and I have had a wonderful few days together."

The veneer of control shattered in a million pieces.

Her parents were supposed to be on a cruise. Why hadn't she called until she reached them? Why hadn't she made sure they were safe?

What had she done?

"Where are my parents? What have you done to them?"

His cruel laugh filled her ears. "Meet me tomorrow, my love."

His sudden silence burned through her.

Adam grabbed the phone from her hand. "Ashley? What in the world did he say?"

A thousand questions rammed against the obsidian blackness taking the place of her brain and heart.

Adam turned to Margo. "Call Patrick. I need to call Marshal Taylor back. We have to move now."

Ashley grabbed both of their arms in a death grip. "What if my parents are already…?"

Margo took hold of her hand. "He could be lying, Ash."

"You're right." She should have known that. She punched in her mom's cell number. There was an easy way to find out.

No answer.

She tried her dad's.

It rang and rang. Then his recorded message.

She hung up. "They're not answering. We have to get down to the station now. See if the police can locate my parents."

Adam pointed to the phone at his ear. "We'll handle it, Ashley. Trust us."

Trust them? Not happening.

"Ashley, honey. Patrick's coming. Let's pray."

Trust God? Not when He allowed her fiancé, her friends, and now her parents to be dragged into this life-and-death game.

She hated games. But she'd play this one. Her way. For her parents.

Patrick held an expressionless and petrified Ashley in his arms. Petrified as in stone stiff. Resolute. Nowhere near terrified.

Her response frightened him more than anything else. That and the possibility of Mr. and Mrs. Walters being in the hands of a violent stalker.

"Talk to me, Ash."

"About what? That my parents might have been in this delusional man's clutches this entire time? That they could be dead? Or pawns to be dangled in front of the cops and killed then?"

"You're assuming the worst. He could be playing games. Trying to convince you of their presence here, so you'll come. The police haven't corroborated any of what the stalker insinuated."

"He didn't insinuate. He was clear. He's watched me a long time, remember? That means he knows them too. He was on their property. Watching them. He could have moved the second the Atlanta PD cleared out of there. I haven't talked to them since."

"They were leaving for a cruise."

"Not that day. I should have called more. Should have taken them to the airport before I left."

"Ash, this is not your fault."

Her jaw worked back and forth. "I should have known to keep a closer check on them."

"You called them. What more could you do?"

"I left messages. Not the same as making sure they were safe."

Adam and another Shipshewana police officer conferred at the B&B's kitchen table in hushed tones.

Ashley missed nothing.

Margo sat across from them in a rocking chair, eyes closed, mouth moving.

"Sorry to interrupt." Adam cleared his throat and softened his all-business features. "Marshal Taylor wants us in his office."

Ashley jumped up. "Are my parents alive? Has he talked to them?"

"Not yet, Ashley. We're still trying to locate them."

She slipped back into ice-cold focus. "Let's go."

Adam turned to Margo. "Deputy Jessup will stay here with you. We'll be right back."

"Nothing doing. I'm going with y'all." Margo flicked a glance at Jessup. "No offense."

Jessup stood. "None taken."

Patrick motioned to the door. "Adam, this is best. Let's stick together."

The four of them slipped into Adam's SUV and covered the short distance to the small, brick police station in no time.

Ashley flew out of the SUV and through the station doors.

Patrick rushed to catch up. *God, we need You. Please let us find Ashley's parents alive. Please reach Ashley's heart before she locks it down for good. Only You can get us out of this. Show me what I should do.*

"Marshal Taylor, tell me what you know." Ashley stood at attention, only her fists hinting at the war raging inside.

That and telling a police chief what to do.

Adam stood guard in the doorway, his face unreadable. Margo leaned against the back wall of the office, her head bowed. No one moved.

Ashley worked her jaw back and forth, her eyes locked onto Taylor.

"I know you're upset, Ashley, but we have cops from all over the area working on this. We'll find your parents."

"If you don't find them today, I'm going to meet him tomorrow."

Marshal Taylor turned and extended his hand. "You must be Patrick. Good to meet you. Please have a seat."

Patrick shook Taylor's hand and then tugged Ashley into a worn leather chair. He took the matching one next to her. "Thank you for all you and your officers are doing to protect Ashley. And…find her parents."

Taylor shifted a file on his desk. "Ashley, I need you to think about any places your parents might visit. Or people they'd call."

"The Kinsleys. Margo's parents."

"We've spoken with them. They haven't talked to your parents since last Thursday."

"Have you contacted my parents' travel agent?"

Marshal Taylor nodded. "Yes. Margo gave us her name and number."

"Did they book a cruise?"

"No."

Patrick's stomach plummeted. He should have known they'd be as stubborn as Ashley. He should have taken them to the airport the day Ashley fled from their home.

"Did they even call the travel agent?" Fire and ice had nothing on the blistering chill of Ashley's voice.

"Yes. Your parents called about plane tickets and cruise packages. But didn't respond when the travel agent returned their call."

"She didn't think to call the police?"

Marshal Taylor rubbed a hand down his face. The man's bloodshot eyes focused on Ashley. "How would a travel agent know there was a problem?"

"Janice has worked with my family for decades."

"She said they made plans and often changed them at the last minute."

Ashley's stony shell cracked. "My dad's work always interfered with family vacations. Whoever this stalker is, he might have banked on that."

"Both of your parents took emergency leave. No one from their offices has heard from them since last Friday. We're working with their cell phone providers too. They haven't made any calls since Friday. Last known location was their home. But we have Atlanta PD and Fulton County PD checking their house as we speak. They'll let us know when they find them. Can you think of anywhere else they might be staying?"

"They could be at the cabin."

Patrick grabbed Ashley's hand and squeezed. This was killing her worse than anything else could have. And he sat there helpless.

Taylor glanced at a file. "Margo's parents gave police the address and spare keys. They should be contacting us from there any time now."

"So we wait." Ashley crumpled into herself. "They could already be dead."

Then the dam broke, and tears coursed down Ashley's cheeks.

Patrick pulled her into his arms, searching his mind for an answer, a way to lessen her grief.

She clung to him like a life preserver.

"I'll leave you two alone." Marshal Taylor ushered Margo and Adam out the door with him. "We'll be right outside."

"Ash, we can't give up hope. Your parents are as stubborn as you. Smart too. They could be somewhere safe where no one could even find them. Your dad's a district attorney. He's faced down criminals most of his life."

"And one finally got to him. Through me."

He stroked her back, praying without words.

"I've always loved them, Patrick. Even when I hated them. Even when they acted like Eric's murder didn't faze them. Even when Mom tried to control every aspect of our wedding. I'd give anything to hear her demand my attention to the fiber count of the tablecloths."

"Me too, babe. Me too." *God, please. Please let them be alive.*

The office door opened and a grim police chief entered. "Ashley, I need you to look at something now. I'm sorry. We don't have time to waste."

Patrick's insides roiled. This could not be happening.

Ashley grabbed a Kleenex off the desk and stood. "Look…look at what? I can't do crime scene photos. I had to see my brother's…"

"Police have entered the home and are searching for evidence. Nothing on your parents' whereabouts yet."

"Then what do I need to see?" Her features hardened.

Marshal Taylor laid a series of grainy photos and papers on the desk in front of them.

"What in the world…?" Patrick couldn't think. Couldn't move. There in front of him, enclosed in plastic evidence bags, lay wedding photos and a Fulton County marriage license.

With Ashley's name on it.

She covered her mouth. "Oh, no. This can't be…"

"These were mailed to the station from the Shipshewana Post Office. Arrived a few minutes ago. Can you tell me about them?"

"They're not real. They can't be." Patrick jammed his finger into the first fake photo. "You can do anything in Photoshop these days." Marshal Taylor couldn't really buy that there was any grain of truth to these bogus claims. Could he?

"They're real."

Now it was Patrick's turn to go stony. "What?"

She turned to him. "The photos are real. They're from a mock wedding in high school. Tenth grade."

"The marriage certificate?"

"I've never seen that."

Marshal Taylor held up the photo of Ashley with a gangly teen. The boy's thick glasses and bow tie stood out. "Is it Keith Holberg in the photos?"

"Yes."

"Have a seat, Officer Walters. Before you pass out."

Ashley obeyed without hesitation.

Patrick didn't. "This is the stalker? He's a computer geek at best. A ninety-pound weakling who probably never had a date in his life. This is why we're running scared?"

Marshal Taylor sighed. "People change. Ninety-pound geeks grow up to be body builders."

Patrick's rational brain was missing in action. "Yes. You're right." He'd experienced Keith Holberg's fists. He deflated into his seat.

"The GBI are headed back our way. Everyone on our end has been put on alert. What can you tell me about Keith Holberg? Anything at all."

Ashley focused on the pictures in front of them, her hands clamped over her knees.

Patrick focused on Ashley, waiting to jump in and stop the questions if it became too much for her.

"Keith was a nice kid. Asked me out once after this mock wedding for Home Ec class. I said no. But he showed up at the dance and I danced with him one time. That's it. That's all the interaction we had."

Patrick's stomach rebelled. He'd do more than break this guy's ribs if he had the chance.

"He never bothered me after that. Never called. I never saw him again actually. We heard his dad lost his job so they had to move away."

Marshal Taylor leaned into his desk.

"Why couldn't the stalker be Dillon Matthews? Him I could understand." Ashley's green eyes pleaded for the impossible.

Patrick had no answers. Nothing to lessen the fear pulling at Ashley's features.

"Dillon Matthews is serving in Iraq. We located him yesterday." Marshal Taylor searched Ashley's face. "Why do you wish it was him?"

"Because Keith Holberg was suspected of killing his abusive father."

Chapter Twenty-five

Ashley pushed away the sickening cinnamon roll and club sandwich. "Come on, hon. You have to eat. Rise 'n Roll Bakery's food is amazing." Patrick glanced at Margo.

Margo flicked her head to the side. As if Ashley wouldn't catch the two of them discussing her eating habits in silence.

Adam dug into his Dagwood sandwich without a care in the world.

Except that wasn't true. Adam kept a close eye on their surroundings and stepped away every few minutes to check in by phone.

People came and went. In and out of the treasured Shipshewana bakery. But there she sat, doing nothing, the heat pressing in on her despite the bright red awning overhead.

Where were her parents? Were they alive? Why would Keith kidnap them? What else could she do to find them?

She'd given Marshal Taylor all the information she could dredge up from over a decade ago. Things she'd shoved so far back in her memory when Eric was killed that she'd have never recalled them if not for Keith's picture.

To think she'd once sympathized with Keith's sad family life, all the rumors of his relationship with his father.

The one who turned up dead not long after Keith's family moved away.

The one whose mother had recently passed away, leaving them no hope of finding out Keith's twisted game.

"It would help to talk, Ash. I'm here." Patrick's warm hand rested on her ice-cold knee. Despite the heat, everything inside of her had gone cold with the first glance at her "wedding" picture.

Every photo from the first set Keith sent rolled through her brain. She should have known then he'd focus on her parents. So many happy family photos. Pictures of everyone she loved.

At the beach. At her parents' home.

How could Keith have overpowered her dad? Kept them quiet all this time? Brought them here to Shipshewana without anyone knowing?

"They're alive, Ash."

She swallowed a long drink of lemonade. The tartness burned all the way down. "You don't know that, Patrick. No one does."

"Okay, so tell me what you think is going on."

Margo touched Patrick's arm. "That's not such a good idea. The police are taking care of this. We need to talk about the truth, somewhere good to set our minds."

"Don't, Maggie. I can't do this now. I'd rather follow Patrick's advice than listen to your whole 'Trust God even in the dark' speech."

Margo's eyes watered and she dabbed them with a napkin. "I believed I was listening to God when Patrick, Jonathan, and I came up with the escape plan that would keep you safe. But we couldn't keep tabs on everyone. I never even considered that your parents...I wasn't trusting God's protection. I didn't listen well enough."

"Neither was I." Patrick's defeated blue eyes stared up at the overcast sky. "I figured I'd pray and God would show me where the stalker was. I should have stopped him when I had the chance. Then none of this would have happened."

Ashley floated somewhere above the depressing conversation of the people she loved. She understood their pain. If only she could speak to their hurts. If only she'd been smart and taken off right after the pictures had arrived. Hidden until she could remember the shy, backwards boy who got picked by their homeroom teacher to play the groom in a wedding. A stupid, fake wedding that changed their lives forever.

A wedding that might have cost her parents theirs.

"Ashley." Adam's deep, commanding voice dragged her back to the present.

"What?" She'd rather wallow than listen right now.

"Look, I haven't known any of you very long. But this is what I've observed. Patrick and Margo? You love Ashley with a fierce loyalty that's led you to risk your own lives to protect her. Ashley, you are one of the most instinctual, tough-as-nails cops I've had the pleasure of meeting. But no one—not you, not the detectives or GBI agents, not the FBI agents from the Behavioral Science Unit—no one but Keith Holberg could have known what he was going to do."

Maybe. "So we just sit and wait for him to make his next move?"

"No." Adam rubbed his chin. "We can go back to Patrick's suggestion and see what more we can come up with."

Now someone was speaking her language. "So let's get down to business and figure out how to find Keith."

Adam smiled. "Okay, you're the key figure in this guy's drama. Tell us again what you told Marshal Taylor."

"Keith kept to himself. Only spoke to me a few times after that mock wedding. It must have been so real to him. It *was* pretty close to reality. I wore a bridal gown that had been my mother's. Keith had a suit and bow tie. There was a three-tiered wedding cake, wedding mints, the whole kit and caboodle."

"Only it wasn't real." Patrick took her hand. "It was a stupid school project."

"But Keith believed it." Ashley searched her memories and pushed aside the panic at wasting time when she could be out looking for her parents. She'd get to that. Soon. "I remember Keith from middle school. He never smiled. The kids teased him about his scrawny dad, who they said he looked just like. I'd forgotten that until now."

"This scrawny dad who beat him and his mom up?" Patrick succumbed to the psychological fishing expedition.

"Yeah. I remember a work picture of the dad that ran in the papers after he was found in the woods. The guy was normal. Nondescript."

Adam pursed his lips. "You never know what's hiding in the hearts of the most innocent-looking people."

"Great. Thanks." Margo shook her head. "From this point on, I'm going to suspect everyone I ever meet of heinous crimes."

"You don't have to succumb to it, Margo. It's all about where you allow your mind to go." Patrick finished off his Hungry Man sandwich.

"How did the dad die?" Adam checked his phone and motioned for her to continue.

Ashley strained to remember the details. "Hanging, I think. Short suicide note. Open and shut case back then. The police had probable cause to believe suicide. The guy had lost his job and his wife took over working to provide for the family. It was only the kids at school who believed Keith was guilty of murder. I dismissed all the talk as mean gossip."

"Why?"

"Because Keith was smarter than the rest of us. I figured the guys spreading the rumors were jealous and bored, and then I never gave it another thought. Keith dropped off the map. No one at school talked about him anymore." She grabbed a handful of chips and forced herself to swallow them.

"But now?"

"Now I wish I'd paid more attention back then."

Adam nodded. "With what we have to go on, what do you think his next move is?"

"Based on the mailed photos, I'd say Keith is trying to reenact our fake wedding and is convinced I want that too. Maybe that's what he meant by the messages he left. Why he'd kidnap my parents. Why he'd try to get Patrick, the competition, out of the way. Given he's attacked my loved ones and probably kidnapped my parents and Chester too and avoided detection, he's likely planned this for a very long time."

Patrick's blue eyes lit up. "Then your parents are definitely alive, Ash. He would want them there to see their daughter married."

"But my dad's not a little guy. Both of them have stayed physically active and strong."

"He could've drugged them."

Margo kicked Adam's shin.

"Hey." He rubbed the spot. "That was uncalled for."

"Sorry." Margo didn't bother batting her eyes this time.

Patrick coughed to cover a laugh. "Gotta watch those Southern belles."

"That's it." Ashley stood. "Adam, give me your keys. I know where my parents might be."

"Nothing doing." Adam stood. "I'll drive."

She squared off with him. "I don't have an address, but I'll know it when I see it. Trust me." She was back. And ready with a new plan.

Patrick wished for the hundredth time Ashley wasn't a cop. Bull-headed. Self-assured. Right too many times for her own good.

"Let's stop by the police station and fill Marshal Taylor in."

"Too late, Patrick. Adam has already called." She glanced in the rear-view mirror. "Haven't you, Adam?"

"Yes, I did."

"Margo here helped. Dragging me into the restroom and pretending to have a meltdown."

Margo huffed. "I wasn't pretending all the way, Ash."

"I can drop you off at the B&B." Ashley glanced in the rearview mirror once more.

Adam slashed his hand from his chest to his knee. "No way. My job is to keep an eye on both of you. I'd say *keep you two out of trouble*, but I've failed at that today."

"You've protected us for three days, Adam, and no trouble has befallen us." Margo flashed a sweet smile Adam's way.

Patrick had never seen Margo sugar sweet without some bite to her. Maybe this Indiana cop had really snagged her attention.

Guess they all needed some form of diversion. Some mental protection to face what was ahead of them.

Ashley drove past hundreds of white farmhouses. Subdivisions. All Patrick could do was divide his attention between Ashley and the houses. But Ashley gave nothing away, and none of the houses screamed *stalker* and *kidnap victims*.

What if Ashley found the house where her parents were being held? What then?

All Hades would break out.

He slipped his hand across the console and squeezed Ashley's thigh. "I trust you, hon. But this is foolish. You could be leading some good cops away from their work, preparing for tomorrow, and on a wild goose chase."

"You're either in or out, Patrick. I *am* going to tear the countryside apart to find my parents. I'm not waiting for tomorrow to be locked away at the B&B while the chance to save my parents disappears."

"You would do this without me?"

Ashley's thigh muscle tensed to the point of snapping. Her skin had even grown colder under his touch. But she met his eyes. A war raged behind those sharp, pensive, terrified green eyes.

"No. I need you."

"And we need someone bigger than us in charge of this. We're all emotionally invested and not thinking straight. You haven't slept in over a week, have you?"

"No."

"You haven't served on any hostage rescue teams or worked SWAT, have you?"

"No."

"You don't really know Keith or a delusional, obsessive, violent stalker's mind well enough to know without a doubt what he would do, do you?"

Her teeth clenched and her jaw muscles jumped. "No."

"You wouldn't want to risk your parents' lives by storming into a trap unprepared, would you?"

He had counted the cost of this line of questioning for days.

His awareness of the weight of Ashley's answer grew with each tick of his watch's second hand.

She could push him out of her life for good, she was so invested in being the hero of this story. Without a rational plan. Without a care for her own survival. Without God.

But she hadn't counted on the depth of his love for her. Or God's.

He prayed she'd see that now.

"Ashley, honey." Margo leaned up and touched her shoulder. "Listen to him."

"I am."

Patrick released the breath he'd held.

"An hour. That's all I'm asking." At a stoplight she turned to him. "Go with me one more hour and let me look. They're my parents, Patrick. I need to do something."

His shoulders loosened a fraction. He'd laid himself and their relationship bare and survived. Not a contest of wills, but a battle that could mean their very lives.

Ashley slowed down as they passed the Hidden Creek B&B. "Three miles is what he said. I'm to run three miles north. Then he'd meet me there. I still think Marshal Taylor should wire me up and let me meet him. It could be the only way he keeps my parents alive."

Adam entered the battle of wills now, his dark eyes locked with Ashley's in the rearview mirror. "You've risked your life enough. Becoming a sacrificial lamb is not going to save your parents or anyone else. So much could go wrong in the blink of an eye."

"It could all go wrong anyway."

Margo cleared her throat. "Y'all might believe I have rocks for brains and a bleeding heart, but I've seen the Word of God and faith triumph over oppressive darkness and evil. Nothing we do tactically will matter one whit if we don't pray and follow the Holy Spirit."

The admiration on Adam's face grew.

The tense lines on Ashley's face deepened.

This battle belonged to Someone else now. The three of them had used logic, authority, and faith to no avail.

Ashley focused straight ahead. Resolute stiffness protecting a frail hold on self.

Patrick willed her to choose wisely. If he could have, he would take her place a hundred times over.

So would Margo.

So would Ashley's parents.

But only Ashley could decide who was in charge here. And what the next step would be.

The outcome, however, belonged in God's hands alone.

CHAPTER TWENTY-SIX

She intended to shoot someone today.

But for now, Ashley stayed put at Hidden Creek, only venturing to the command post three miles down the road to check for updates. GBI, CRT, SWAT, a vegetable soup of agents and cops swarmed the commandeered house. Each visit she'd prayed for good news—the securing of her parents' location or the slim chance that Keith had been taken into custody due to a random traffic stop.

Nothing like that had occurred.

Her parents remained at large.

So did Keith.

And she had a plan that would test her mettle to the core. And risk her badge.

"You must eat something, Ashley." Mrs. Yoder placed a platter of meats and cheeses and fresh fruit on the table. "The morning is coming soon, no matter how hard you will it not to come."

"Thanks. I wish I'd never brought this danger to your home. Your town. I'm praying today will see an end to it, and your lives can return to normal."

Margo exited her room, a huge yawn escaping before she could well manner it away. "Oh, I didn't realize y'all were up and about yet. You know it's only five."

"Come eat, Margo." Mrs. Yoder set out another plate and poured a mug of coffee. "You've lost weight these long days here. I must not feed you enough."

"No, Debra. You've been a perfect hostess. Thank you for bringing breakfast early."

"More like the middle of the night." Ashley piled food on her plate. Useless waiting had drained her desire to eat, but the hope that this nightmare would end today left her starving.

Debra turned on shaky legs toward the staircase but stopped before ascending. "Ashley, I do not wish these past days away. It has been a privilege to have you and Margo in our home. Philip and I believe God brought you here for a good purpose."

Ashley smiled. "Thank you. That means a lot to me."

Even if she couldn't agree with the good purpose part.

Adam and Patrick, with Adam's key, entered the basement apartment. Adam shot straight for the coffee pot. "Morning, ladies."

Ashley managed a wave.

Patrick beelined it to her side and pulled her into a kiss.

She wasn't in the mood. Her focus was a million miles away. More like three miles.

"Is this how you're going to be when you make detective?" Patrick held her face in his hands.

"Sergeant. In Montezuma I don't need a detective's exam. Just a hard-earned promotion." If she didn't throw it all away today.

Patrick pulled up a chair. "Play things smart, Ash. The GBI's and CRT's rescue plans rest on how things go down today. You understand that, right?"

She nodded. Her parents' lives depended on the events set to unfold two hours from now.

Adam joined them at the table. "Have you heard the latest?"

"No. Probably not."

"We've searched all the abandoned homes within a ten-mile radius. None showed any signs of inhabitants."

Margo poured orange juice into everyone's cup. Always the mom.

She'd taken on that role since grade school. Or tried to. Ashley preferred playing the eccentric aunt. Or the GI Joe commando. She quit playing house before they'd turned eight.

Most days, anyway.

"What's a CRT?" Margo turned to Adam. "Some top secret cop speak?"

He smiled. "You got tactical right yesterday. I figured you'd be up to speed on the rest by this morning."

"This dog don't hunt."

Adam blinked a few times.

Patrick chuckled.

Ashley flat out laughed. "You done gone too Southern for this Yankee."

"Sorry." Margo smiled at Adam. "My granddaddy's sayings pop out sometimes. The closest translation is when pigs fly."

"I get that one."

"You still haven't defined CRT for me." Margo buttered her toast with a heap of Amish peanut butter.

"Critical Response Team." Adam focused back on his food. "Our CRT consists of SWAT and negotiators. Right now, SWAT is gearing up and scoping out the best position of attack. The negotiators are standing by."

Ashley sobered fast. "If I don't show up, you all won't see Keith. And then we may never know where he's keeping my parents."

"If you show up, you'll be arrested."

She studied the clock in the kitchen. "Best not take any chances then."

They finished their food in silence.

Her window of opportunity was fading fast.

At three this morning, she'd played out the schematics of handcuffing Patrick and Adam to the dining room chairs.

But she'd be arrested in no time flat and fired when she got home. Not to mention how that would destroy the trust she and Patrick had built together.

At four, she'd hit on a better option. They'd still be mad, but without the same level of risk to her job and upcoming marriage. It might just give her the edge to track down her parents too.

And now it was time.

She stood and yawned the biggest yawn she could muster.

"You didn't sleep at all last night, did you?" Patrick stood too. "Want to watch some TV? You might fall asleep if we find the right movie."

"I doubt it. But I'm going to fall over on my face if I don't try and lie down." She avoided everyone's eyes.

Margo cleared the table with Adam's help.

"I'll see you in a little while, okay?" She leaned up on her toes and kissed Patrick with all the energy she could muster.

He responded in full measure. Heat flushed her face and arms as Patrick pulled her close.

She could get lost here. So much so that she almost forgot what she was about to do.

"I doubt I can sleep now."

Patrick smiled. "Sweet dreams."

Once inside her dark bedroom, she closed the door and leaned against it. Deep breath in. Deep breath out.

She started the shower and stripped off the jeans and T-shirt she'd worn to breakfast, replacing them with black running shorts and a dark blue GCPD T-shirt. Her go-to pj's.

Today they'd be cover.

Along with her gun.

One more check at the door. The TV was on and Margo was chattering about a story involving her and Ashley's parents when they were kids. Good.

She made short work of the high window lock and eased the glass open.

Nothing changed in the cacophony of TV and conversation and dish-washing outside her door.

In less than twenty seconds she was out the window and crouched in what had to be some sort of deep window garden. The vines scraped at her ankles and exposed arms.

But she was free.

Allowing her eyes to adjust to the dark, she focused on her breathing and the early morning noises.

Then she sprinted toward the road, watching far down the way for any approaching cars. The last thing she needed was to get caught now.

No cars.

Only folks on the Amish farms stirred.

She set a ground-eating pace, not caring where her tennis shoes landed.

Gravel pinged behind her.

Not Adam. Please, God. Let me do this.

A low whistle came next.

Then familiar legs drew even with hers. "Go back."

"Not on your life." Patrick's face contorted with pain, but he matched her stride for stride, his voice strong.

She struggled to sustain the pace. Forget talking.

At least he wasn't making her turn around.

They continued running for twenty minutes, the slow-rising sun filling in more and more details of the gray landscape.

At the twenty-minute mark, she pulled up short. "There's the house. No chance the SWAT guys haven't picked us up. Best get inside and face the music."

"Agreed."

"You could turn back now."

"Not a chance."

The last few yards stretched out like a gauntlet before her.

She stopped at the steps of the back door and waited, her breath still ragged from the run and the demons chasing her.

The posted guard shook his head and slipped inside.

None other than Marshal Taylor himself met her at the door. "I warned Winslow you'd give him the slip."

"Does he know I'm here?"

"Turning on the shower to keep a single guy out of your room was a touch of genius." Marshal Taylor eyed Patrick. "I expected this from her. Not you."

"Almost one flesh and all."

"Bit of stupid thrown in there." Marshal Taylor held the door open. "As a superior officer and a man old enough to be your father, do me a favor and let this stunt be the end of your heroics."

Ashley nodded.

"Duly noted that there was no promise in there."

Patrick grinned. "You've raised a strong-willed daughter?"

"Three of 'em." Marshal Taylor returned to the front room and sat before a bank of computers and phone lines. "Make yourselves comfortable. But stay out of the way. All we need is for him to show up and drive away. Tails are posted at every street branching off from State Road 5."

Six o'clock met them with a less than stellar sunrise. Gray dawn and drizzle. Patrick extended a bottle of water Ashley's way.

"Thanks." She twisted the top and downed the liquid in one gulp.

A whole new perspective on his fiancée opened up before him. This was her turf. How she must appear to every criminal she threw in her cage or talked down from some upper ledge of desperation.

Equal parts awe and apprehension filled him.

He joined her on the leather couch. "Someone is pretty trusting of the SPD to loan out their home like this."

"That would be Corporal Winslow's sister. Once Adam tells her what you did, I doubt you'll be as welcome as you are right now." Marshal Taylor's eyes never left the monitors.

She didn't flinch.

"Guilt isn't eating away at you?"

"Yes. It is. But not about ditching Winslow. About leaving my parents unprotected. I can't imagine what they've endured."

"No one's substantiated that suspicion. They might be hiding out in Georgia for all we know."

"We'll know something soon."

The Indiana SWAT team leader and the CRT commander flanked Taylor at the command post. Two GBI agents, Edwards included, and the DA's investigator added their gadgets and expertise to the mix. Adrenaline tinged the air, but none of the officers' body language communicated anything but confidence.

Same with Ashley.

Same with the CRT and SWAT members that checked in routinely. Their hushed, code-numbered communication fell like bullets at a shooting range.

Each word hit its mark.

Six thirty and no movement outside.

Cars rattled by the house, but none stopped and no increase in radio chatter.

Buggies clip-clopped past the house too. For their sakes, he hoped Keith didn't show up and then take off, leading the police on a high-speed chase. Buggies couldn't swerve to the side fast enough to avoid danger.

"Do you think he'll show?" He catalogued every nuance of Ashley's face.

"Yes."

"What about when you're not there?"

"I should be out there."

Taylor cleared his throat. "But you won't be. You can bet your badge you're staying right there."

"Yes, sir."

Patrick's old cell phone's vintage rotary ring exploded in the controlled silence of the command post.

Ashley yanked it out of her shorts pocket and lasered Marshal Taylor.

He nodded. "Answer it. We're ready."

Were they?

∞

"Hello." Ashley held her breath and waited.

"Ashley? Baby, is that you?" Her mom's weathered voice brought tears to her eyes. She'd not been called baby since she and Eric were in grade school.

"Mom, where are you?" Ashley paced the floor, tears burning her eyes. "Are you okay? Is Dad there? Is Keith listening in?"

"He left…a phone. Told me to call you. Then he was…gone."

"Is Dad there?"

"Your dad is here…somewhere. Can't see him. We're…tied. Hands. Feet. Hurts. Your dad thinks…we've been…drugged. Can't remember…how we got here…what happened…after you left."

Her worst nightmare sprouted fangs.

Mom's halting whispers stole her ability to understand everything said. So many questions. Not enough time.

Keith could return at any moment.

Sounds of her mom weeping filled the line. She was far away from the phone. Or maybe Ashley was losing the connection.

"Mom? Mom, are you hurt?"

"No, baby. I just didn't know…if…I'd hear…your voice again."

"Is Keith there?"

"No. He left…a long time ago. Said something about…a…missing puzzle piece."

She focused on Marshal Taylor. "Can you find them?"

"Working on it." Taylor's fingers clicked over his keyboard. One of the other cops was on another line running down this new cell number. "Keep her talking."

A loud coughing pierced her ear.

"Dad?"

"He's not doing well…sick…since we woke up…first time."

"Can you give me any clues about your surroundings?"

A whooshing filled the lines now.

"Mom? Talk to me. Mom?"

"It's cold. Hands are tied…it's dark…all the time…no cars around. Farm animals. Horses. Cows. Lots of banging. Like you and Eric… when you were little."

"Good, Mom. You're doing great." She grasped Patrick's hand and hung on. His rock-solid grip provided an anchor. "Keep going."

"That's all. So sorry, baby."

It wasn't enough. "No, Mom. You did great." The images filling Ashley's mind left her dizzy and numb.

But they were alive.

"We're coming, Mom. Hang on a little longer."

"Need to rest…eyes sore…so tired."

"I love you, Mom. We're coming. Stay on the line. We'll find you."

Cops scrambled into action, team leaders, Marshal Taylor, and Agent Edwards barking out orders in turn.

She stood motionless.

Marshal Taylor stepped toward them. "Your mom is one tough old bird. Smart too. SWAT has been dispatched to the most probable locations given the cell tower data. There are only a handful of Amish farms with new construction in the target area."

"What if Keith comes back too soon for your guys to move in?"

"One step at a time, Ashley." Marshal Taylor turned away and resumed a stream of orders, most of which guaranteed her spending the next few hours doing nothing but waiting.

Patrick wrapped his arms around her. "They're alive, Ash. We could see them in a matter of hours."

"If we aren't too late."

Chapter Twenty-seven

From his secure perch, Keith smiled at Saturday's dawning light. Today would be a good day. The day of his dreams. He had only one more piece of the puzzle to fit into place and his masterpiece would be complete.

His and Ashley's wedding day would be perfect. Just what they deserved.

After all these years, all his planning. His success was almost too good to be true.

But he'd made his dreams happen. He'd watched every CSI and police show on TV and cable. Read every book at the library on investigations and psychology and medicine.

Ashley's parents were proof of his success. Find the perfect dose of the right medicine and they'd follow him anywhere. The Internet made so many things easy these days. Now his in-laws loved him. They were ready to release Ashley into his care.

Images of their bound and bleeding wrists cut into his happy thoughts. It had taken time to convince them. That was all. Mr. Walters especially needed a great deal of persuading. But after that first day, Randall had figured things out nicely. He was a reasonable man. Smart too. Just not as strong as he believed himself to be.

Keith slipped down from the large oak and faded into the grayish light. A storm brewed overhead. No one had driven by in an hour. No one had found his borrowed buggy either. He tipped his black Amish hat to the oblivious SWAT officer in the distance and drove his horse away. Not the fastest mode of escape, but the smartest given the police crawling all over the place. One more Amish man raised no suspicion.

His mind drifted back to the wonders he had waiting for Ashley.

Her simple but elegant dress.

Roses by the dozens.

Candles.

Randall's Bible.

Wouldn't Ashley be a vision coming down the aisle in her wedding dress, smiling on her father's arm?

Keith checked his other disposable phone. By now Jacquelyn had phoned her daughter and given her the information Ashley needed to find them.

Once Ashley spoke the words he'd longed to hear again since tenth grade, the police would leave them alone. Randall and Jacquelyn would forgive him for his necessary harshness and send the happy couple off on a dream honeymoon.

His hands trembled in anticipation.

Only one more stop to go.

Ashley paced the command post living room. "Marshal Taylor, you have to let me go with you. They're my parents. I need to see them."

Patrick grabbed her hand and pulled her to him.

His comfort didn't still the shaking.

"Ashley, we've been over this a million times." Taylor rubbed a rough hand down his face. "There is no way under God's green earth I'm letting you anywhere near the place your parents are being held."

"Are you sure you have the right place?"

"Yes."

"How can you know?"

Taylor sighed. "I've been a police officer a very long time. Too long I think some days. In addition, we have the best of the best on this."

"But you haven't secured the exact location from their phone signal."

"No time. We have a general radius and two homes that fit the description your mother was able to provide."

Ashley toed the Oriental rug in the living room. "But what if he's there? He'll kill my parents before he surrenders to the police."

"SWAT trains for this. Hostage negotiators too. It's their job. They'll make sure Keith is stopped and your parents kept alive."

"I've been a cop long enough to know you can't guarantee that."

Taylor flashed a half-hearted, sympathetic smile her way. "I've heard Patrick praying all morning. You two keep that up. It can't hurt."

Ashley noted the two SPD officers and GBI Agent Edwards left at the command post computers. More babysitters. Plus the CRT commander poring over the maps spread on every flat surface. A SWAT team leader focused on the computer maps and the steady stream of radio chatter. Even more officers from other counties would arrive soon.

She studied the floor plans of the two homes the police had honed in on. One near an Amish toy maker's shop and a dairy farm. The other an empty brick home for sale since January with construction of a new barn going up this week at a neighboring farm.

Her mind flipped through her options.

Stay put and pray. For what, safety? That hadn't happened. She couldn't form words to the One who could have kept her parents out of this.

Stay here and pace, listen to the radio.

Scenarios of rescues gone wrong filled her mind. All the TV reports. Memories from the barn fire that had almost claimed Patrick's, Brad's, and Jonathan's lives. The fire at Mrs. Adams's home that left her and her wheelchair-bound husband scarred for life. The many nights someone had snuck into her backyard, evading all detection. That man wasn't in jail. He was here.

And she had to get to her parents before the police did.

God forgive her for the information she'd withheld from Taylor and the rest. They believed the noises Mom heard originated from construction or woodworking. But she and Eric hadn't made that kind of noise. They'd played in relative quiet. In a basement with a noisy old furnace.

The first home she remembered.

And she'd found one just like it while driving around yesterday. An older stone home with lights blazing during the daytime but no movement inside or outside. No cars during the day or when they'd driven by again last night. Of course that would be the one Keith chose. His attention to every detail of her growing up wouldn't have allowed him to miss the resemblance to Ashley's first home.

She hoped Adam wouldn't remember how many times she'd driven around that neighborhood. Or realized which house she'd focused on. That had to be the place. Mom's clue cinched her decision.

She flopped back down on the leather couch. Patrick joined her, neither of them saying a word. But he knew her too well not to understand what had to happen.

The babysitting police officers didn't even glance her way.

Patrick watched the clock.

She watched the cops. She had to leave soon.

Keith tied his horse to a tree and left him munching on some feed.

Picking his way through the field adjoining the Hidden Creek Bed and Breakfast, he forced himself not to whistle. A habit he'd broken in high school.

Among many other changes to his life.

Dark clouds hovered overhead and in his mind. Such an awful time of life to constantly replay in one's mind. Why did he do that? The only moment worth remembering was the one in which Ashley said those beautiful words.

"I do." She had grinned and squeezed his hand. *"Don't pass out on me now. We have to finish this right."*

Even back then, she'd been a levelheaded, reasonable girl with a kind heart. Her encouragement had gotten him through standing in front of his usually taunting, cruel classmates. Her greetings in the hallway after that upped his status enough to avoid the worst of the bullying.

But not at home.

He'd taken care of that too.

An ambling cow drawing near jerked him into the present. He halted by a border tree and scrambled up. Through his binoculars, he found his target. The last piece to the puzzle.

And her bodyguard.

Not the mountain of a cop that had kept Ashley prisoner for days. Good.

Keith patted the weapon in his pocket and blessed his mother for leaving him such a good inheritance.

He missed her. But he'd made her proud. He'd followed his dream and captured it.

Today.

Blending in with the stormy day, he drew near the basement apartment. Close enough to hear everything.

People seldom realized how their voices carried.

"Miss Kinsley, I do understand how hard this is on you." The short, skinny cop brushed his fingers through dark floppy hair. "But we have to stay here for now. Ashley is safe. The cops and feds are taking care of everything."

The basement door clicked open.

Keith flattened against the warm bricks and held his breath.

"What? What are you doing?" Margo's pinched voice dripped with her Southern roots.

"Nothing. Just checking outside is all." The police officer closed and relocked the doors. "Can't be too careful, can we?"

Margo's heels clicked over the uncarpeted kitchen. Dishes clattered.

Perfect.

"I'm making myself a sandwich. Are you hungry, Officer Jessup?"

"No, ma'am, thank you." The police officer's shoes slapped against the tile and then trailed off.

Could this day get any better?

He fingered the spare key he'd had made days ago. Days when they weren't looking for him as they were today. How had Ashley not noticed him? She must have lost herself in dreams of freedom. Dreams where he would show up and rescue her from her controlling fiancé and take her to a place where they could be together, unbothered by her crazy schedule and any so-called friends who would stand in their way.

I'm coming, sweet Ashley. Soon.

With swift and practiced movements, he slipped to the door and turned the key, making no sound. The door lock unlatched.

Margo continued fixing her sandwich.

The police officer was nowhere to be seen.

A dangerous unknown.

He crept up to his target and slipped a hand around her mouth, jerking her backward and out the door before she could conjure a response.

Through the grass and into the field they flew.

Margo put up no resistance whatsoever. She must have understood his plan and sympathized. Good. She was the one expendable puzzle piece of the set.

Once they were hidden by trees, he slowed his steps.

"Are you going to cooperate, dear Margo?" He held her tight to him, his hand still clamped around her mouth. He wasn't stupid.

She nodded. And shuddered.

He'd questioned himself on the wisdom of bringing Margo into this day. She could be kind like Ashley. Sometimes. Right now her fear kept her in check.

"We'll be off to my buggy. There you will slip into a beautiful Amish dress I've purchased just for you. Later you will don your lovely bridesmaid dress. Do you understand?"

Another nod.

"If you cooperate, you live. Besides, you wouldn't want to mess up your best friend's beautiful and long-awaited wedding day, would you?"

She shook her head.

But Margo was smart. Much more intelligent than he'd given her credit for years ago. She'd managed to keep her plans for Ashley hidden well. For a time.

They tromped through the tall grass until they reached the buggy.

"Are you sure you will cooperate?"

She nodded.

Even so, he handcuffed her right wrist to the buggy wheel before he let go. Releasing his hold on her mouth, he reached into the floorboard and retrieved a duffel bag.

Her scream pierced the day, shattering his good mood.

He swung and backhanded her.

She fell to the ground and clutched her jaw.

"I expect no more trouble from you." He pulled out some clear tape anyway. "This should do the trick." Leaning over the sobbing Margo, he ensured her cooperation by binding her ankles and covering her mouth. That would secure peace and quiet on their journey to the perfect wedding location.

From a distance, no one would suspect any trouble.

"Will you change into this dress like a good best friend or do I need to do it for you?"

Her blue eyes widened and blazed. She shook her head and held out her free hand for the simple blue dress he now held.

Choosing to slip the dress over her clothes rather than truly change didn't bother him one bit. But he did turn her around and handcuff the other hand before releasing her right one. She'd given him no reason to trust her again.

"It would look better without your immodest tank top and shorts underneath. But no matter. You will be clothed in your favorite bridesmaid dress soon. The rich, blue, full-length one. The one I believe you called *absolute perfection*. Isn't that right?"

Margo didn't move her head at all. But her eyes told the whole story.

He studied the red-faced, angry young woman before him. She'd neither cooperate nor help with his wedding today.

He would handle that as planned. She'd learn.

Maybe then his day would return to perfect.

CHAPTER TWENTY-EIGHT

Patrick busied his shaking hands with food prep. He'd never, ever, not in his wildest dreams believed he'd assist Ashley with a criminal act.

But it was help or be left behind. So he'd help. This one time. Or so he prayed.

He also prayed for Marshal Taylor's compassion. The man held Ashley's future in law enforcement in his hands.

No. God did.

Would God be honored by what they were about to do?

Ashley stood beside him. "Are you almost ready?"

"No whispering." The young volunteer officer observing them had no idea who he was messing with. Poor kid.

Ashley spun around. "I am not a prisoner here. I can speak at any volume I choose." Said volume rose with each word.

Patrick hid his nervous grin. This was not happening. Not really comfortable praying their deceptive game would work, he hoped instead for the thousandth time he was doing the right thing.

Ashley advanced on the young cop, her face fire truck red. "I am sick and tired of being told what to do and being cramped up in this tiny house under your babysitting. I can't cry. I can't talk. I can't even go to the bathroom alone." She poked a finger into his chest. "I am not a baby. I'm a cop."

Maybe she wasn't acting after all.

The volunteer cop stepped back. "I understand, ma'am. If you'll just step back to what you were doing."

"I was fixing you and your silent partner a snack. Remember? And even then I have to have a kid babysitting me."

The kid couldn't have been more than a handful of years younger than Ashley.

"Ma'am, I apologize." He held up his hands. Not too much experience with women or hysterical, potentially violent escapees.

"Look." The kid bumped into the hallway wall. "I'll back off. Stay in the hall here. You go back to fixing food."

"With you breathing down my neck from one more foot away? Not happening. Fix your own food." She dialed back the emotion and retied her ponytail.

And sniffled. Twice. With a long pause in between.

She was too good for her own good.

He should have stood up to her and insisted they pray. But a sense of peace deep in his gut—and the fire in Ashley's eyes—convinced him to stick by her side. She'd be in danger alone. So would anyone in her path.

At least this way, he could keep his eyes on Ashley and be lookout or whatever it was criminal sidekicks were supposed to do.

No. Not criminal. They were the good guys.

As Ashley fought for self-control over her tears, real or pretend, the young cop laid a hand on his weapon and glanced back toward his partner, eyes wide. The kid had no idea his unconscious habit would only goad Ashley on. He telegraphed fear.

The cop's hand remained on his duty weapon.

Patrick focused on Ashley, waiting for her signal. They'd face more than a nervous cop if they got away from here.

Keith had guns. Most likely many.

But the good guys took a bullet if necessary. That was also Patrick's role today. To get between Keith and Ashley, no matter what. He clenched his hands and teeth. Better. More in control. Yes, he'd take a bullet if it came to that.

But he prayed it would not. Prayed that God would protect them despite the way they were going about their plans.

Despite the fact they had no backup. And only the weapon in Ashley's possession. No experience. Told to stay put and stay safe.

But Ashley believed with all her being that if the cops got involved in a standoff with Keith, without allowing her to speak to him, the man would kill her parents and himself before he surrendered.

Patrick agreed. Keith fit that profile to a T.

For that reason alone, he was willing to risk the consequences.

The young officer cleared his throat and held up his hands again. "Don't cry, ma'am. I know this is hard on you and your family. We'll bring them home safe. You'll see."

Ashley swiped at her eyes. "Just give me a minute, okay? Please."

The cop glanced over his shoulder again. The radio chattered. "I'll be right back."

He scurried to the front room.

Ashley motioned toward the door.

It was time.

Ashley's legs burned. But their window of opportunity would slam closed any minute.

In between the play-acting turned reality, she'd heard the voice of reason. The cops could handle this. She'd been stupid to give them the slip again. Because this could all be a trap.

But it was too late to turn back now. One bad choice deserved another.

If it saved her parents.

"We're coming up on two miles. Where's the house?"

"A little farther."

They continued running down gravel roads. Through patches of woods.

Most of the cops were congregating miles away from there, not crawling these streets anymore. Unless her two babysitters had called the escape in. She hoped they were too busy following the rescue attempt.

"Do you know where you're going, Ash?" Even Patrick breathed hard this time.

"To Winslow's house."

"What?"

She pointed. "Did you bring your keys?"

"Yeah. Habit. Why?"

She slipped around the cop's nice one-story starter home. "Winslow told Margo...about his house." She gulped in air. "About the garage being his next repair project. Which means...we don't have to commit a B&E to get your car."

"We just hoist the garage door?"

"Yep."

"If it used to be electric, it'll take a Hercules to lift it."

She patted his chest. "Good thing I have you then."

"If adrenaline counts for anything." Patrick slipped his hand through the rusted door handle and heaved.

The door slammed up like a giant flicking a card house.

Ashley moved to the driver's door. "Keys?"

His second of indecision rankled her. "We have to move. I'll be careful with the car."

He tossed the keys over. "I care more about your life than this car. Are you sure we shouldn't call Taylor and tell them where we're headed?"

"You call. I'm not waiting." She revved the engine and Patrick slipped in beside her. They were off.

Patrick clicked on his seat belt and punched numbers into his phone. She didn't bother with the belt. She followed her memory and found the right neighborhood. Thank God for cars.

The smallish prayer pierced her cold armor.

But the conviction wouldn't stop her. The Shipshewana police could have the rescue and capture of Keith Holberg. All she wanted was eyes on her parents and the chance to get them to safety before Keith returned.

She drove by the medium-sized stone house. In the gray rain, the house lights burned brighter.

What if she was wrong? What if this wasn't the house?

She had to take that chance.

Pulling off to the side of the road and parking at the edge of a small field, she retrieved the handgun Patrick always carried on long trips. Especially this one.

She handed his XD over.

He nodded.

They jogged down the paved road, dressed perfectly for their parts today. At the stone house, she sprinted down the closest side to the back.

Patrick followed.

"Stay here." She pointed to the back door.

Deep breath in.

It didn't feel like a trap.

Deep breath out.

Time to find out.

She tried the door first. It was open. Horror music soundtracks played in her memory.

Stepping slow and staying low, she entered the silent home. Nothing stirred.

The small kitchen was immaculate. No one had eaten there in a long time. No upstairs to worry about. No noise from out front.

She slipped against the far wall and waited.

The basement door sat two feet away.

Please let it be unlocked. Please let me rescue my parents. Please, God.

Emotion clogged her throat and cut off the internal prayer.

She had no time for tears now. Instead, she sprang for the door and turned the handle.

It opened.

Not willing to risk an ambush, she flipped on the basement light and the room came to life.

"Please let us go. Please let us see Ashley," Mom begged from the far side of the unfinished room.

An oldtime furnace in the corner sat silent. But it had done its duty.

"Mom, it's me." She rushed around a stack of shoulder-high boxes to her mom's side.

The sight stopped her cold.

Her mom's head drooped to the side, eyes closed. Face dirty and black hair in shambles. Tear tracks and streaked mascara cut a path down her ashen skin.

A cell phone stood guard on the floor. "Officer Walters? Are you there?" Not recognizing the tinny voice, she ignored the phone. It could be Keith.

Ashley set to work on the duct tape binding her mom's hands and feet. "Mom, it's me. Talk to me, Mom. Where's Dad?"

Her mom mumbled incoherently.

Stalking blackness closed in on her. What she'd do to Keith when she saw him…

A sound off to her left behind another stack of boxes raised the hair on the back of her neck.

Not him. Not now. Not yet.

She had to hurry. She ripped duct tape away from Mom's hands and ankles. Her mom didn't flinch.

Drugged. But alive.

"Mom?" She pulled her mother into her arms. "Wake up, Mom. Please."

A moaning sound to her left reached her ears.

"Dad?"

She swept her mom in her arms and moved around another stack of musty boxes. There lay her dad. Bound. Gagged. Bruised. Bloody.

Oh, Daddy.

She fought to breathe.

Laying Mom down as easy as possible, Ashley listened for any other noises. Nothing. She tore into the brittle and spiky rope binding her dad. It cut her hands, but she had to keep moving. They didn't have much time.

She ripped off the ropes and removed the gag.

Her dad coughed and choked. She helped him sit up straight and held him there. "I'm here, Daddy. I'm so sorry. So very sorry."

Tears burned down her cheeks.

"Ashley? Is it really you?" His voice cracked.

"Yes, Daddy. I'm here." She nudged him to stand. "Can you walk?"

He leaned into her but stood. "Yes. To get out of here. Yes."

She bent down to hoist her mother onto her shoulder.

"Is she...?" Her dad's voice caught on a gasp.

"No."

"Thank God." He inched forward, grabbing at boxes as they moved toward the stairs. "If your mother could see you now."

"She'd kill me for carrying her like this."

Dad cracked a smile.

The weight of the world lifted a little.

Sirens in the distance lit a fire under her. They had to get out of this house before Keith snuck back and had them all.

"Grab the rail, Dad. We have to get out of here."

His turtle pace set every impatient nerve ending on fire. The full weight of her unconscious mom dragged her down.

But she had to get out.

They gained the basement door, Ashley's radar on high alert. "Hang on, Dad. Stop."

She adjusted her mom's limp form on her shoulder and paused to listen for an ambush.

Nothing but sirens.

The most welcome sound of all.

Ashley nudged her dad. "Okay. Let's go."

They made it to the back door.

And into the barrels of a dozen black guns.

∽

Patrick froze as the SWAT team aimed at Ashley's head. A Shipshe-wana cop tightened the hold he had on Patrick's arm.

There Ashley stood in the back door of the stone home, one hand on her father's bloodied arm, the other holding tight onto her mother's ragdoll form.

Oh, God, no. Please. They couldn't be too late.

"My parents need ambulances." Ashley's voice sent ice splinters flying. "Tell me they've been called."

She stepped forward and laid her mom in the grass. The SWAT guys were nothing but a pack of annoying gnats. "Get an ambulance!" She glared down the men with guns.

Marshal Taylor rounded the house, part bull, part 007 control. "Ambulances are on their way." He motioned to the black vested, heavily armed men, including the one holding Patrick in a vise grip. The men stood down.

"I should let them haul you away." Taylor knelt by Mrs. Walters's side, across from Ashley.

Patrick rushed to her dad's tilting side. "I've got you, sir."

"Patrick. I knew you'd be here." He helped Mr. Walters to the ground.

Ashley smoothed the hair away from her mother's face. "Do what you have to do, sir. I had to follow my gut."

"And not tell me until you were already in the house. It could have been a trap." His words landed like blows.

"I was willing to take the risk." She met Taylor's narrowed eyes. "Sir, he would have killed my parents to get to me. I couldn't let that happen."

More sirens split the commotion surrounding them. Paramedics rushed into the fray and took over.

Ashley stumbled back. Patrick was there to catch her.

Marshal Taylor joined them. "You belong in the back of a squad car. But you can accompany the ambulance." He motioned one of the cops over. Winslow. "Corporal Winslow will stick by your side."

Great.

But Adam's eyes held no malice. His body language remained all business, no hint of barely controlled rage for evading him.

Ashley's eyes stayed glued to the men working on her parents. "Thank you, sir."

Marshal Taylor studied Ashley's now shaking form. "Winslow, fill her in when you get there."

"Yes, sir."

"Did you apprehend Keith?"

"No." Marshal Taylor stood like a statue. "He has Margo."

Chapter Twenty-nine

Ashley slammed her hand into the hospital corridor's sterile wall.
Once.

Twice.

Patrick intercepted the third time. "You'll be in an ER bed unable to help your parents…or Margo if you keep that up."

Ashley jerked away and hugged her ribs, holding in the scream that clawed for release. *Why, God? Why Margo? Why couldn't this nightmare be over?*

If the police didn't play this whole situation razor-edge perfect, her best friend would end up like her parents.

Or worse.

She'd risked it all to rescue her parents. She'd never get away again to help Margo. And Keith would dispose of Margo at the first hint that they wouldn't allow Ashley on scene.

Patrick wrapped his arms around her. "We did what was best, babe. Your parents will recover."

"After years of counseling, maybe."

"Good thing I have connections to some great ones."

She cracked a smile for Patrick's sake. And wrapped her arms around his strong and solid form, drawing strength for the upcoming nightmare now gnawing her soul.

She spotted Winslow's black shoes before she heard them. Any hope she had of helping Maggie fled. She couldn't even hear a huge cop in a hospital hallway. What good was she now?

"Drink up. You both need it." Winslow extended two steaming brown cups.

"Thank you." Ashley warmed her hands around the base of her cup, still leaning into Patrick's strength. The ER nurse had wanted to treat her for shock. She'd refused, holding out hope she'd be allowed back in the field. All she wanted was to talk to Keith. Convince him not to kill Maggie.

"Docs said your parents can have company soon. They're almost done."

Yeah. Stitching up lacerations. Cleaning and bandaging and monitoring for internal damage.

Her stomach pitched. This wasn't the end she'd envisioned.

"Your dad is a great guy. Sense of humor even after all he's been through." Winslow settled against the wall next to her.

"Yeah." Tears threatened again. She was too tired to swipe them away.

"We'll find Margo."

"How?"

"I care about her too, Ashley." Adam hung his head. "Nowhere near what you feel, I get that. But still…"

A shudder tore through her. "Then let me call Keith. He'll tell me where he is if I say I'll meet him."

"Neither Marshal Taylor nor the GBI will authorize anything of the sort. You have to know that."

"He'll kill her if the cops move in and refuse to let him speak to me. I know he will."

"How certain are you?"

"One hundred percent." Ashley pushed off from the wall. "And we all know the ticking clock is never on our side with a kidnapping. Ever."

∽

Patrick stood apart from the frantic tableau in front of him.

The conference room table sprouted wires and maps and all manner of manuals and tactical gear. The men seated or standing around it, all tense and vigilant.

Ashley glared them down in turn, pushing ahead with her case, pleading for their understanding.

Adam was a pushover compared to Marshal Taylor, and it'd taken Ashley more than thirty minutes to convince Adam to take them back to the police department. Before that they'd spent time with Ashley's parents, and she'd promised she'd return as soon as she could.

Not a word about Margo or Chester to Randall or Jacquelyn.

Which meant Ashley believed Chester was already dead, or…

Patrick was beyond guessing at Keith's bizarre behavior.

"He will kill her." Ashley jammed her fists on her hips.

Marshal Taylor, a bulldog of a SWAT commander, and the older hostage negotiator all studied the lone female officer in the room. GBI Special Agent Jim Edwards shook his bald head.

The cool air and hot tensions whipped around them.

"Look, I understand I have no role in this situation and am here only because of Agent Edwards's and Marshal Taylor's discretion."

"Which I'm questioning every minute."

Patrick braced for explosion.

Ashley returned to his side. "But I know Keith. I'm his whole reason for living. Read the file that law enforcement from three different states and multiple departments have compiled. It's all there."

Marshal Taylor scrubbed his buzz cut hair. "There is no way I'm allowing a loose cannon like you, Walters, to insert yourself into this situation."

"If I don't at least talk to Keith, he'll choose his own gun or death by cop. But he'll take Margo with him. Ask Patrick. He's a licensed counselor."

Patrick waited, his mind racing with what facts or credentials he could offer to tilt the scale in Ashley's favor.

"I'm positive Patrick's opinion is in no way biased." Taylor closed his eyes. "Sorry, Patrick. Please, go ahead."

Patrick hesitated a moment before speaking. "We've spent the day running toward trouble, and I know, disregarding orders to stay in a contained situation."

"Twice."

"But Ashley's presence on scene resulted in the locating and rescuing of her injured parents. As dehydrated and drugged as they were, waiting any longer than we did could have cost them their lives."

Ashley tensed. He had to lay it out straight if they had any hope of resolving this standoff with the clock.

"Keith Holberg has spent the better part of twelve years stalking Ashley. Documenting her every move. Learning everything about her family and friends. He's not a man deterred from his plans or his fantasy." The words burned all the way through Patrick. "Ashley's not being as emotional as you suspect. It's my opinion, based on our knowledge of Keith and what we've seen today, that Ashley is the key to his thin hold on reality. If you shut her out, Keith will implode."

The SWAT commander broke eye contact and rubbed his clean-shaven face. "If someone has eyes on her at all times, I'll concede her presence at the scene. But..." His steel gaze locked onto Ashley. "I will not hesitate to tackle you myself and haul you off to jail if you try to interfere. Again."

Ashley met his rigid posture. "Understood."

The hostage negotiator leaned forward. "I've listened to the last sounds of life through a telephone connection more times then I care to recount. This Holberg has likely not slept in days, could be using a spectrum of pharmacopoeia, and is delusional to the point that any poking of that fantasy could cause his rapid deterioration."

Pretty much what Ashley had just said with fewer words. But this guy had the clout to get things done.

Agent Edwards gathered the paperwork in front of him. "As lead investigator, I'm in agreement that if we want to find Miss Kinsley before any harm befalls her, we should allow Officer Walters to make her phone call."

Ashley collapsed back into her chair. She'd won this battle.

Patrick squeezed her hand. But what would it cost her in the end?

∽

Ashley griped Patrick's cell phone with sweaty hands. Everything rested on this one call.

Maggie's life.

The SWAT and hostage negotiators. The GBI agents and the DA investigator. They might handle death daily, but even they couldn't escape the consequences. If they witnessed a homicide and death by cop today, their lives would never be the same.

Neither would Patrick's.

Or hers.

Right now hers mattered least of all. Still, she had to get this call right. She punched in the last number Keith had used to contact her.

His phone rang.

And rang.

Every ring jangled her nerves.

"Ashley, my love. I trust you're well. I haven't seen you today. Pity."

She hated his gravel-filled voice, the slick words. The delusion she had to play to. "I'm sorry about that, Keith. I tried to get away to meet you."

"I know you did."

"Can I have a second chance?" The bitter appeal stung her mouth.

"Your best friend has continued to ruin my plans. I'd really like to be done with her. Your parents weren't this uncooperative."

Ashley's breath caught. Maggie was still alive. She had to keep her that way. "Please. Don't hurt Maggie. I need my best friend at my wedding."

"Yes. Yes, I figured you'd feel that way." His voice echoed. An empty house? A barn? Where was he?

"Can I talk to her?"

"No. That would not be wise. She's dressed for the wedding and is a bit nervous. I think we should move up the sunset nuptials and proceed with the wedding, don't you?"

"Where? I can be there fast."

"I have your dress, Ashley. I'm sorry I had to see it before our big day, but I knew you had to leave in a hurry to draw the police away from me. Thank you for that."

He had her wedding dress? How much deeper could his violation go? Acid churned in her empty stomach.

This time she waited for him to answer her question. If he even remembered it.

"Margo looks stunning in her bridesmaid dress, just like you said. I do hope you'll come soon, my love. I can't wait much longer."

"Tell me where and I'm on my way."

The police officers listening in held their collective breath.

"I cannot wait to see you, my love. I can hardly believe I'll have you in my arms before sunset today."

In his dreams.

"Yes, well. Head to Goshen via US-20. Turn left onto Indiana 13. Be careful or you'll miss it. I so wish we could have married at your church in Atlanta. Eric would have loved that."

She'd claw his eyes out.

Patrick pulled her close. Only his strength and Margo's life kept her from spewing every vile thought in her head.

"When you find Indiana 4, turn right. Our wedding destination will be down the first road to your right. Margo and I will be waiting for you. Oh, and Ashley? Do not allow Patrick to join us. Do you understand?"

"Yes."

"I trust your parents are feeling better at the hospital now. Dreadful what the damp night air up here can do to an old person's constitution. I had hoped you'd bring them to the wedding with you."

Patrick squeezed her hand.

"I will see you soon, my love." He inhaled low and long. "I should not have to tell you this, but your police friends are not invited. The first sign of them, I shoot Chester. At the second, I shoot Margo."

The phone line went dead.

∾

Keith stared out the front windows, his hands trembling with anticipation.

Margo stood granite still at the center of the abandoned farmhouse's bay window. Her beautiful blue dress covered in sweat stains. Her arms and legs still bound. Her mouth still covered.

Their relationship benefited from strong tape.

Candles lit what used to be a dining room area behind them. Rose petals covered the floor. In the back bedroom, Ashley's dress and red Vino Rosso bouquet awaited her.

Chester barked uncontrollably from the backseat of Keith's rental car. Ashley must be near.

That or the stupid mutt was intent on ruining the day.

He would show the mangy animal. The one who tried to bite him every time he offered it a bit of food. Outside was good enough for the dog. Cleaner too without the mutt's fur all over the place.

Plus, he had a perfect shot should any police pop up from the surrounding fields.

But they would not. Ashley wouldn't allow them.

Keith picked up one of his favorite weapons. The simple but effective handgun that had almost ended Patrick James's life.

Too bad he had missed. Ashley would have been his much sooner.

Today Patrick would not be in attendance for the real wedding. The one Ashley had dreamed about since high school.

If he showed his face, he would die.

Keith's phone rang.

"Hello, Ashley, dear. I see you've arrived." She crouched in the field across the street from his newly acquired farmhouse. "No Patrick. Very wise of him. And now all the pieces are in place. Come in the back door. Your dress is waiting for you in the bedroom to your right. Do hurry."

"I want to see Margo."

"She will stand at your side for the wedding."

Ashley hesitated. He hated that. Her one flaw. Not speaking her mind. Had she done that years ago, he would have swept her out of the deep depression she'd fallen into after her brother's death.

"I'll come in only when Margo is released."

Playing hard to get. He liked that. She wanted him all to herself.

Chester's howling split the serene evening.

"Is that Chester?"

"Yes. He's in the car."

Ashley gasped. "He'll suffocate. Let me at least open a door."

If he died before this day ended, so much the better.

"No. Wedding first. Unimportant details later."

Ashley hesitated again. His nerves stood at attention.

"Stand up for me, my love. I want to see you."

No answer.

"Ashley, you must learn to obey me right away. If I tell you what to do, you must do it. Do you understand?"

"Yes."

"Stand up."

Ashley rose from the field. Her long black hair waved in the breeze. She'd grown from a captivating teen into an exquisite woman. His bride to be.

Chester's howling played a discordant background to his big day.

"Come inside now, Ashley."

She stood her ground. "Please come outside with Margo. An outdoor wedding is what I've always wanted. You know that, right?"

He hated the lesson she must experience on her wedding day. He nudged the curtains aside a fraction on the open window to his left.

Chester's crate came into sharp view.

He fingered the trigger.

CHAPTER THIRTY

Sweat poured down Ashley's back. The Kevlar vest didn't help matters any. But it could keep her alive. If she played this day right.

If she played according to the new Elkhart County Emergency Services Unit in addition to the Indiana State Police and the Northeast Indiana SWAT team and her GBI handler's instructions. Any more alphabet soup agencies and she risked mental overload.

As if waiting outside a stalker's hideout wasn't already pushing her beyond the breaking point.

GBI Agent Jim Edwards's words ricocheted through her brain, *"Do as I say. Say only what the trained hostage negotiator says. Stay alive."*

He was like the little angel of light on her right shoulder. Only Edwards barked commands into her earpiece with a mouth no angel would dare.

A SWAT takedown team was in position and sniper teams had fanned out and circled the abandoned farmhouse, standing guard over a lonely stretch of road. They hid in tall grasses. Massive trees.

She never saw them. Only sensed their presence.

Patrick waited in a house a quarter mile down the street. Safe.

"Ask him again about the outdoor wedding." Alan Reeves's butter smooth voice filled her earpiece.

It was her idea to push for an outdoor wedding. She didn't need this hostage negotiator calling her shots.

Shaking hands told a different story. She wiped one, then the other on her sweat shorts, the silent phone still death-gripped in her left hand.

All her plans. All the waiting. All the fear. All the faith she'd claimed in herself. And here she stood, poised to save a life and she couldn't stop the shaking.

"Ask him. Keep him talking. We need a visual."

Her cotton-filled mouth wouldn't cooperate.

Chester howled.

The unmistakable rack of a weapon's slide sounded over the phone line.

Please, God. No. "Keith? Please talk to me. I need to hear your voice." Her stomach roiled at the lies spewing forth. At the reason for the lies.

God, where are You?

Silence answered her from all sides.

"Keith, please. Talk to me." Ideas zipped through her brain like bullets. "I'm afraid I'm going to faint. Wedding day jitters. Talk to me, Keith. Tell me it will be okay."

His ragged breath stood the hairs on her neck at attention. As if he hovered right behind her. Ready to pounce.

She had to keep her head.

Come out of this alive.

With Maggie. With Chester.

"Keith, please. You don't want to do this." Was his weapon pointed at Maggie? She was too far away to make out any details. Keith hid in the shadows. The gray day and threatening blackness overhead didn't help one bit.

"I'm sorry, my love." Keith steeled his voice. "But I must teach you a lesson. One I hope you never forget."

"Hold your position." Another man telling her what to do. The SWAT commander yelled again. "Do not engage. Do you hear me? Do not engage."

Her ears rang.

Time stood still. Her vision tunneled.

Her badge on the line. Her friend's life in the balance.

Chester. Her eyes found her trusting boxer. His chestnut form slammed against the top of the crate. His howls grew in volume.

Keith would shoot Chester first. In that split second, she could create a diversion and maybe save Maggie's life. If she was fast enough, maybe help Chester too.

If it wasn't too late.

Indecision froze her to the spot. Risk death to provide a distraction? Risk her entire career? Maggie's life?

All at once, fire filled her.

Seconds raced.

Stretched.

Her muscles burned.

This ended now.

Patrick held his breath and clamped his hands around the binoculars. Officers barked orders all around him—an angry beehive of movement. Controlled chaos.

His eyes stayed glued to Ashley's statue in the field.

His mind replayed the sickening sound of a racked gun that had blared through the command post and Ashley's desperate voice.

Keith's deranged answer.

No, Ash. Don't move. Please, God. Don't let her die.

No other words. No other thoughts. Nothing.

Everything focused on Ashley. On the next second.

Then déjà vu.

God, You could stop this!

But He did not.

Ashley ran across the street. Crouched.

A flash of activity at the farmhouse window.

A black muzzle. "He's going to shoot her!"

Patrick couldn't look away.

He couldn't think.

Keith fired.

The explosion rocked Patrick to the core. And the bullet tore through the rental car in the farmhouse driveway. But he couldn't locate Ashley. Where was she? Why couldn't he find her? Was she hit?

Silence washed over him. Pressed in on him. Dead silence.

Cops shouted in the background. Barked orders. But nothing registered in his brain.

Where was Ashley?

"Return fire." The SWAT commander's iron order sliced into Patrick.

"No! Ashley's out there. You can't shoot! You'll kill her." Patrick fought against the bile rising in his throat.

Granite hands clamped down on his arms. "Sit down. Stay out of the way." Marshal Taylor turned back to the monitors and wires filling a makeshift desk.

Patrick shot up again, binoculars back in place.

He'd find Ashley.

But what his eyes landed on sickened him into silence.

Ashley raced across the street. But she was too late. The bullet tore through the rental car door and found its mark.

Chester's horrifying yelp gargled in his throat and died.

She slid to a stop and tried to get a bead on Keith. But he'd slipped into the shadows, and she couldn't risk hitting Margo. The snipers would take Keith down. She'd given them a needed diversion.

Now she had to help Chester. She threw open the door, and heat blasted her face. The acrid tang of blood slammed into her next.

Sniper bullets singed the air. Her mind added twenty bullets to each bullet fired, jacking her heart rate higher and higher.

She attacked the metal crate lock. "Don't die, Chester. Don't die on me."

She snatched his still form from the crate and crumpled into a ball, as small as she could go. Chester whimpered in her arms. His blood soaked into her shorts.

They huddled by a tire. No place to go. No good place to stay. One shot could pierce the wheel and end her life.

"Take your shot." The SWAT commander's voice boomed over her earpiece.

They'd missed the first time.

Another sniper fired.

The sound of ripping metal. Boards splintering.

But no human sound. No Margo screaming.

Thank You, God.

No Keith shrieking in pain either.

Chester's breathing slowed.

Please, God. Don't do this to me. Don't take his life to show me I failed. I should have waited. I should have listened.

Foxhole confessions melted into tears and inaudible groans.

In the silence, reason snapped her back to sanity. She had to get out of there. Had to let the police handle the rest. But she couldn't let them risk their lives to save hers. She had to get away. Get to safety.

Empty farmland on both sides of the road surrounded her.

Correction. One lone barn on the same side of the road stood halfway between her and safety.

Could she make it there without drawing fire?

Would Keith kill her?

What about Maggie?

The impossible questions knotted a blazing rope of fear around her.

Think!

She was a cop. She'd trained for situations like this. But it wasn't the same when it was her family with guns to their heads. Her beloved pet dying in her arms. Her life shattered by one stupid split-second decision.

Or a series of foolish choices.

Get to safety now. Get Chester help. Deal with the consequences later.

She could do this.

"Hang on, Chester."

He didn't move. But he still breathed. She had to get out of there now.

Setting her eyes on the barn, she crouched into a run.

Burning legs. Bent back. Leaden arms.

Wind rushed past as she flew to the barn.

Voices whipped at her ears.

Staying low, she raced around the front of the barn and collapsed into the hot wood side.

Nothing moved. No sirens. No ambulance. No gunfire.

Was it over?

She couldn't take that chance.

Back in a crouch, sweat pouring down her back, she rushed forward again. Zigzagging through the tall green grasses. The farmhouse shrank into the distance, moving farther and farther away.

Still she pushed on. She had to make it there.

Keep running. One foot forward. Duck and run one way. Stay down and run the other.

The makeshift brick command center grew closer this time. She locked onto the far corner of the drab brick. Bolting for safety, she clutched Chester tight.

Arms reached out for her, pulling her into the house. Pulling Chester away from her.

"Of all the harebrained, stupid…" Blazing curses filled the front room. A Mac truck form loomed over her. Edwards. "So help me, I will…" More flaming words.

She shot to her feet. "I gave you a window. You had a visual. You missed the open door I gave you."

"You defied orders." Edwards's hot breath scorched her face.

Patrick stepped in between. "Sir, she's in shock."

No, she had full command of her faculties now. And because of that she clamped her mouth closed, allowing Patrick to pull her away.

"Are you hurt?" He moved ice-cold hands down her arms, her sides.

"No. He shot Chester. I had no chance to return fire."

"I know, Ash. One of the cops has Chester. They've called in a vet. We'll get him help. I promise."

She wiped her hands, the weight of what remained to be done

falling on her like an avalanche. "I have to find out what's happening with Maggie."

She ripped the earpiece from her ear and let it dangle over her dirty black vest. "Has the entry team moved in? Is Margo injured?"

No one met her eyes.

She forced down the emotion clogging her throat. "Has SWAT moved in?"

Edwards faced her. "They tried. Shots were fired."

"Margo?"

"Her scream backed everyone off."

Ashley clenched her fists. She could see it all in black and white. The terror on Margo's face. Keith's filthy hands around her neck. His gun pointed at her temple.

God, what have I done?

"What did she say?"

Marshal Taylor's baritone grabbed Ashley by the throat. "He said he'd kill her and take the rest with him. She begged for them to leave."

"Why didn't a sniper take him?"

"He has a living shield." The SWAT commander bit down hard on words that didn't need a voice to shred her insides.

"Now what?"

The SWAT commander, Blake something, backed down and returned to his seat beside Marshal Taylor. "We wait. Regroup. All our cards are on the table. Holberg's are not. We can't risk the life we're trying to save by rushing in there like last time."

Because of her.

Patrick's cell lay in the muddy field across from the farmhouse. Her dog lay dying in a back room. She'd thrown it all away for a razor's-edge shot at saving both Maggie and Chester.

Patrick tugged on her waist. "Come back here with me. Chester could use some of your fight."

She stepped ahead, her mind and gut hollowed out, her body moving on autopilot. She wasn't cut out for police work. Never enough. Not a protector. A fool. An emotional, inexperienced failure.

"They're in here." Patrick opened a door and nudged her inside. Two men were working over Chester's still form. One cop. A volunteer, off-duty deputy. One of the ones she'd given the slip earlier today. She hadn't cared enough to remember his name.

"I believe he'll make it." The cop flashed her a cautious grin. "This guy's a tough one. A fighter. But he needs to hear your voice."

The other man, dressed in a green golf shirt and tan pants, bent over Chester, never taking his eyes off his work. "I've given him a sedative, but he can still hear you."

She knelt by Chester's head and stroked his sticky fur. "Come on, boy. You have to pull through this. I need you."

"Mike Miller, Shipshe vet. Good thing my favorite golf course is nearby."

His attempt at humor died a silent death.

"Ashley Walters." She stroked her boxer's fur and tried to pray something more substantial than a demand for help. "His name is Chester."

"Well, Chester's a bit of a puzzle to me. Some would call it a miracle. I've only heard of a handful of dogs that pull through a situation like this one."

"But he'll be okay?" She met Patrick's hopeful blue eyes.

The vet pursed his lips and continued stitching. "I'd like to keep him for observation. Treat him for infection. With diligent supervision, he stands a good chance of recovery."

"What happened?"

"Can't tell you one hundred percent that no bones were affected without X-rays, but it appears the bullet passed through his chest webbing and arm webbing. Superficial to his pectoral muscles. Clean exit."

She inhaled a ragged breath. At least she'd have Chester when this nightmare ended. But what about Maggie? *Please, God. Protect Maggie.*

What if this nightmare never truly ended?

The front room scrambled into activity. "We got him on the line! Walters, get in here!"

She rushed into the chaos of cops. Edwards, in all his GBI glory, smiled. "You got another shot at redemption." He pointed to a cell phone resting on what was once a coffee table. "Holberg hung up on us again, but you can get him back on the line. He'll talk to you. Draw him out, so SWAT can end this. With no wild card cop going off halfcocked."

Ashley licked her cracked lips. "No flash bangs or SWAT robots to go in instead?"

"My guys have already been shot at enough today." SWAT commander Blake worked his jaw back and forth. "Body armor can't always save you."

Edwards sized her up. "If you can't do this…"

"No. I can."

The older hostage negotiator, Alan somebody. Reeves. Yes, Reeves. Reeves, the calmest cop in the room, held out the phone. "He won't answer my call again. I've had him on the line twice, but as soon as he heard my voice, he demanded you or he'd start shooting."

"He's shot at my recon team after each call." Blake flicked a glare her way. "We need to know where he is so we can get in place for the termination phase."

Ashley snatched the phone, then slowed her fingers. Slowed her breathing.

Nothing else mattered but getting Margo out. Safe.

She made the call. Each unanswered ring chipped at her icy nerves. "Answer it."

No one spoke.

But they moved. Like a well-trained team, every cop on deck worked their job.

"This had better be Ashley." Keith's gravel voice morphed into a snarl. "Or this is the last time I'm answering."

"It's me." Margo squeaked in the background. "Easy, Keith. Please."

"Ashley, my love. You and your friend are still alive only because I believe with all my heart that you want to marry me today. This will happen."

"Yes. Yes, Keith."

Alan Reeves pointed to a list of questions he held high.

"You will not betray me again, my love."

"I understand. I won't." But she would. She had one more chance to redeem this nightmare. She'd do whatever it took.

Reeves waved the list of questions. *Are you okay?* was right at the top. Like she cared if Keith was okay. "Keith? Are you okay? Are you hurt?"

"No, my love. I am waiting for you to come to me."

"Is Margo hurt?"

"Not yet."

"What happens now, Keith?"

No answer.

"Keith? Are you there?"

Seconds ticked by.

Still nothing. Nothing but screaming silence.

Chapter Thirty-one

Keith pulled Margo tighter to his chest as they huddled in an interior room. No windows open. No sound to lead those vicious, gun-wielding madmen to his whereabouts.

His rescue of Ashley had gone so very wrong.

He held the major cause of disruption in his aching arms. "You will not fight me any longer, do you hear me?"

Margo nodded.

Her earlier scream had at least provided breathing room. Made the SWAT fools back off. Now the ample supply of bullets and weapons at his disposal would finish the job.

Soon he would walk out of here a free man. Once Ashley stood at his side. She would make all the uninvited police nuisance go away.

He redialed the number Ashley had called from. He had hated to hang up, but he'd needed time to think. Time to stay on the move. Stay out of sight. Until Ashley learned to obey him at his first command.

A sinking, gnawing thought dragged his energies away from where they were most needed. What if Ashley didn't come?

No. She would come. He had not gone through twelve years of training and preparations for this day to end without a wedding.

Sweat dripped into his eyes. Candle smoke and the bitter smell of gunpowder filled the air with a sickly black, charred ambiance. Not the right atmosphere for a wedding.

He'd run this day over and over in his mind.

Never once did it include a gun battle.

The phone rang and Ashley picked up, a little breathless. "Hello? Keith, you scared me. Are you okay?"

This was why he would fight for Ashley. Fight until the end of the police's reign of destruction. The love of a good woman led a man to triumph.

"I'm fine, my love. Thank you for caring."

"Can you tell me where you are now?"

Still continuing with the questions? The police must have betrayed her too and now held her captive, demanding she extract the information they'd use to kill him.

He could not allow that to happen.

"I am safe, my love. I know you're being held against your will. I will rescue you soon. Free you from the evil men holding you captive."

"How, Keith? There are so many of them."

She sounded terrified. His blood flamed. He should never have left her alone. He should have stayed by her side. "I will wait and use their supposed intelligence and tactical superiority to my advantage."

"I don't understand."

Wouldn't Ashley be thrilled when he told her she no longer had to work as a police officer? She had no reason to continue a job she hated and didn't understand in the least.

"I'll let them come to me. Then finish them off."

"Do you have enough supplies?"

"Yes. I appreciate your consideration. You could bring me more though. I can always use more if they won't go away."

"You know I can't come near." She drew in a quivering breath and lowered her voice. "They won't let me leave."

New scenarios crashed into his brain. They sliced like machetes. Every one ended in him holding Ashley's dying body in his arms, gasping for breath.

He had to think. Reason a new method of attack. He could demand a car or helicopter and leave the police destruction behind. But they wouldn't let Ashley go so easily.

Maybe if the police believed he was softening. Yes. That might buy him some time to prepare for an escape.

"I'm truly sorry about Chester. It was not my intent to end his life."

Ashley sniffled. "I know you didn't mean it. I understand that now."

He waited in a coiled silence.

Margo squirmed.

"Do not make me shoot you limb by limb."

"No! Don't hurt her." Ashley inhaled and exhaled. "I…I know you wouldn't do that, would you, Keith? You won't harm my best friend?"

"No. Ashley. I'd never do anything to hurt you."

"Can I see Margo? I need to be sure she's okay. With all the excitement of the day, she might need medical treatment, Keith. She's not as strong as she appears."

This was true. "She is fine. Anxious for the wedding to get underway."

"Please let me see her."

Ashley was far too focused on her best friend. She should be focused on him alone. His instincts gnawed at him to consider the possibility Ashley would try to trade her life for Margo's. A sacrifice of love. But a foolish one.

"Come out where I can see you, my love." That would get her away from the police. A frisson of pleasure shot through him. "Tell the police to send you out with some food. I'm looking at Margo and it appears she will pass out soon without nourishment."

"Yes. Yes, I'll talk to them. Give me some time, okay? I'll call you right back."

All he needed was one good look at Ashley. He'd gauge her true motives. Prove to himself that his suspicion was unfounded.

Or else his sad smile would be the last her eyes would see.

Patrick stood outside the wall of blue surrounding Ashley.

"I can do this."

Agent Edwards shook his stoic head. "No way. You've already shown you can't be trusted in close quarters. We'll send another agent with food and a delivery team. Approach from the front."

The SWAT commander bristled. "I say when my men go or stay. And I'm not willing to risk this. This stalker is higher than a kite on his own adrenaline. He'll shoot whoever shows up."

"Unless it's me."

Patrick breeched the blue wall and grabbed Ashley's arms. "Stop, Ash. Let the negotiator take over. You're not thinking straight."

Her foggy eyes cleared. "Patrick. Stay on my side here. I need to go back out there. If I don't, Keith will shoot Maggie and all our work today will be for nothing."

"I'm on the side of those trying to keep you alive."

An explosion of gunfire dragged his attention outside.

"Officer down." The radio crackled. "Officer down!"

SWAT members sprang into action.

Patrick pulled Ashley out of the scramble. "It's almost over. They'll go in and finish this off now. He's gone too far. Threatened too much. Surely they'll move in now and end it."

Ashley's jaw muscles popped. "And Maggie will be dead."

He followed her eyes to the front window. Like a kicked-in anthill, black bodies moved at lightning speed and perfect formation toward their injured team member.

He couldn't look away. Couldn't form words.

Gunfire reverberated through the room.

"Pull back now! Get out of there!" The SWAT commander's sheen of confidence broke.

The black antlike forms retreated, a body in tow. And then nothing. No movement outside.

Chaos inside. Police pulled the wounded man into the command post and worked over him to staunch the bleeding. The SWAT commander bellowed orders into his mouthpiece. "Get an ambulance here. Now!"

Patrick rushed over to help, releasing the wounded man's headgear so he could breathe.

"Guy's got an arsenal." The injured cop was a kid. Sweat poured down his blotched skin and into his wide-open eyes.

Patrick eased his head down to the floor. "Tell me what you saw."

Twice in the span of a week, he'd knelt next to a bleeding man and tried to keep him talking as other more experienced professionals tried to save his life.

"Black in there. Smoky." The kid's face contorted. His shallow breaths came more rapidly. "No sightline to fire. No hostage in view."

"Okay. Okay. Tell me your name."

"Danny."

"Okay, Danny. Tell me about your family."

"My wife is Darcy. We have a little girl, Daria. She's two." Danny's breathing slowed down.

His abdominal bleeding did not.

Sirens pierced the chaos. "The paramedics are here, Danny. Hang on, okay? They'll take good care of you."

Danny's dark eyes followed Patrick across the room.

But soon Patrick's view filled with men and women in uniform starting an IV, taking over for the officers still wanting to save their friend.

He reached for Ashley's hand.

But she wasn't there.

He searched the back of the living room where SWAT team members conferred.

No Ashley.

He rushed to the door after the paramedics.

No Ashley.

A tanned hand grabbed his bicep. "It was the only way, Patrick. I'm sorry."

Patrick stared into Marshal Taylor's steady eyes and found no comfort there.

They'd sent his fiancée into the hands of a deranged killer.

∽

Ashley's hands hung steady at her side.

Her breathing regulated. In and out. In and out.

Her focus the white farmhouse five hundred feet ahead of her.

Mud streaked her bare legs. Chester's dried blood still clung to her vest and running shorts.

But she could do this.

She had to.

"Stick with your slow approach." Edwards chimed in her earpiece.

A delivery team approached, hidden, matching her step for step. Surrounding her on all sides.

Blake Tucker's voice cut in. "Stop at the barn. That includes you, Walters." The SWAT commander took no confidence in her show of bravado earlier.

Neither did she.

"Yes, sir."

But she had to do this for Maggie. One last hope of securing her survival. One very large possibility this would be Ashley's last day on earth.

The plan buzzed around her brain. Simple steps. Far easier to think than do.

The cell phone burned in her hand.

She ducked behind the barn and rested her stiff back against the solid wood.

"Time to call." Edwards again. She would not miss his domineering drawl.

She punched in the numbers and hit the call button.

Wind whistled through the tall grasses. Heat encircled her and wound around her chest.

"Ashley, my love. Did you see what I did for you? I believe this is almost over. We will be married today after all."

Slick slime oozed from his words. Pure evil. His excitement drained hers.

"Yes, I saw it all, Keith." She forced fake joy into her words, forcing down the burning bile in her gut at the same time.

"Come to the back porch. Your dress will be waiting there."

She slipped to the far side of the barn and peeked around the corner. Sure enough, a white sheath flapped in the breeze.

Her wedding dress. Once a symbol of undying love and joy. Now a prop in a psychotic play, featuring her in the starring role.

"I see that. I can't wait to put it on." Lying tinged her tongue like battery acid. "Then where will we go? The house must be trashed."

By bullets that almost killed a fellow officer.

She had to turn off all thoughts. Become steel like the other cops sitting in the command post, eyes glued to her performance.

"I will meet you in the back, my love."

"An outside wedding? The one I've always dreamed of?"

"I would do anything to make you happy."

She couldn't ask about Margo again without risking Keith's ire. *God, I can't do this. I wanted to be the hero, but my feet won't move forward. Today's not a good day to die.*

No. Not for her. Not for Margo. One last Hail Mary attempt for the end zone. Strange the thoughts flying through her brain.

"I'm coming, Keith."

"No request to see your petulant best friend?"

Ashley checked the desperation boiling inside. "She'll stand by me for my wedding. That's all I need to know." An idea arrowed through her. "Can Margo assist me with my dress? She's the only one who's been able to handle the buttons at the back."

Only his breathing filtered over the line.

"Keith? I just want to look perfect for you."

Her earpiece came to life. "Good. Good move. We're in position. You have a green light."

She held the phone away from her. No way could Keith hear that she was miked.

"Yes, Ashley. I will allow you to unbind Margo when you arrive. If…"

She held her breath.

"If you both cooperate with full sincerity. Something I'm not sure I can depend on anymore. You have so much to learn, Ashley. But we will have years to repair the damage you've done today."

His twisted fantasy slammed against the lies she already fought.

The damage you've done.

The damage you've done.

She had to still the singsong taunt, the breath of an enemy bent on destroying her. Keith had crawled into her head.

Time to dislodge the slithering snake.

"Come, Ashley, my love. Come to your wedding feast."

"Yes. I'm coming, Keith." She left the phone line open, but slipped the cell into her running shorts. She couldn't stand one more gravel-filled, poison-laced word.

"Proceed slow and steady." Marshal Taylor's compassion tinged voice spurred her on.

As if she were gliding down the aisle of a church, she forced a smile onto her face.

Margo's blonde head peeked out of the back door.

Her blue eyes locked onto Ashley's.

Go back, Ash. Turn around. Margo's mouth moved, but no sound escaped.

She stepped up the first step of the back porch.

Keith's black-smeared, muscled arm snaked around Margo's red neck. Tears traced each other down her cheeks.

Peace settled over Ashley's heart. An unfamiliar, beyond-comprehension peace. Not the cold of stepping into battle.

"Can I…" Ashley gentled her voice. "Can I please take off her duct tape now?"

"Yes, my love. I'm so glad you're finally where you were meant to be."

He was still hidden by the sturdy doorframe. Guarded by Maggie's trembling body. And now Ashley's.

She stepped up another step. And another. Until she could touch Maggie.

"Do hurry, Ashley. It's almost sunset after all."

The gray sky spit rain.

"Maggie, remember that pitcher you tried to buy for me at Lambright Woodworking?" She freed a corner of duct tape at the edge of her friend's mouth. "How I said it would be a perfect wedding gift?"

Confusion lit Margo's eyes.

Ashley yanked off the tape.

Margo started to scream.

"Oh, no, dear Margo." Keith covered her mouth. "I will not listen to that screech again."

Ashley moved to Maggie's wrists. Blood and bruises marred the surface.

"When we're done here, I hope you'll find that pitcher. The one I almost dropped. Remember that one?"

Recognition unclouded Maggie's blue eyes.

Ashley peeled the clear tape, taking skin with it. "I'm so sorry."

Margo blinked and more tears fell.

Ashley held her breath. It was almost time.

The splintering wood under her creaked.

Seconds stretched.

Her vision tunneled and her whole world became Maggie's eyes. Keith's forehead.

"Come now, Ashley. We have a—"

Ashley ripped the last of the tape off and jerked Margo down to the floor with her.

A crashing thud.

Scrambling to cover Maggie's shaking body.

The air humming with incoming fire.

Straight and true, the sniper's bullet found its mark.

CHAPTER THIRTY-TWO

Ashley held tight to Maggie's right hand, unwilling to let her best friend out of her sight. A female medic checked Margo's condition and poked and prodded her friend as the ambulance sped down the country roads.

"Ash, stop watching the monitors. I'm okay." She winced. "At least I will be okay. Soon. Once I'm out of the ER."

"Ma'am, I need to start an IV. I can't get a vein on this side." The bossy brown-haired medic loosened Ashley's fingers, one by one.

"I'm fine, Ash. You made sure of it." Maggie's blue eyes overflowed with tears.

Ashley's did not. "I never should have dragged you into this. He…" She bit down on the words that didn't need saying.

Maggie would have so much to work through in the coming months. But she was alive. Ashley had accomplished the task set before her and managed to rescue Maggie after all. Nothing else could come against them that compared to the day she'd survived today.

At the hospital, Maggie was wheeled away where Ashley couldn't follow. She stood in the drizzling rain. Every nerve ending dull and lifeless.

"Ashley!"

She jumped at the male voice. Her heart raced once again. Her hand flew to her gun even as her mind screamed at her to stop. The nightmare was over.

Adam jogged into view. "Patrick's right behind me. Did they say anything about Margo's condition?"

"No."

"Come on, let's go inside. Get you cleaned up. You look—"

"Don't. I can't take any more flattery today." An attempt at a smile fell flat. She just couldn't muster it.

"You know there are reams of paperwork." He patted the duffel bag flung over his shoulder. "I brought extra pens for you."

"Ha-ha."

Adam cupped her elbow and steered her toward the waiting room. "You were amazing today. Rescuing your parents. Stepping into the sights of a delusional stalker. Cool and steady, that's what you were. I don't know many cops who could have pulled that off with such finesse."

"Then you need better friends, Adam."

Patrick rushed into the ER waiting room and stopped, his dull blue eyes scanning the crowd. The second his gaze landed on her, his face lightened. At least he wasn't yelling at her like she deserved.

"I love you, Ashley Renee Walters." He wrapped his arms around her and pulled her tight to his chest.

Tears threatened. "I love you too."

When he pulled back, she studied his face. Dried blood streaked his cheek. New lines appeared at the corners of his eyes and mouth.

Until right this second, she hadn't given enough thought to what today had cost Patrick. What he had witnessed. What he would say about her job now. How could he still choose to marry a cop?

Adam cleared his throat. "I'll leave you two alone." He held out the duffel bag. "But I suggest getting into a restroom soon. You could both use some cleaning up."

She could only imagine.

Patrick smiled. "I don't have any idea what he's talking about."

"You wouldn't. And I love you for it." She unzipped the duffel. Her jeans, a clean GCPD T-shirt, and a washcloth called her name. A hairbrush too. Adam's sister must have helped him pack this bag. Or Debra. A lifetime had unfolded since she'd laid eyes on Debra this morning.

Had it really been only this morning?

Every second of it crashed in on her again.

"Don't, Ash. Don't relive it."

As if that would keep the specters at bay. "Adam packed you some clothes too. The guy thought of everything."

He grabbed shorts and a T-shirt from the bag. "Hope he and Margo work out. It'd be good for both of them."

Or else Maggie would fight her demons alone.

Ashley sped into the bathroom and jerked to a stop in front of the mirror. How had they allowed her to leave the scene?

Ashen face.

Sunken eyes.

Blood in her hair.

Her hands itched to yank out the stained tresses. Keith's blood.

She flooded the sink with water, trying to scrub away all traces of evil that horrible man had left. But she couldn't scald the stain off her soul.

The memories of his words. And hers. The pictures of her parents bound and gagged. Maggie bruised and bleeding. Snapshots of terror that time wouldn't erase.

"*Come now, Ashley. The damage you've done. The damage you've done.*"

The words punched her in the gut. Over and over.

She had to get away. Get help. Or today would bury her.

Snatching up the duffel, she tried to calm her ragged breathing. A towel. She needed a towel.

Her hair dripped all over the floor as her feet stalled with indecision.

The bathroom door creaked open. A woman with a crying toddler stopped and blinked at her. "I…are you okay? Do you need me to call someone?"

"No. No. I'm fine." She tightened her hold on the duffel and rushed into the nearest stall.

The lock clicked in place and for a second she could breathe.

Water dripped down her back, ran over her calves.

The washcloth. Of course. She should have remembered it.

The toddler's crying lessened to a sad mewl coming from the hand-icapped stall. Then both mom and toddler disappeared out the door.

Back at the sink, she scrubbed her hair with the washcloth and rinsed it out. Pink tinged water swirled down the drain. A quick scrub of her face, neck, legs, and she retreated back into the stall.

Robot-like calm reigned. She slipped her weapon into the duffel bag, along with filthy shorts and black shirt, socks.

Her jeans raked over her scratched-up legs. But she dismissed the burning. Next came her shirt. Then she ran a brush through her hair.

Back at the mirror, she dared another look.

Normal.

Almost.

Maybe never again.

Patrick catalogued Ashley's every move. Every word. No one else noticed the hollow ring.

He did.

"Mom, you look so much better. The doc says you'll be ready to go home tomorrow." Ashley brushed her mother's dark hair.

"Did you arrest that awful man, honey? Tell me he's behind bars."

Patrick caught Ashley's eye. She shook her head. "Yes, Mom. He's been taken care of. He won't hurt us ever again."

Not a lie. But nowhere near the truth either.

Ashley's dad stirred in the bed next to them. "We're here, Dad." Patrick laid his hand on the groggy man's arm.

"Don't touch me!" Randall scooted to the edge of his bed and jammed his finger into the nurse's call button. "Help! He's going to kill me!"

Tears dripped down Ashley's face.

Two nurses rushed into the room. "Please step back, sir." With that, the taller of the two nurses jerked the curtain closed around Randall's bed.

But not before Patrick caught a glimpse of the huge needle and the fear in Randall's eyes.

"He was going to kill me." Randall's voice quaked. "Is he gone?"

"Yes, sir. You're safe."

No. Not yet. And all Patrick could do was pull Ashley to him as Randall's shaky voice stilled and the room settled back into silence.

Nurse number one stepped from behind the curtain, her face a picture of compassion. "He'll sleep well for a while now, folks."

"And when he wakes up again? What then?" Ashley's words held no fire, no life.

Nurse number two drew the curtain back and avoided Ashley's stare. She turned his way. "We'll put in a call to his doctor. He should be here shortly to answer any questions you all may have."

Ashley turned toward the window.

Jacquelyn's watery eyes followed Ashley.

Patrick collapsed into a chair on the far side of the room, as far from Randall as he could go. He never wanted to cause him that kind of pain again.

"It's not you, dear boy." Jacquelyn reached out a frail hand. "We will get through this with you at our side."

He couldn't even muster a smile.

"Let's talk about the wedding, shall we?" Jacquelyn's green eyes sparked.

"Mom."

"Yes, dear. I'm sorry. I hoped it might cheer everyone up to have something to look forward to."

Jacquelyn was on the right track. But not a wedding. Not even theirs. Maybe they'd talk about that in a week or two. Maybe plan a quiet ceremony at the courthouse.

A knock sounded at the door. Adam stepped in, his eyes downcast. "Mrs. Walters. Ashley. Patrick. Sorry to interrupt."

Ashley's mom turned to Ashley, her face drawn into a question.

"This is Adam Winslow, Mom. A friend of ours. A fellow police officer."

Adam toed the ground.

Patrick sat up straighter. "What's wrong, Adam?"

"Is it Maggie? Is she okay?" Ashley crossed the room in two strides.

Adam blocked her way. "Margo is fine. At least that's what Marshal Taylor said after he talked to her. She's asking for you."

"Okay." Ashley looked from Adam to the hall. "So I'll go see her."

"Well…" The mountain of a police officer shrank in stature.

Patrick's gut tightened. They couldn't handle any more bad news today.

"Spit it out, Adam."

"Ashley's police chief is headed this way with some other GBI bigwigs. There'll be a disciplinary review first thing Monday morning. I thought you should know."

Ashley rummaged through Margo's smallest suitcase. "You're sure your phone is in here?"

"Yes. I've talked to my parents a number of times while you were visiting with your folks and talking to the police." Maggie struggled to sit up in her hospital bed. "And I'm sure Adam placed my cell right where I requested."

They should all be going home tonight. Not staying in the hospital for observation. Not her parents. Not Maggie. But here they were. All three remained tethered to IV fluids due to severe dehydration and shock and a whole host of other things Ashley's mind refused to remember.

At least she was free, not confined to a hospital bed.

Not really free either.

Maggie held out her hand. "I don't need the phone right now anyway. I'll call Candice back in the morning. Would you like to talk to her too?"

And hear all about Candice dropping the charges against her psycho stalker husband? No thanks. Ashley couldn't handle finding a phone, let alone face her failure to make Candice see the truth.

"Please say you'll talk to Candice with me tomorrow."

"Maybe next week or the week after. You need time to recover."

"So do you."

Easier said than done. "Soon I may have plenty of time to stare at my bedroom walls. Depends on how things go at the disciplinary review Monday."

"Come sit with me, Ash. Stop finding things to do to keep your hands busy."

Better to stay busy and ahead of the memories.

"We need to talk. You need to talk."

Ashley squeezed her best friend's hand. "No. You need to rest. Get better soon so we can all go home and put this nightmare behind us."

"Stop running, Ash. Only God can—"

"What? Heal us? Fix what Keith shattered?"

Maggie inhaled and exhaled slow and steady. "Whether you see it now or later, I'm praying you realize what evil attempted to destroy, God protected us from."

And still the tentacles of today's events remained. Might never go away.

Maggie's phone blared the beginning notes of Martin Luther's "A Mighty Fortress Is Our God."

"Really? You changed your ringtone when?"

"Adam changed it for me. That hymn is helping me remember the truth."

Ashley pulled the annoying phone from the outside pocket of Maggie's suitcase. If only a song could fix it all. "It's Candice."

"Talk to her, Ash. Please. For me."

It was a step above talking to Patrick or Maggie about her feelings. Or another doctor about medical treatment she didn't need. Or a police counselor sure to show up any minute now.

With the flick of her finger on Maggie's iPhone, Ashley answered the call. "Hello?"

"Margo? Is that you? Are you okay? I heard the awful news and couldn't stop thinkin' about you and Ashley. I just had to know y'all were okay."

"We're as good as can be expected."

"Ashley? Is that really you?" Candice's racing voice pulled up short.

"Yes. I'm in Maggie's hospital room. She was planning to call you back tomorrow."

"Oh. Good." A long pause. Ashley was too tired to fill the quiet with polite, surface chitchat or a recounting of today. "Well...if you two really are okay, I'll just wait for y'all to call me back tomorrow."

Maggie shook her head.

Exhaustion pulled at Ashley's good sense. She should just say good-bye and hand Maggie the phone. They'd all be better off for it.

Instead, she did what Maggie would do, so Maggie could rest. "No, I can talk for a minute. How are you doing?"

"I'm...well...I should be askin' about you. Are you sure you're okay? You don't sound like yourself."

True. Keith had managed to rip that away too. "I'm fine. I could use some good news though. Tell me how your counseling is going."

"Seriously?"

As long as it was good news, yes. "You know we care about you, right? I care."

"I know." Candice sniffled. "You wouldn't have risked your life if you didn't care."

True. Too bad that hadn't made a difference.

Maggie's mouth moved in silent prayer. Even after all they'd faced, Maggie prayed.

"Ashley?" Candice swallowed hard. "I've been thinking about what you said last time we talked. You know? About how I'd be dead if I got back with Justin again."

"I shouldn't have been so harsh about that."

"But you were right. My counselor said you were a wise friend to tell it to me straight. What you said made me see that I belonged in Kentucky with my family...and Justin belongs in jail."

Yes. Yes, he did. For the rest of his life.

"I...I think I'm gonna stick with this decision this time. Hearing about what happened with you, how you faced your stalker the way you did and saved Margo's life, made me see I can be stronger than I've been. Maybe even as strong as you someday."

As strong as she had been. Once. Before Keith's systematic destruction.

At least she'd helped Candice see the truth after all.

Now if that truth could work for her...

Chapter Thirty-three

Ashley fastened the last button of a borrowed suit early Monday morning. No uniform. No sidearm. Vacant eyes met hers in the mirror. So much for making the truth work for her situation.

How could she trust a God who hadn't walked her through the fire without her getting burned? Thanks to Maggie's note last night that verse in Isaiah had tumbled through her brain all night long.

When you walk through the fire of oppression, you will not be burned up; the flames will not consume you.

She'd walked through fire and been burned. Consumed. Nothing left. How could she trust God now? He hadn't stopped the nightmare. He could have.

Weeks ago, she'd stood before her mirror in uniform and drilled her routine pre-shift questions. Back then she'd answered a confident "yes" to each and every one of them.

Could she stay safe and protect fellow officers and the public? Yes.

Even if it meant using the gun she'd just strapped on? Yes.

But today?

Today her hands shook. Could she do it today? Could she stay safe?

No. A deranged stalker had stolen every bit of her confidence in her ability to remain safe and protect those she loved.

Her parents lay battered and bruised in the Songbird Ridge B&B.

At least they were out of the hospital. Dad was more in his right mind but still so far from healing.

Maggie slept late in her room next door. Equally battered, both inside and out. But still clinging to God and her belief that He had come through for them. Protected them. He'd done what Ashley couldn't do.

And the officer shot in the line of duty Saturday was still in the hospital. Alive. But his recovery would be long and difficult. All because of her.

Even Chester bore the scars from her inability to protect them. He remained at the vet's, struggling to regain lost weight and strength to heal from a bullet wound that should have taken his life.

She turned away from the mirror and stared out the little window she'd used to escape an eternity ago. Then she'd been so sure she could handle it.

But the nightmare had handled her.

And today, she'd face a board of her superiors to determine her future as a police officer.

If today's review progressed to a formal hearing, it would be an open and shut case. She'd disobeyed direct orders and would be charged with obstruction of justice. If found guilty, her badge and sidearm would be stripped from her.

Then Keith's conquest would be complete.

A knock rattled her door. "You ready, hon?" Patrick. She still had Patrick.

"Come on in."

His handsome face and piercing blue eyes begged her to find hope even now. Even if the worst happened today.

But every thought of wedding dresses sickened her. She'd never get through a wedding now. How could she? How could Patrick? Maggie?

From beyond the grave, Keith had won.

A tear slipped down her cheek.

"Ash, don't." Patrick pulled her into his arms. But nothing touched the iceberg filling her chest. "The worst is over. We'll get through today. You'll see. God hasn't abandoned us."

But she had still failed. She'd given her all. Risked everything to save the people she loved. Sacrificed her life and career. But it wasn't enough. Her faith wasn't enough. *She* wasn't enough.

Today she'd stand in front of a group of men saying out loud what she knew in her heart.

Patrick's warm hands cupped her face. "I love you, Ashley Renee Walters. Nothing will ever change that."

"I love you too."

"And nothing on earth, nothing that's happened or will happen can separate us from God's love. From His ability to redeem even this."

She pulled away. "We need to go. I can't be late."

They drove to the Shipshewana Police Department in silence. Patrick probably prayed. She couldn't even form the words. She should thank God for her parents' lives. For Margo's. For Patrick. For the good news about the injured SWAT officer.

But all she could see were the scars.

She entered the quiet police station.

"Officer Walters." Corporal Adam Winslow stood behind his desk, in uniform. "They're waiting in the conference room. If you'll follow me…"

What choice did she have?

Patrick squeezed her hand and whispered in her ear. "You can choose how you face this. Protect your heart and shut down. Or trust that the God who *did* protect us all is still in control."

Choose wisely. Ageless words of wisdom.

Adam held the door open for her. His brown eyes warm and kind.

All the players on the stage of her future stood as she entered.

Montezuma's Police Chief Fisher. His dark eyes smiled. Then his well-lined face emptied of emotion. His hair had grayed more since she'd last been called into his office.

Marshal Taylor stood by Fisher's side. He too met her eyes and nodded. No trace of disdain or approval. Just a long-time cop with weary eyes. She'd added years to those kind eyes.

GBI Agent Jim Edwards softened his features as she passed. Which only served to unnerve her more. She'd have preferred he retain his Mac truck approach to her and the investigation he'd spearheaded.

Of the remaining men, SWAT Commander Blake Tucker, DA Investigator Jack Danson, and Hostage Negotiator Alan Reeves, only her shift commander, Sergeant Sam Culp, had the nerve to smirk. And she could hug him for it.

By the time she'd reached her lone chair facing the line of decorated police officers, her hands no longer shook.

Nothing but numb remained.

These men held her future in their hands. So be it.

A still, small voice poked its way into her heart. No, only One held her future in His hands. Only One.

The One who loved her more than His life.

The One who had stood before powerful men, His future in their hands. Their sins and hers etched all over His whipped and bloody back. His nail-scarred hands.

Maybe she could trust that Man.

As she took her seat, a little of the chill inside thawed.

Marshal Taylor alone remained standing and faced her. "Officer Walters, you understand why we're all in attendance today."

"Yes, sir."

"Every agency representative here has conferred on this case and stayed up to date every step of the way. We've spent the last twenty-four hours in discussion regarding your actions throughout this investigation and on Saturday, the sixteenth of June. We meet today only as a disciplinary review. The result of today's review will determine whether there will be a formal hearing. Do you understand, Officer Walters?"

"Yes."

"Do you still waive your right to legal counsel?"

"Yes."

The conference room door opened, and one man and two women, all in dark suits, entered.

The board members present all shifted seats so she was left facing three strangers. This new, fully impartial board pierced the cold calm of the room.

Maybe she shouldn't have waived legal counsel.

"Officer Walters, I'm Georgia Bureau of Investigations Agent Stan

Sullens. This is Agent Tessa Ramirez…" Agent Sullens motioned to a dark-haired woman in her mid-thirties. "And Agent Rashida Washington." Agent Sullens nodded to the lone woman willing to meet Ashley's eyes with a smile.

Ashley did her best to respond with what she hoped resembled a smile.

Agent Sullens waved in another group of people. Besides Patrick, Ashley didn't expect any of them to come, let alone be allowed entry to these proceedings. But here they were. And she loved them even more for it. Maggie. Her parents. Elizabeth Rey, her shift partner, Detective Rich Burke on crutches, Emma Diggins, and Brad, Anna, and Jonathan Yoder.

Ashley's insides thawed completely.

Whatever the outcome of this meeting, she wasn't alone.

Where Marshal Taylor had stood, Agent Sullens now presided. "My team and I have listened to the testimony of each person present and learned a great deal of your character and commitment, Officer Walters."

She had to remind herself to breathe.

"While the charges you face are serious, obstruction of justice at the forefront, the evidence offered in your favor and the outcome of a perilous hostage situation far outweigh, in our opinion and the opinion of all the officers present, the requirement for a formal disciplinary hearing."

Had she heard that right?

"In addition, based on your cooperation and sacrifice in an intense and fatal SWAT operation, the charges brought against you have been waived."

Ashley blinked against a rush of emotions.

The remainder of official words jumbled with the watery view of family and friends surrounding her, now smiling. Even domineering Jim Edwards and the bulldog of a SWAT commander she'd faced down and disobeyed.

Agent Sullens's final words pierced deep and reverberated through her mind. "You are free to return to duty, pending mandated counseling."

Free.

Free.

Not guilty.

Free.

And for the first time since the nightmare began, she wasn't afraid.

CHAPTER THIRTY-FOUR

S he could do this. She had to do this.

Ashley stood outside Davis Mercantile, her hands sweating. Her jeans hanging loose around her waist. Her stomach in knots.

She had to survive this reentry into life, this outing with family and friends. If not, she'd let everyone down. And if she couldn't handle this, how would she face the rest?

This was only the first of three places she'd face today before she and her family headed home tomorrow. Then there was the wedding...

Patrick kneaded the steel sinews of her neck. "You don't have to do this yet. We can come back. You've already proven your mettle."

"Not to myself. Not yet."

Family and friends crowded around her.

Anna hugged her again. "I am thankful to spend time with you before you return to Montezuma."

"Thanks for being there today, Anna. What you said to that disciplinary board about how I saved your life..." Ashley fought for control. "I know what that cost you to go back into those memories. That day."

Anna shook her gray head, her wise eyes brimming with tears. "A sacrifice to the Lord always costs us something. You have given so much. How could I not give my small portion in your time of need?"

Jonathan, Beth, and Brad followed Anna inside. Brad turned back. "We're going up to the top for lunch and a carousel ride. You'll be there?"

"Yes."

Maggie and Ashley's parents entered together, each kissing her cheek as they passed. All three wore long shirts to cover their scars. They had such a long way to go.

"They'll make it too." Patrick pulled her close.

"I know. I just can't shake..." She followed her mom's example and stood straight, but not stiff. No bowing over for the Walters clan. No hiding reality either.

"The bruises will heal. The scars will fade. The pictures will too. In time."

"And in the meantime?" The mental images from Saturday shot around her brain. They'd kept her awake for days. Fading wouldn't happen soon.

"We find joy wherever we can. In the little things. Laughter. A good meal. An afternoon with friends."

Culp adjusted his leather belt as he approached with Elizabeth.

Ashley hugged them both. "I know I said it all day yesterday, but thank you both for driving all the way up here. For making it possible for Brad to come. For all you've done..."

The rest of her words got stuck in her throat.

Culp stepped back. "Still think admin duty shoulda been your consequence. I have reams of paperwork waitin' at home."

A chuckle escaped. Always the same old Culp. "Maybe I'll help with those."

"Maybe nothin'." He smirked. "So let's go eat. I've been hearin' about all this good A-mish food."

"Especially the peanut butter." Elizabeth ran a hand through her short red hair and grinned. "The Yoders said they'd have some for us before we left."

Such a picture of normalcy. Some things she never wanted to change.

So far, so good. She could handle the rest.

Ashley and Patrick brought up the rear of their huge group. The gun in her ankle holster weighed her down as she stepped into the building.

People brushed by her.

Laughter. Crying. Ringing phones. Footsteps on wooden floors. Music. The scent of salty pretzels and sweet candy. More people pressing in on all sides.

Her senses blazed.

"I think I'm going to be sick."

Patrick wrapped his arm around her again. "Let's go back to the B&B then."

"No." If she didn't walk up those steps by the massive Douglas fir, she'd forever watch over her shoulder, fear snapping at her heels.

Defeat dogging her.

Once again, she wiped her hands down the front of her jeans. *Lord? I'm trying here. I need Your help.*

One step at a time she forced her feet forward. Last time here, she'd raced out the doors with a lumberjack of a man following fast.

She'd survived that.

And kept Candice alive.

Only by the grace of God.

Each step loomed ahead, an icy impassable mountain or a memorial stone of freedom.

She chose freedom.

At the top, her heartbeat a bass drum in her ears, she faced the area where she'd taken down the lumberjack.

Strangers swept by, barely noticing the sweating cop frozen in their midst.

"Ashley, come on!" Brad stood by the huge carousel and waved a token.

Invisible fingers tightened their grip around her arms. A chill spread from shoulder to shoulder and she shivered.

Why was this so difficult? Two weeks ago, none of this would have fazed her. None of it. She'd faced down criminals in the streets and again in court on a regular basis.

Today, she fought to cross a memory to regain her freedom.

But God was here. He would carry her through the recovery as He had the nightmare.

One step at a time, she crossed the honey-colored floor, Brad's youthful brown eyes drawing her forward. He grabbed her hand.

"The first time back in Montezuma, it was the same for me."

Her heart filled. Of course he understood. And he'd healed. So would she.

The carousel lurched forward, the happy organ music of state fairs and cotton candy Saturdays wrapped around her.

Brad's smile topped it all off.

Around and around her tawny mount danced. Her hair swayed in time with the carousel music. Healing had begun.

Patrick braced for impact, but Ashley continued the long walk from the former command post. Ahead of them, yellow crime scene tape flapped in the breeze. Birds cawed from surrounding trees.

The ugly white farmhouse loomed. Reality and memory swirled together.

Tactical rifles exploded all around him. Police orders fell like bullets. Thunder rolled.

He could still smell the smoke of gunfire and extinguished candles. The metallic tang of blood. The stench of death.

He could still see Ashley's bloodstained wedding dress flapping in the stormy winds.

His breathing came in shallow bursts and he had to focus to even out his inhale and exhale.

Ashley didn't speak. No telling what horrific details slammed around her brain. He had his own memories to fight through to be of any help to her.

They had survived. God had carried them to the other side of the valley of the shadow of death. He latched onto that anchor.

Ashley grabbed his hand. Her fingers trembled. "If we face the haunting shadows and stay standing, they lose their power."

Bit by bit they chipped away at them.

At Davis Mercantile Ashley had conquered her first crowd, her first public meal, first conversation with a stranger since the nightmare started.

Then she'd confronted the house where she'd rescued her parents and faced sniper rifles.

There he had to tamp down the fury and helplessness of that scene. But he couldn't allow anger's scalding fingers to lock him in the past as the Shipshewana cop had held him in place.

The police did their job. Ashley had done hers. And he'd been there to catch her when she fell.

Twenty yards now separated them from the ugly white farmhouse. He stepped forward, Ashley at his side.

A valiant warrior quaking in her shoes.

A little girl, wide eyed and swallowing hard.

Patrick was caught between the raw fear of Saturday—watching the woman he loved race into danger—and an unshakable resolve that God was there. Then and now. They could have lost everything. But they hadn't.

Time to stare into the pit one last time.

He rounded the house, following the crime tape until they stood opposite the bloodstained back porch.

He could still see and hear it all.

Margo trembling in the hands of a psychopath.

Ashley advancing right into his domain.

The singular rifle explosion.

The blood.

The interminable silence.

SWAT engulfing the porch, hiding Ashley from his sight.

Over and over, he replayed the scene. His pulse raced. His mind narrowed to include only the black.

Ashley's grip tightened around his hand. She had to be experiencing even worse, and he wasn't in a place to help. He needed to get there.

He squared his shoulders and adjusted his focus to include more than the darkness. Margo's tears as she and Ashley clung to each other amid a swarm of police and medical professionals, strobing lights and crunching tires.

"You were so brave, Maggie." Ashley smoothed rain-soaked hair out of Margo's face.

Margo wrapped Ashley in a hug. "I knew you'd rescue me, Ash. I knew you'd come."

Tears of joy, not terror.

A police cruiser slowed to a stop on the road next to them and Ashley tensed. Patrick slipped a protective arm around her.

Marshal Taylor opened his door and leaned against it, his posture relaxed. His smile subdued but evident. "Figured I'd find you two here."

"Conquering some dragons, sir." Patrick nudged Ashley toward the present.

"Tom. Call me Tom."

"Still conquering dragons, Tom."

"Wise of you both." He and Tom exchanged a world of words in a short glance.

Tom pointed to a box in the passenger seat. "I have a few things that I wanted to return to you."

"What things?" Ashley's green eyes narrowed.

"Patrick's phone, your phone and wedding dress. Margo's clothing. Your mother's purse and your father's wallet." Tom reached into his car and pulled the box out. "Would you like me to put them in your car?"

Ashley shook her head. "Just my parents' things and the phones. Though I don't know how long it will take before I can use my cell again."

"I've paid for three wedding dresses. You sure you don't want this one back? You could sell it online."

Patrick couldn't imagine. What woman would want a dress that had been used in such a demented drama?

Ashley shivered and turned away, then wrapped her arms around herself. "No. I don't ever want to see that dress again."

Would she ever want to see another wedding dress? Had Keith stolen their wedding from them too? Patrick's mind whirled. One more bitter defeat. Or could it be a smart steppingstone into the future? "If I pay for cleaning, can you find somewhere to donate it?"

Tom set the box back down. "I'm sure I can. There are plenty of churches around here that give away all sorts of clothing and household things. Somebody might be looking for a nice wedding dress like this one."

"It could be an answer to someone's prayers." Patrick measured Ashley's response.

"Sure." She turned back to them. "That's one way of looking at it."

"I'll take care of it then." Tom studied the house as he spoke. "You had a lot of folks telling you things back at that hearing. But I didn't get a chance to say all that was on my mind."

Patrick wanted to step in front of Ashley and tell the marshal to stop right there. But the tone of Tom's voice held him in place.

"Ashley, you're the age of my oldest daughter. Just as strong-willed and full of life. When you first arrived here, I wasn't sure how to take the glint of trouble in your eyes or the warnings from your chief."

"I'll be sure to thank Chief Fisher for his glowing recommendations."

Tom chuckled. "I might have pegged you as a hotheaded rookie with a selfish bent toward snatching glory and leaving trouble in your wake."

"That pretty much fits."

Patrick cringed. Only God could fix Ashley's mistaken view of herself.

"But those characteristics don't fit the person standing in front of me. Ever since that first meeting, I've noticed more and more what you're made of. More steel and instinct than many officers I've trained."

Patrick urged Tom on with his nods. Ashley needed to hear this.

"More heart and guts than most." Tom pointed to her eyes. "And now there's a tested and tried courage and tempered fire in there. Don't let what happened here steal that. Use it to become more of the person you already are."

Ashley drew in a long breath. "Thank you, sir. Thank you for everything."

Tom tapped the door of his cruiser. "Well, it's back to work for me. I'll drop those personal items at your car minus the clothing. You two don't be strangers to Shipshewana. We'd be honored to have you stay for a real visit sometime soon."

Patrick waved and waited for Tom's car to disappear behind them before he turned to Ashley. "You ready to head back?"

"Yes." This time, she wrapped her arm around his waist and set them to walking forward. Away from the ugliness. Toward tomorrow. "Are you ready to talk about the wedding?"

She'd raised the one question he dreaded asking. That had to be a good sign.

They reached his Mustang before he answered. He stepped in between Ashley and the farmhouse, so he could study her eyes. "Not unless you are."

"We need to."

"We don't have to yet."

"We should."

Patrick could fire off a list of *shoulds* with the best of them. He rehearsed them all the time, had for as long as he could remember. The *shoulds* of life kept him on the right track, right along with clocks. They kept life in nice, neat order. As they strangled the life out of him.

What had he always counseled his patients to do? Put away the *shoulds* and dwell on Christ, be where they were today.

Life on this side of the counseling desk wasn't that easy.

But if he'd learned anything from these last few weeks, he'd learned that he couldn't package real living in neat forty-five minute appointments or wrap up healing with a few wise words.

Reality was messy.

Living well took time. Healing took work.

He and Ashley would figure out the how together.

"Let's talk about our honeymoon first." He tucked a stray strand of black hair behind her ear.

The edges of her mouth turned up slowly and her eyes brightened, like an ocean sunrise not quite pushing back the dark night. Not yet anyway.

They both needed this reminder to help soften the stray memories of dark that still clung to the image of a wedding.

"I'm thinking we should forget Jamaica and just run away to a little mountain cabin in the middle of nowhere."

"Why?"

He cupped her face in his hands and bent down until they were nose to nose. "I can think of a few ways to pass the time. And I don't need a cruise ship or exotic locale."

Understanding pinked her cheeks. "I'm sure you can."

"Can't you?"

She wrapped her arms around his neck. "Absolutely."

CHAPTER THIRTY-FIVE

The day had finally arrived.

A day Ashley had dreamed and daydreamed about for months now.

With the smallest tinge of knee-shaking jitters, she paced the length of the Traveler's Rest Bed and Breakfast, her simple, white, ball-gown style dress gliding along the floor. Deep breath in. And out. She smoothed the delicate A-line waist and adjusted the lace sleeves one more time. And her short train. And her loose chignon. And the silk veil with lace edge that matched her dress to a T.

She'd never felt so beautiful in her life.

"You're stunning, Ashley dear." Maggie's misty blue eyes danced with anticipation. "I can't believe today is finally here."

"It's really real, isn't it?"

Maggie nodded.

The entire first level around her shone with white lights and maroon, mango, and chocolate ribbons and flowers. So very beautiful. So beyond her ability to have pulled off. Only God could have provided all they had needed for this wedding. Including the perfect weather.

The October evening rivaled an Impressionistic painting—dusty blue and orange clouds, trees bursting with yellow, scarlet, and orange leaves. A perfect nip in the air but warm enough that her lace sleeves would feel just right.

Emma bustled in, Mom at her side. "Oh, my, but you two are lovely." Emma turned to Ashley's mom. "We four have pulled together an exquisite evening. It will be the most amazing fall wedding ever."

"I'm sure I've said it a million times, but thank you. Mom, Maggie, Emma, this day wouldn't have happened if not for you three."

More hugs and dabbed eye makeup. And smiles. *Thank You, Lord.* It was time to smile again.

Dad stepped into the wedding wonderland. "It's starting to fill up out there."

Maggie inhaled. "And it smells like confectioners' heaven in here. Brilliant idea to have a candy and pastries buffet for the reception."

Patrick's one request for the entire day. That and his sports-themed groom's cake. And a short wedding and reception. That she couldn't deliver. But what he wouldn't get in terms of fast, they'd made up for in food. Emma and a team of bakers had crafted cupcakes with sugar mums and calla lilies in carrot cake and chocolate flavors, candied apples, mini pumpkin cheesecakes, and of course, Ashley's favorite chocolate croissants. Glass candy jars were filled with favorite candies: red hots, candy corn, Whoppers, mallow-crème pumpkins.

Her stomach growled at the reminder of food. Soon she and Patrick would fill their plates with sweet treats to celebrate a day long in coming. Then they'd dance the evening away with friends and family under a lit canopy of twinkling lights.

They'd had time to hammer out every tiny detail, in between work and counseling and learning how to live in each God-given moment. Learning to accept that God was good even when life was not. That was so hard. Her mind still wandered back sometimes…

She shook her head gently. Rather than allow her mind to revisit the past, she refocused on the details of today. She'd never believed anything in life could really be perfect.

But this day had shaped up to be as close to perfect as possible.

Manicures, hair appointments, and laughter. Her counselor had said to fill this day with as much laughter as possible. And they had.

"It's almost time for me to make my way outside." Mom stood and smoothed out the full skirt of her stunning maroon ball gown. Not quite Maggie's floor-length satin dress with matching jacket, but close. All their dresses were one of a kind, Ashley's one concession to the day.

Ashley twirled for one last motherly inspection.

"Perfect." Mom smoothed a hand down Ashley's cheek. "I'm so proud of you, baby. And so thankful you're my daughter."

"Don't make me cry again, Mom." She blinked away a sheen of tears. "I love you, and I'm thankful every single day for you."

"I know." Mom turned to catch Dad wiping his eyes with his maroon handkerchief. "Randall Walters. Don't you dare mess up that impeccable tuxedo."

They shared a tender kiss, and Mom headed out to the glassed-in back porch.

"We've all come such a long way." Maggie adjusted Ashley's train. "I can't wait to hear you and Patrick exchange vows. And then watch you dance."

They shared a mischievous grin. Only Maggie and Patrick's sister, Kathleen, knew that Patrick had cut out of work early for the last month to take dancing classes. Well…the ladies and Adam. He'd come into town a week early and attended a few of the classes with Patrick. He and Maggie were a striking couple.

"Is today everything you dreamed?"

Ashley glanced at the four-tiered wedding cake with a spray of cascading fall flowers, arranged like a Dutch still life painting. She touched the diamond combs in her hair, and smelled the pomegranate tulips and mango calla lilies in her bouquet.

"More. Today is more than I ever dreamed possible." She met Maggie's eyes. "I asked God to tell Eric all about it. Maybe silly, but I hope my big brother knows I made it to this day."

"I think he does. But he'd pull your hair just a little and tell you to lay off the chocolate."

Ashley stuck out her tongue. So mature. As always.

Pachelbel's Canon in D drifted into the room. "That's you, Mags. Go wow them."

Maggie slipped her arm through Chip's tuxedoed one. "That's all for you to do today. Enjoy it to the fullest."

As Margo and Chip glided away, Dad took her hand and kissed it. "I haven't seen you much today, but I wanted to tell you…" He blinked and coughed twice. "I may not have always been the dad you needed. But I love you more than life. You've always been the delight of my heart. Like your mother, I'm so very proud of you."

"I love you, Daddy."

He wrapped his strong arms around her and held her tight.

Wagner's Bridal Chorus began. "That's us, Ashley girl. Are you ready?"

Without a shadow of a doubt. "Yes."

The rows of guests stood as she and her dad took one slow and measured step at a time down a path of fall colored mums outlined with large hurricane vases and floating candles. She wasn't rushing this day, not by one step.

It was too perfect.

Patrick, in his new tux and maroon vest and tie, captured her attention from the start. So very handsome. The slight quirk of his smile was only for her, holding a million brilliant memories and causing every nerve ending to come alive.

She pulled her eyes away from Patrick to smile at the rows of police officers, from Montezuma, Atlanta, and a handful from Shipshewana. Marshal Taylor's grin beat them all.

Candice beamed from her seat next to Marshal Taylor. They'd spoken much in the last few months, and Candice's hope-filled eyes reminded Ashley they'd both come through the fire, been tempered, and were ready to embrace what lay ahead.

The Yoders, newlyweds Jonathan and Beth, Anna, Brad, and Brad's mom, Joyce, filled another row. Brad had put his tux to good use, ushering rather than standing up front. A place the Mennonite teen no longer seemed eager to occupy. But he beamed from his seat and gave her a thumbs up.

So much to be thankful for, Lord. So very much.

Patrick's niece, still a little too young to walk down the aisle in front of Ashley, tossed more mums from her seat in the front row. Everyone giggled. A glowing Kathleen grinned and maintained a hold of Susie's arm.

She and Dad continued up to the vine and marigold covered arbor. Patrick's misty eyes drew her in, his full lips mouthing words for her heart only.

"You are gorgeous, and I'm a goner."

She winked and tore her gaze away one last time.

Pastor Barnes addressed the entire gathering, his gray hair slightly ruffed in the evening breeze. "Please be seated." He turned to Dad. "Who gives this woman to be married to this man?"

Dad lifted her veil and then cupped her cheek in his hand before placing a kiss on her forehead. He spoke no words, but his misty green eyes said it all. He placed her hand in Patrick's. "Her mother and I."

Once Dad was seated next to Mom, Pastor Barnes proceeded with the ceremony. Ashley's eyes never left Patrick's again. He was so strong, so confident, so handsome in his crisp tux and mischievous grin. His tender blue eyes only for her. He mouthed again. "I'm a blessed man."

All the sudden, Pastor Barnes spoke about lighting the unity candle, and Maggie stepped forward to take her bouquet.

When Maggie stepped back, Ashley whispered in Patrick's direction. "Is he skipping some parts?"

Patrick leaned in. "Only the first few paragraphs." His voice sent tingles up and down her spine. Maybe Patrick was right about the ceremony. Short was better.

Together they lit a carved white candle under a deepening autumn sky, painted in rich and bold blues and gold.

Then it was time. Ashley stared into the crystal blue of Patrick's eyes and listened as he repeated the pastor's words. "Do you, Patrick Douglas James, take Ashley Renee Walters to be your wife—to love and cherish as Christ loved the Church and gave Himself up for Her? To lead with a servant's heart and gentle strength from this day forward, for better or worse, for richer or poorer, in sickness and in health, until you stand face-to-face with Jesus?"

"I do." Patrick turned to Chip for the ring and placed it on her finger.

"Do you, Ashley Renee Walters, take Patrick Douglas James to be your husband—to love and obey, to respect and honor? To walk hand in hand with a servant's heart and enduring grace from this day forward, for better or worse, for richer or poorer, in sickness and in health, until you stand face-to-face with Jesus?"

"I do." Maggie sniffled and handed Ashley the beautiful gold band with the inscription "All God—Perfect." The perfection that can only come from God. As Ashley placed the ring on Patrick's hand, she couldn't miss the smile of God etched across the sky and filling her heart.

Or the nail-scarred hands wrapping around this day, holding her and Patrick.

Pastor Barnes placed a hand on both of their shoulders. "Every couple, like every masterpiece, requires enough dark to shine the light, enough scars to highlight the victory, and the sacrifice of love to reveal the beauty within. You two have given us all a clearer picture of this truth. And so, what God has joined together, let no man put asunder. And now, by the power vested in me by the State of Georgia and Almighty God, I pronounce you husband and wife. You may *now* kiss the bride."

Patrick brushed a single tear from her cheek with his thumb and drew her into his arms, his lips covering hers and sealing the promise of the future yet to come.

One that didn't scare her the tiniest bit.

Patrick picked her up and twirled her around, his lips deepening the kiss until everything else faded away.

Except for the laughter of God encircling them—deep and rich and filled with joy.

AUTHOR'S NOTE

Dear Reader,

Thank you for journeying with me through a harrowing adventure that touched on two deep subjects that affect many of our lives: What happens when faith fails? And the struggle between selfishness and sacrifice.

The reason these two issues were forefront in this book is because, like every book I've ever written, these stories contain snatches of my wrestling matches with God. I wrote *Nowhere to Run* in the midst of one of the biggest health crises of my life and an accompanying struggle with the question about failing faith, only worded a little differently: Where is God when life hurts?

This book also forced me to go back to my college days when I was stalked. It wasn't hard to write Ashley's fear. I remembered well how night and shadows took on sinister shapes because someone watched my every move. I lived in fear for my life.

And, like Ashley, I survived a dangerous stalker and carried on with my life, not letting the stalker ruin my future. But I hadn't fully healed. So God in His great mercy and grace took me back so I could heal as I wrote and prayed over a story that could help others down the path of healing.

Traumatic experiences, like stalking or a health crisis, color who we are and affect who we become. If we allow them, they can distort the image of God and leave us with a nagging fear that thrives just below the surface of our lives.

That fear can lead to selfish living. We focus on keeping control over our circumstances or even doing a lot of good things, like Ashley's protecting her loved ones, for the purpose of providing security. We subtly begin depending on ourselves to make life work. And then something else happens and we wonder where God is. Or a major crisis occurs and we wonder where our faith has gone.

The good news is that God never lets go of us. He isn't surprised by our questions or angry at our attempts to control and fix it all. The bad news is that God never lets go. Okay, that's not bad news really, but it's a tough truth. God never lets us stay locked in our fear or selfishness, trying to control our world and find security there.

Sometimes He makes us write a book that forces us to see the truth. Sometimes He makes us read a book that touches something deep inside. God works in myriad ways to draw us closer to Him, to pry our fearful hands off of our lives and the lives of our loved ones, and learn to trust Him.

It sounds too easy to be an answer. Trust God. We hear "trust God" and think it's somehow up to us to make ourselves trust more. To have more faith. Or that trust will fix the hurt or answer all the questions. It doesn't.

Trust does help us see God for who He is and turn to Him.

Psalm 56:3-4 is a good place to start. "When I am afraid, I will put my trust in you. I praise God for what he has promised. I trust in God, so why should I be afraid? What can mere mortals do to me?"

Feelings aren't reality. They're flags. Warning signs for us to heed. Our feelings of fear can lead us back to God's Word instead of selfish living. Because the reality is there are no other answers than to go back to who God is and what He says. The truth is we can't make life work without God. We need God. We need to be clinging to Him and praising His name and being thankful and trusting that He is good when life is not. We need to be honest when we don't have the strength to read or pray or praise. He understands. And He is there to carry us. To give us the faith to believe He is who He says He is. God has not left us alone.

Yes, trials and troubles will come. God's Word promises that. But God also promises He will never leave us. The One who knit you together, who knows everything about you and the very number of your days, is also the One who loves you more than you can imagine.

We don't have to live in fear. We can sacrifice our will, our ways to fix things, and the fear that living selfishly causes and cling to Him. He is good. He is for us.

I spent much of this book living in fear. I'm learning there's a better way because of this same story. I pray you'll join me. God is here and He is for us. He will never let go. Ever.

Because of His grace,
Amy

Discussion Questions

1. Ashley believes it's up to her to protect her loved ones. How was she right? How was she wrong? What would you have done in her situation?

2. Ashley wasn't the only one to protect herself or others in this story. Who else behaved in protective ways? What did they do? Which one most resonates with you and why?

3. Patrick deals with the *shoulds* of life—he should have done this or that and then things would have been better. Can you relate? What *shoulds* drive your life now?

4. Many people in this story risked their lives for someone they loved. Ashley, Patrick, Joyce, the Yoders. Since most of us won't have to fight off a stalker like they did, how can we live out John 15:13? ("There is no greater love than to lay down one's life for one's friends.")

5. Ashley believed she was handling her fear by protecting others, fighting, and trusting in herself. Was she handling her fear? Why or why not? How would you counsel Ashley to deal with her fears? What has God used in your life to free you from fear?

6. Despite the difficult circumstances, Margo continued to point Ashley back to God. Is there a Margo in your life? How can you be that kind of friend to those you love?

7. One question raised in this story is: What happens when faith fails? When Ashley's faith in herself failed, her answer was to turn from selfish independence to God, to sacrifice her way to find God's answers. When have you risked that scary path? How did God show Himself faithful?

8. Sacrifice is a key theme in this story. What did each of the characters sacrifice? What was the result? How about you—what does sacrifice look like in your life?

9. At the beginning of this book is a quote from Marianne Williamson. "Our deepest fear is not that we are inadequate. Our deepest fear is that we are powerful beyond measure. It is our light, not our darkness, that most frightens us. We ask ourselves, Who am I to be brilliant, gorgeous, talented, and fabulous? Actually, who are you *not* to be? You are a child of God. Your playing small doesn't serve the word." What does this quote mean to you? How can you live out this truth?

10. What does it mean to accept that God is good even when life isn't?

Meet Amy Wallace

Amy Wallace writes Dark Chocolate Suspense—high-action suspense that delves deep into heart issues. Amy is a homeschool mom, author, speaker, co-leader of a young writer's club, and avid chocoholic.

Her novels include the Defenders of Hope Series—*Ransomed Dreams, Healing Promises,* and *Enduring Justice.* Amy is also a contributing author of *A Novel Idea: Best Advice on Writing Inspirational Fiction, God Answers Moms' Prayers,* and *Chicken Soup for the Soul Healthy Living Series: Diabetes.*

Says Amy:

"If I could be remembered for only one thing, it would be that I glorified God by enjoying Him to the fullest and that I showed by example what it means to dream big and live a life that touches hearts and leads people into a deep relationship with Christ."

What about you? What sentence would sum up who you are and how God is using your life?

I'd love to hear from you!
Please visit me at my website, Dark Chocolate Suspense:
www.amywallace.com

— OR —

Come connect with me on Facebook:
https://www.facebook.com/amywallaceauthor

— OR —

Hang out with me at my Heart Chocolate blog:
http://peek-a-booicu.blogspot.com/

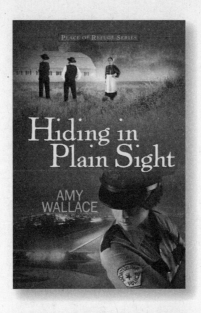

HIDING IN PLAIN SIGHT
By Amy Wallace

Secrets of the Heart Never Stay Hidden

World-weary and down to a threadbare faith, police officer Ashley Walters seeks refuge in Montezuma, Georgia, a quiet town with a thriving Mennonite community. Yet even in the peaceful surroundings, she can't escape the haunting memories of crime-ridden Atlanta.

Then marriage-and-family counselor Patrick James partners with a teenaged Mennonite runaway to offer Ashley a second chance at redemption...and romance. But when violence erupts over revitalization plans that pit the Montezuma and Mennonite communities against each other, Ashley vows to stop the person responsible—even if he is someone she's come to love.

As God unlocks the secrets darkening Ashley's heart, she must answer two crucial questions: Who is in control? And can she trust Him?